S.M.
Vidaurri

Hannah
Krieger

All My
Friends
Are Ghosts ™

Published by

kaboom! ™

Designer
Scott Newman

Editor
Matthew Levine

Special Thanks to Lauren Affe, Ensley Chau, Cassandra Tassoni, Feliza Vidaurri, **and** Cameron Chittock.

kaboom!™

BOOM! Studios, 5670 Wilshire Boulevard, Suite 400, Los Angeles, CA 90036-5679. Printed in China. First Printing.

ISBN: 978-1-68415-498-2, eISBN: 9781-64144-656-3

All My Friends Are Ghosts ™

Written by
S.M. Vidaurri

Illustrated by
Hannah Krieger

Colored by
Hannah Krieger
with **S.M. Vidaurri**

Lettered by
Mike Fiorentino

Cover by
Hannah Krieger

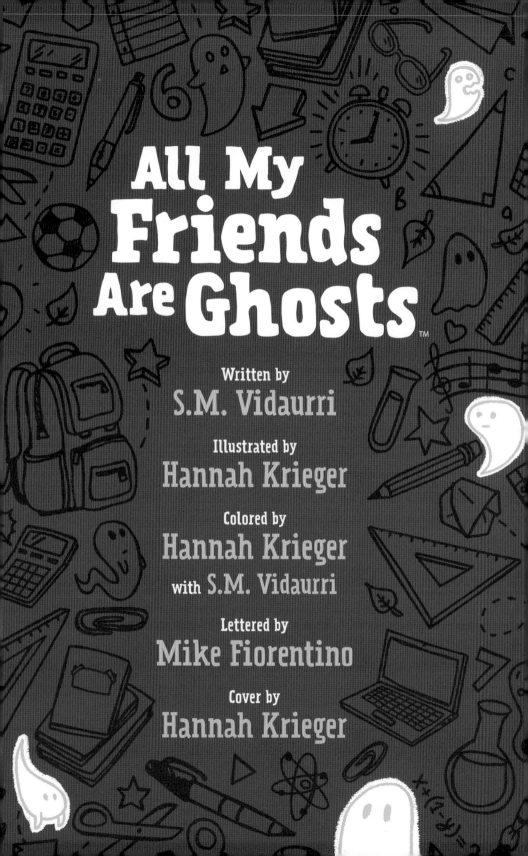

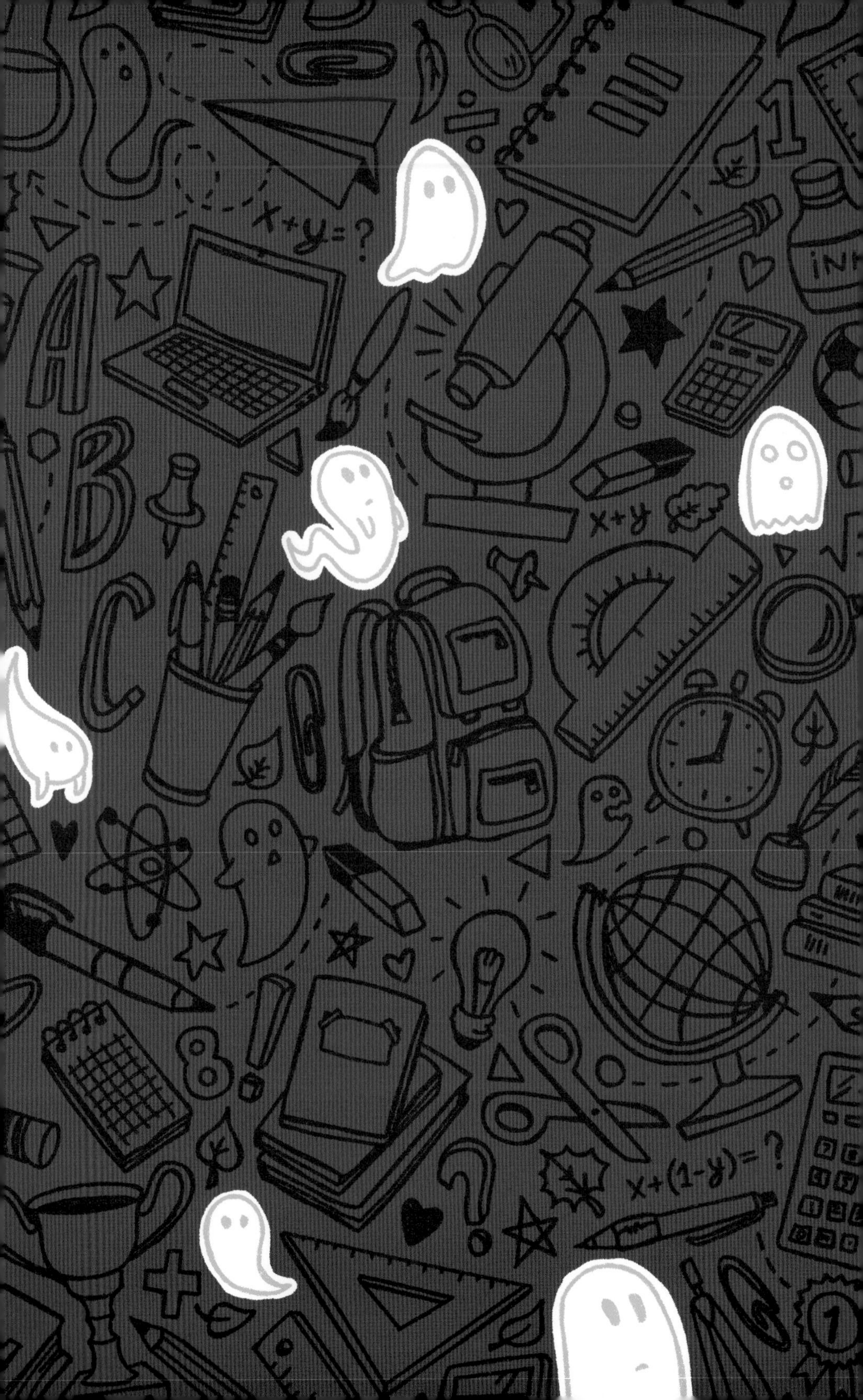
x+y=?
x+y
x+(1-y)=?

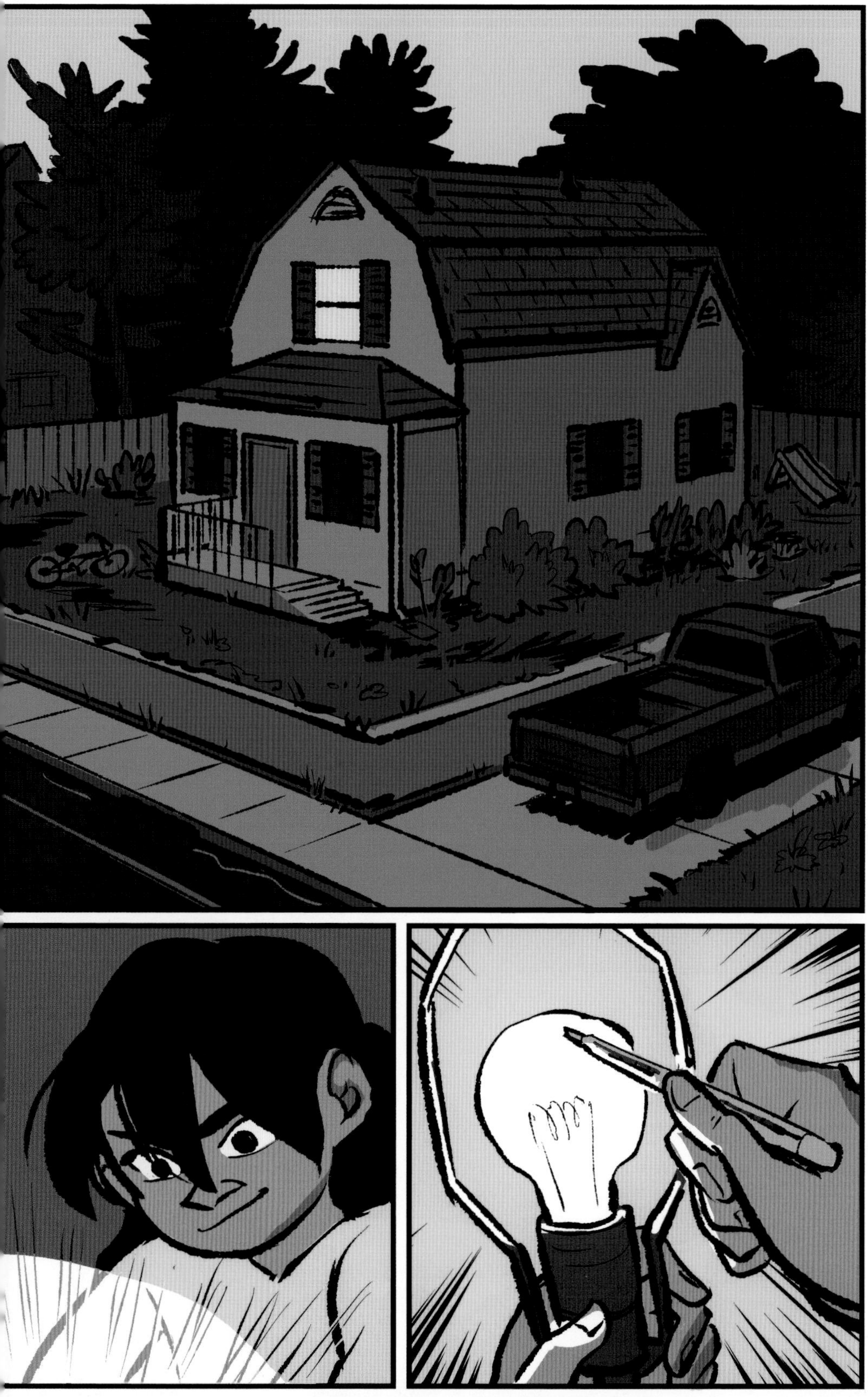

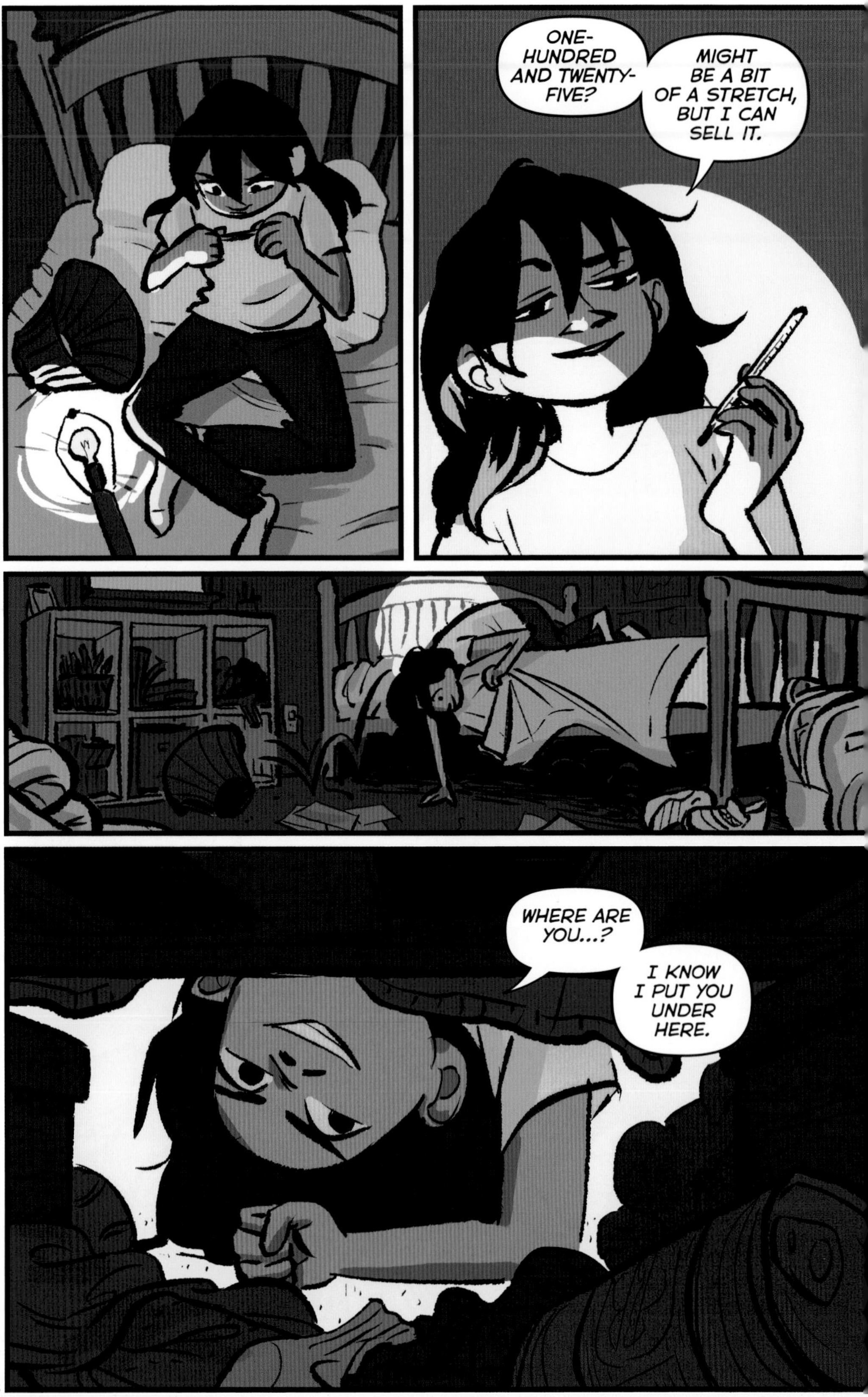
ONE-HUNDRED AND TWENTY-FIVE?
MIGHT BE A BIT OF A STRETCH, BUT I CAN SELL IT.
WHERE ARE YOU...?
I KNOW I PUT YOU UNDER HERE.

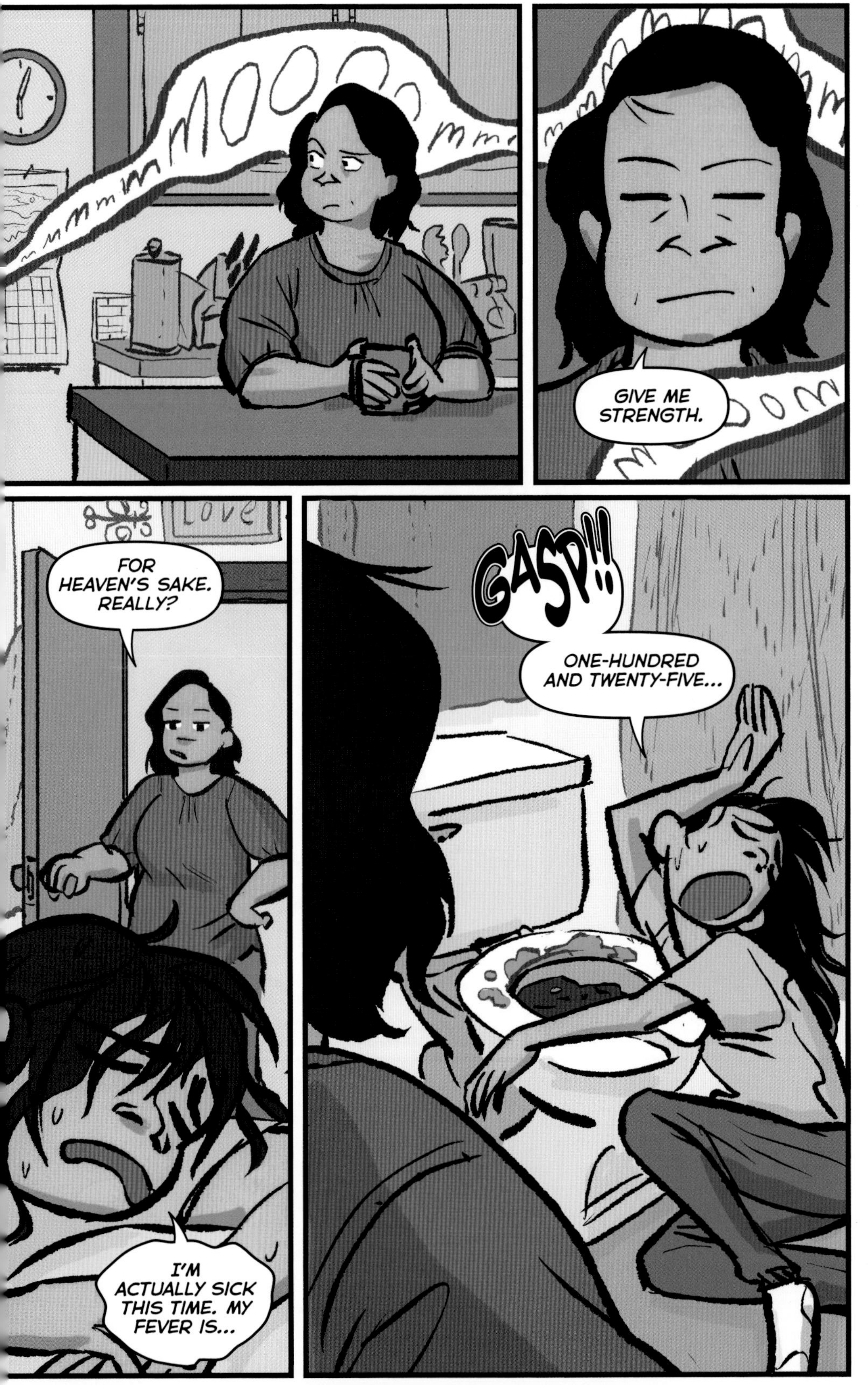
mmmmmMOOOOmmm
GIVE ME STRENGTH.
LOVE
FOR HEAVEN'S SAKE. REALLY?
I'M ACTUALLY SICK THIS TIME. MY FEVER IS...
GASP!!
ONE-HUNDRED AND TWENTY-FIVE...

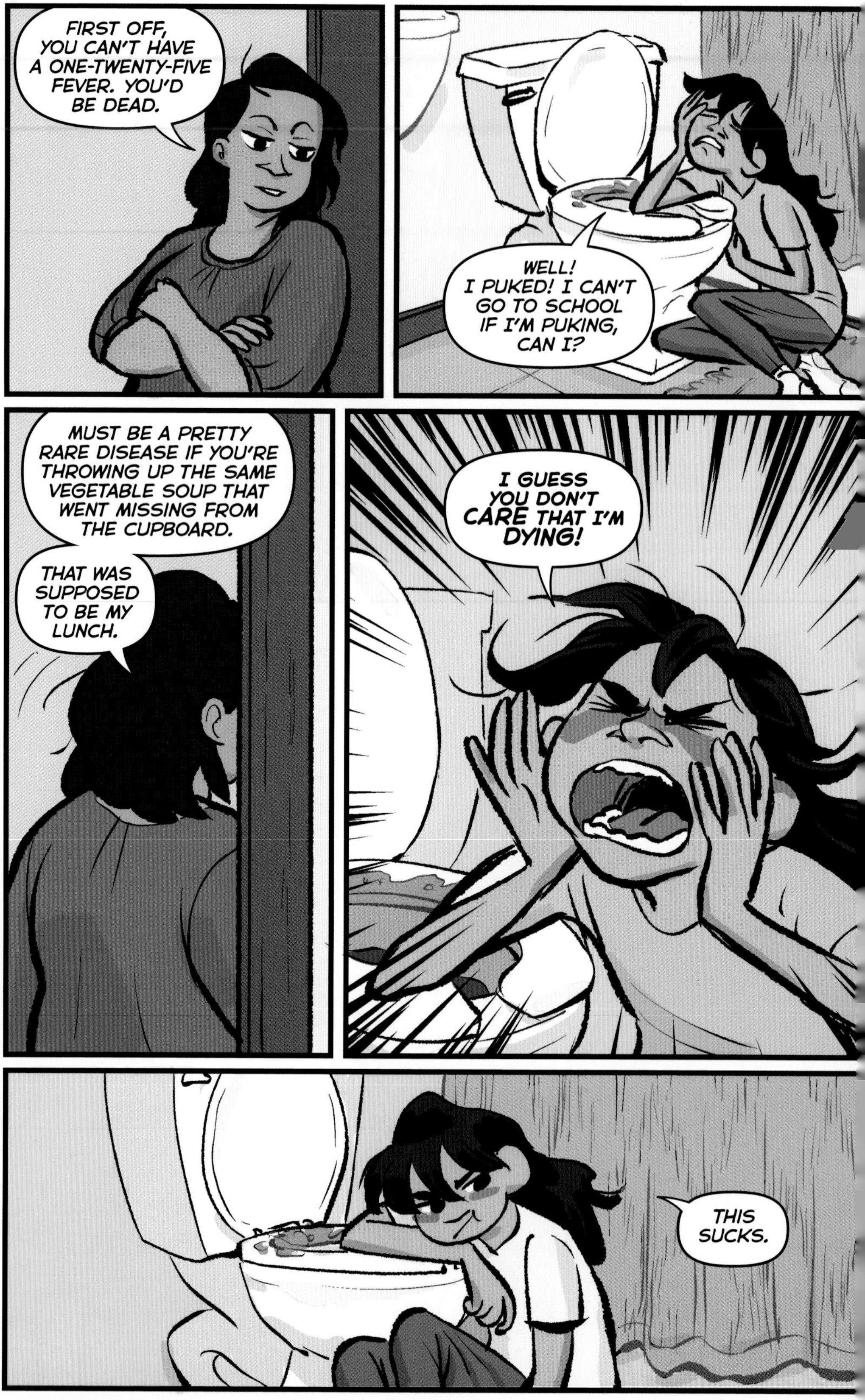
FIRST OFF, YOU CAN'T HAVE A ONE-TWENTY-FIVE FEVER. YOU'D BE DEAD.
WELL! I PUKED! I CAN'T GO TO SCHOOL IF I'M PUKING, CAN I?
MUST BE A PRETTY RARE DISEASE IF YOU'RE THROWING UP THE SAME VEGETABLE SOUP THAT WENT MISSING FROM THE CUPBOARD.
THAT WAS SUPPOSED TO BE MY LUNCH.
I GUESS YOU DON'T CARE THAT I'M DYING!
THIS SUCKS.

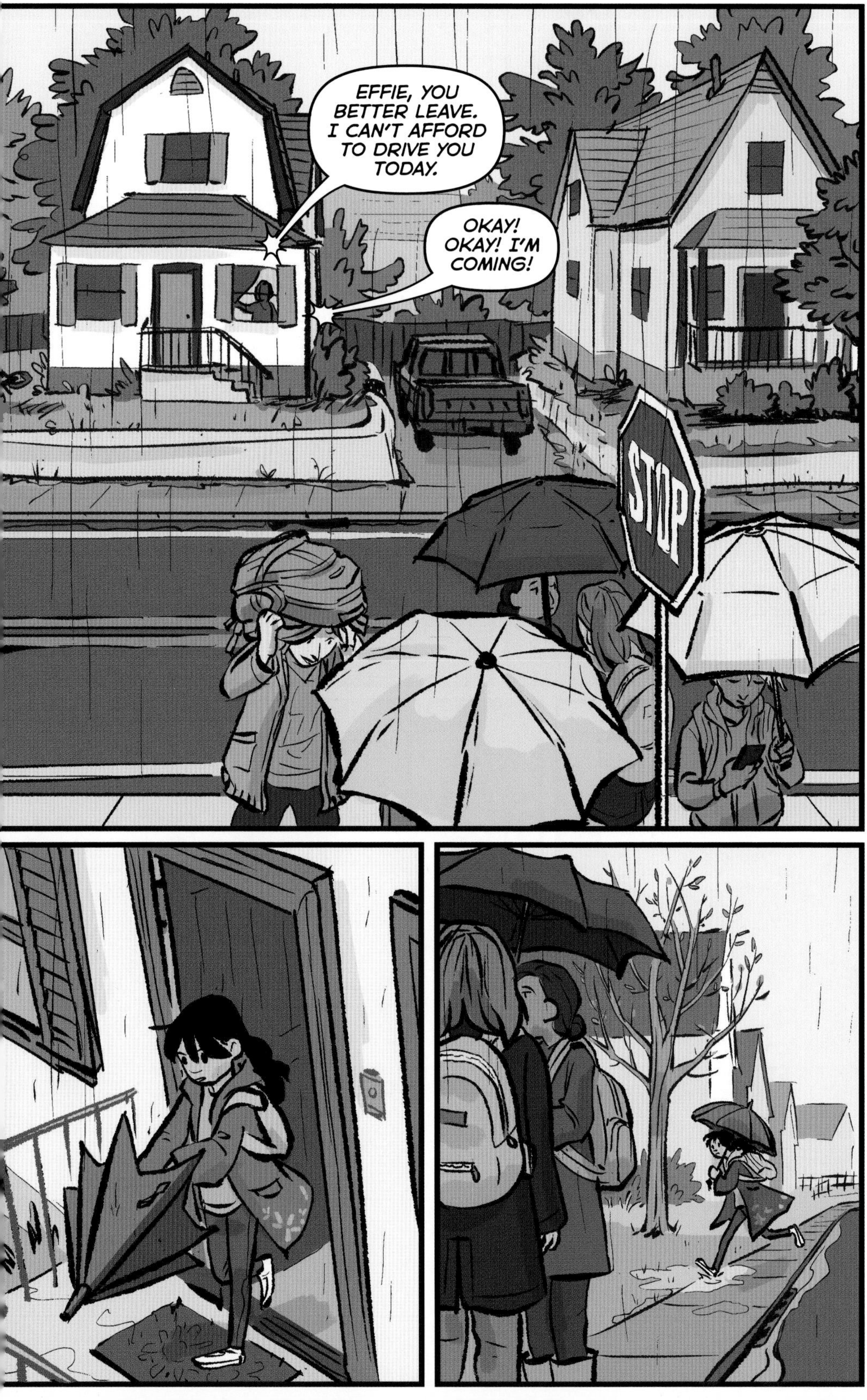
EFFIE, YOU BETTER LEAVE. I CAN'T AFFORD TO DRIVE YOU TODAY.
OKAY! OKAY! I'M COMING!
STOP

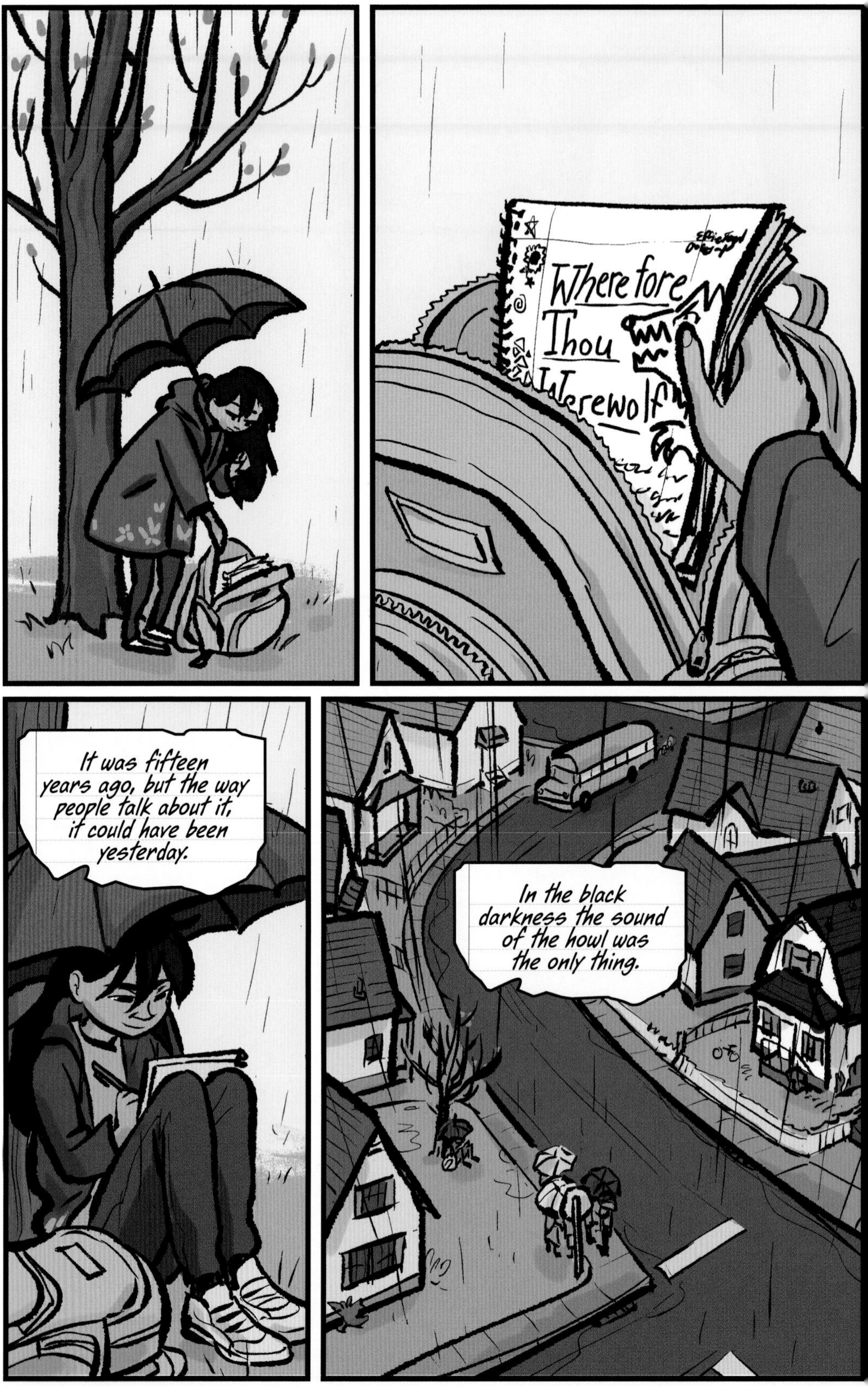
Wherefore Thou Werewolf
It was fifteen years ago, but the way people talk about it, it could have been yesterday.
In the black darkness the sound of the howl was the only thing.

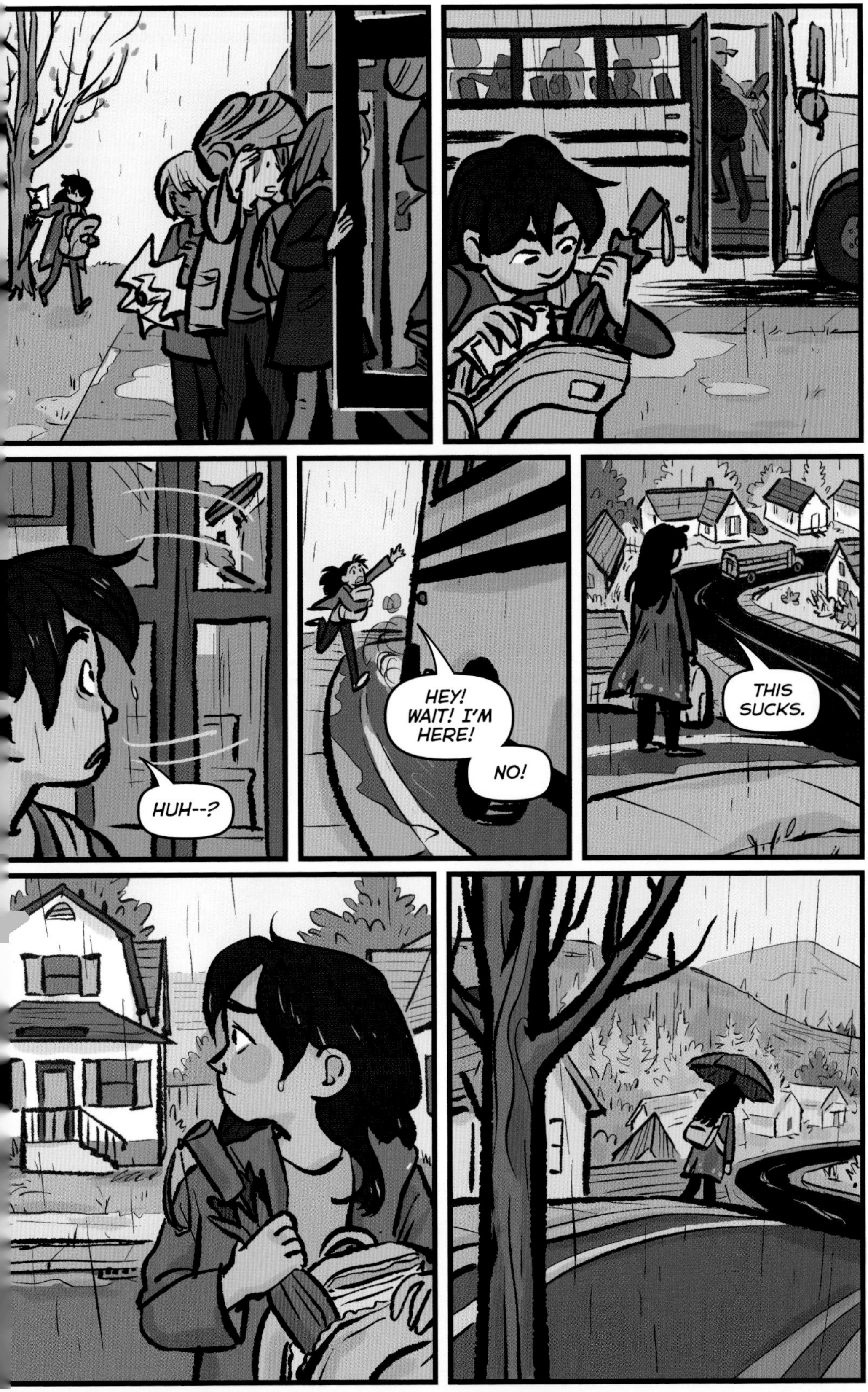
HUH--?
HEY! WAIT! I'M HERE!
NO!
THIS SUCKS.

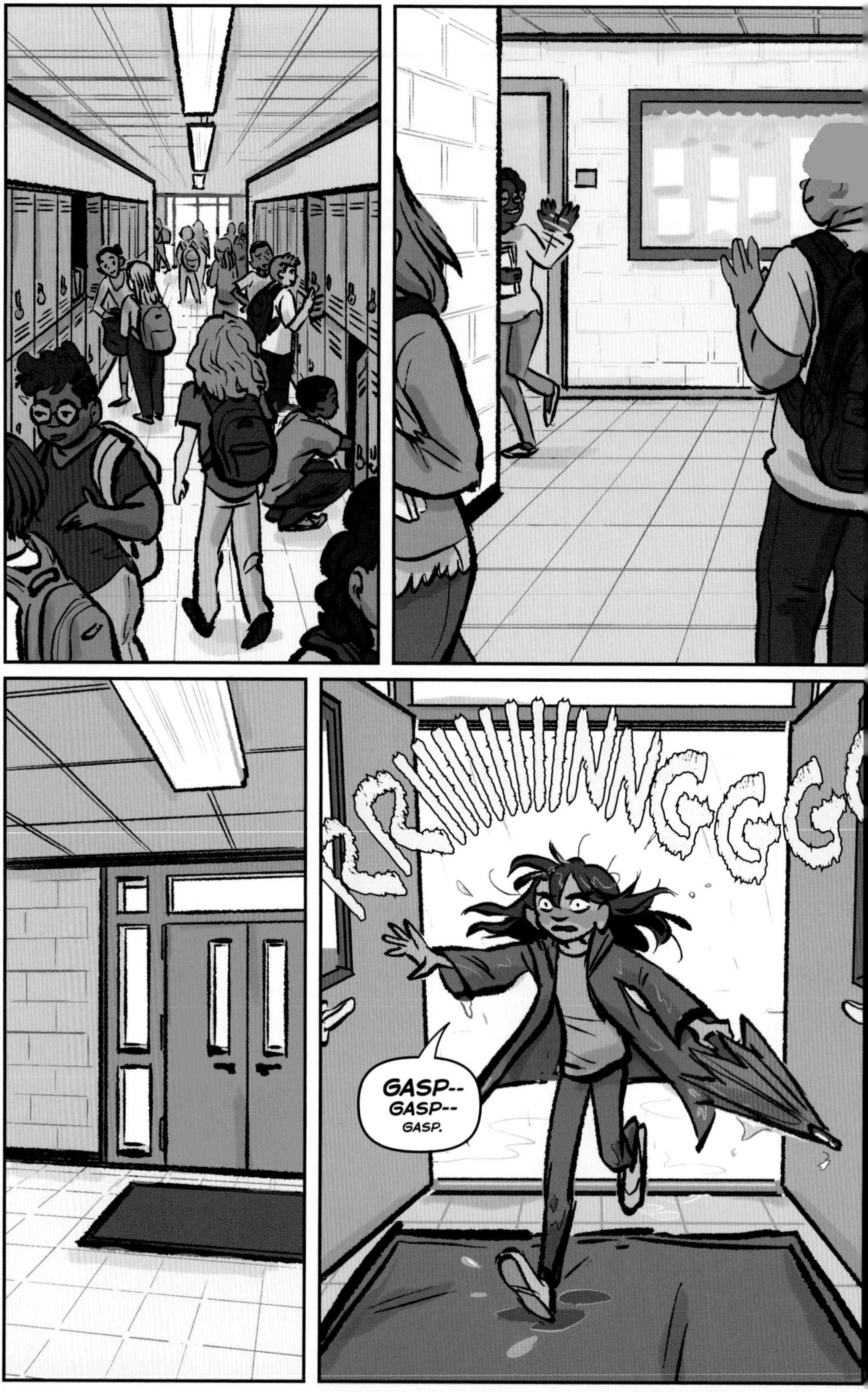

SQUIIIIIIIIINNGGGG
GASP--
GASP--
GASP.

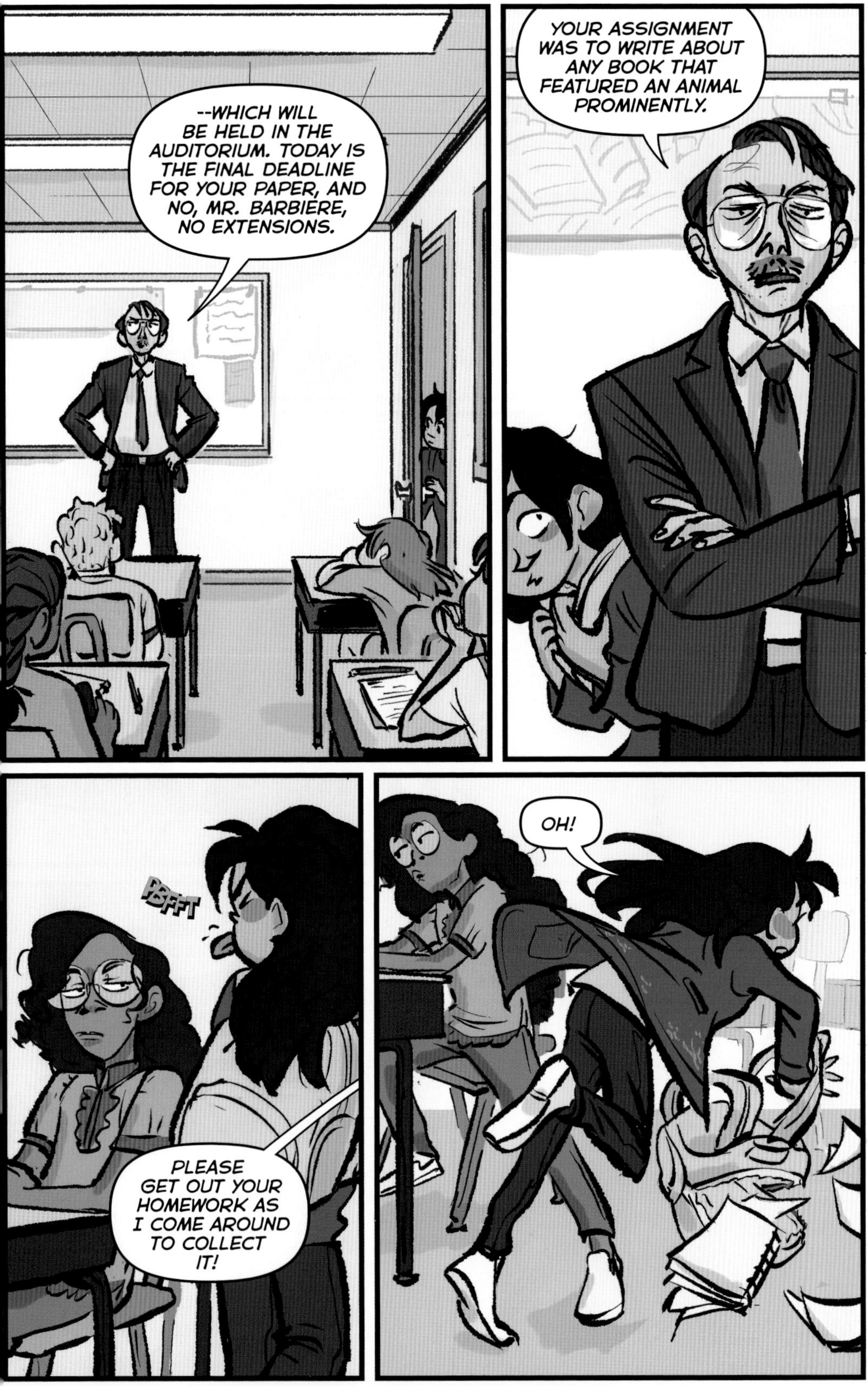
--WHICH WILL BE HELD IN THE AUDITORIUM. TODAY IS THE FINAL DEADLINE FOR YOUR PAPER, AND NO, MR. BARBIERE, NO EXTENSIONS.
YOUR ASSIGNMENT WAS TO WRITE ABOUT ANY BOOK THAT FEATURED AN ANIMAL PROMINENTLY.
PBFFT
PLEASE GET OUT YOUR HOMEWORK AS I COME AROUND TO COLLECT IT!
OH!

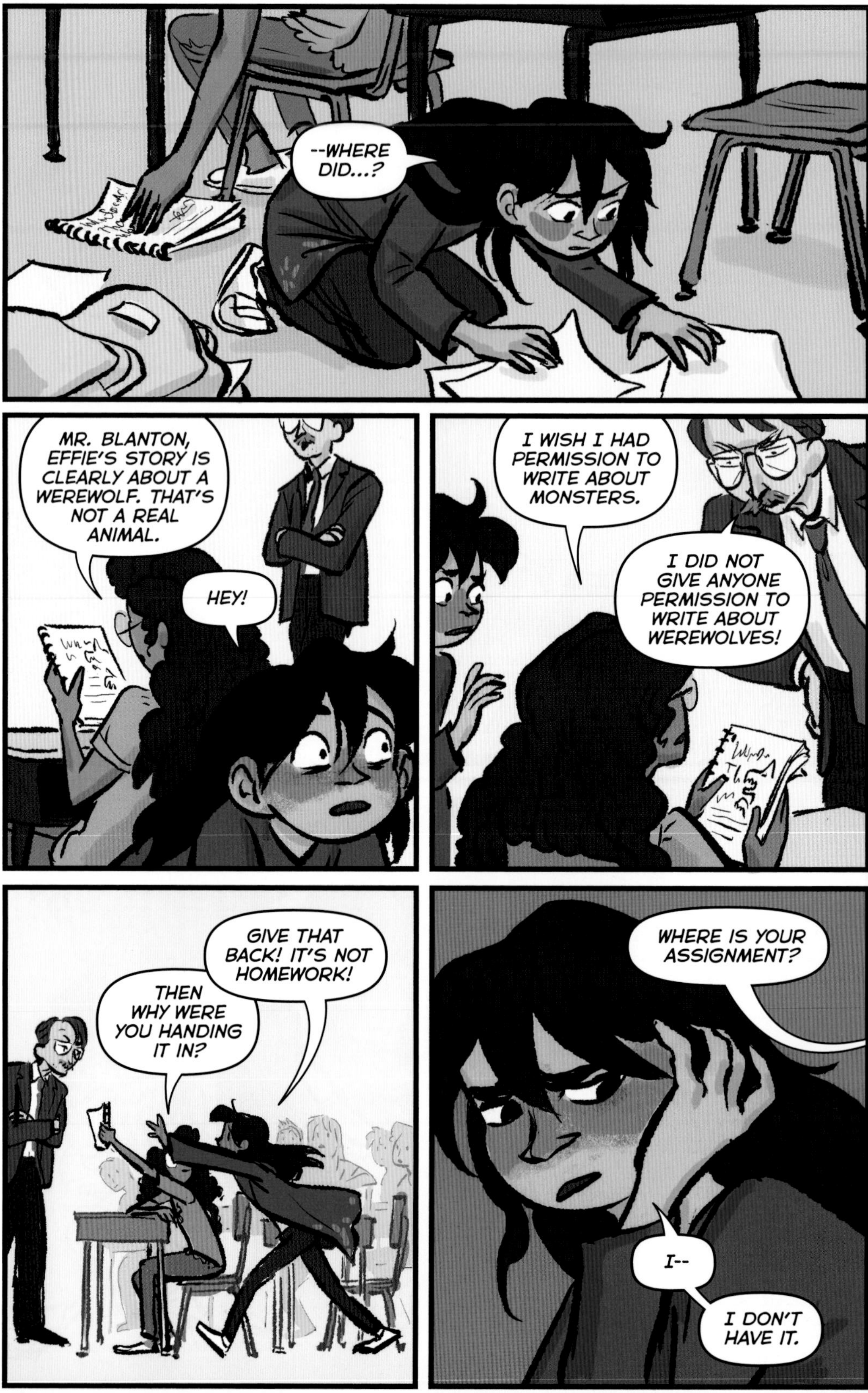
--WHERE DID...?
MR. BLANTON, EFFIE'S STORY IS CLEARLY ABOUT A WEREWOLF. THAT'S NOT A REAL ANIMAL.
HEY!
I WISH I HAD PERMISSION TO WRITE ABOUT MONSTERS.
I DID NOT GIVE ANYONE PERMISSION TO WRITE ABOUT WEREWOLVES!
GIVE THAT BACK! IT'S NOT HOMEWORK!
THEN WHY WERE YOU HANDING IT IN?
WHERE IS YOUR ASSIGNMENT?
I--
I DON'T HAVE IT.

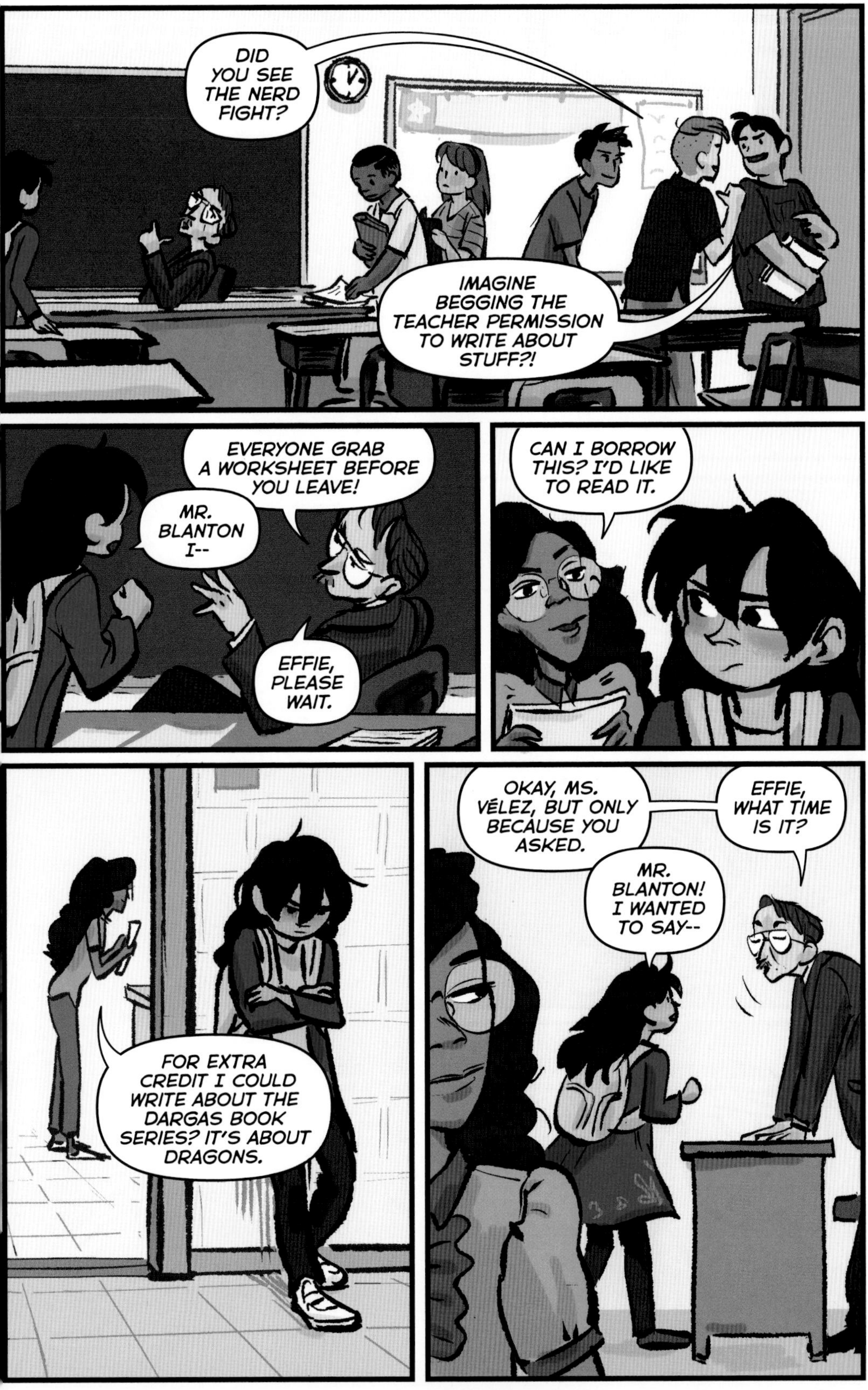
DID YOU SEE THE NERD FIGHT?
IMAGINE BEGGING THE TEACHER PERMISSION TO WRITE ABOUT STUFF?!
EVERYONE GRAB A WORKSHEET BEFORE YOU LEAVE!
MR. BLANTON I--
EFFIE, PLEASE WAIT.
CAN I BORROW THIS? I'D LIKE TO READ IT.
FOR EXTRA CREDIT I COULD WRITE ABOUT THE DARGAS BOOK SERIES? IT'S ABOUT DRAGONS.
OKAY, MS. VÉLEZ, BUT ONLY BECAUSE YOU ASKED.
EFFIE, WHAT TIME IS IT?
MR. BLANTON! I WANTED TO SAY--

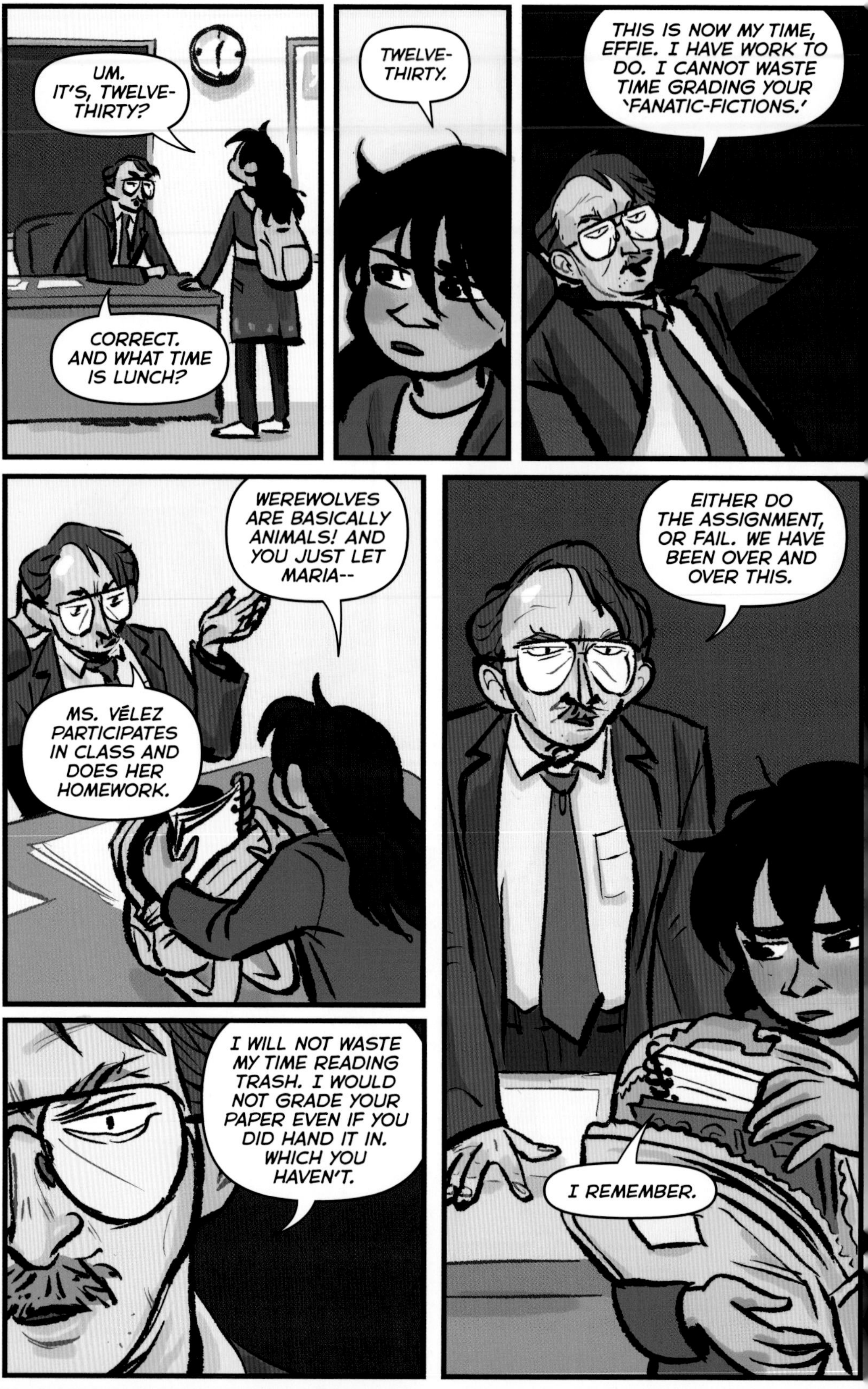
UM. IT'S, TWELVE-THIRTY?
CORRECT. AND WHAT TIME IS LUNCH?
TWELVE-THIRTY.
THIS IS NOW MY TIME, EFFIE. I HAVE WORK TO DO. I CANNOT WASTE TIME GRADING YOUR 'FANATIC-FICTIONS.'
WEREWOLVES ARE BASICALLY ANIMALS! AND YOU JUST LET MARIA--
MS. VÉLEZ PARTICIPATES IN CLASS AND DOES HER HOMEWORK.
EITHER DO THE ASSIGNMENT, OR FAIL. WE HAVE BEEN OVER AND OVER THIS.
I WILL NOT WASTE MY TIME READING TRASH. I WOULD NOT GRADE YOUR PAPER EVEN IF YOU DID HAND IT IN. WHICH YOU HAVEN'T.
I REMEMBER.

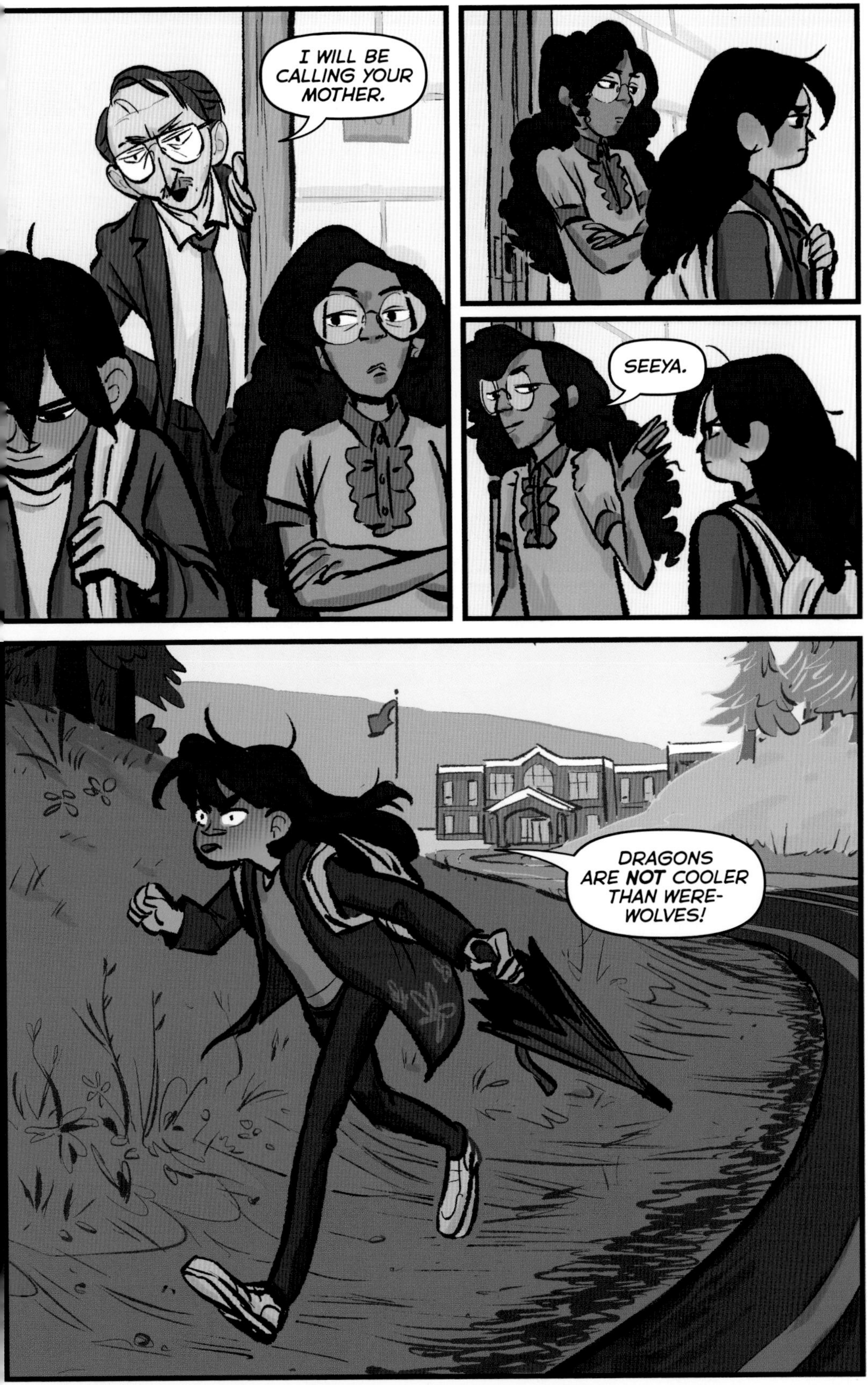
I WILL BE CALLING YOUR MOTHER.
SEEYA.
DRAGONS ARE **NOT** COOLER THAN WERE-WOLVES!

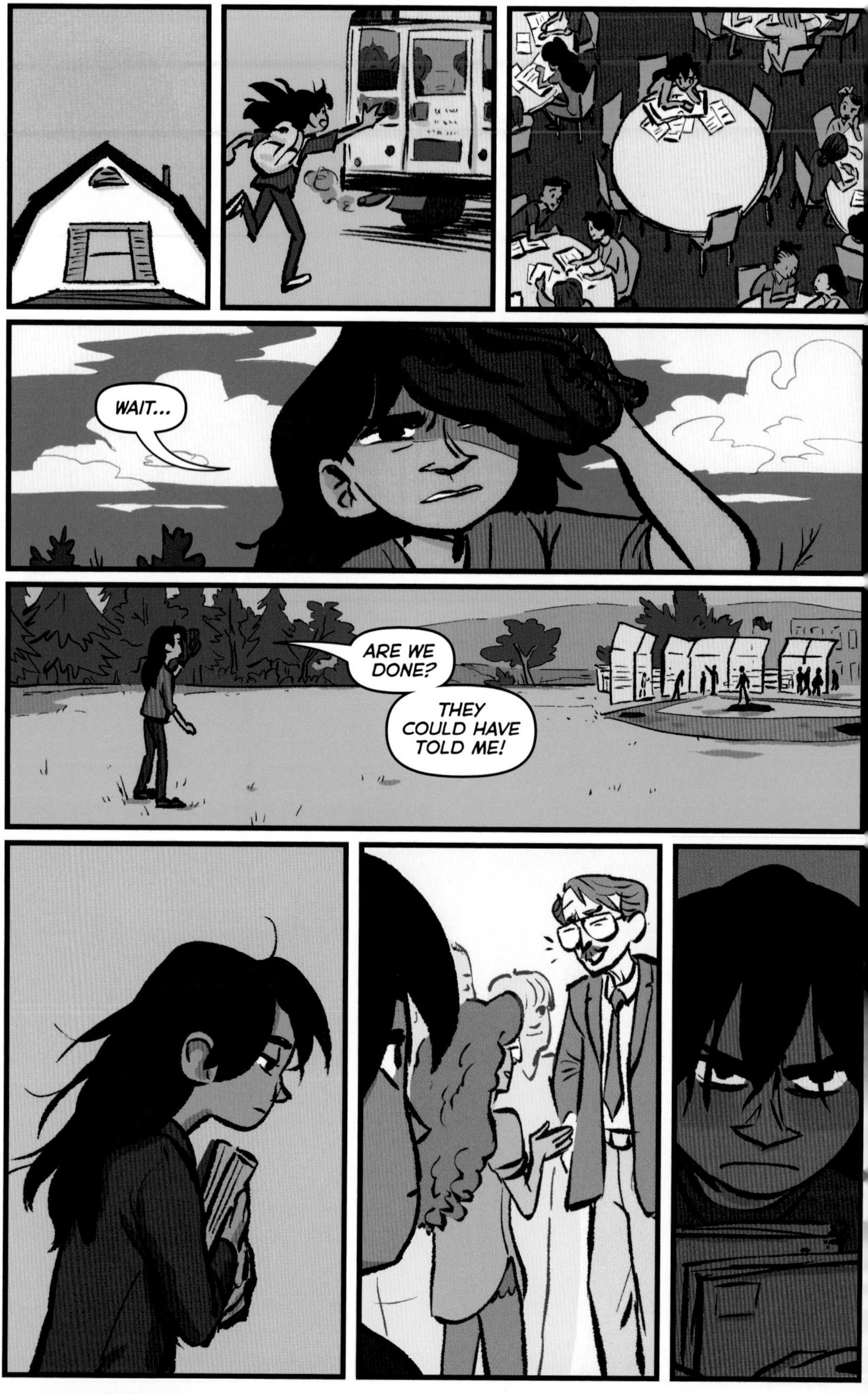
WAIT...
ARE WE DONE?
THEY COULD HAVE TOLD ME!

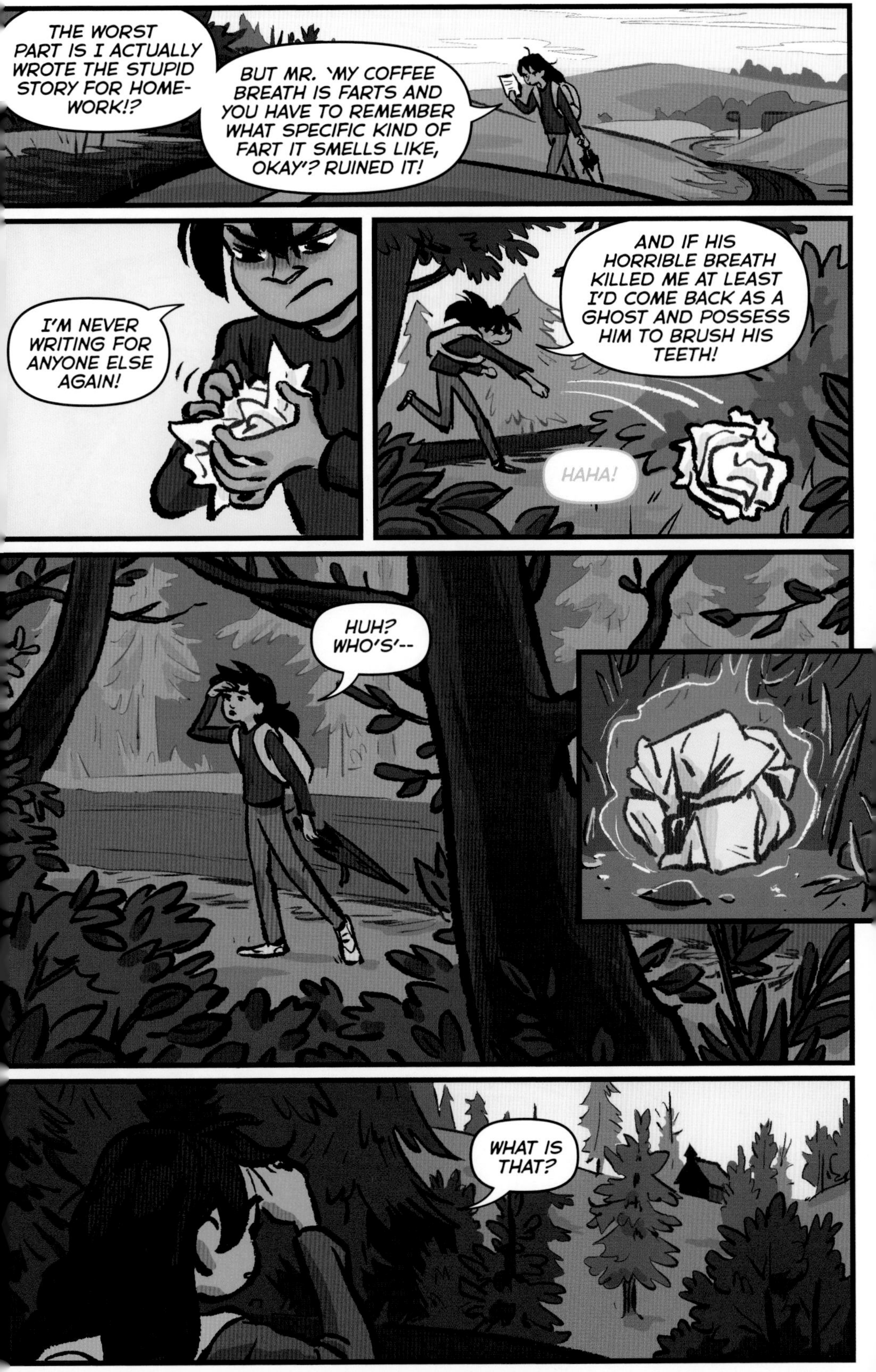
THE WORST PART IS I ACTUALLY WROTE THE STUPID STORY FOR HOME-WORK!?
BUT MR. 'MY COFFEE BREATH IS FARTS AND YOU HAVE TO REMEMBER WHAT SPECIFIC KIND OF FART IT SMELLS LIKE, OKAY'? RUINED IT!
I'M NEVER WRITING FOR ANYONE ELSE AGAIN!
AND IF HIS HORRIBLE BREATH KILLED ME AT LEAST I'D COME BACK AS A GHOST AND POSSESS HIM TO BRUSH HIS TEETH!
HAHA!
HUH? WHO'S'--
WHAT IS THAT?

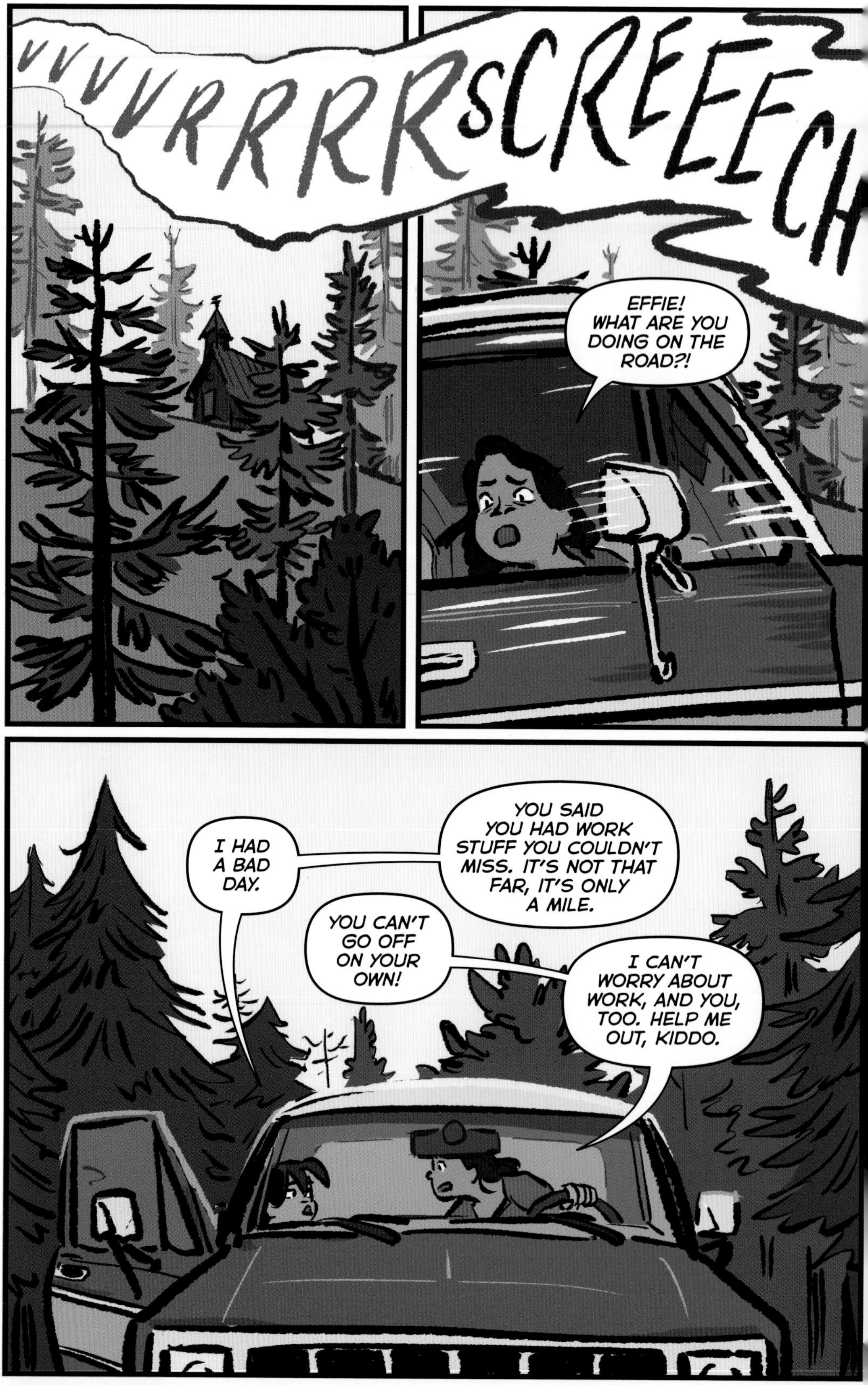
VVVVRRRRR
SCREEECH
EFFIE! WHAT ARE YOU DOING ON THE ROAD?!
YOU SAID YOU HAD WORK STUFF YOU COULDN'T MISS. IT'S NOT THAT FAR, IT'S ONLY A MILE.
I HAD A BAD DAY.
YOU CAN'T GO OFF ON YOUR OWN!
I CAN'T WORRY ABOUT WORK, AND YOU, TOO. HELP ME OUT, KIDDO.

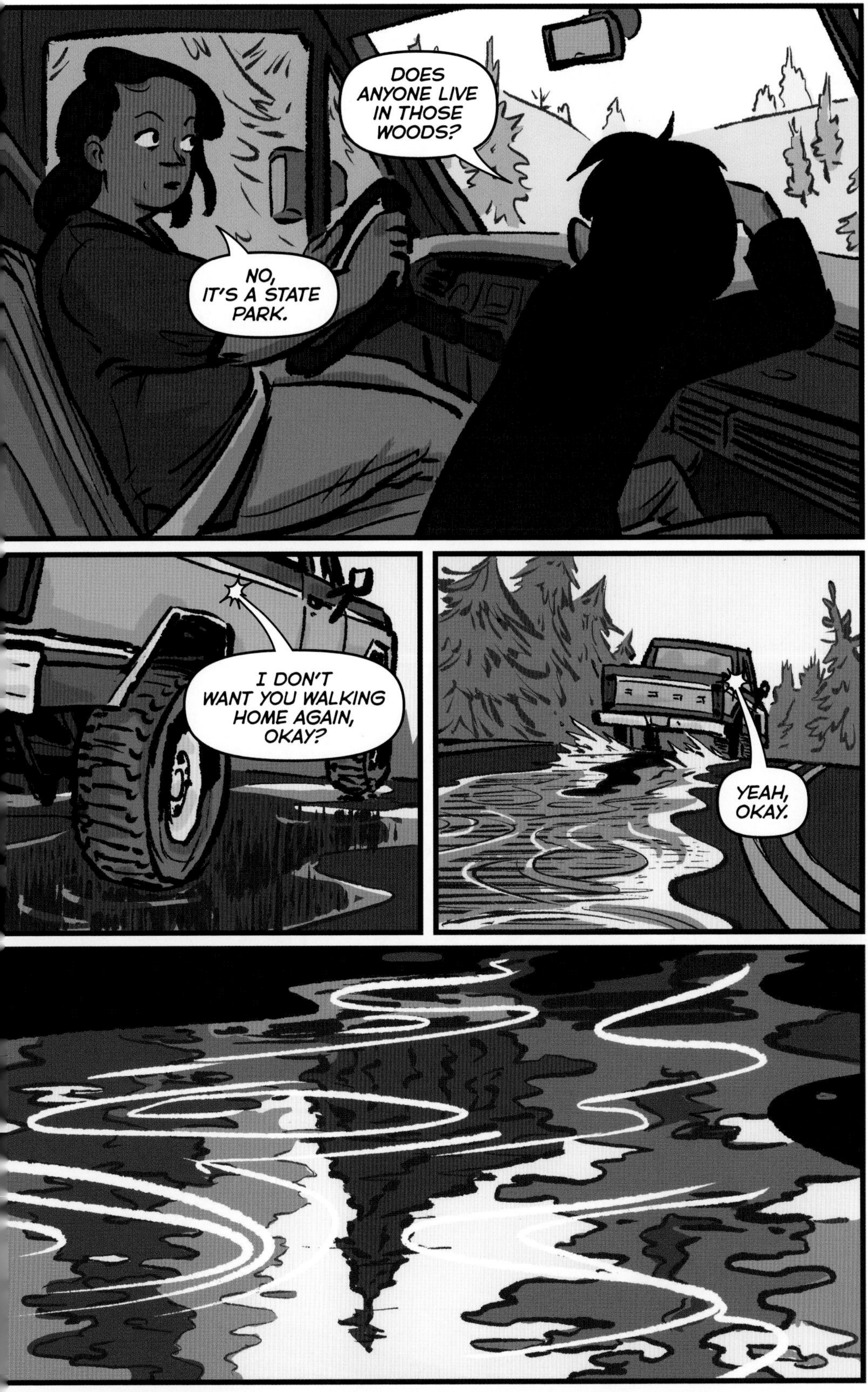
DOES ANYONE LIVE IN THOSE WOODS?
NO, IT'S A STATE PARK.
I DON'T WANT YOU WALKING HOME AGAIN, OKAY?
YEAH, OKAY.

About this Park
History

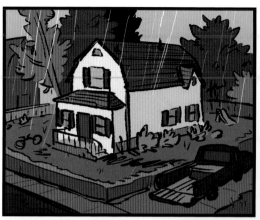

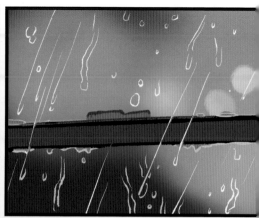

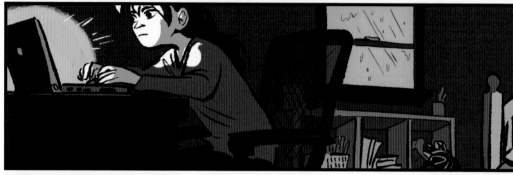

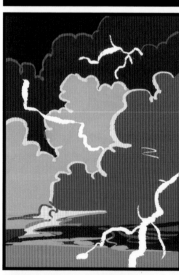

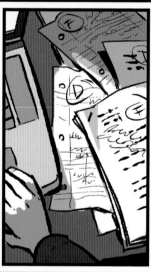

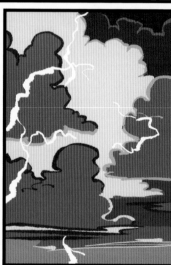

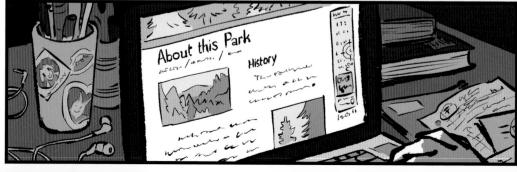

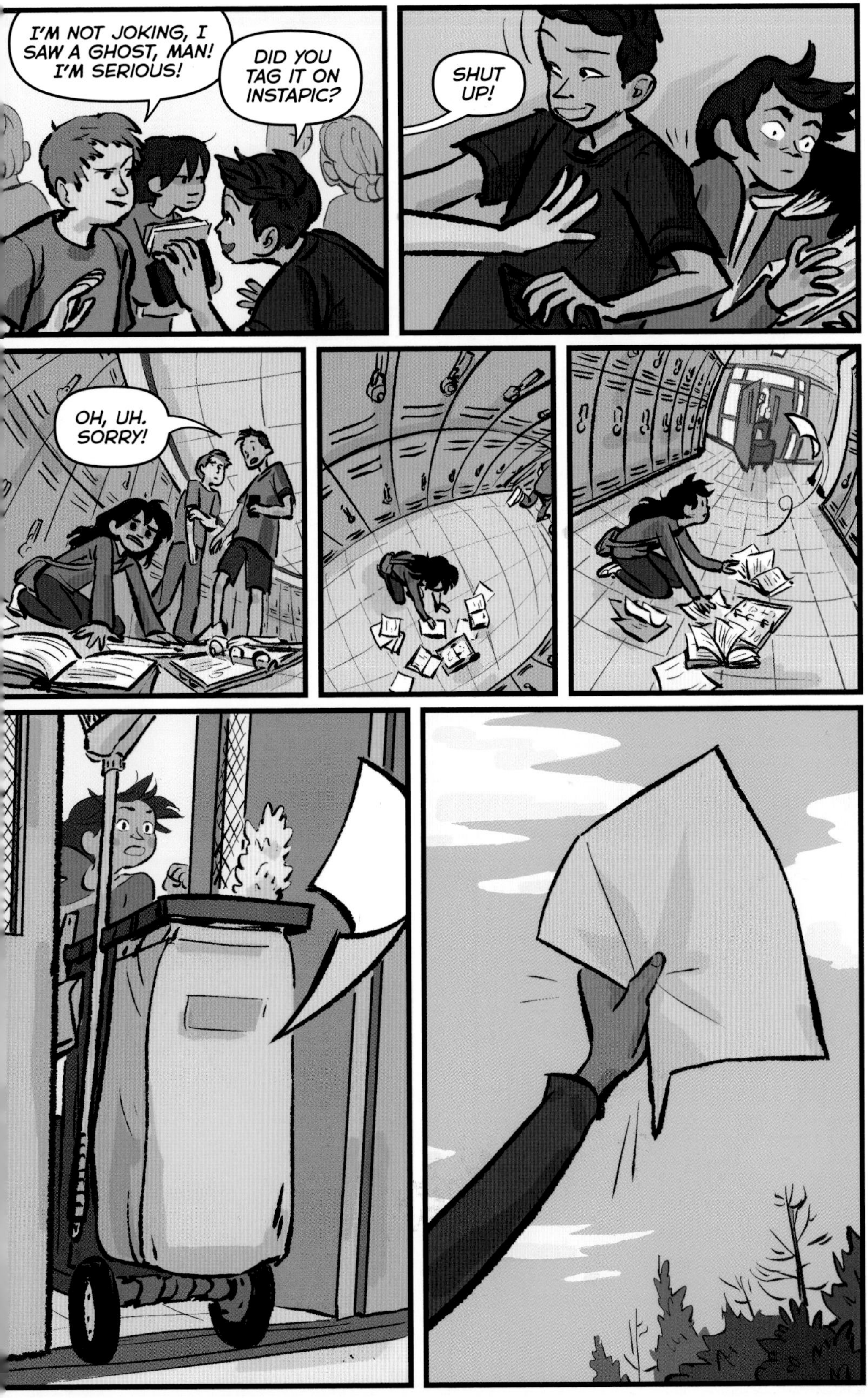
I'M NOT JOKING, I SAW A GHOST, MAN! I'M SERIOUS!
DID YOU TAG IT ON INSTAPIC?
SHUT UP!
OH, UH. SORRY!

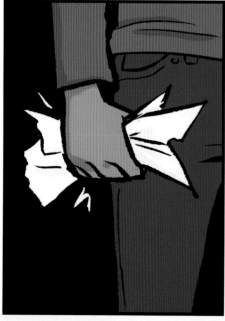

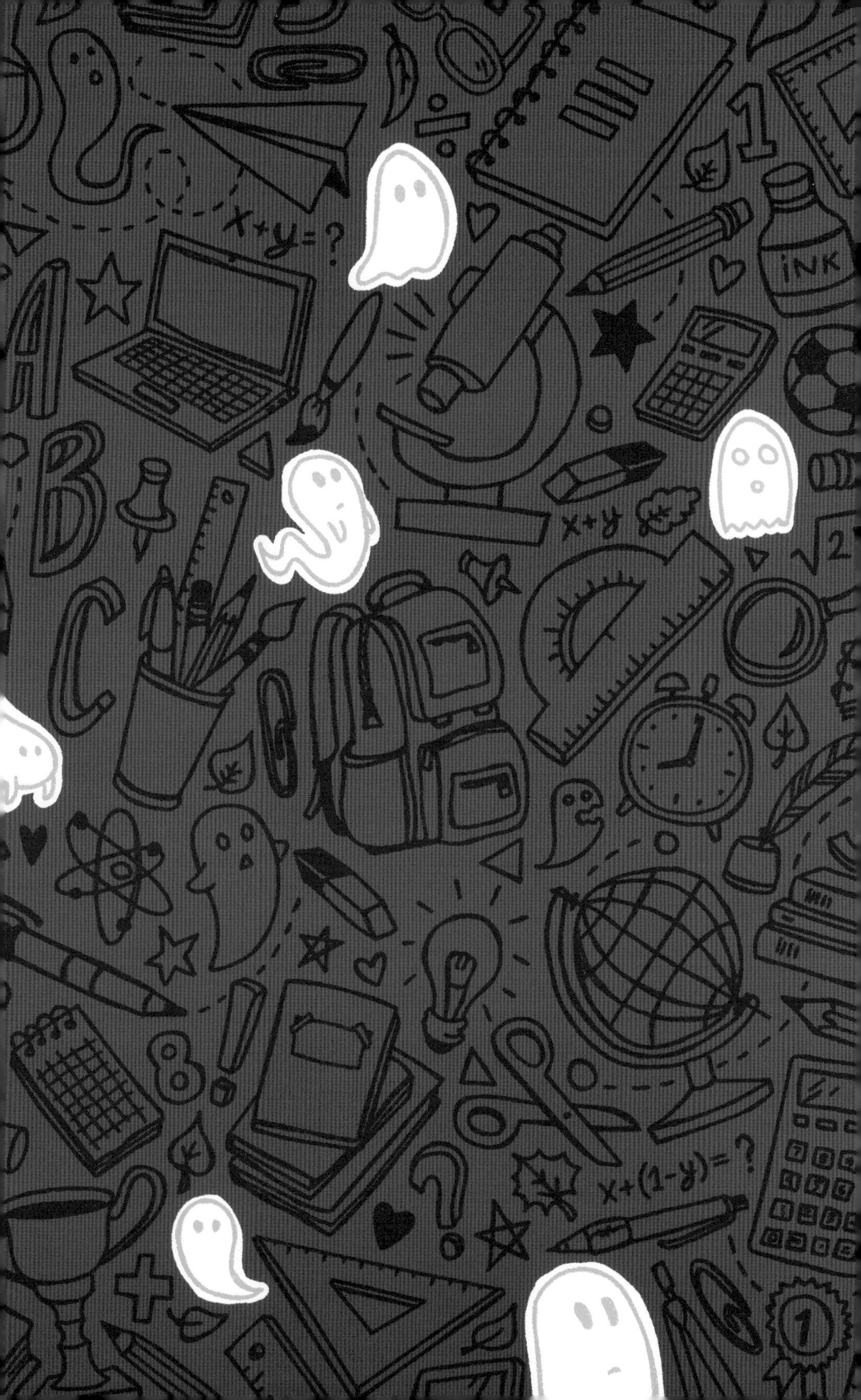
x+y=?
iNK
x+y
x+(1-y)=?

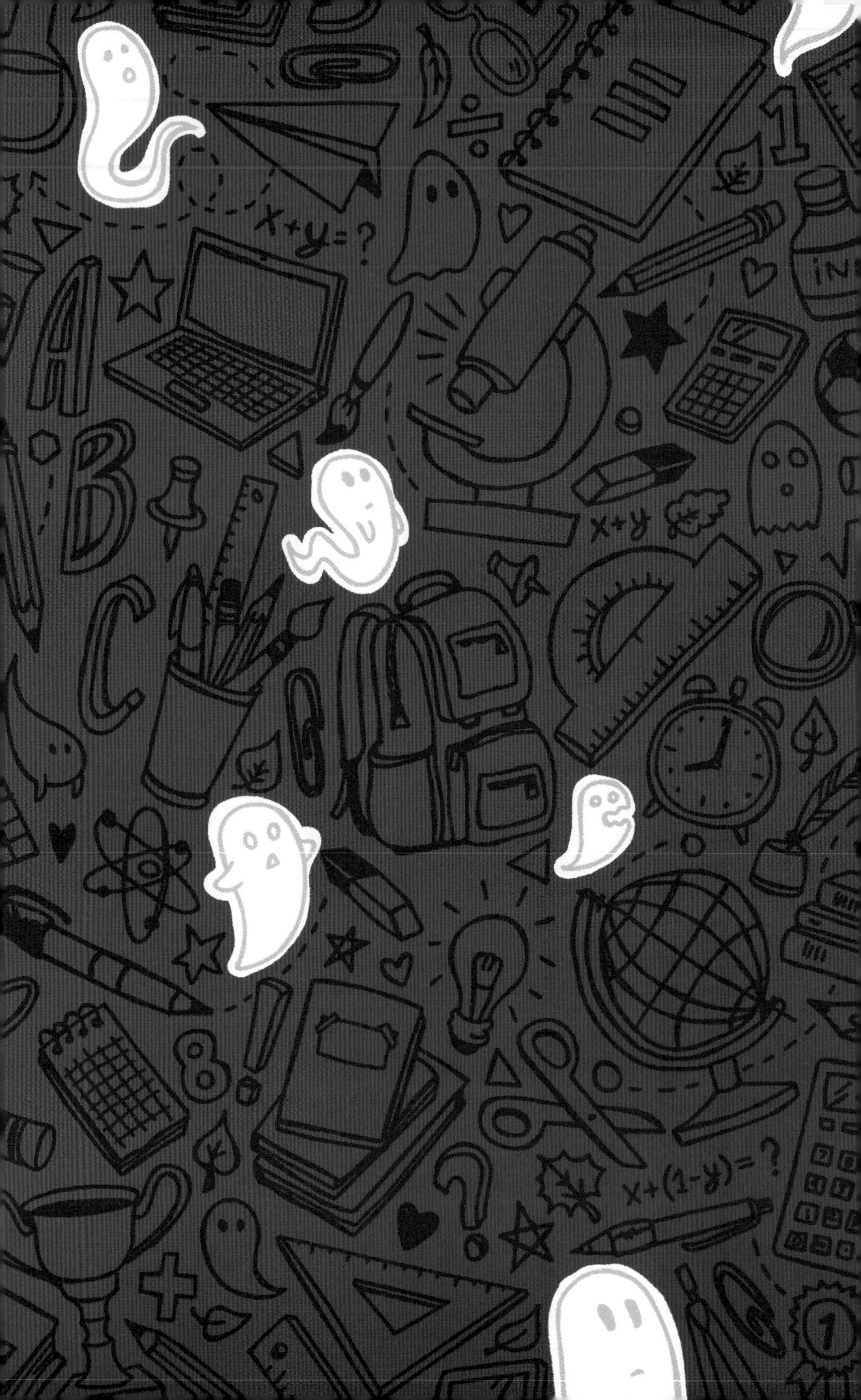
x+y=?
x+y
x+(1-y)=?

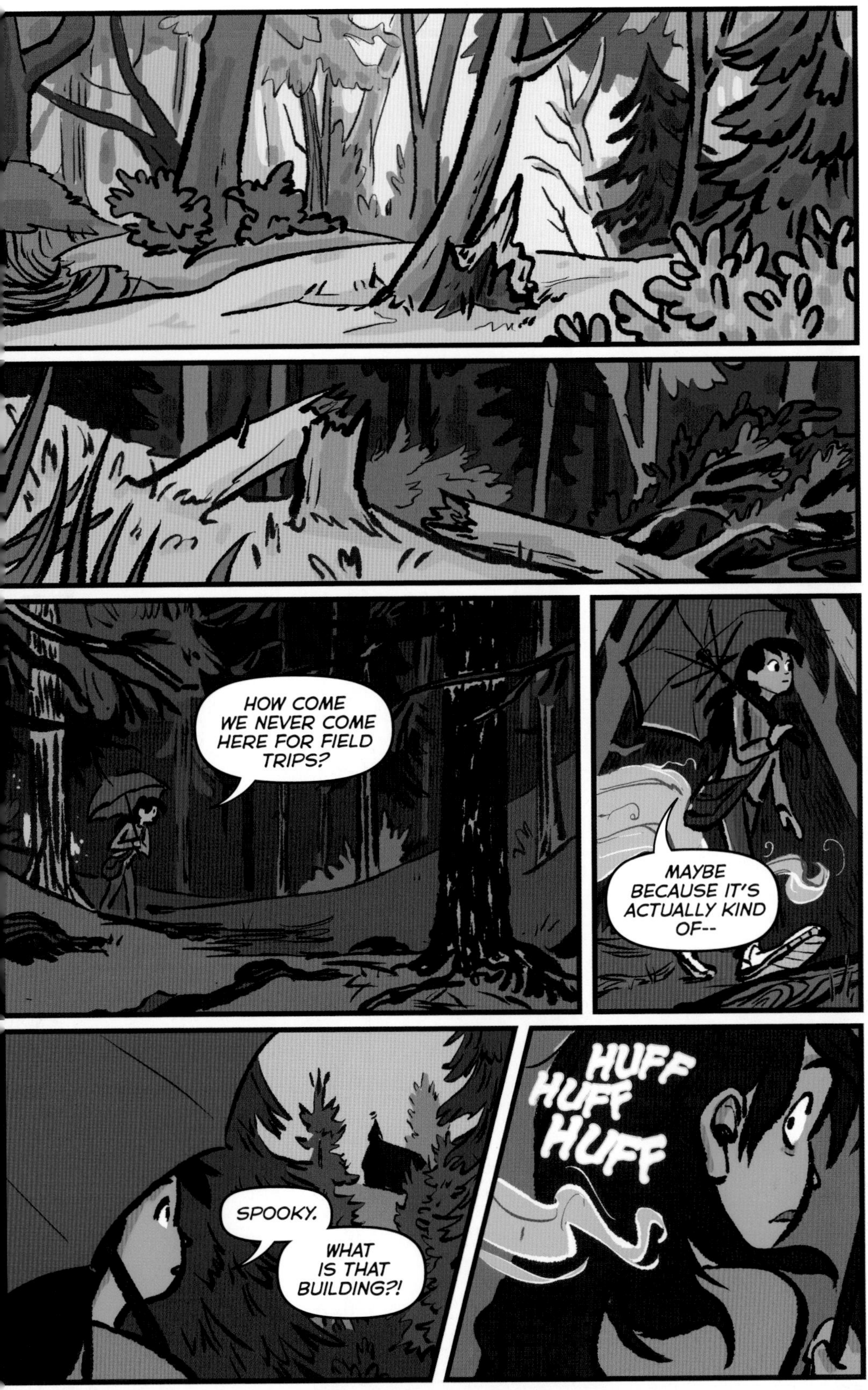
HOW COME WE NEVER COME HERE FOR FIELD TRIPS?
MAYBE BECAUSE IT'S ACTUALLY KIND OF--
SPOOKY.
WHAT IS THAT BUILDING?!
HUFF HUFF HUFF

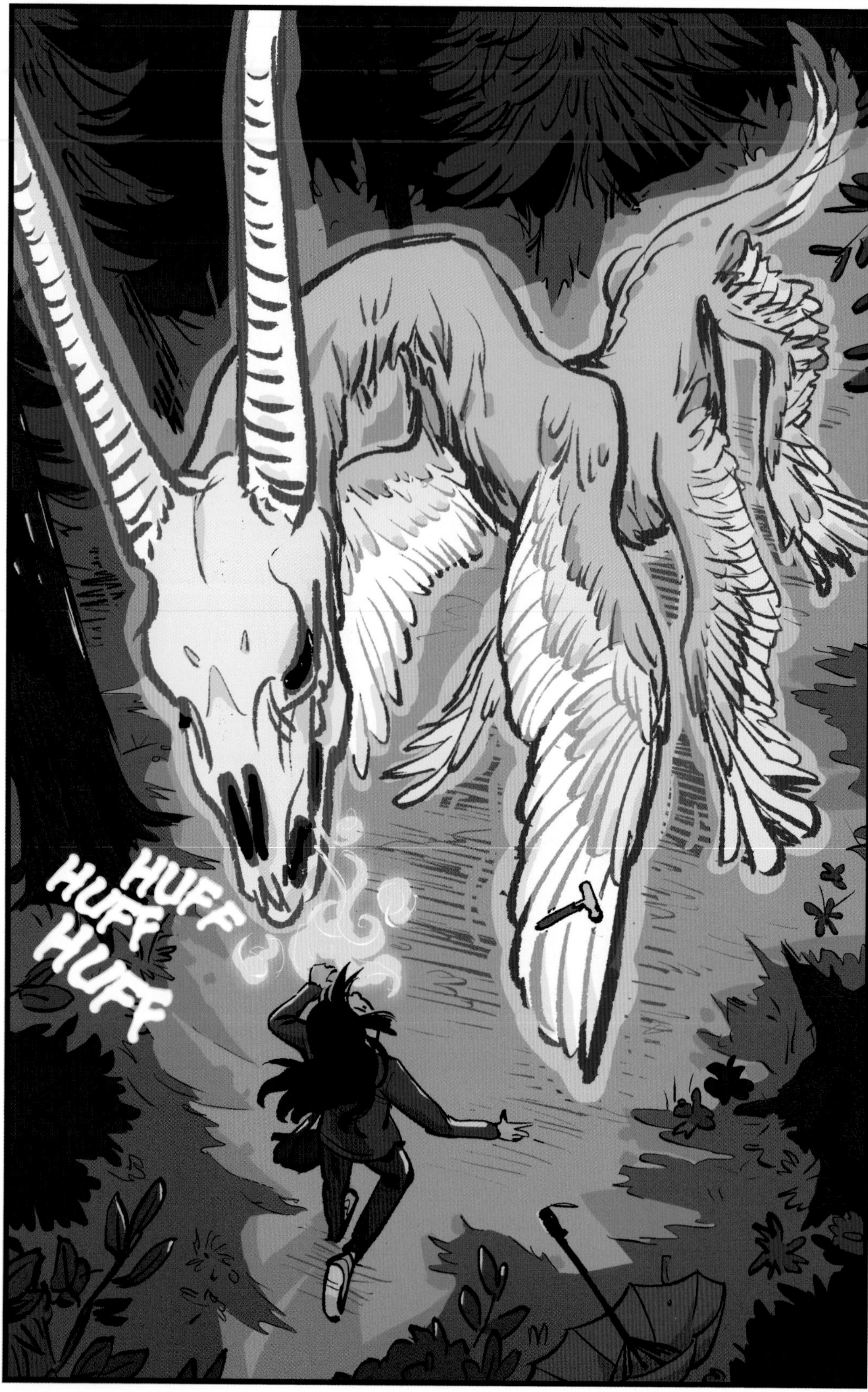
HUFF
HUFF
HUFF

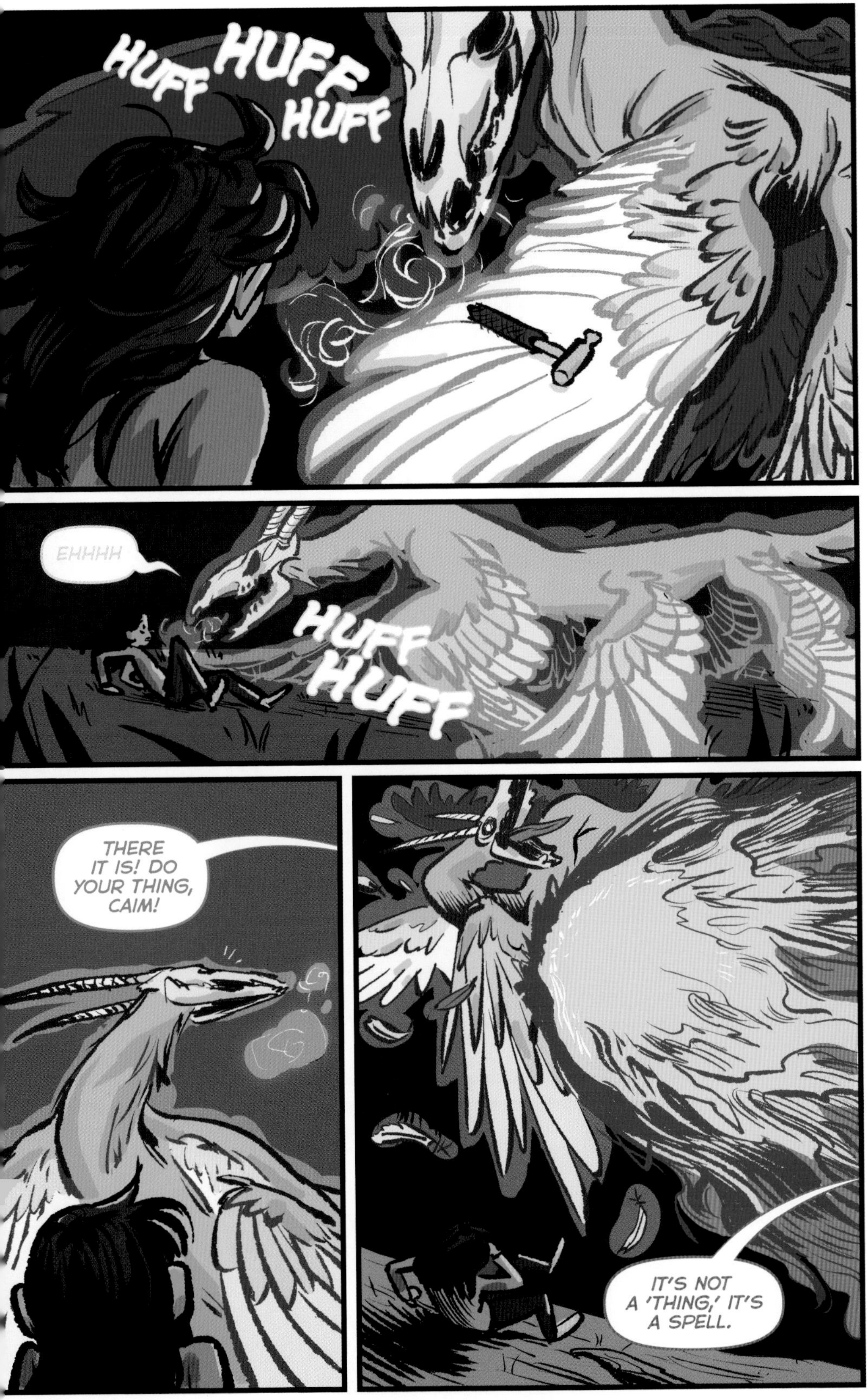
HUFF HUFF HUFF
EHHHH
HUFF HUFF
THERE IT IS! DO YOUR THING, CAIM!
IT'S NOT A 'THING,' IT'S A SPELL.

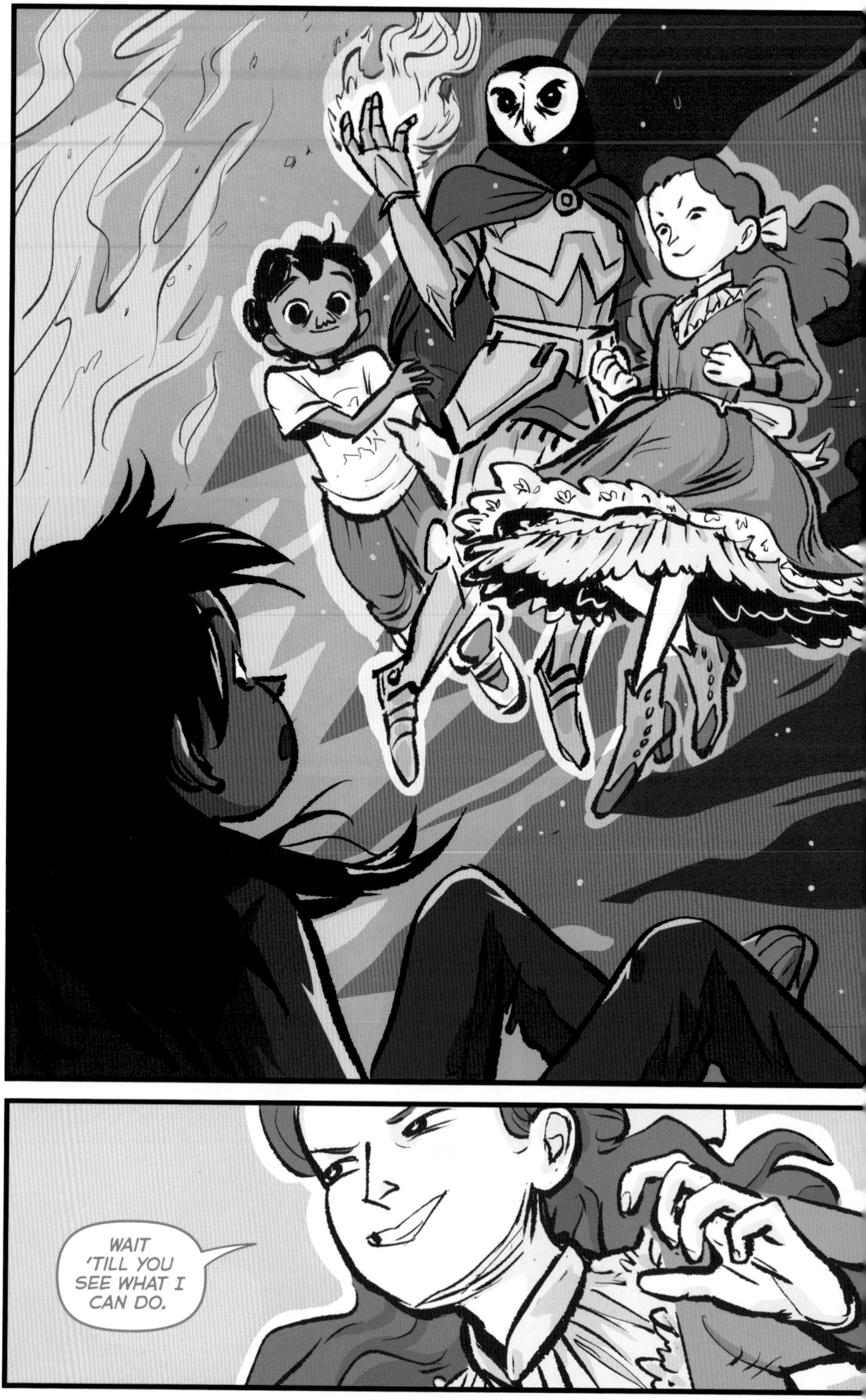
WAIT 'TILL YOU SEE WHAT I CAN DO.

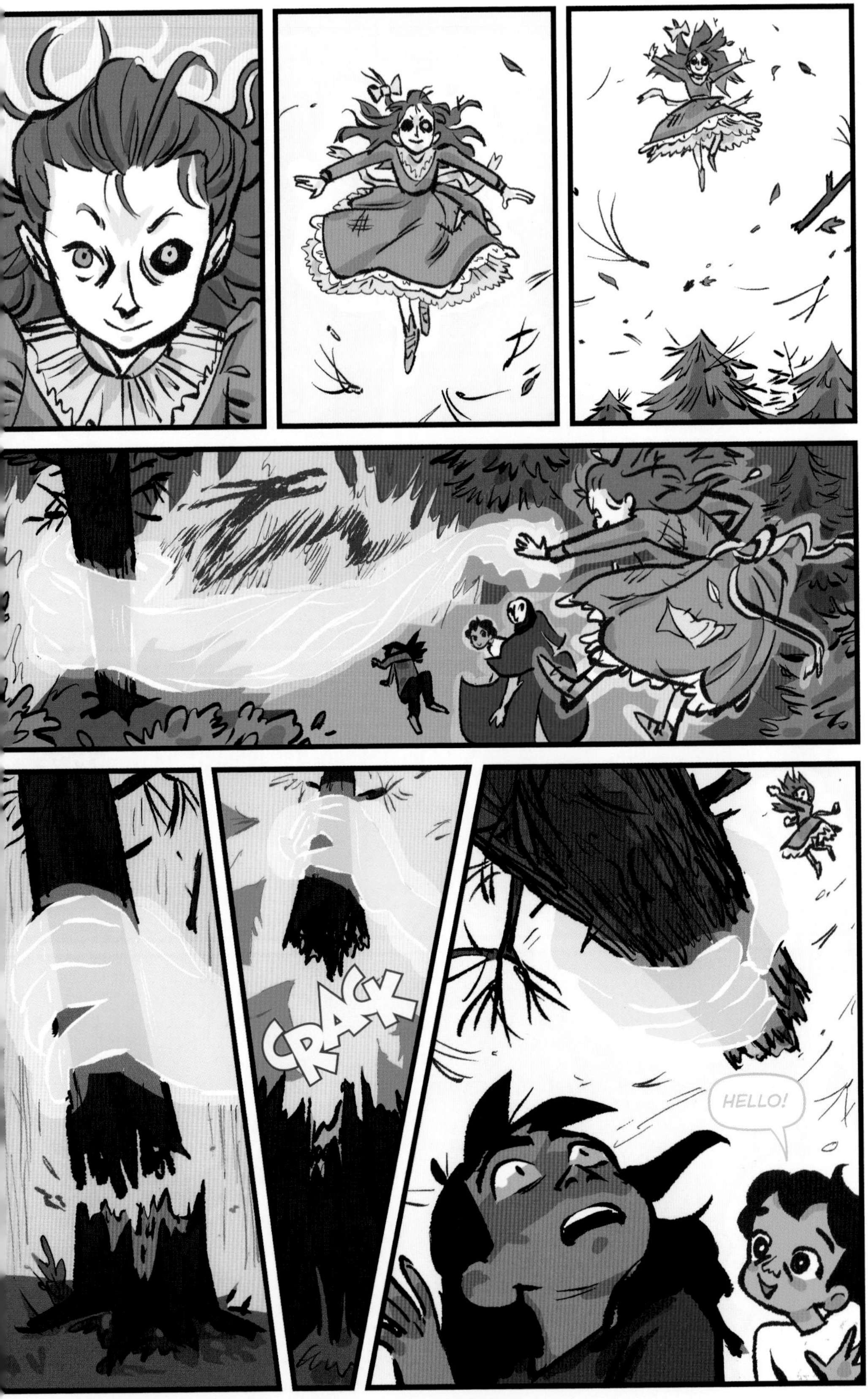
CRACK
HELLO!

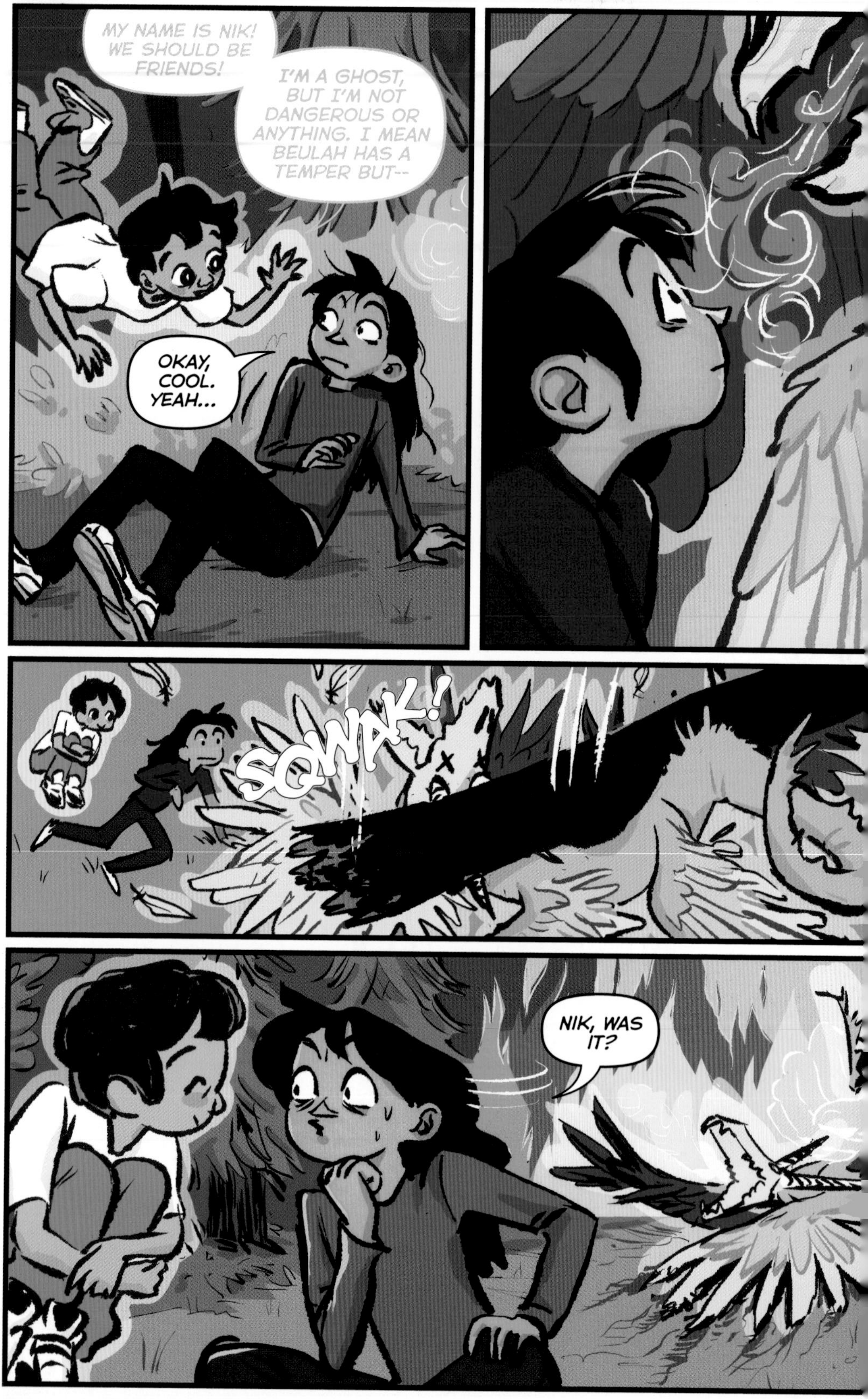
MY NAME IS NIK! WE SHOULD BE FRIENDS!
I'M A GHOST, BUT I'M NOT DANGEROUS OR ANYTHING. I MEAN BEULAH HAS A TEMPER BUT--
OKAY, COOL. YEAH...
SQWAK!
NIK, WAS IT?

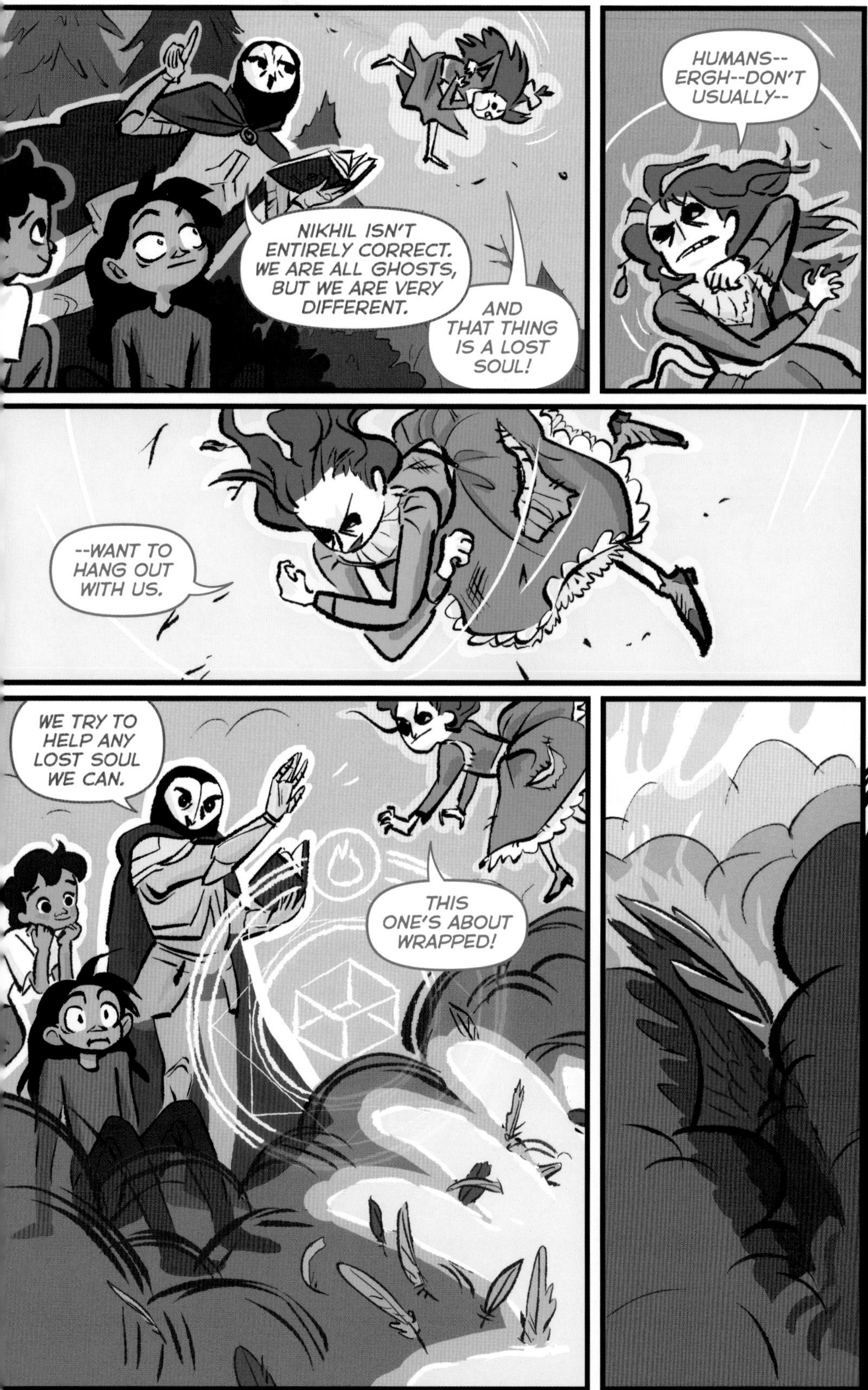
NIKHIL ISN'T ENTIRELY CORRECT. WE ARE ALL GHOSTS, BUT WE ARE VERY DIFFERENT.
AND THAT THING IS A LOST SOUL!
HUMANS-- ERGH--DON'T USUALLY--
--WANT TO HANG OUT WITH US.
WE TRY TO HELP ANY LOST SOUL WE CAN.
THIS ONE'S ABOUT WRAPPED!

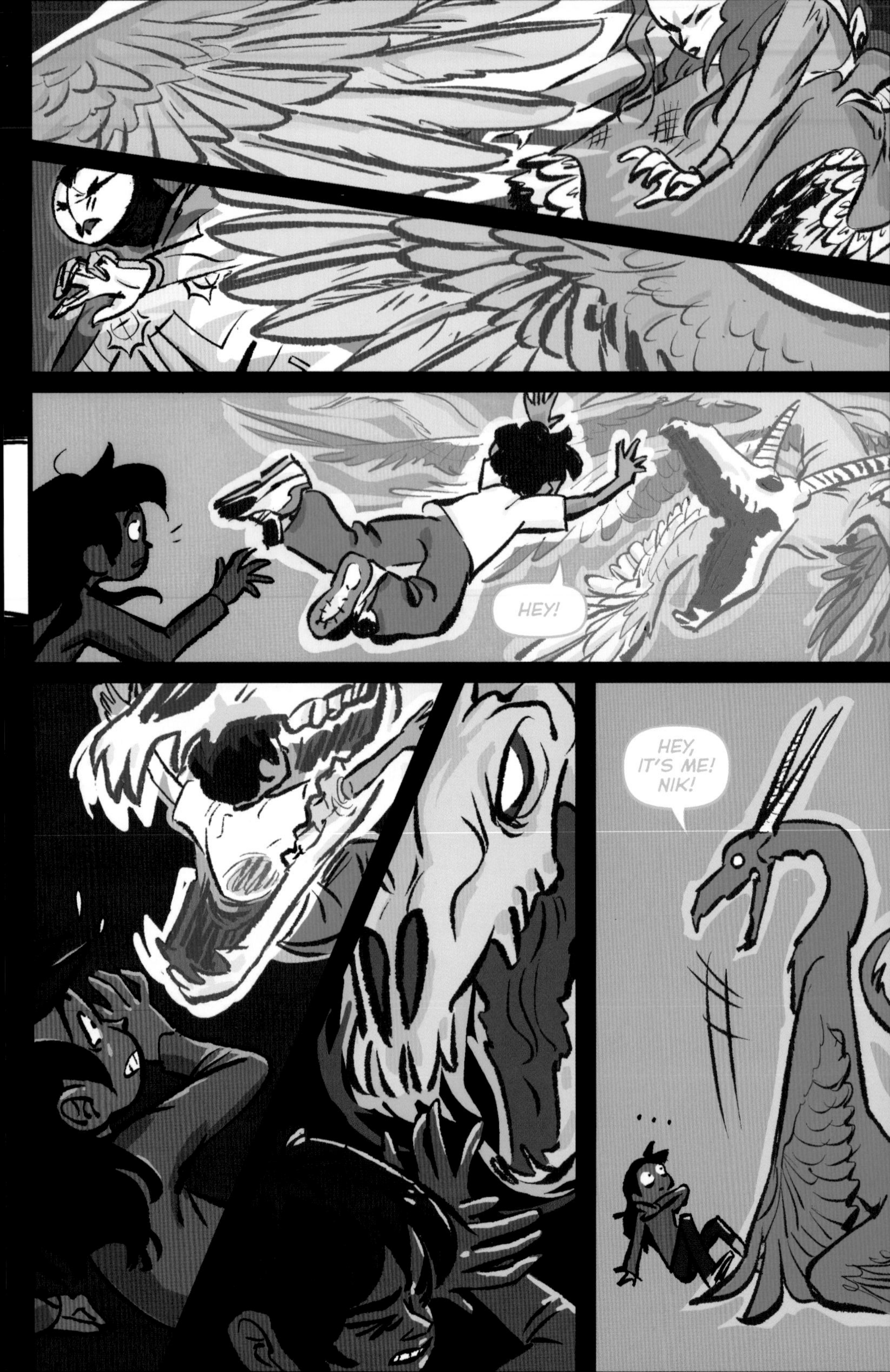
HEY!
HEY, IT'S ME! NIK!
. . .

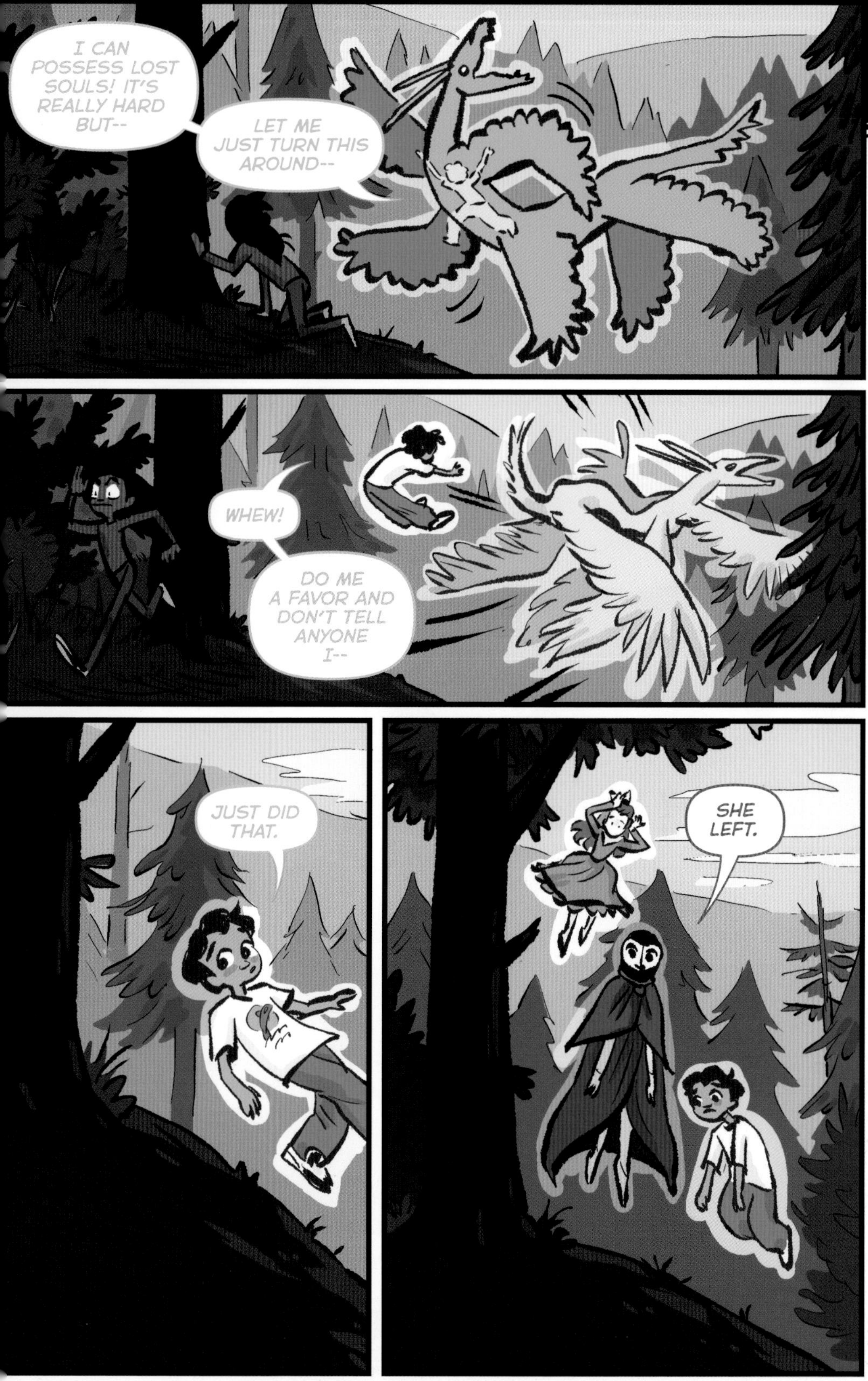
I CAN POSSESS LOST SOULS! IT'S REALLY HARD BUT--
LET ME JUST TURN THIS AROUND--
WHEW!
DO ME A FAVOR AND DON'T TELL ANYONE I--
JUST DID THAT.
SHE LEFT.

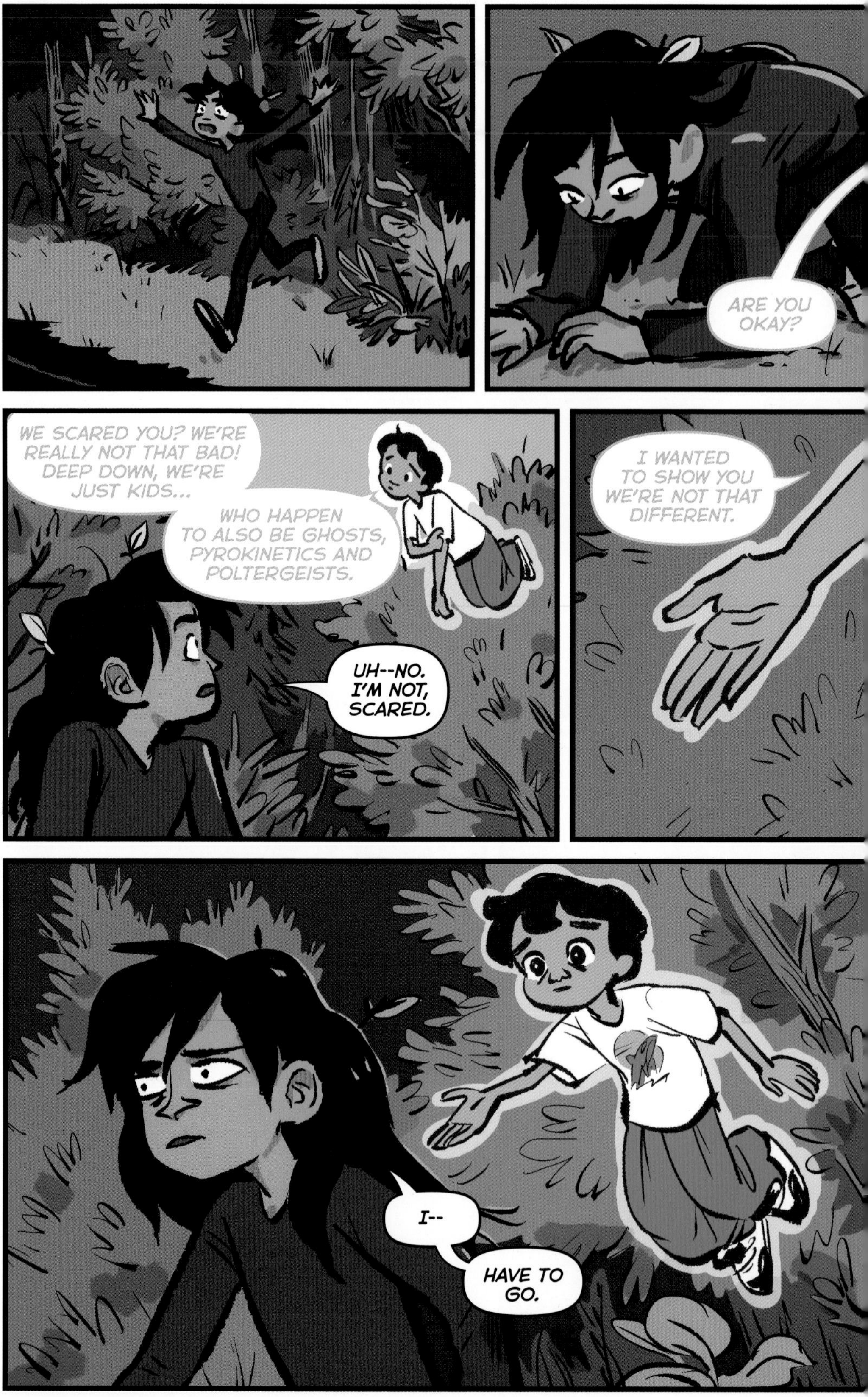
ARE YOU OKAY?
WE SCARED YOU? WE'RE REALLY NOT THAT BAD! DEEP DOWN, WE'RE JUST KIDS...
WHO HAPPEN TO ALSO BE GHOSTS, PYROKINETICS AND POLTERGEISTS.
UH--NO. I'M NOT, SCARED.
I WANTED TO SHOW YOU WE'RE NOT THAT DIFFERENT.
I--
HAVE TO GO.

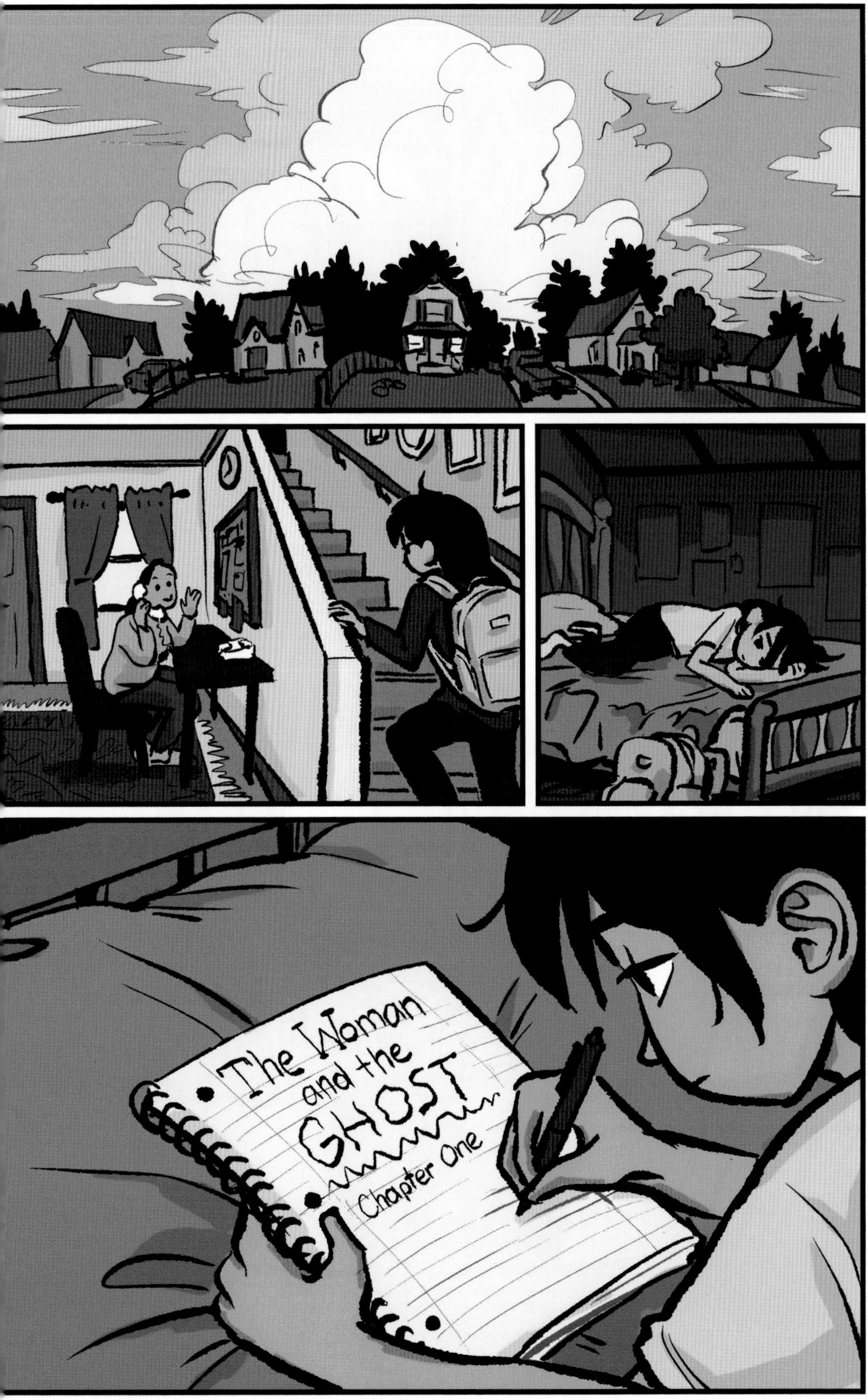
The Woman
and the
GHOST
Chapter One

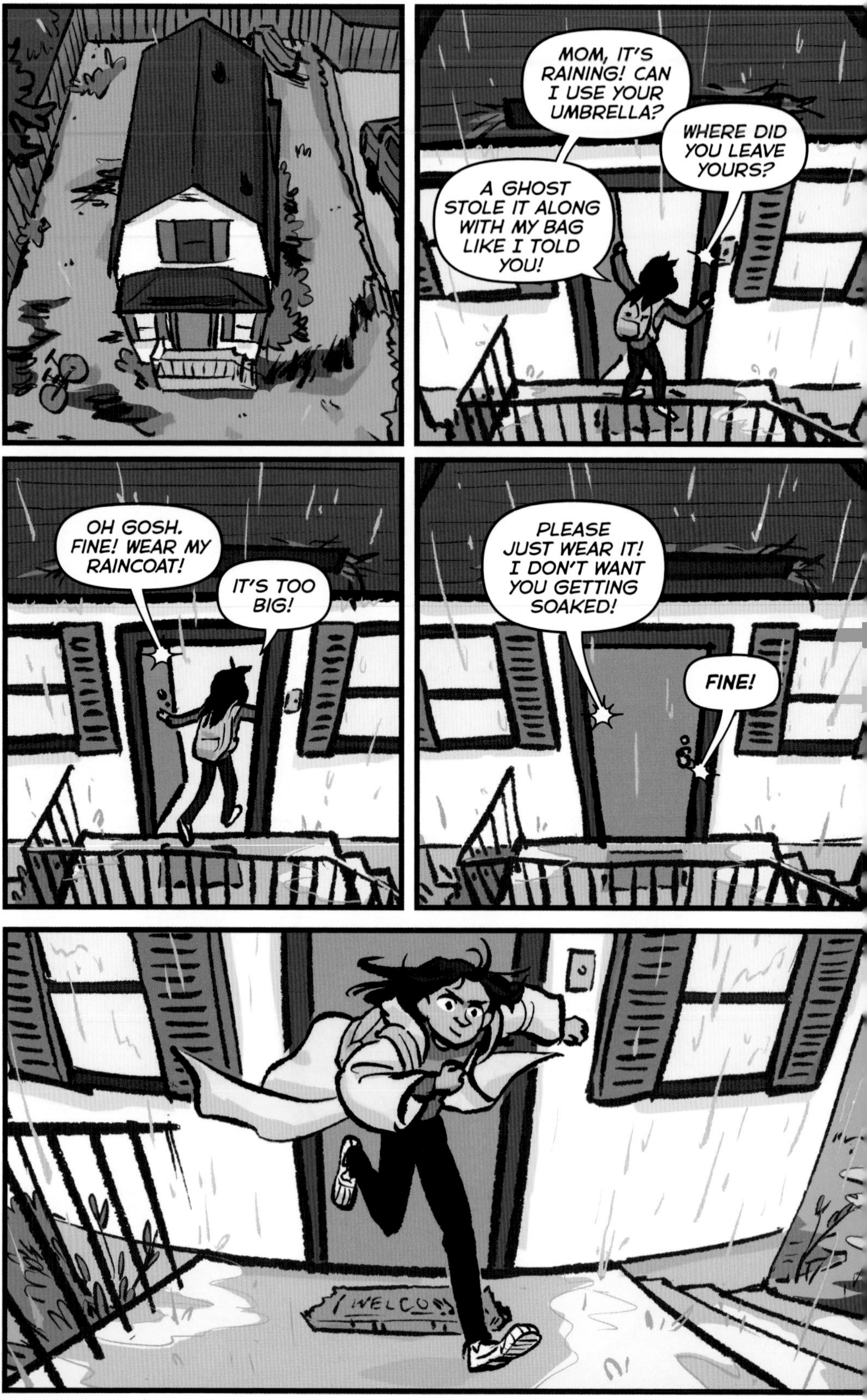
MOM, IT'S RAINING! CAN I USE YOUR UMBRELLA?
WHERE DID YOU LEAVE YOURS?
A GHOST STOLE IT ALONG WITH MY BAG LIKE I TOLD YOU!
OH GOSH. FINE! WEAR MY RAINCOAT!
IT'S TOO BIG!
PLEASE JUST WEAR IT! I DON'T WANT YOU GETTING SOAKED!
FINE!
WELCOM

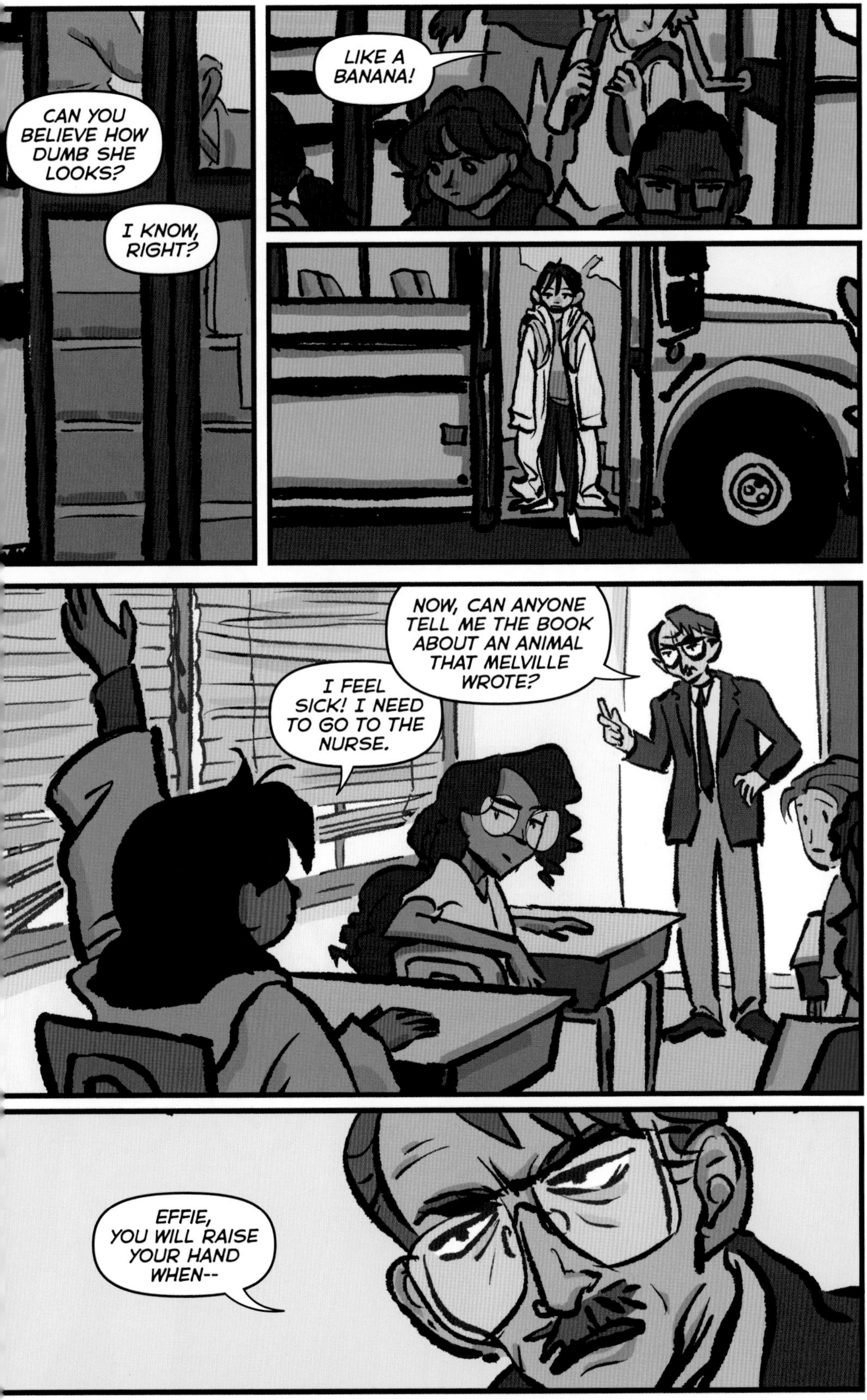
CAN YOU BELIEVE HOW DUMB SHE LOOKS?
I KNOW, RIGHT?
LIKE A BANANA!
NOW, CAN ANYONE TELL ME THE BOOK ABOUT AN ANIMAL THAT MELVILLE WROTE?
I FEEL SICK! I NEED TO GO TO THE NURSE.
EFFIE, YOU WILL RAISE YOUR HAND WHEN--

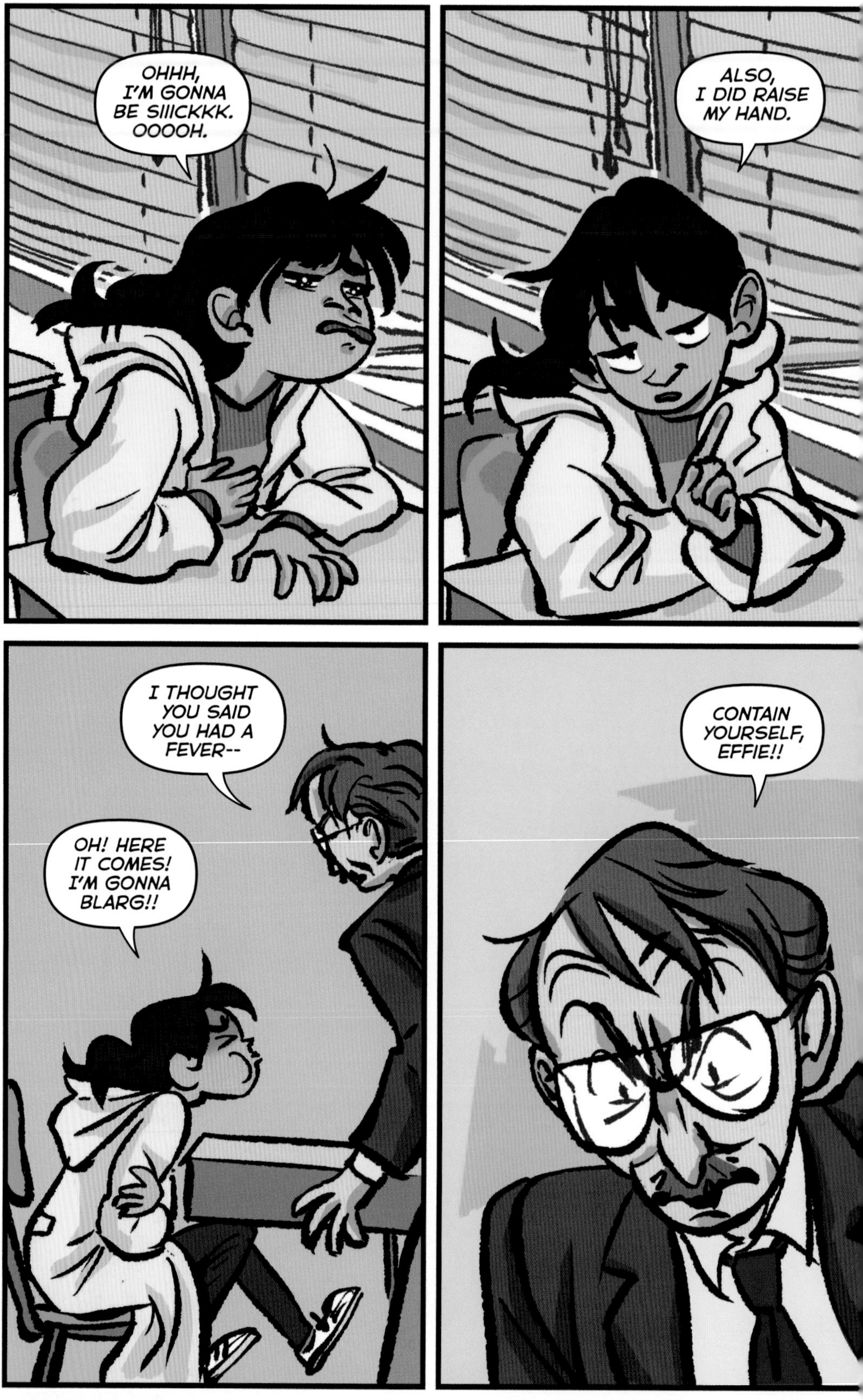
OHHH, I'M GONNA BE SIIICKKK. OOOOH.
ALSO, I DID RAISE MY HAND.
I THOUGHT YOU SAID YOU HAD A FEVER--
OH! HERE IT COMES! I'M GONNA BLARG!!
CONTAIN YOURSELF, EFFIE!!

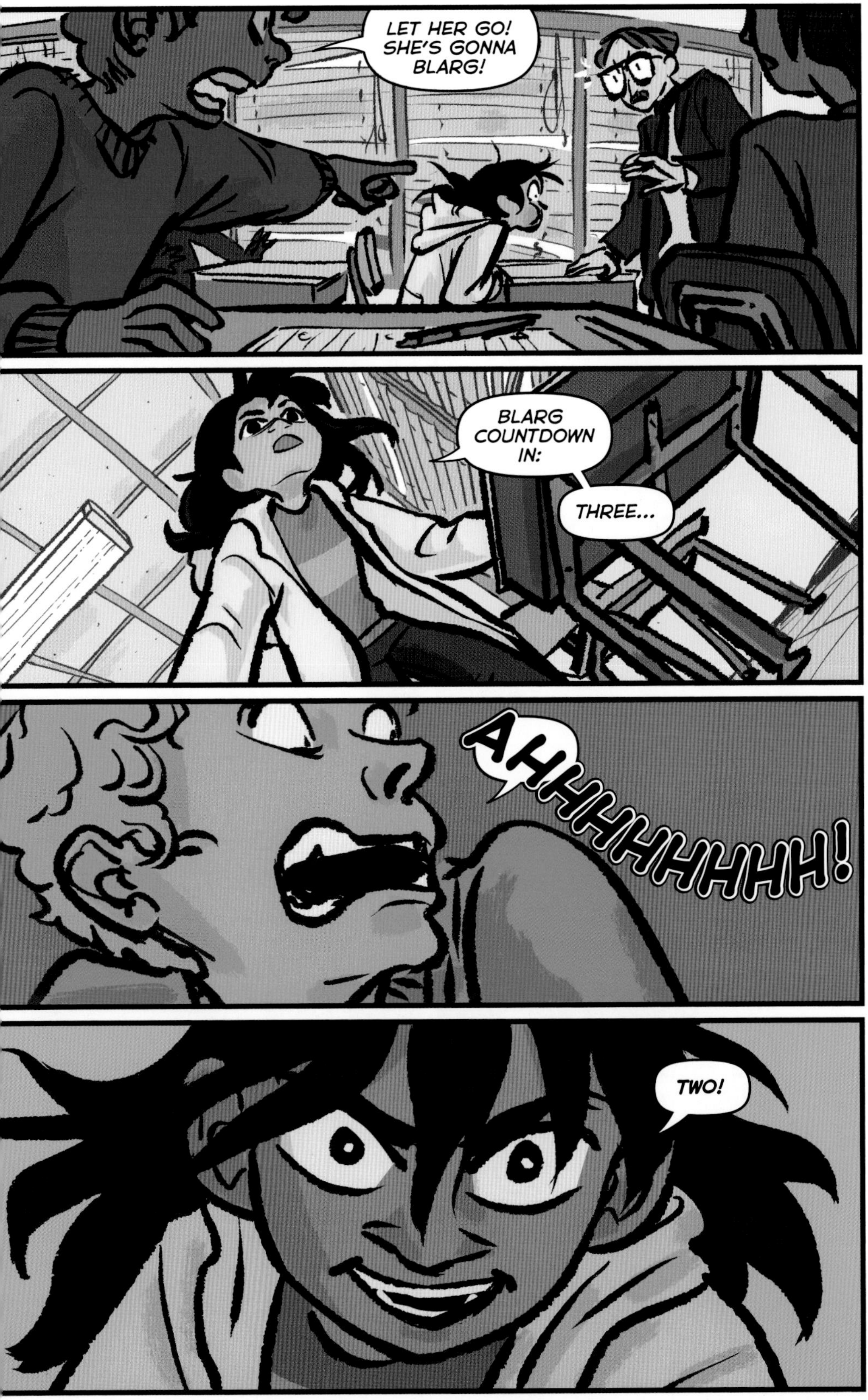
LET HER GO! SHE'S GONNA BLARG!
BLARG COUNTDOWN IN:
THREE...
AHHHHHHHHH!
TWO!

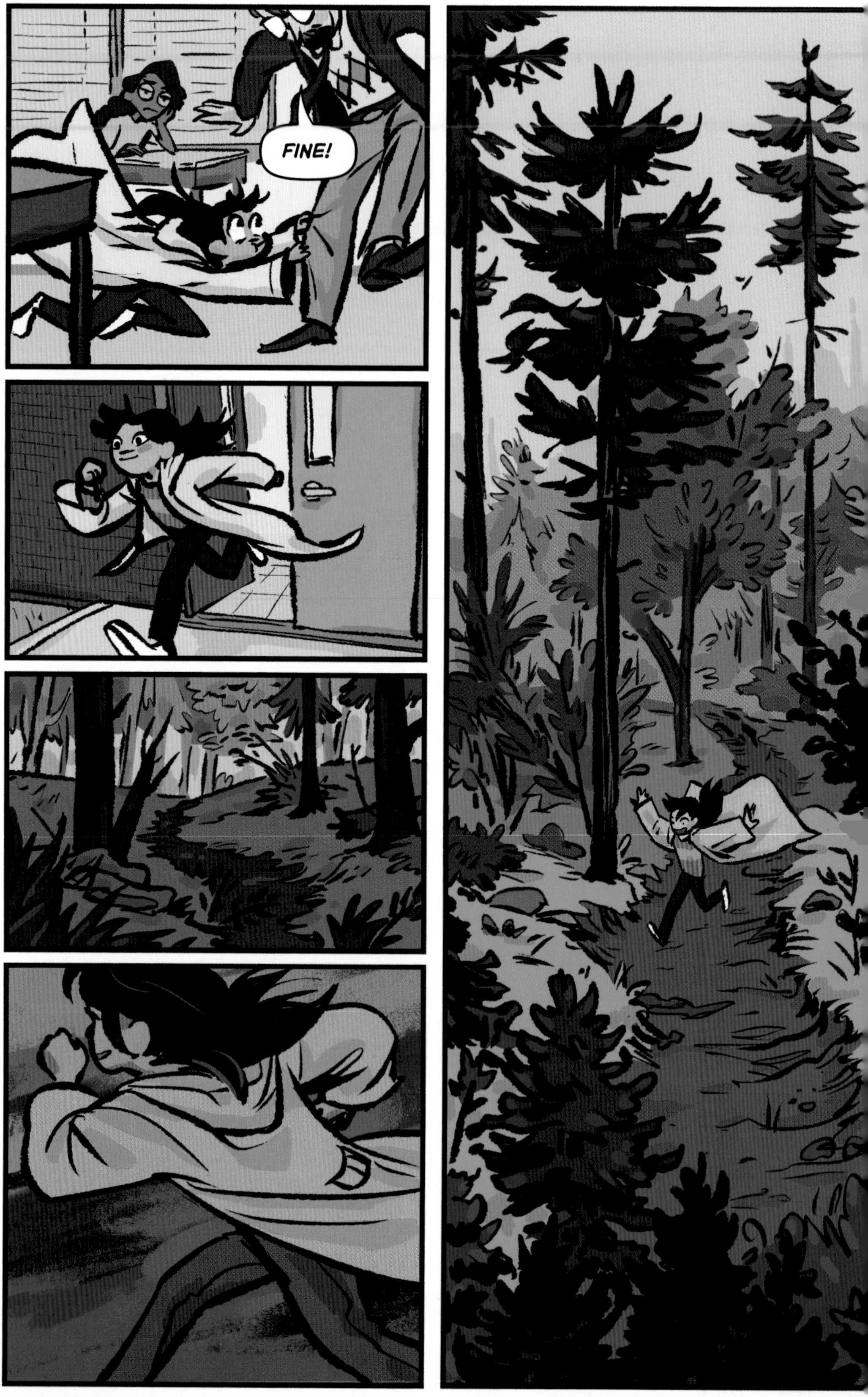
FINE!

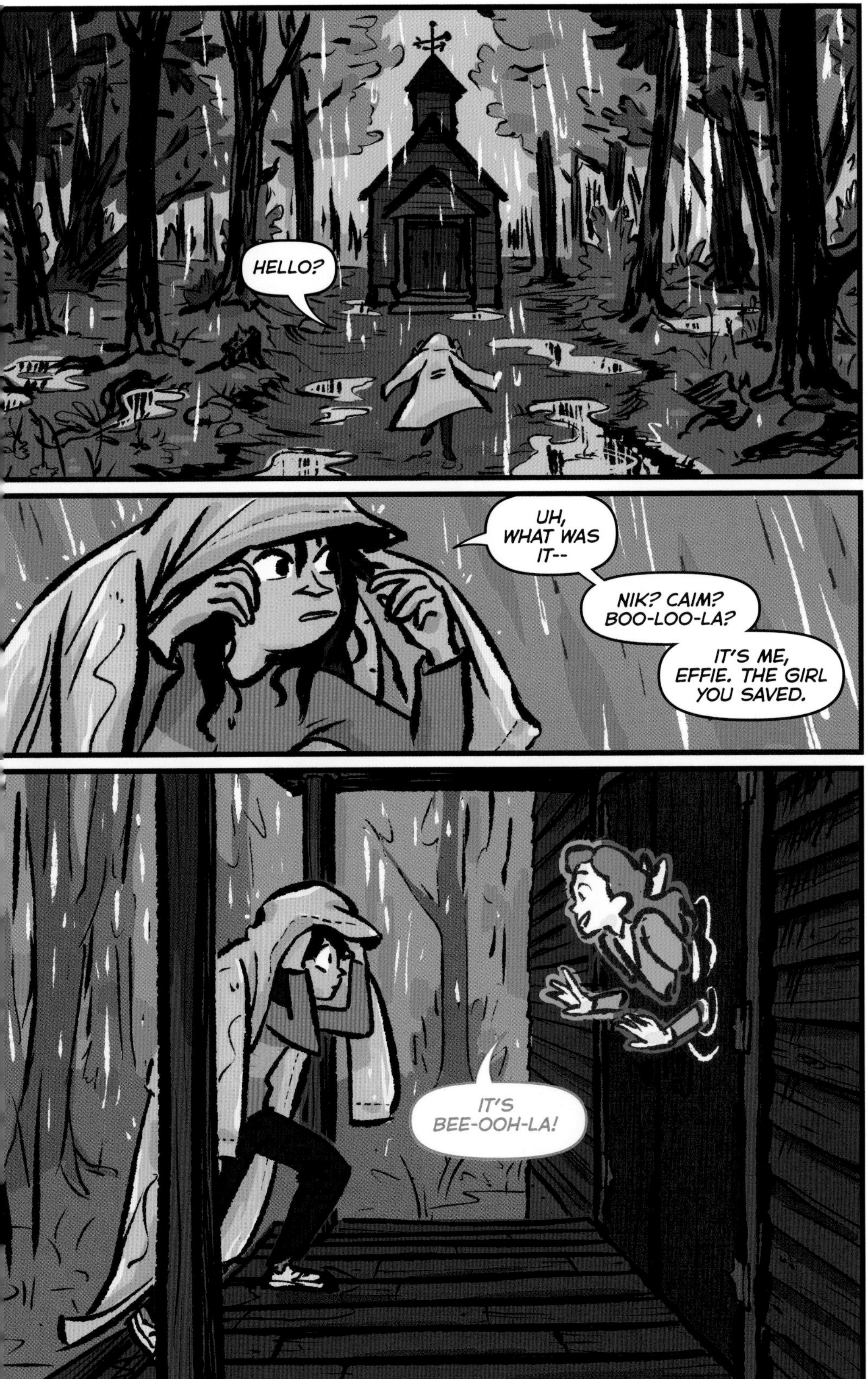
HELLO?
UH, WHAT WAS IT--
NIK? CAIM? BOO-LOO-LA?
IT'S ME, EFFIE. THE GIRL YOU SAVED.
IT'S BEE-OOH-LA!

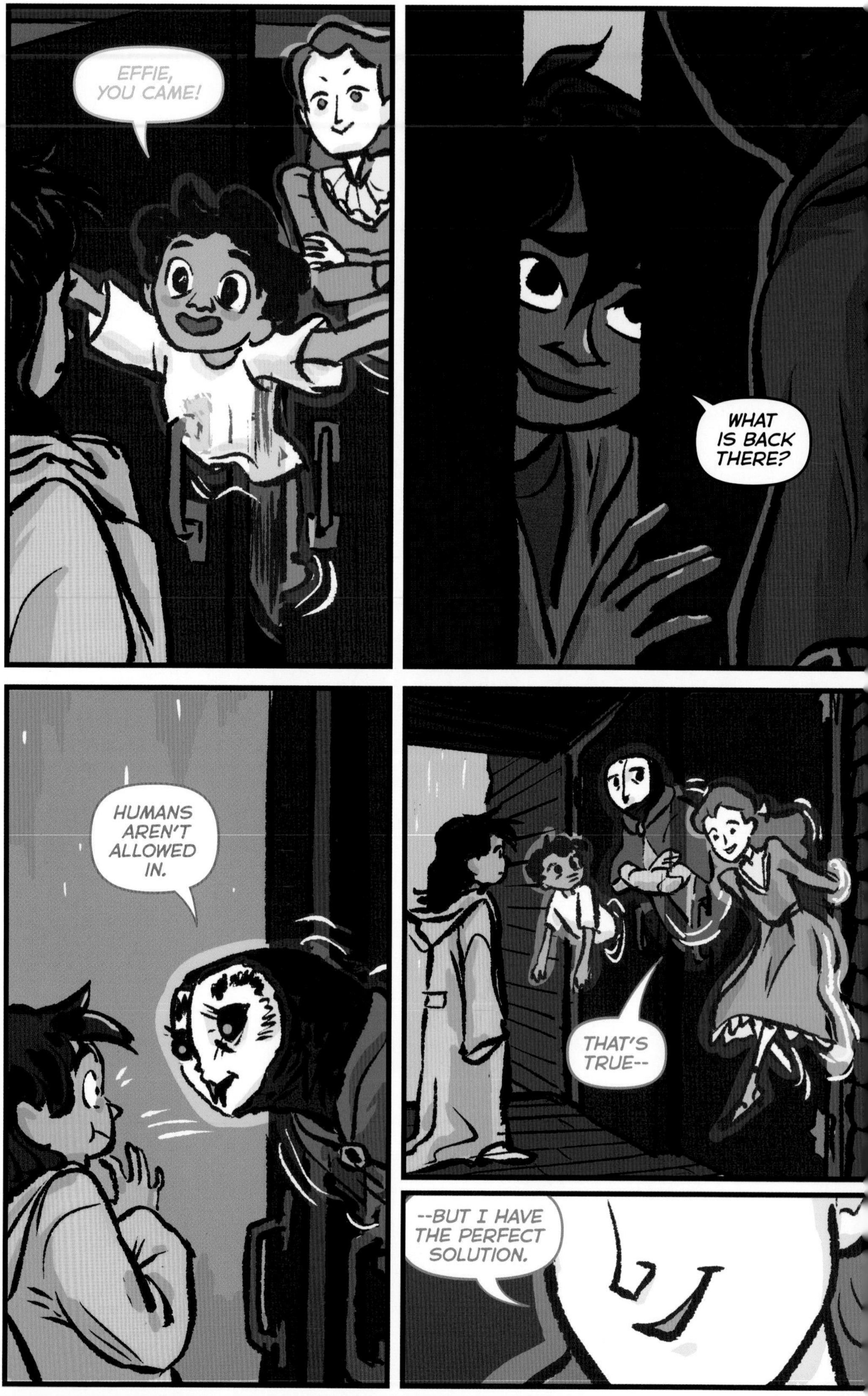
EFFIE, YOU CAME!
WHAT IS BACK THERE?
HUMANS AREN'T ALLOWED IN.
THAT'S TRUE--
--BUT I HAVE THE PERFECT SOLUTION.

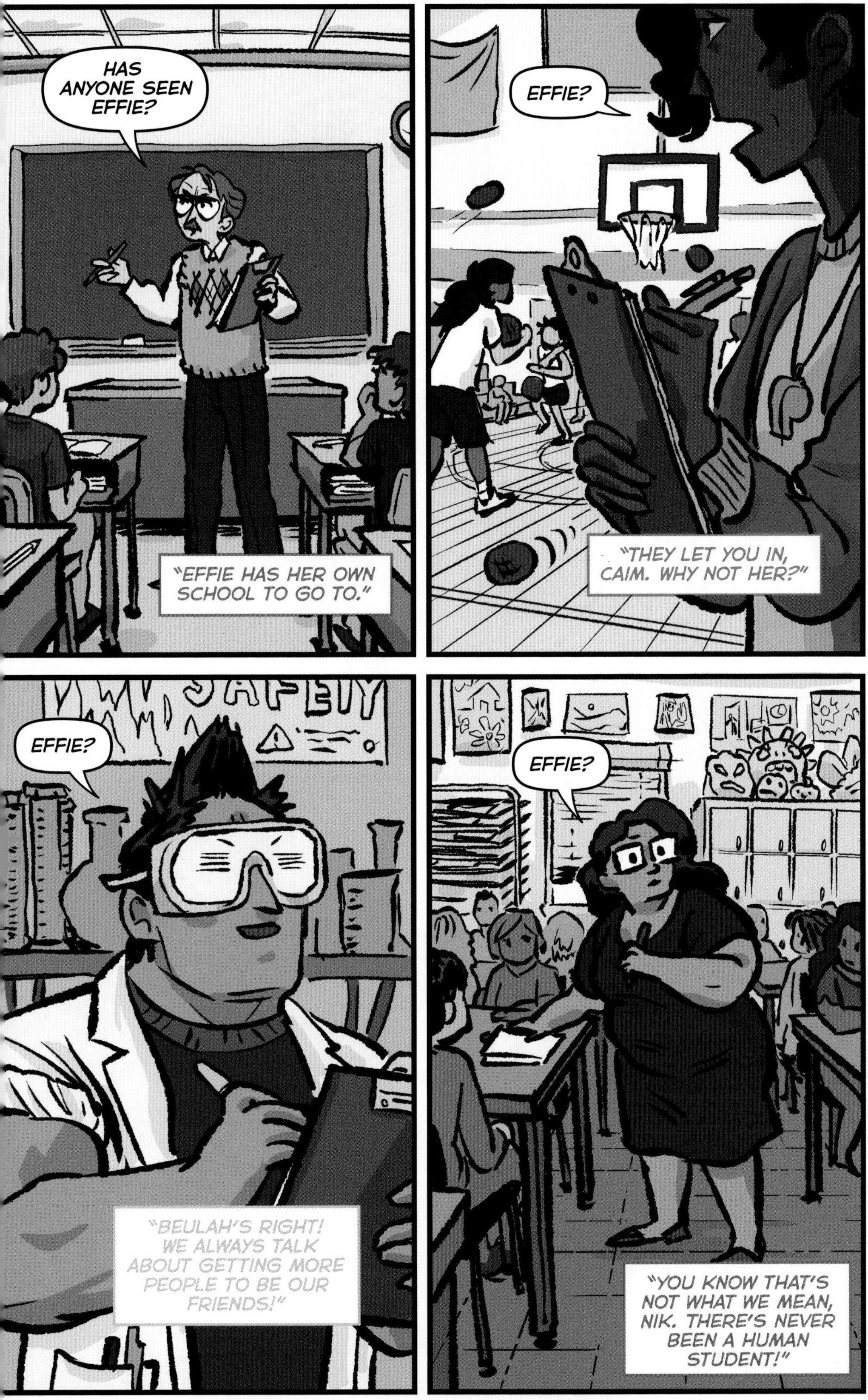
HAS ANYONE SEEN EFFIE?
"EFFIE HAS HER OWN SCHOOL TO GO TO."
EFFIE?
"THEY LET YOU IN, CAIM. WHY NOT HER?"
SAFETY
EFFIE?
"BEULAH'S RIGHT! WE ALWAYS TALK ABOUT GETTING MORE PEOPLE TO BE OUR FRIENDS!"
EFFIE?
"YOU KNOW THAT'S NOT WHAT WE MEAN, NIK. THERE'S NEVER BEEN A HUMAN STUDENT!"

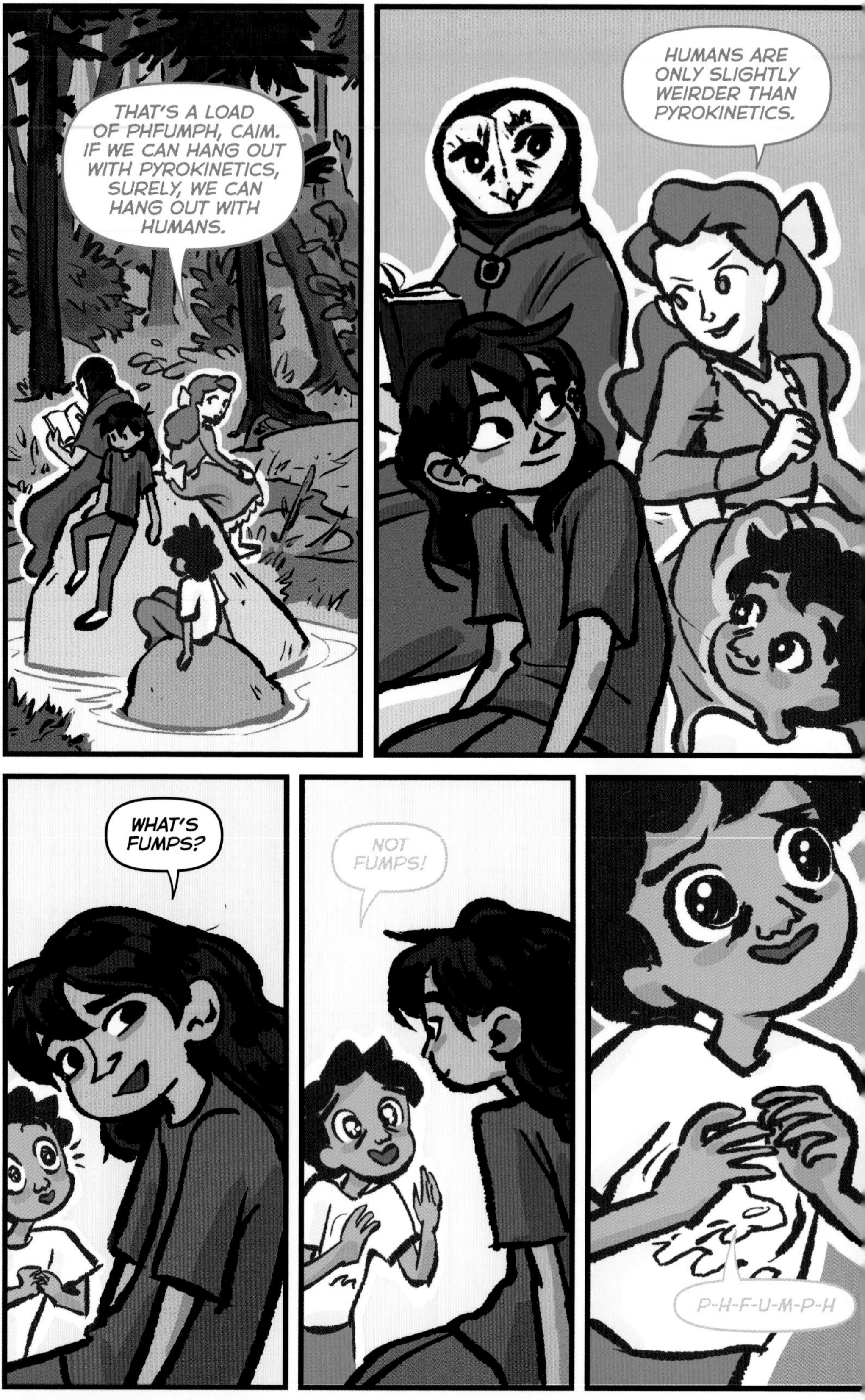
THAT'S A LOAD OF PHFUMPH, CAIM. IF WE CAN HANG OUT WITH PYROKINETICS, SURELY, WE CAN HANG OUT WITH HUMANS.
HUMANS ARE ONLY SLIGHTLY WEIRDER THAN PYROKINETICS.
WHAT'S FUMPS?
NOT FUMPS!
P-H-F-U-M-P-H

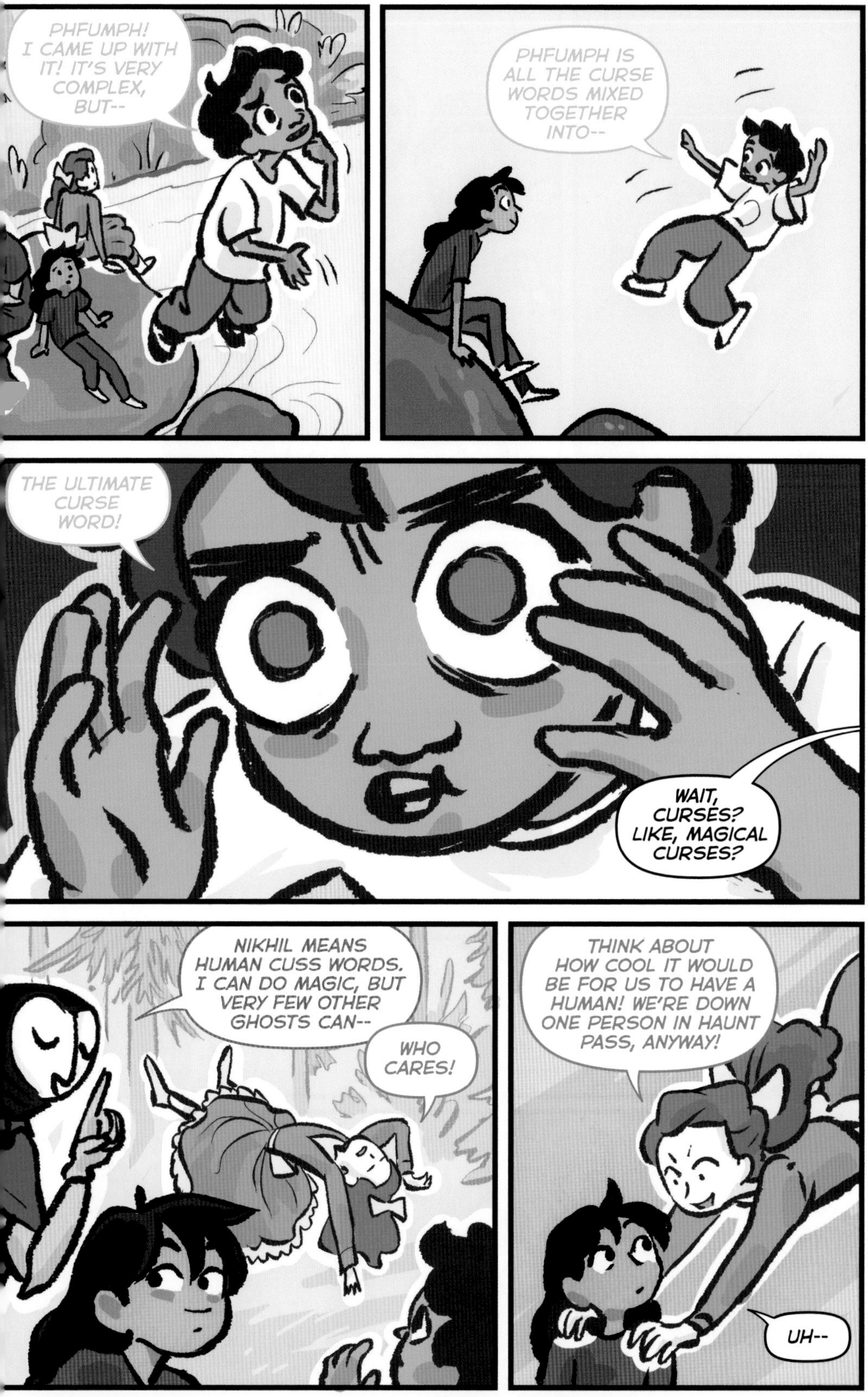
PHFUMPH! I CAME UP WITH IT! IT'S VERY COMPLEX, BUT--
PHFUMPH IS ALL THE CURSE WORDS MIXED TOGETHER INTO--
THE ULTIMATE CURSE WORD!
WAIT, CURSES? LIKE, MAGICAL CURSES?
NIKHIL MEANS HUMAN CUSS WORDS. I CAN DO MAGIC, BUT VERY FEW OTHER GHOSTS CAN--
WHO CARES!
THINK ABOUT HOW COOL IT WOULD BE FOR US TO HAVE A HUMAN! WE'RE DOWN ONE PERSON IN HAUNT PASS, ANYWAY!
UH--

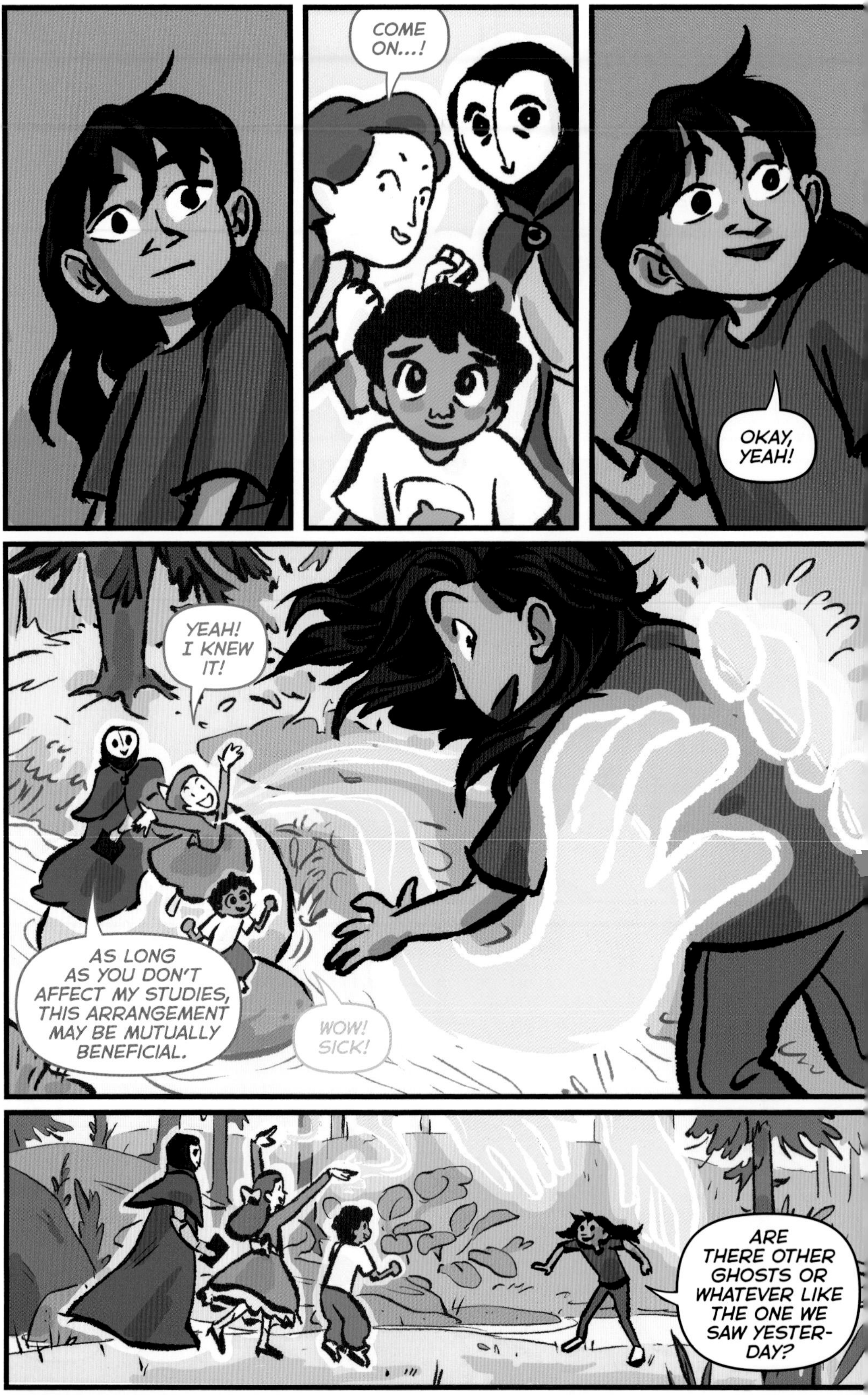
COME ON...!
OKAY, YEAH!
YEAH! I KNEW IT!
AS LONG AS YOU DON'T AFFECT MY STUDIES, THIS ARRANGEMENT MAY BE MUTUALLY BENEFICIAL.
WOW! SICK!
ARE THERE OTHER GHOSTS OR WHATEVER LIKE THE ONE WE SAW YESTER-DAY?

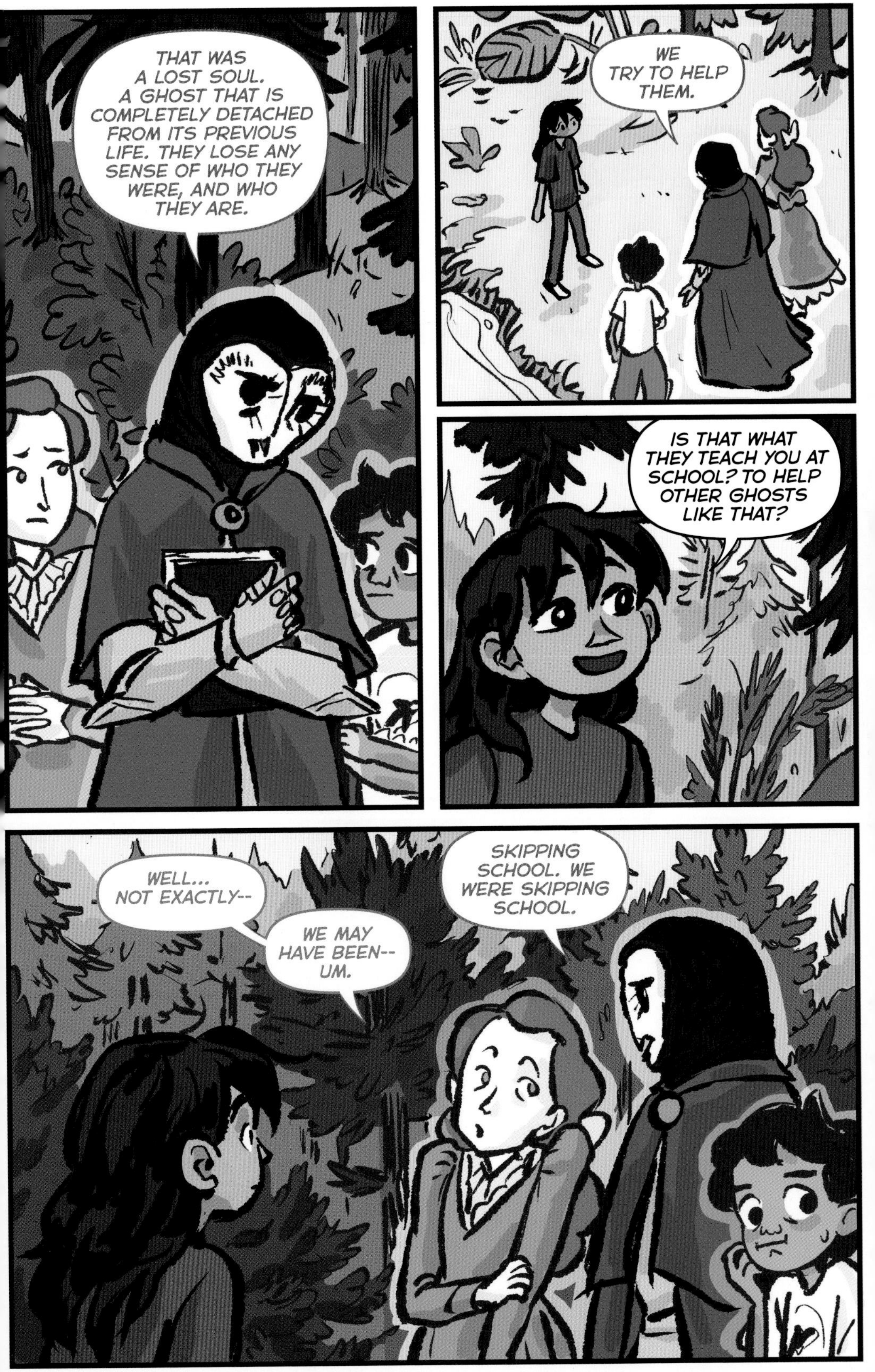
THAT WAS A LOST SOUL. A GHOST THAT IS COMPLETELY DETACHED FROM ITS PREVIOUS LIFE. THEY LOSE ANY SENSE OF WHO THEY WERE, AND WHO THEY ARE.
WE TRY TO HELP THEM.
IS THAT WHAT THEY TEACH YOU AT SCHOOL? TO HELP OTHER GHOSTS LIKE THAT?
WELL... NOT EXACTLY--
WE MAY HAVE BEEN-- UM.
SKIPPING SCHOOL. WE WERE SKIPPING SCHOOL.

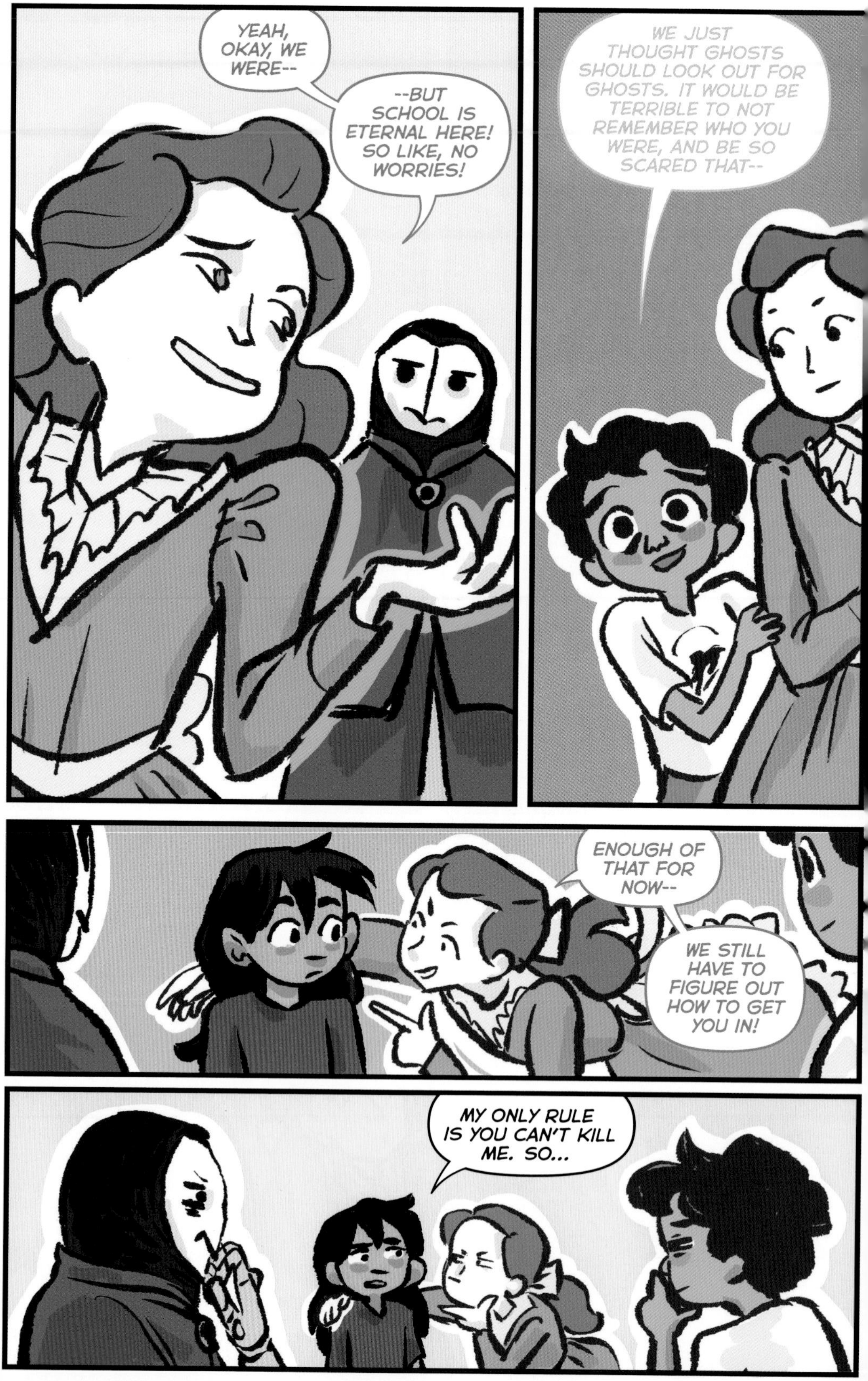
YEAH, OKAY, WE WERE--
--BUT SCHOOL IS ETERNAL HERE! SO LIKE, NO WORRIES!
WE JUST THOUGHT GHOSTS SHOULD LOOK OUT FOR GHOSTS. IT WOULD BE TERRIBLE TO NOT REMEMBER WHO YOU WERE, AND BE SO SCARED THAT--
ENOUGH OF THAT FOR NOW--
WE STILL HAVE TO FIGURE OUT HOW TO GET YOU IN!
MY ONLY RULE IS YOU CAN'T KILL ME. SO...

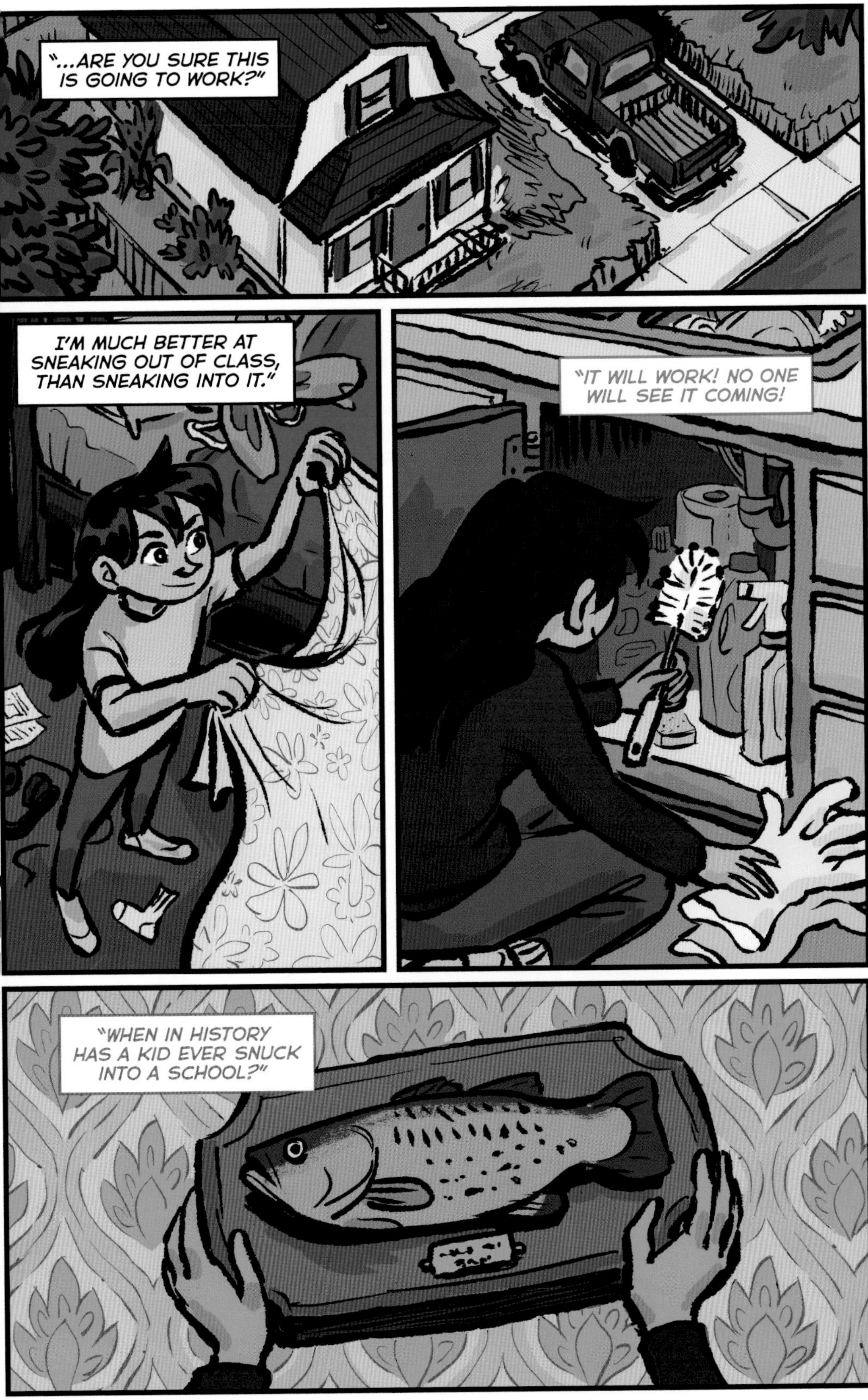
"...ARE YOU SURE THIS IS GOING TO WORK?"
I'M MUCH BETTER AT SNEAKING OUT OF CLASS, THAN SNEAKING INTO IT."
"IT WILL WORK! NO ONE WILL SEE IT COMING!
"WHEN IN HISTORY HAS A KID EVER SNUCK INTO A SCHOOL?"

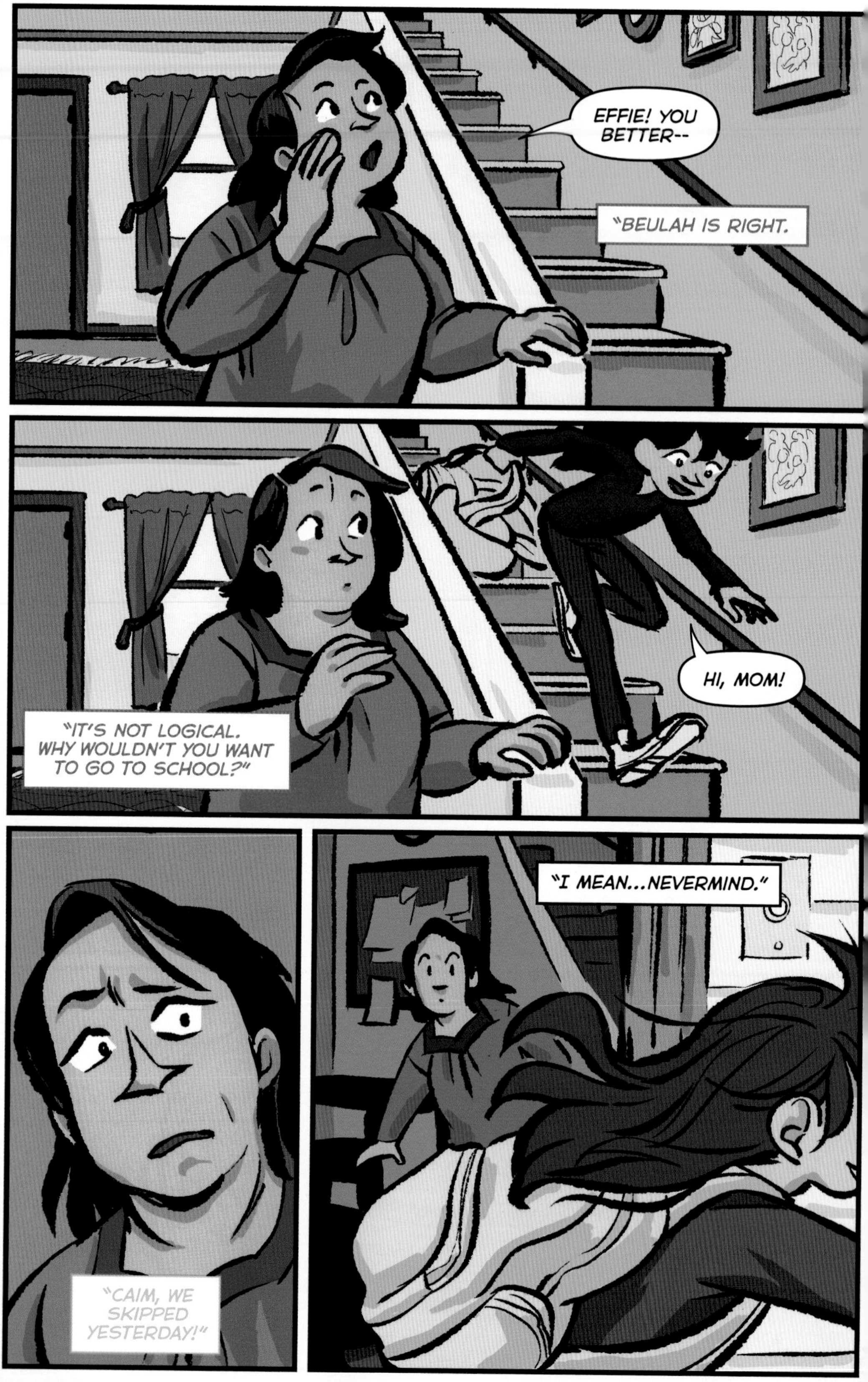
EFFIE! YOU BETTER--
"BEULAH IS RIGHT.
HI, MOM!
"IT'S NOT LOGICAL. WHY WOULDN'T YOU WANT TO GO TO SCHOOL?"
"CAIM, WE SKIPPED YESTERDAY!"
"I MEAN...NEVERMIND."

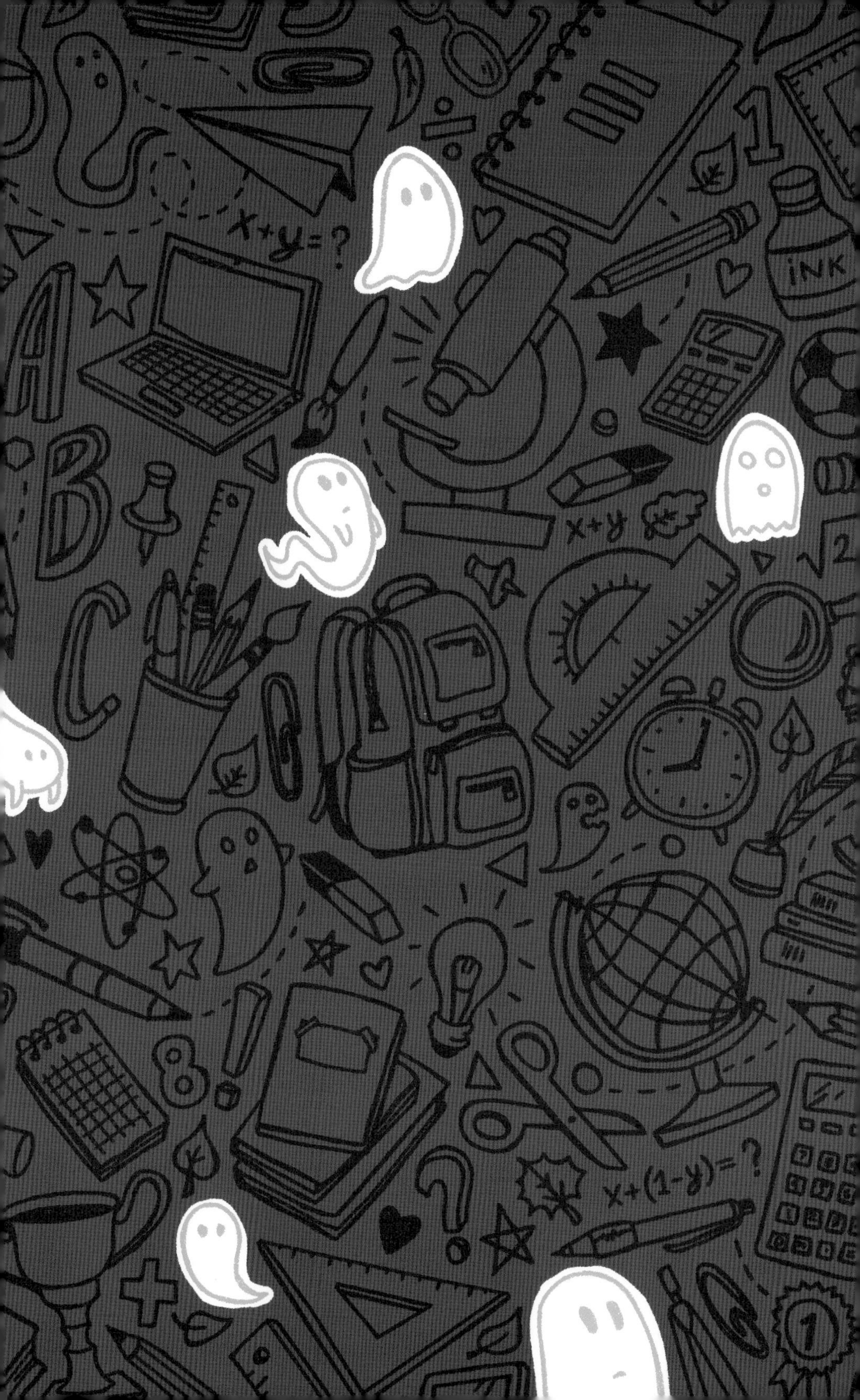
x+y=?
INK
x+y
x+(1-y)=?

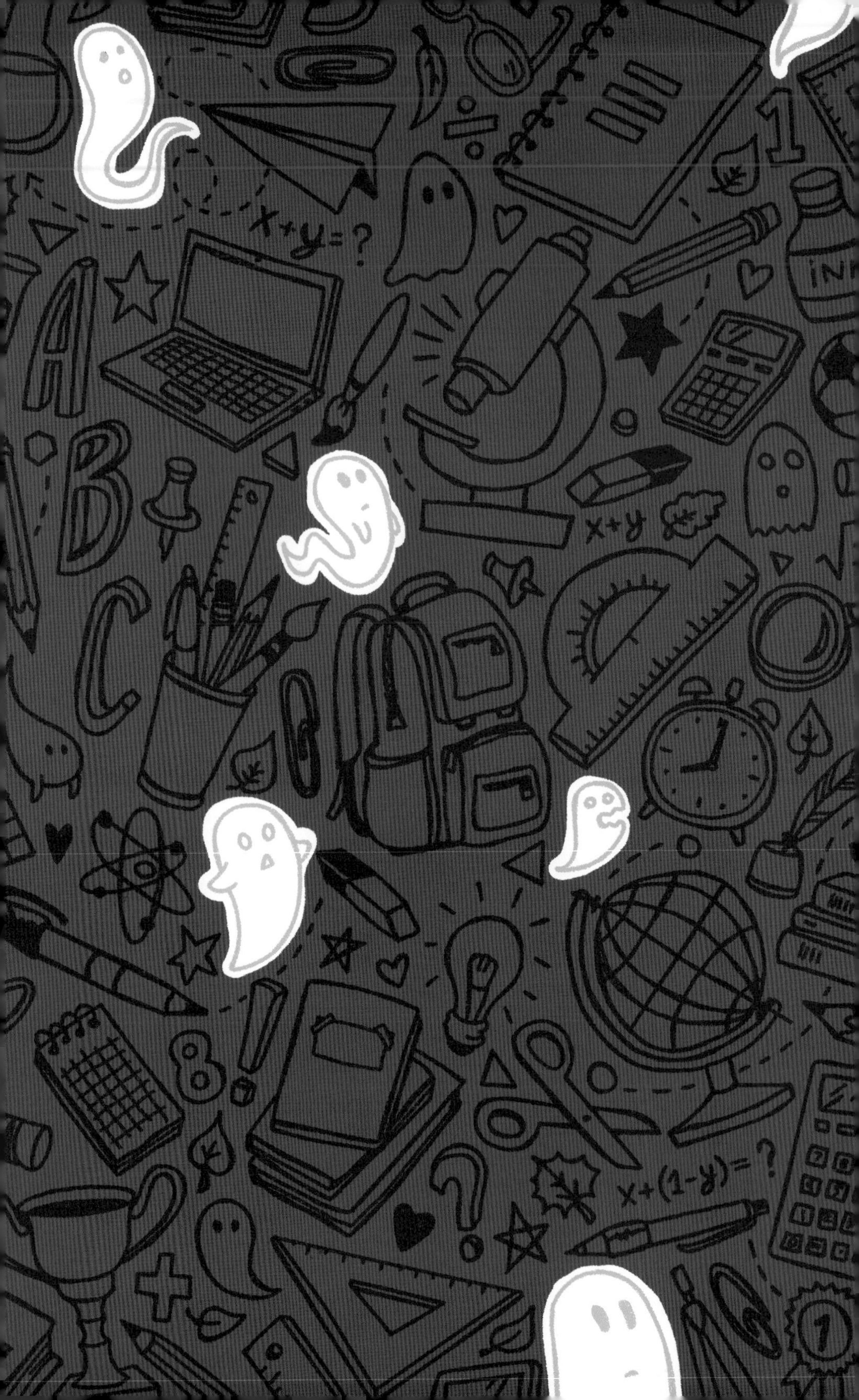
x+y=?
x+y
x+(1-y)=?

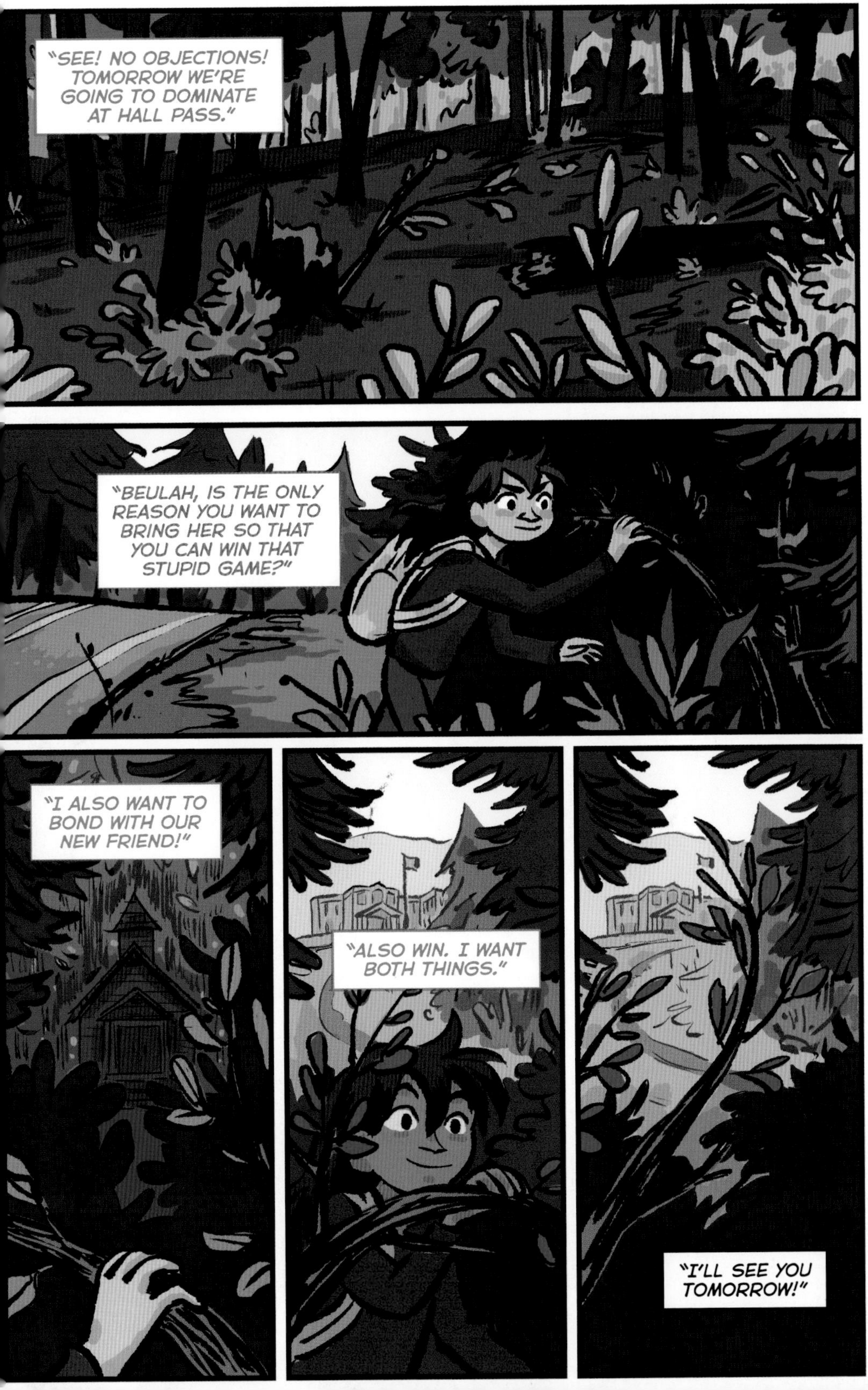
"SEE! NO OBJECTIONS! TOMORROW WE'RE GOING TO DOMINATE AT HALL PASS."
"BEULAH, IS THE ONLY REASON YOU WANT TO BRING HER SO THAT YOU CAN WIN THAT STUPID GAME?"
"I ALSO WANT TO BOND WITH OUR NEW FRIEND!"
"ALSO WIN. I WANT BOTH THINGS."
"I'LL SEE YOU TOMORROW!"

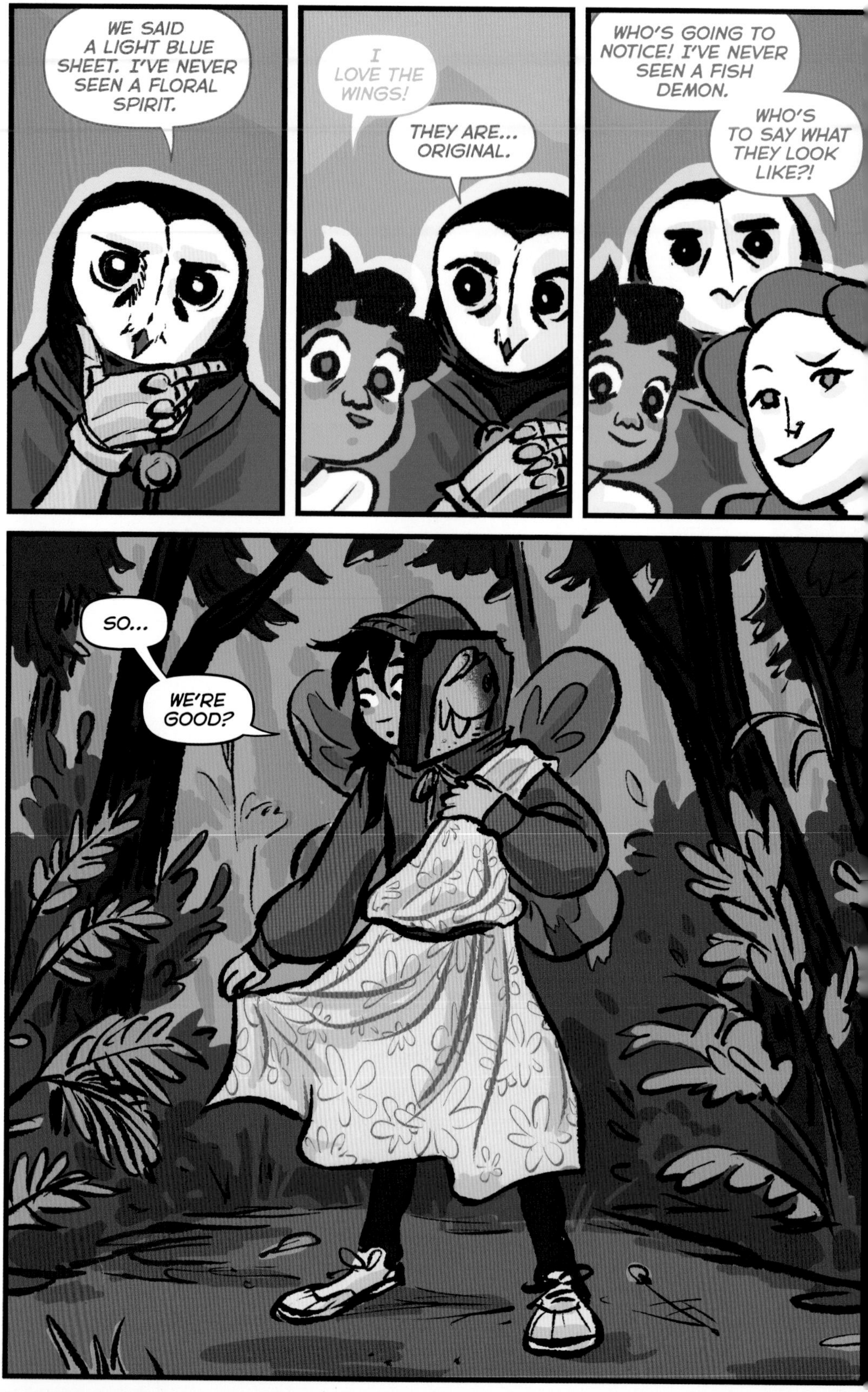
WE SAID A LIGHT BLUE SHEET. I'VE NEVER SEEN A FLORAL SPIRIT.
I LOVE THE WINGS!
THEY ARE... ORIGINAL.
WHO'S GOING TO NOTICE! I'VE NEVER SEEN A FISH DEMON.
WHO'S TO SAY WHAT THEY LOOK LIKE?!
SO...
WE'RE GOOD?

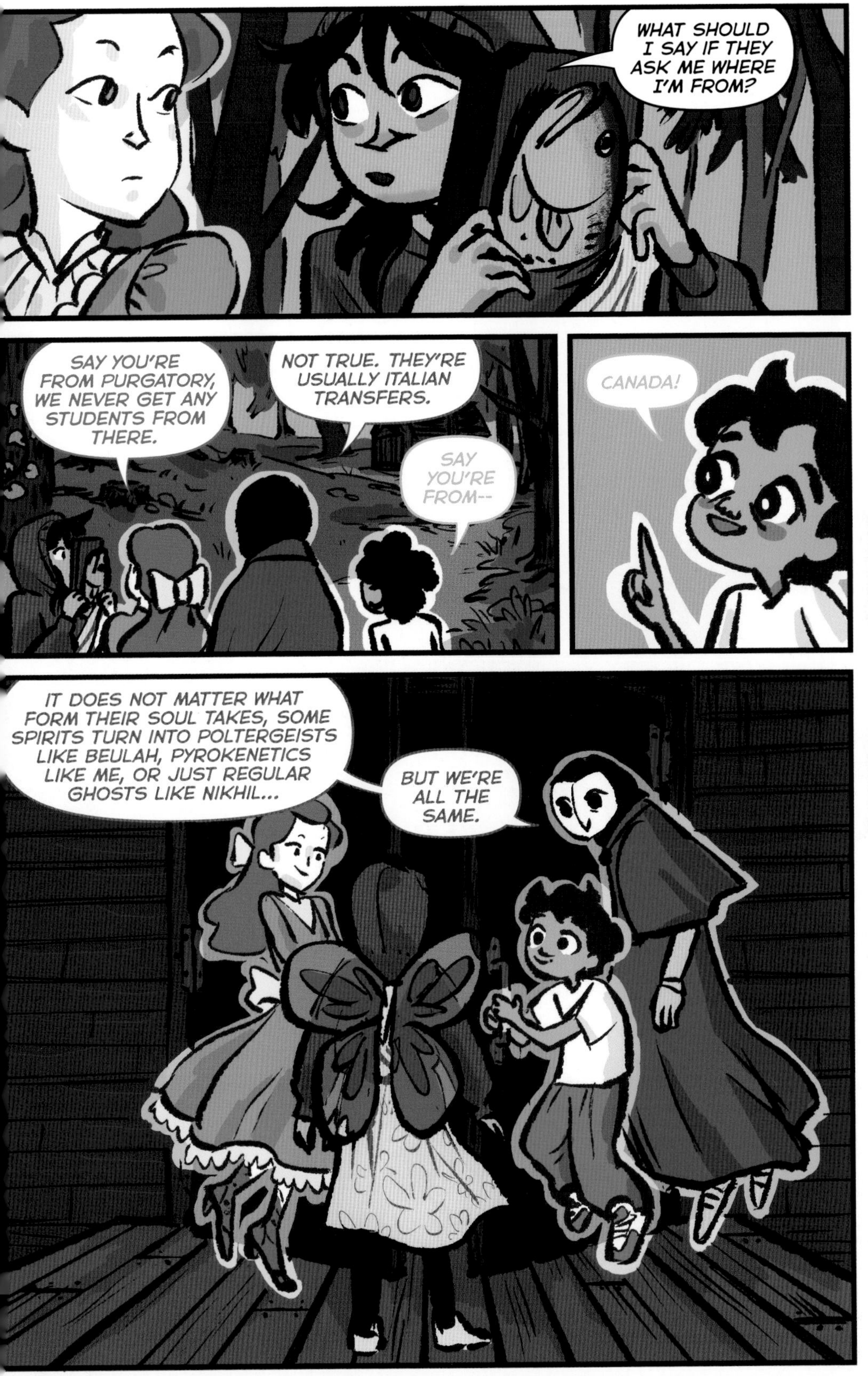

WHAT SHOULD I SAY IF THEY ASK ME WHERE I'M FROM?
SAY YOU'RE FROM PURGATORY, WE NEVER GET ANY STUDENTS FROM THERE.
NOT TRUE. THEY'RE USUALLY ITALIAN TRANSFERS.
SAY YOU'RE FROM--
CANADA!
IT DOES NOT MATTER WHAT FORM THEIR SOUL TAKES, SOME SPIRITS TURN INTO POLTERGEISTS LIKE BEULAH, PYROKENETICS LIKE ME, OR JUST REGULAR GHOSTS LIKE NIKHIL...
BUT WE'RE ALL THE SAME.

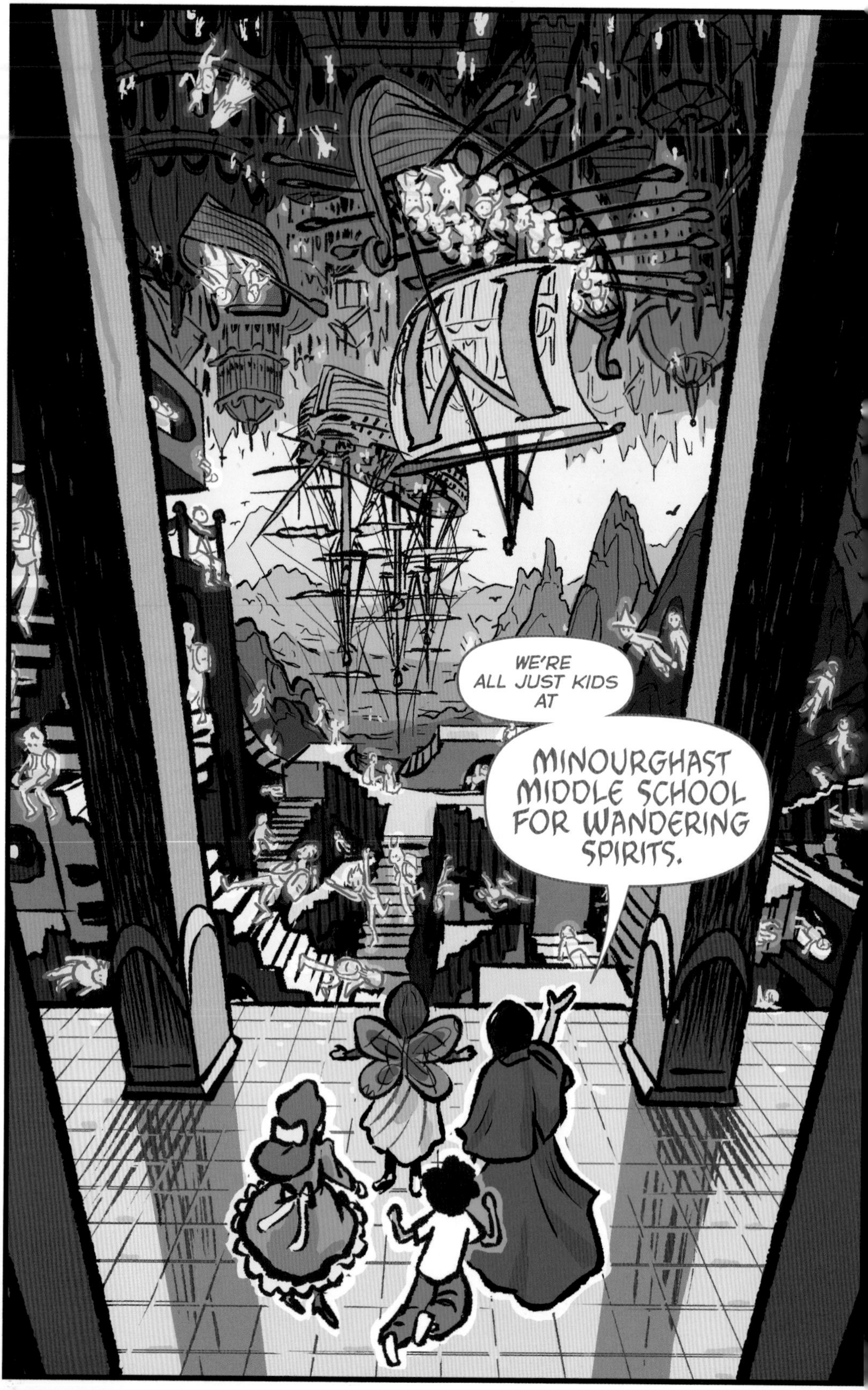
WE'RE ALL JUST KIDS AT
MINOURGHAST MIDDLE SCHOOL FOR WANDERING SPIRITS.

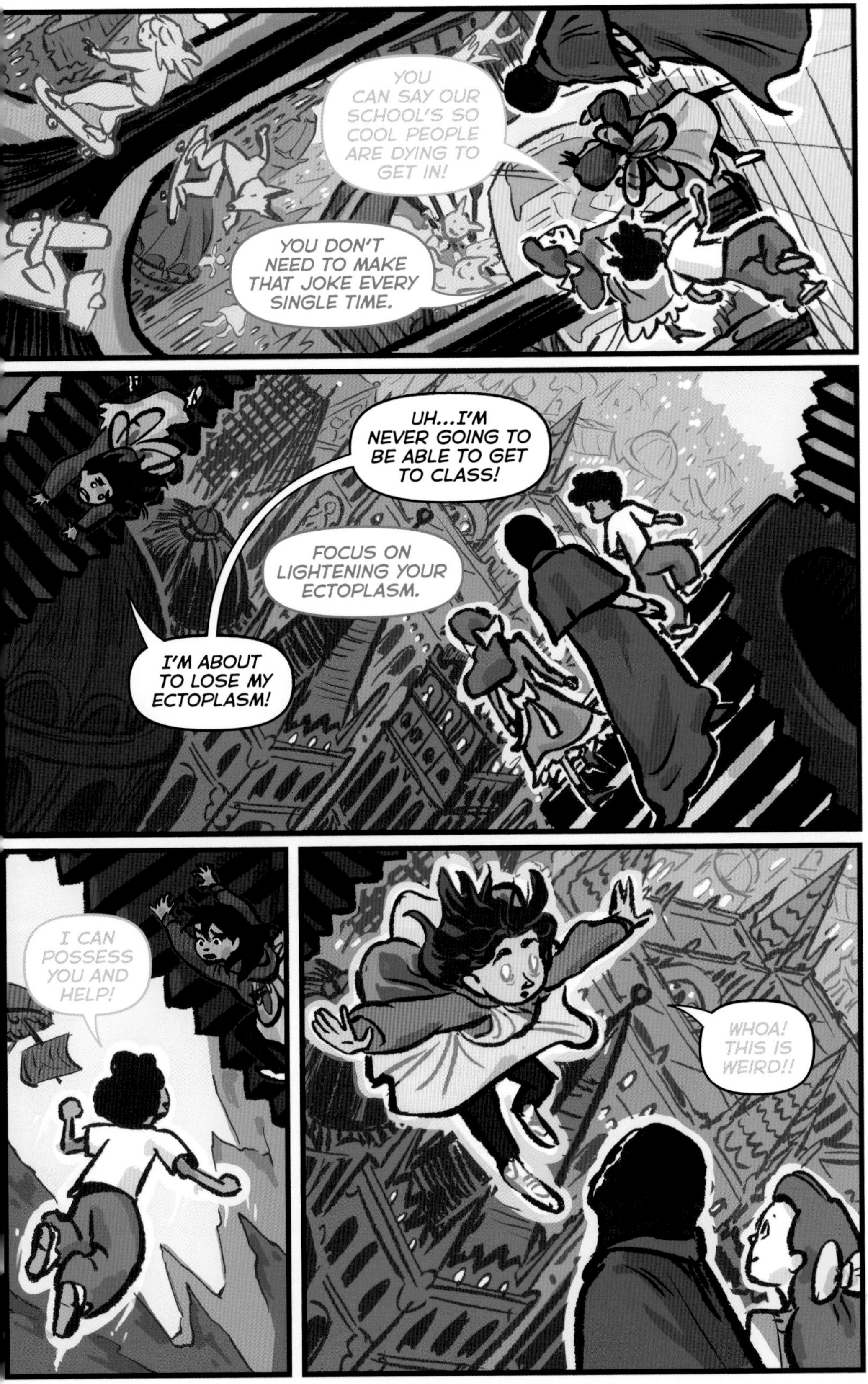
YOU CAN SAY OUR SCHOOL'S SO COOL PEOPLE ARE DYING TO GET IN!
YOU DON'T NEED TO MAKE THAT JOKE EVERY SINGLE TIME.
UH...I'M NEVER GOING TO BE ABLE TO GET TO CLASS!
FOCUS ON LIGHTENING YOUR ECTOPLASM.
I'M ABOUT TO LOSE MY ECTOPLASM!
I CAN POSSESS YOU AND HELP!
WHOA! THIS IS WEIRD!!

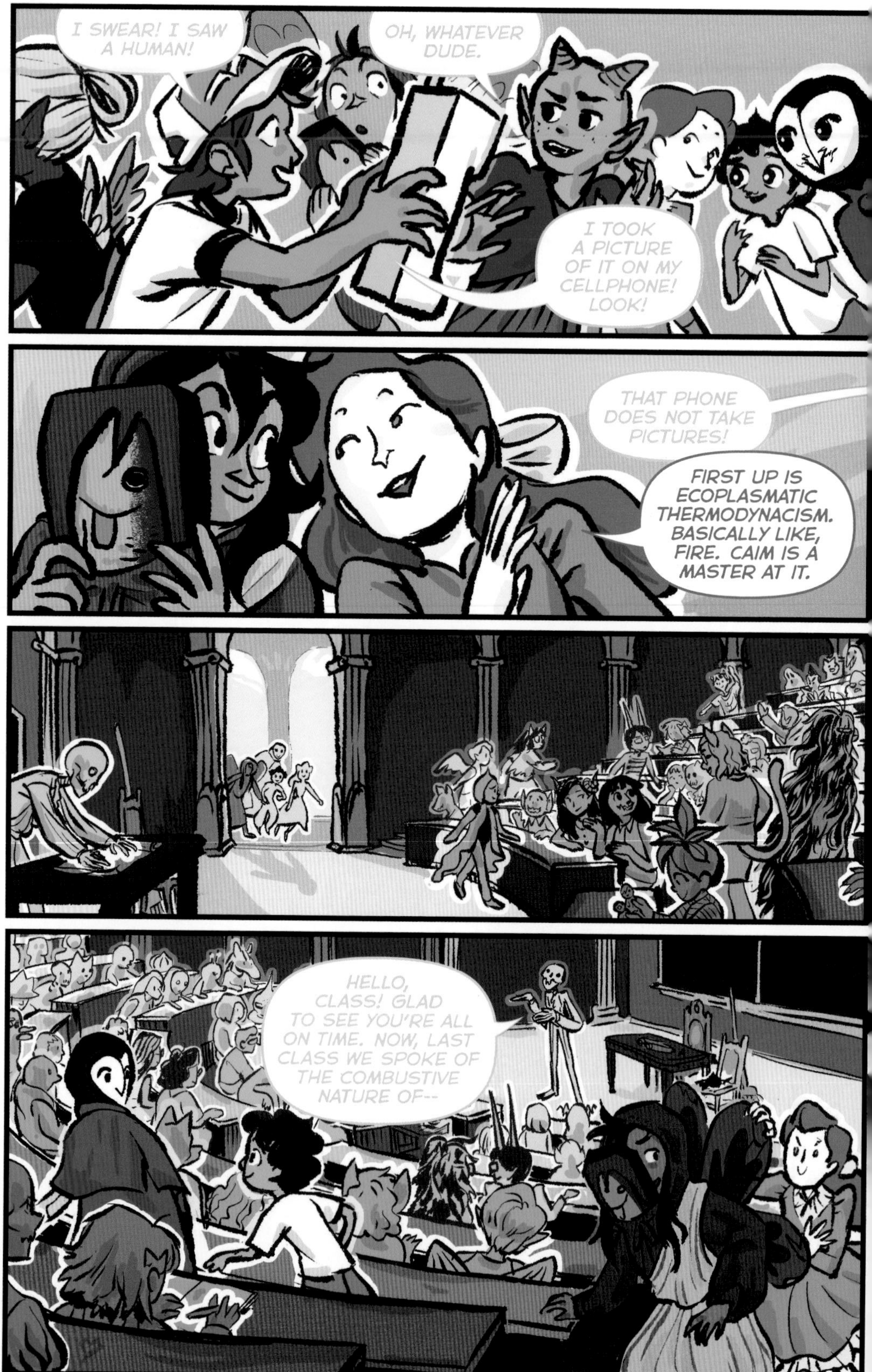
I SWEAR! I SAW A HUMAN!
OH, WHATEVER DUDE.
I TOOK A PICTURE OF IT ON MY CELLPHONE! LOOK!
THAT PHONE DOES NOT TAKE PICTURES!
FIRST UP IS ECOPLASMATIC THERMODYNACISM. BASICALLY LIKE, FIRE. CAIM IS A MASTER AT IT.
HELLO, CLASS! GLAD TO SEE YOU'RE ALL ON TIME. NOW, LAST CLASS WE SPOKE OF THE COMBUSTIVE NATURE OF--

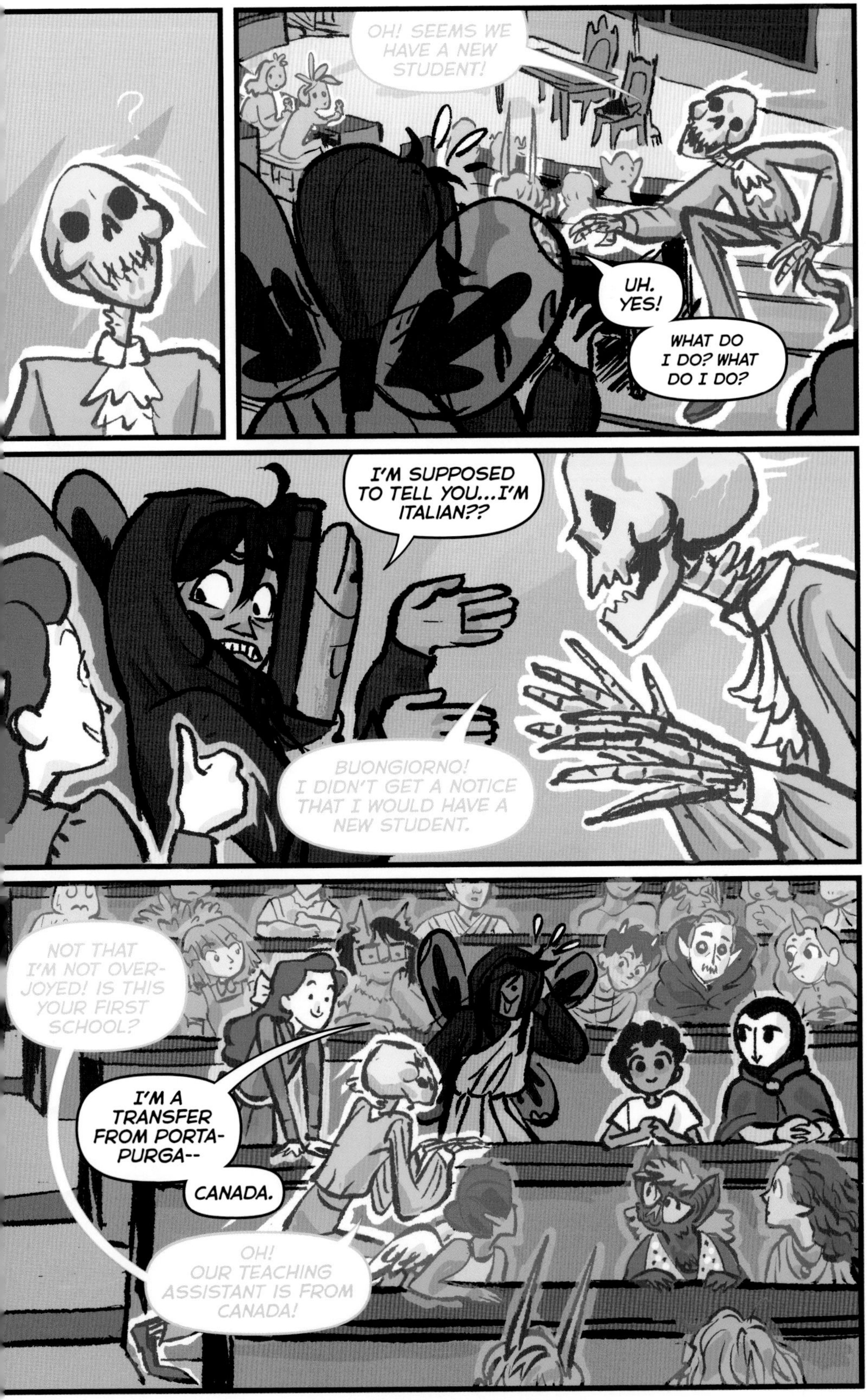
?
OH! SEEMS WE HAVE A NEW STUDENT!
UH. YES!
WHAT DO I DO? WHAT DO I DO?
I'M SUPPOSED TO TELL YOU...I'M ITALIAN??
BUONGIORNO! I DIDN'T GET A NOTICE THAT I WOULD HAVE A NEW STUDENT.
NOT THAT I'M NOT OVER-JOYED! IS THIS YOUR FIRST SCHOOL?
I'M A TRANSFER FROM PORTA-PURGA--
CANADA.
OH! OUR TEACHING ASSISTANT IS FROM CANADA!

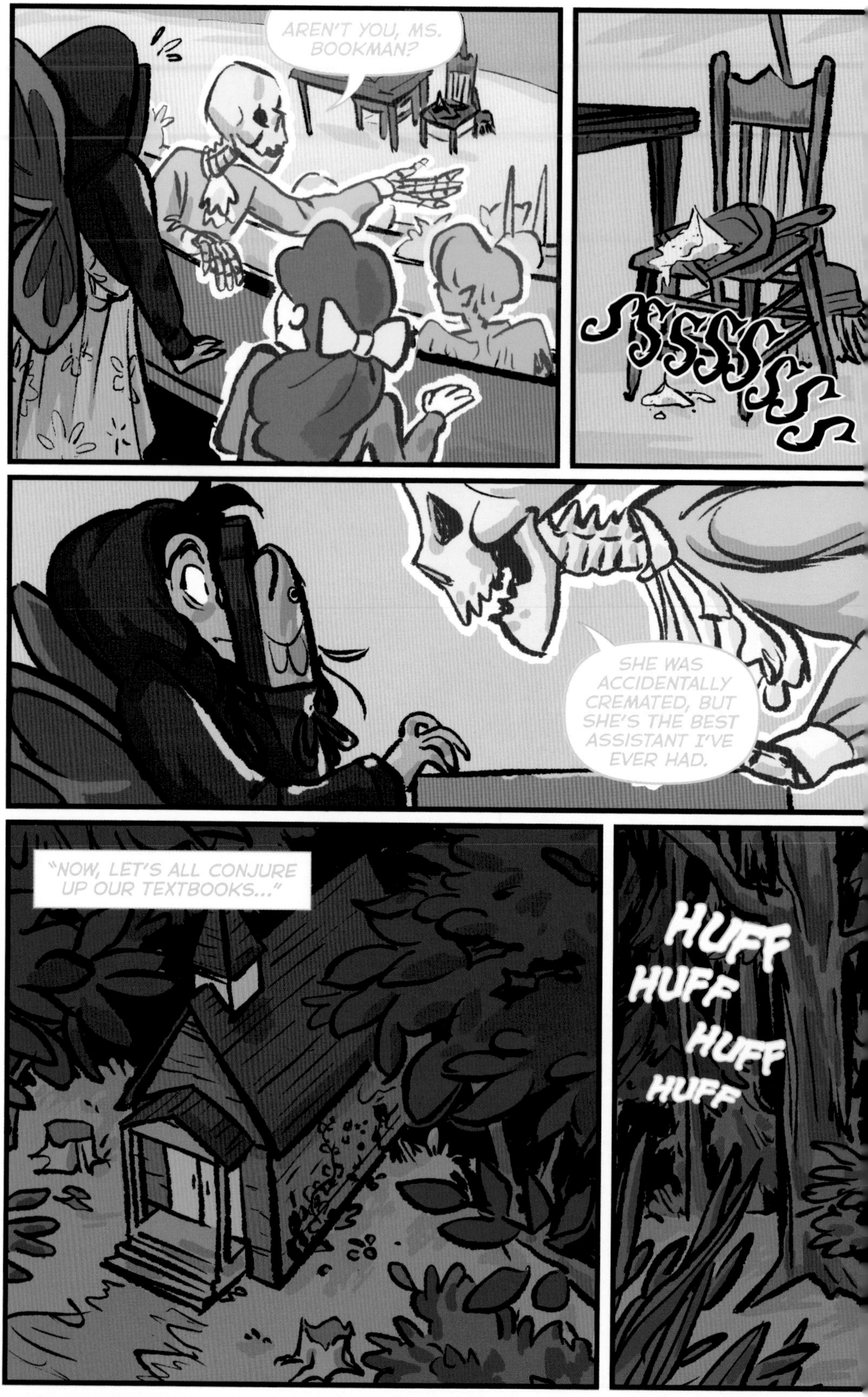
AREN'T YOU, MS. BOOKMAN?
SSSSSSS
SHE WAS ACCIDENTALLY CREMATED, BUT SHE'S THE BEST ASSISTANT I'VE EVER HAD.
"NOW, LET'S ALL CONJURE UP OUR TEXTBOOKS..."
HUFF
HUFF
HUFF
HUFF

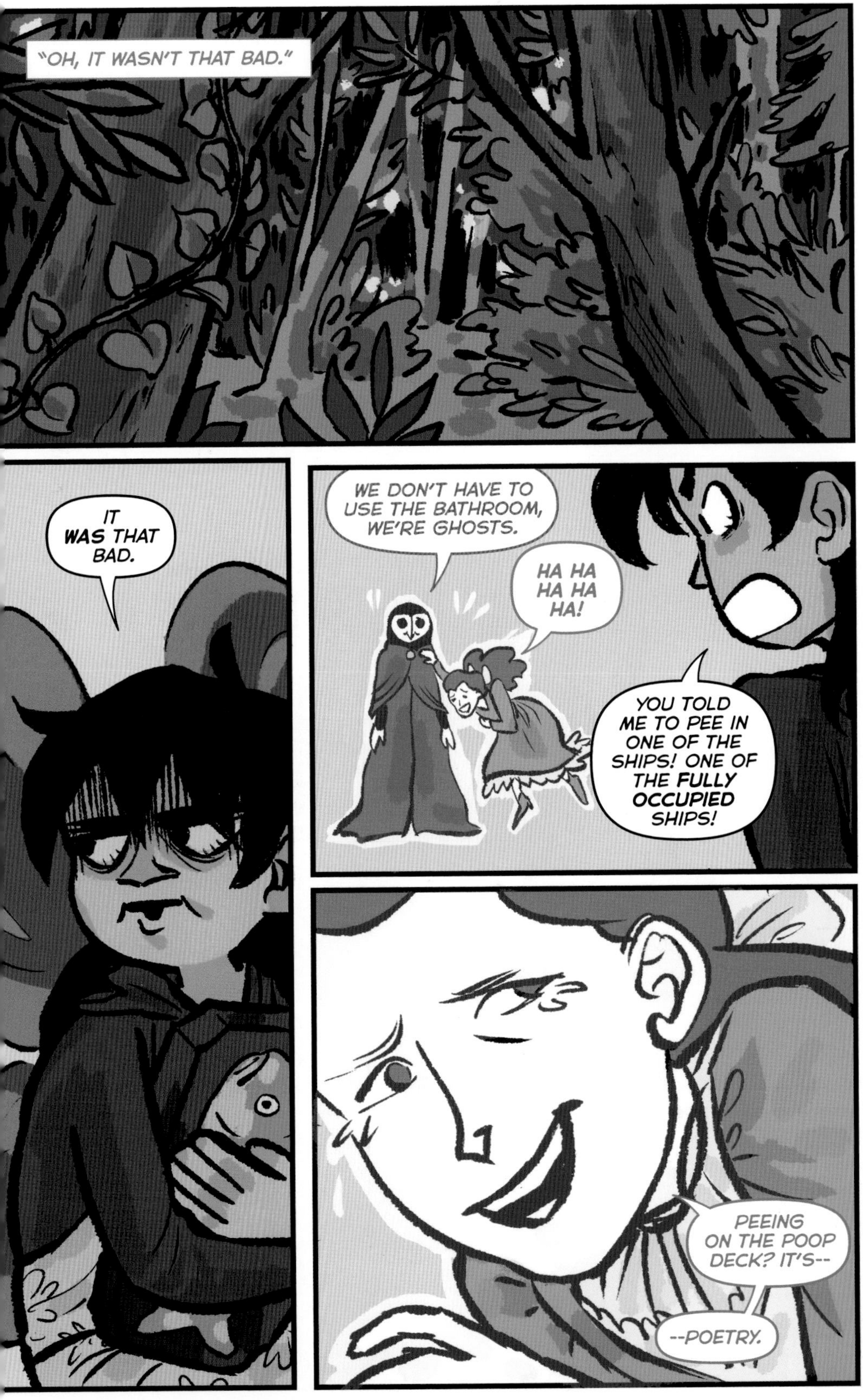
"OH, IT WASN'T THAT BAD."
IT WAS THAT BAD.
WE DON'T HAVE TO USE THE BATHROOM, WE'RE GHOSTS.
HA HA HA HA HA!
YOU TOLD ME TO PEE IN ONE OF THE SHIPS! ONE OF THE FULLY OCCUPIED SHIPS!
PEEING ON THE POOP DECK? IT'S--
--POETRY.

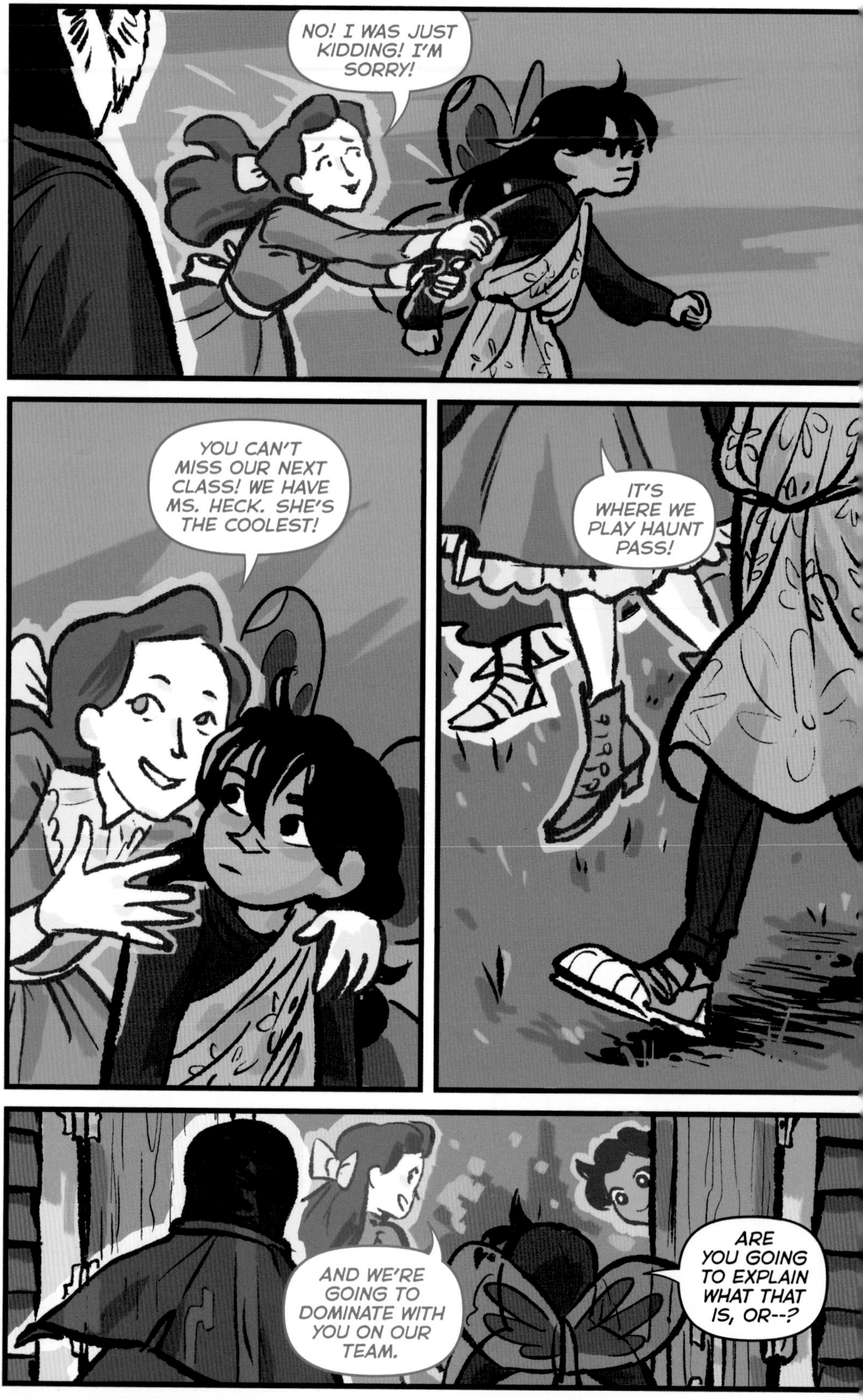
NO! I WAS JUST KIDDING! I'M SORRY!
YOU CAN'T MISS OUR NEXT CLASS! WE HAVE MS. HECK. SHE'S THE COOLEST!
IT'S WHERE WE PLAY HAUNT PASS!
AND WE'RE GOING TO DOMINATE WITH YOU ON OUR TEAM.
ARE YOU GOING TO EXPLAIN WHAT THAT IS, OR--?

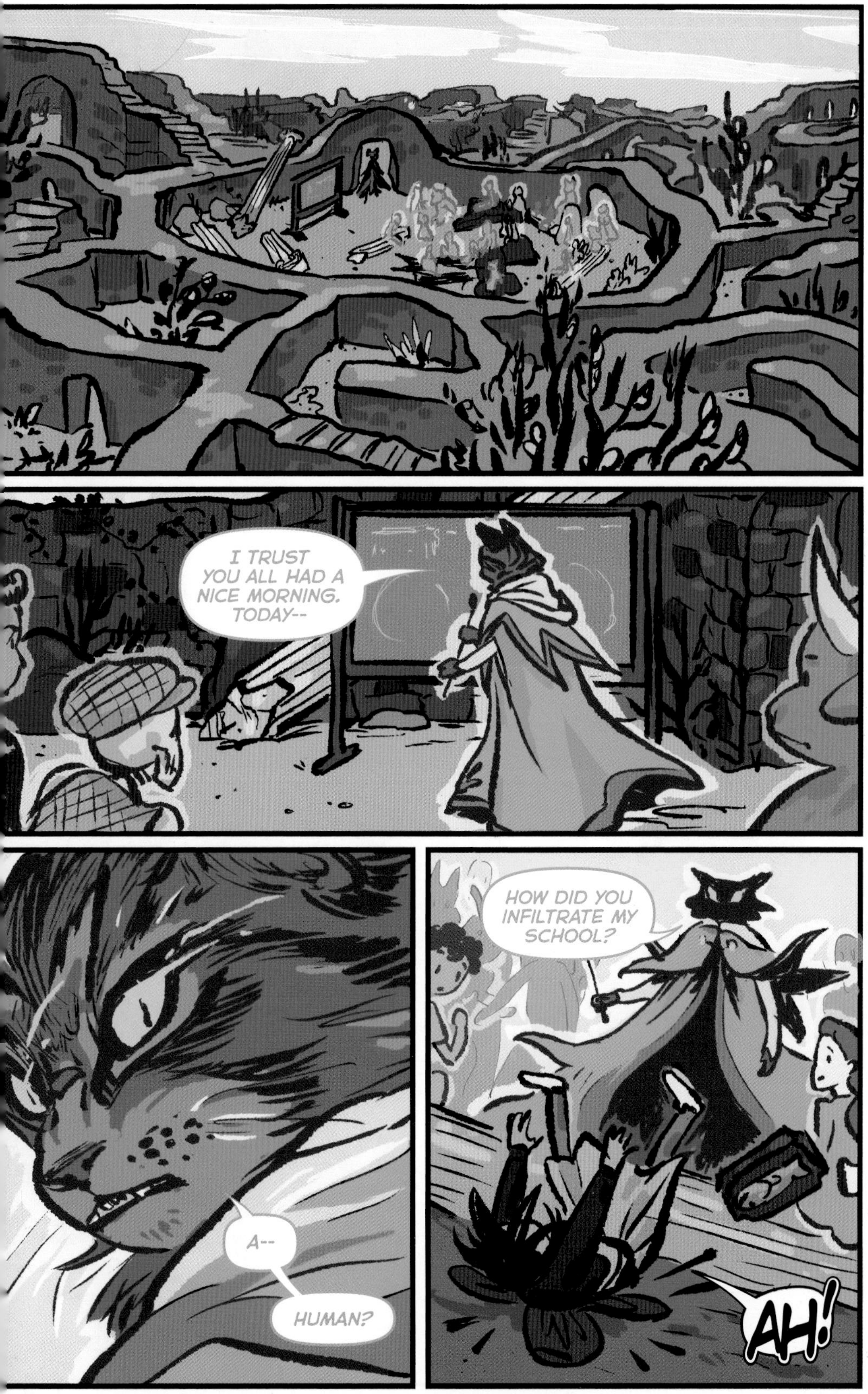

I TRUST YOU ALL HAD A NICE MORNING. TODAY--
A--
HUMAN?
HOW DID YOU INFILTRATE MY SCHOOL?
AH!

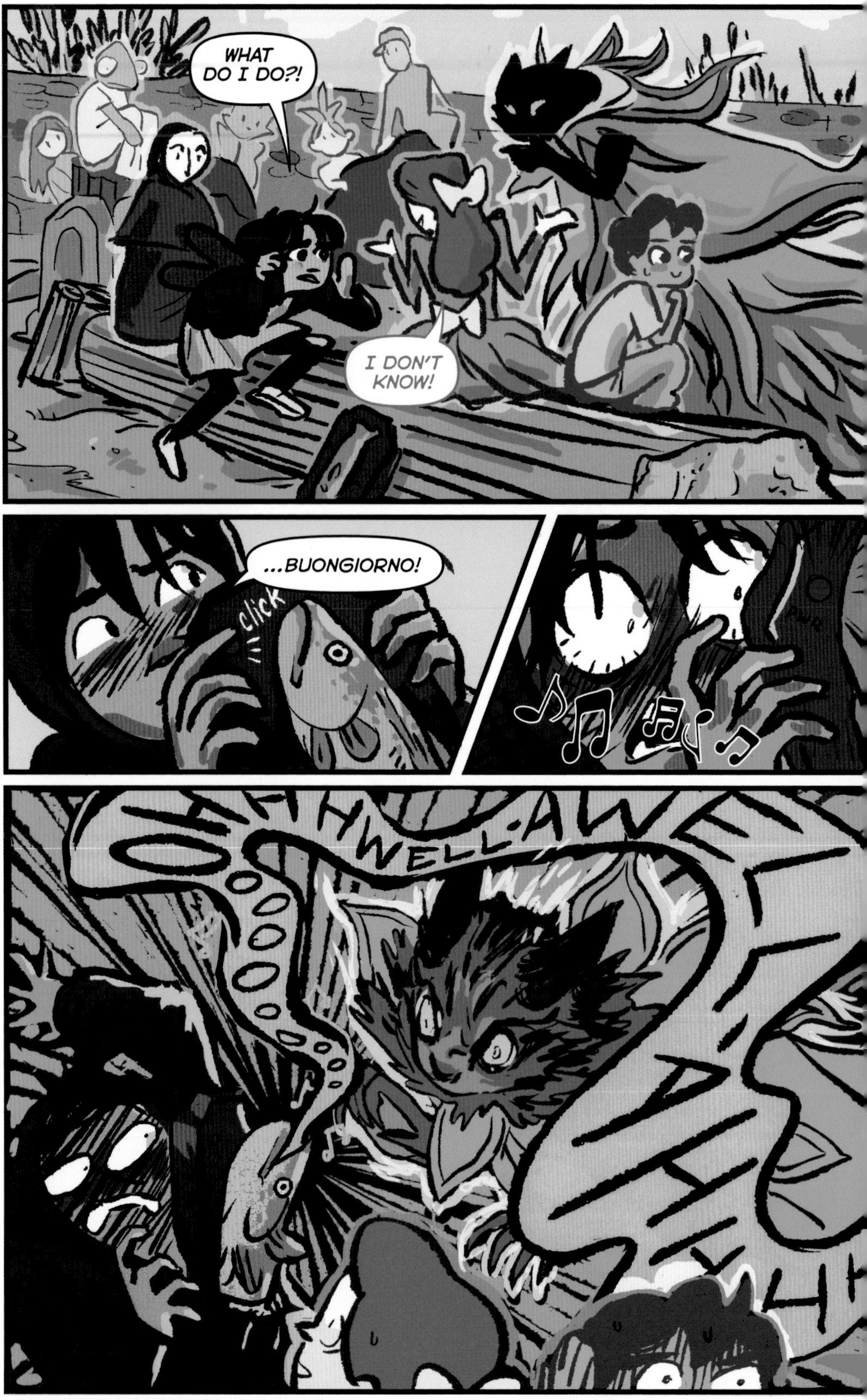
WHAT DO I DO?!
I DON'T KNOW!
...BUONGIORNO!
click
HWELL-AWE

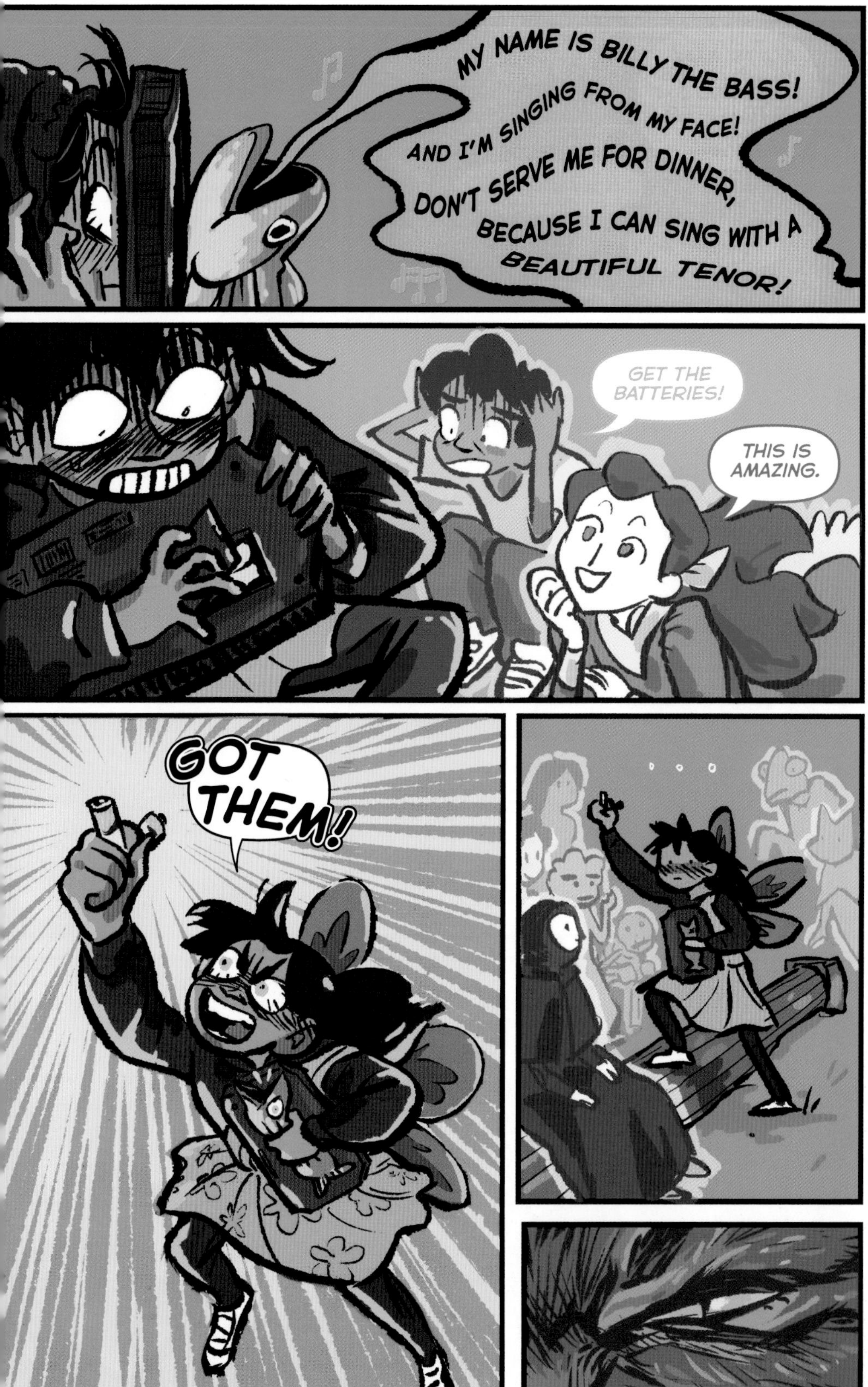
MY NAME IS BILLY THE BASS!
AND I'M SINGING FROM MY FACE!
DON'T SERVE ME FOR DINNER,
BECAUSE I CAN SING WITH A BEAUTIFUL TENOR!
GET THE BATTERIES!
THIS IS AMAZING.
GOT THEM!

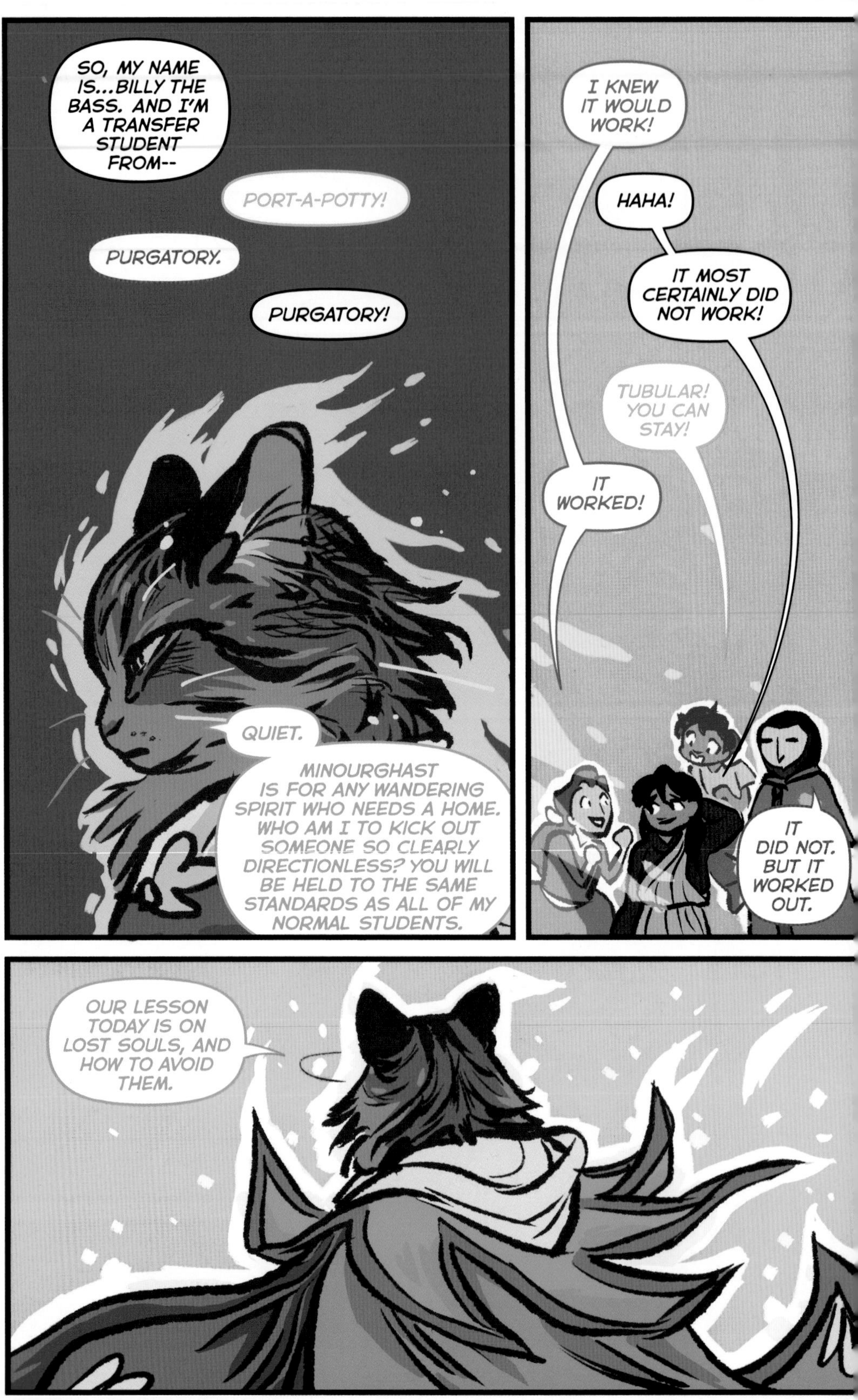

SO, MY NAME IS...BILLY THE BASS. AND I'M A TRANSFER STUDENT FROM--
PORT-A-POTTY!
PURGATORY.
PURGATORY!
QUIET.
MINOURGHAST IS FOR ANY WANDERING SPIRIT WHO NEEDS A HOME. WHO AM I TO KICK OUT SOMEONE SO CLEARLY DIRECTIONLESS? YOU WILL BE HELD TO THE SAME STANDARDS AS ALL OF MY NORMAL STUDENTS.
I KNEW IT WOULD WORK!
HAHA!
IT MOST CERTAINLY DID NOT WORK!
TUBULAR! YOU CAN STAY!
IT WORKED!
IT DID NOT. BUT IT WORKED OUT.
OUR LESSON TODAY IS ON LOST SOULS, AND HOW TO AVOID THEM.

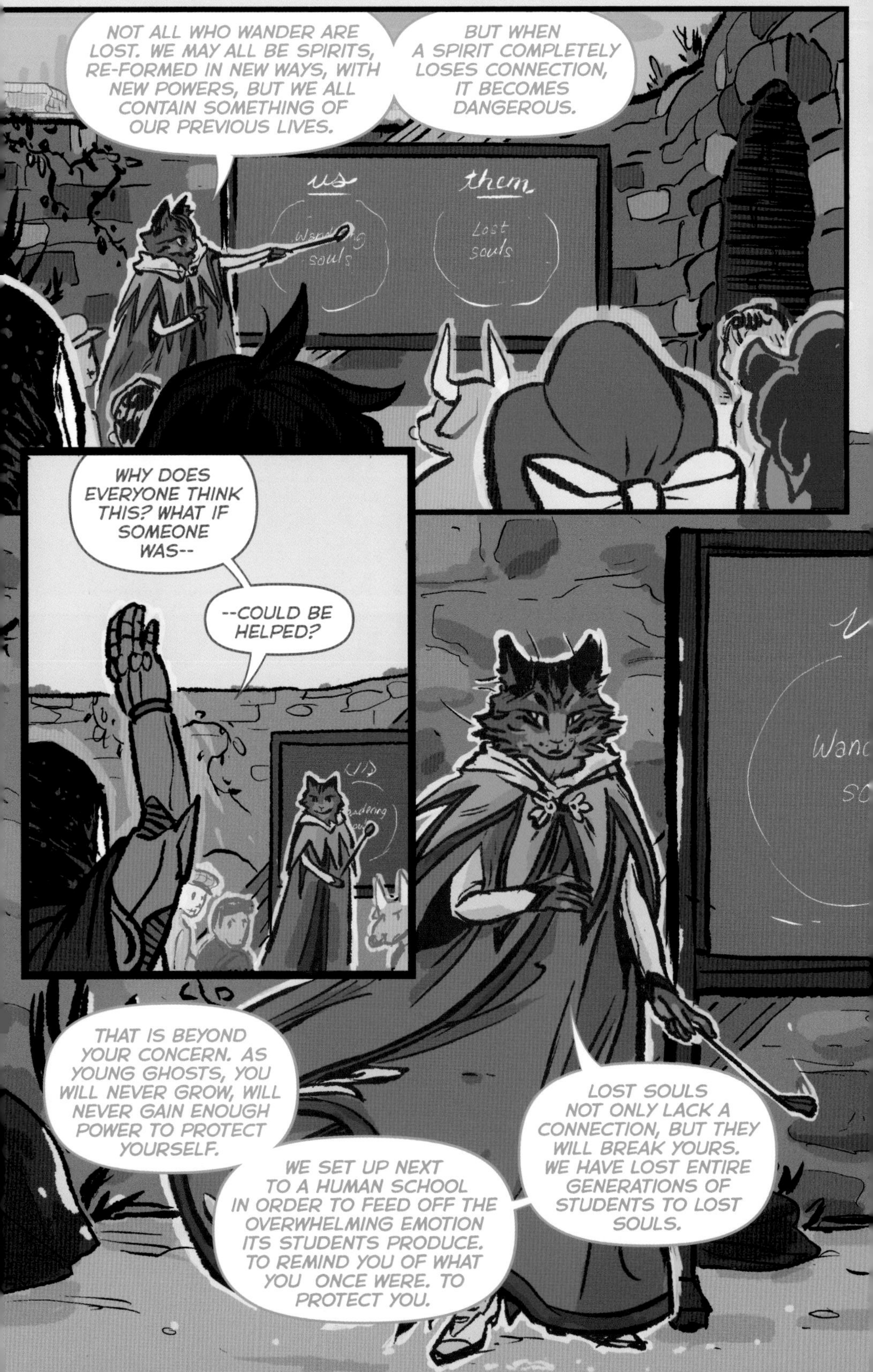
NOT ALL WHO WANDER ARE LOST. WE MAY ALL BE SPIRITS, RE-FORMED IN NEW WAYS, WITH NEW POWERS, BUT WE ALL CONTAIN SOMETHING OF OUR PREVIOUS LIVES.
BUT WHEN A SPIRIT COMPLETELY LOSES CONNECTION, IT BECOMES DANGEROUS.
us
them
Wandering souls
Lost souls
WHY DOES EVERYONE THINK THIS? WHAT IF SOMEONE WAS--
--COULD BE HELPED?
THAT IS BEYOND YOUR CONCERN. AS YOUNG GHOSTS, YOU WILL NEVER GROW, WILL NEVER GAIN ENOUGH POWER TO PROTECT YOURSELF.
WE SET UP NEXT TO A HUMAN SCHOOL IN ORDER TO FEED OFF THE OVERWHELMING EMOTION ITS STUDENTS PRODUCE. TO REMIND YOU OF WHAT YOU ONCE WERE. TO PROTECT YOU.
LOST SOULS NOT ONLY LACK A CONNECTION, BUT THEY WILL BREAK YOURS. WE HAVE LOST ENTIRE GENERATIONS OF STUDENTS TO LOST SOULS.

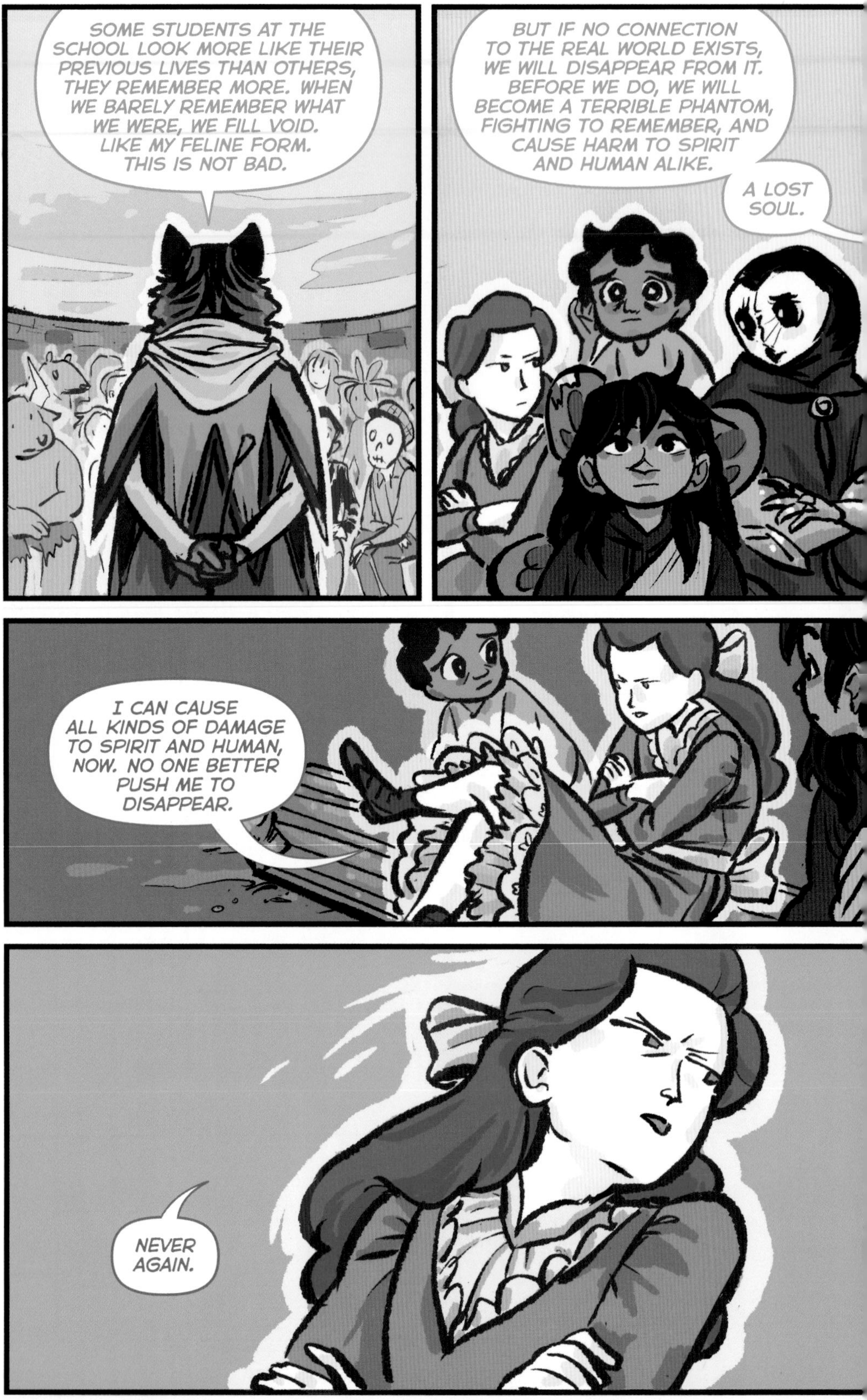
SOME STUDENTS AT THE SCHOOL LOOK MORE LIKE THEIR PREVIOUS LIVES THAN OTHERS, THEY REMEMBER MORE. WHEN WE BARELY REMEMBER WHAT WE WERE, WE FILL VOID. LIKE MY FELINE FORM. THIS IS NOT BAD.
BUT IF NO CONNECTION TO THE REAL WORLD EXISTS, WE WILL DISAPPEAR FROM IT. BEFORE WE DO, WE WILL BECOME A TERRIBLE PHANTOM, FIGHTING TO REMEMBER, AND CAUSE HARM TO SPIRIT AND HUMAN ALIKE.
A LOST SOUL.
I CAN CAUSE ALL KINDS OF DAMAGE TO SPIRIT AND HUMAN, NOW. NO ONE BETTER PUSH ME TO DISAPPEAR.
NEVER AGAIN.

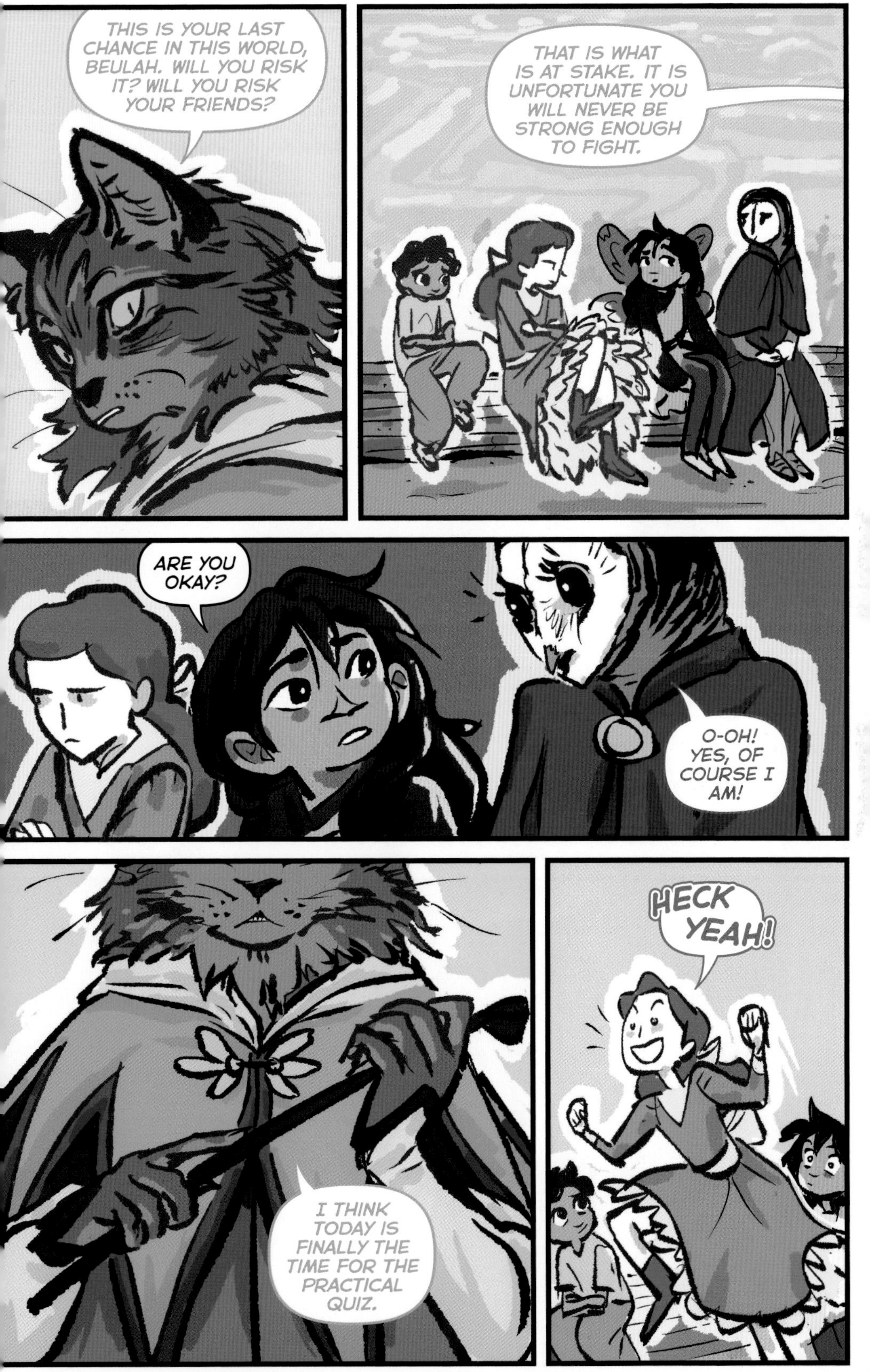
THIS IS YOUR LAST CHANCE IN THIS WORLD, BEULAH. WILL YOU RISK IT? WILL YOU RISK YOUR FRIENDS?
THAT IS WHAT IS AT STAKE. IT IS UNFORTUNATE YOU WILL NEVER BE STRONG ENOUGH TO FIGHT.
ARE YOU OKAY?
O-OH! YES, OF COURSE I AM!
I THINK TODAY IS FINALLY THE TIME FOR THE PRACTICAL QUIZ.
HECK YEAH!

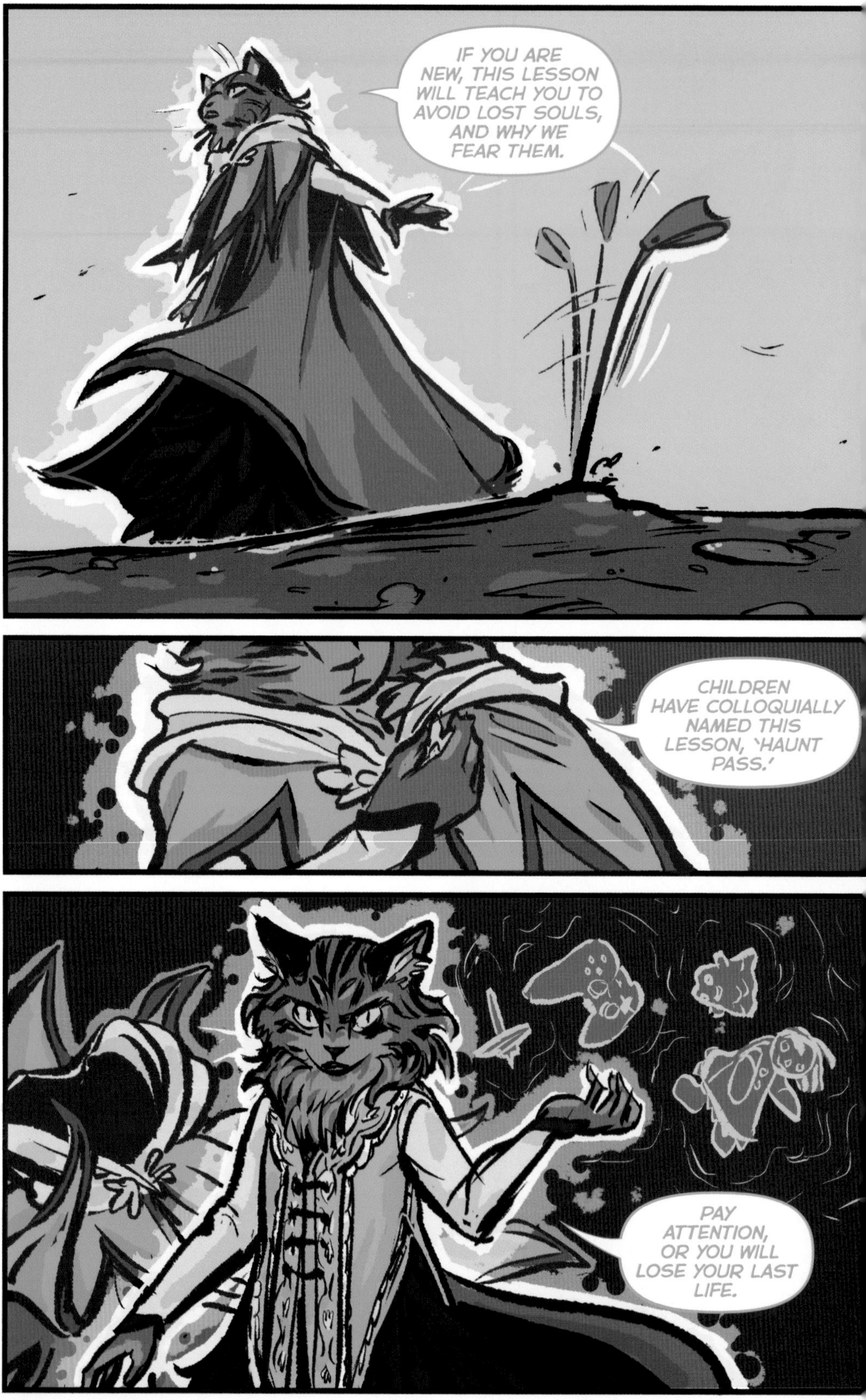
IF YOU ARE NEW, THIS LESSON WILL TEACH YOU TO AVOID LOST SOULS, AND WHY WE FEAR THEM.
CHILDREN HAVE COLLOQUIALLY NAMED THIS LESSON, 'HAUNT PASS.'
PAY ATTENTION, OR YOU WILL LOSE YOUR LAST LIFE.

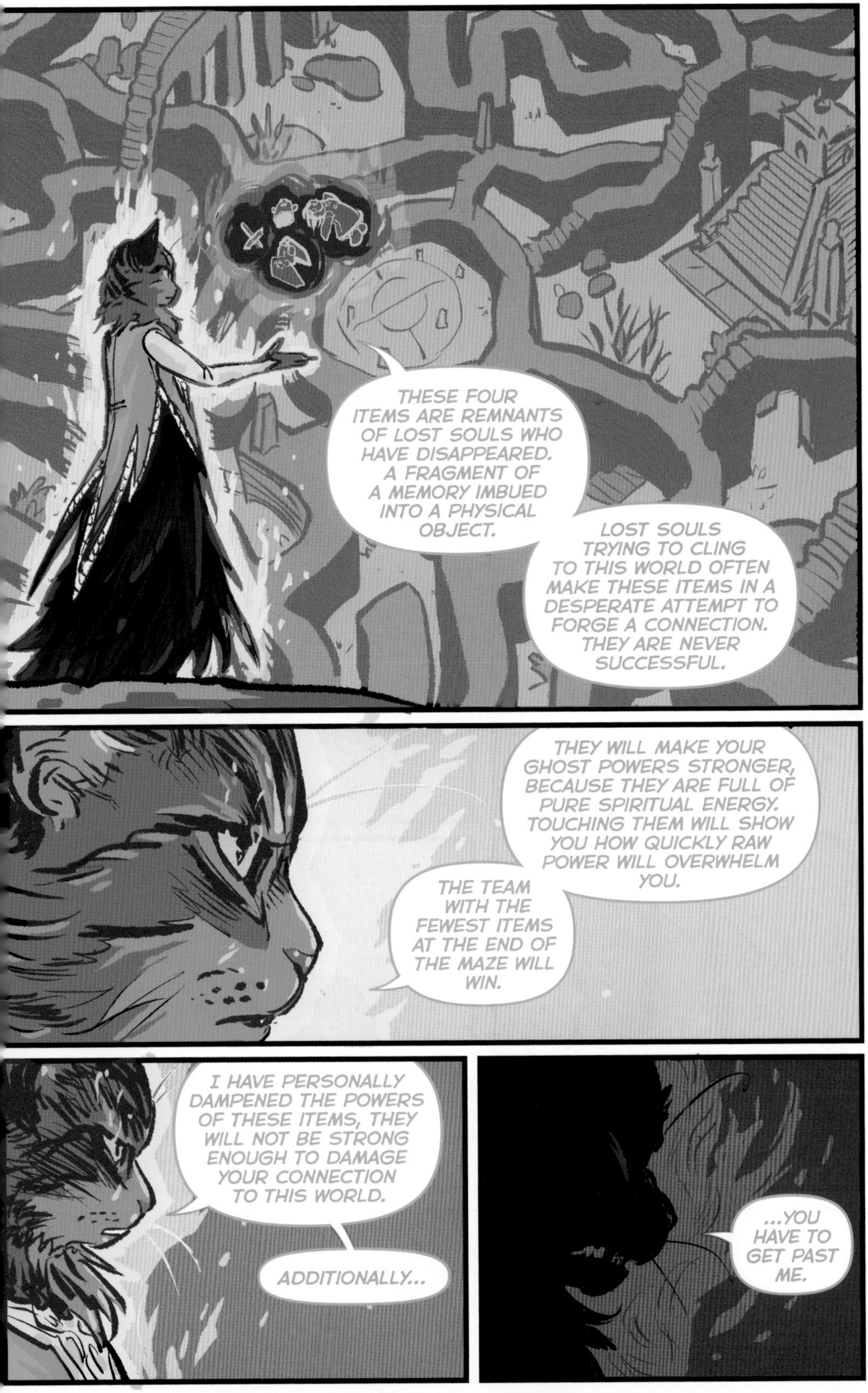
THESE FOUR ITEMS ARE REMNANTS OF LOST SOULS WHO HAVE DISAPPEARED. A FRAGMENT OF A MEMORY IMBUED INTO A PHYSICAL OBJECT.
LOST SOULS TRYING TO CLING TO THIS WORLD OFTEN MAKE THESE ITEMS IN A DESPERATE ATTEMPT TO FORGE A CONNECTION. THEY ARE NEVER SUCCESSFUL.
THEY WILL MAKE YOUR GHOST POWERS STRONGER, BECAUSE THEY ARE FULL OF PURE SPIRITUAL ENERGY. TOUCHING THEM WILL SHOW YOU HOW QUICKLY RAW POWER WILL OVERWHELM YOU.
THE TEAM WITH THE FEWEST ITEMS AT THE END OF THE MAZE WILL WIN.
I HAVE PERSONALLY DAMPENED THE POWERS OF THESE ITEMS, THEY WILL NOT BE STRONG ENOUGH TO DAMAGE YOUR CONNECTION TO THIS WORLD.
ADDITIONALLY...
...YOU HAVE TO GET PAST ME.

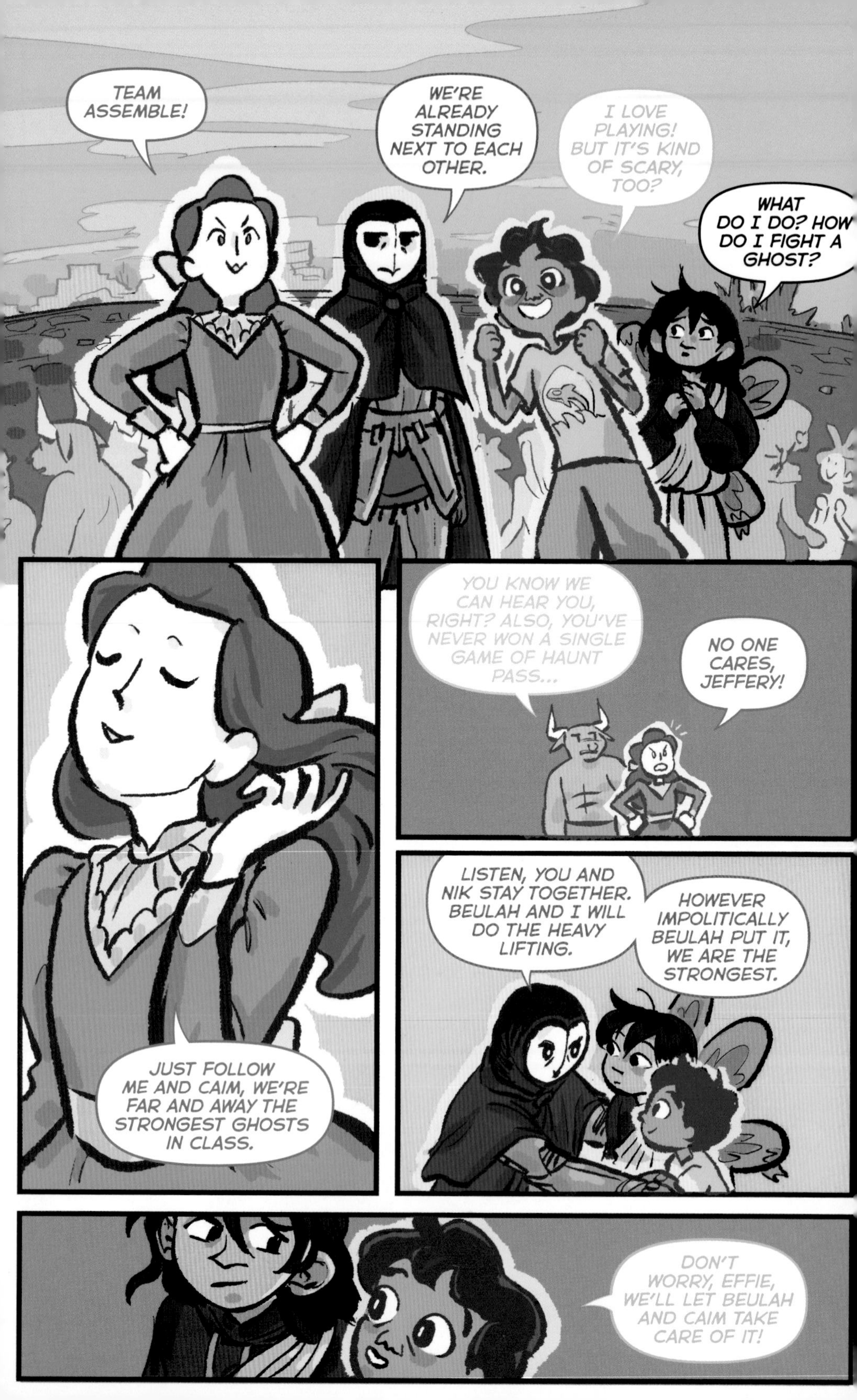
TEAM ASSEMBLE!
WE'RE ALREADY STANDING NEXT TO EACH OTHER.
I LOVE PLAYING! BUT IT'S KIND OF SCARY, TOO?
WHAT DO I DO? HOW DO I FIGHT A GHOST?
JUST FOLLOW ME AND CAIM, WE'RE FAR AND AWAY THE STRONGEST GHOSTS IN CLASS.
YOU KNOW WE CAN HEAR YOU, RIGHT? ALSO, YOU'VE NEVER WON A SINGLE GAME OF HAUNT PASS...
NO ONE CARES, JEFFERY!
LISTEN, YOU AND NIK STAY TOGETHER. BEULAH AND I WILL DO THE HEAVY LIFTING.
HOWEVER IMPOLITICALLY BEULAH PUT IT, WE ARE THE STRONGEST.
DON'T WORRY, EFFIE, WE'LL LET BEULAH AND CAIM TAKE CARE OF IT!

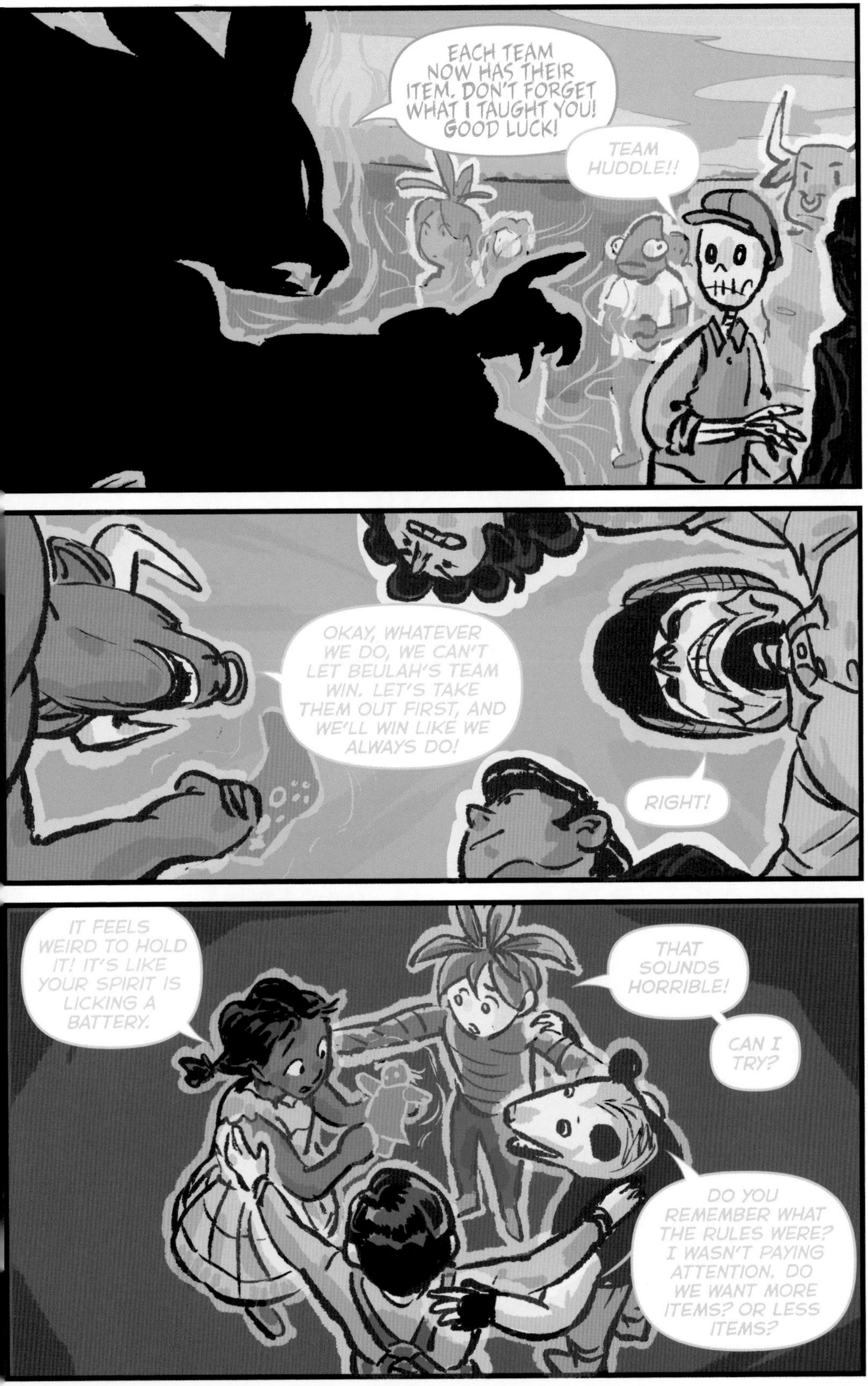
EACH TEAM NOW HAS THEIR ITEM. DON'T FORGET WHAT I TAUGHT YOU! GOOD LUCK!
TEAM HUDDLE!!
OKAY, WHATEVER WE DO, WE CAN'T LET BEULAH'S TEAM WIN. LET'S TAKE THEM OUT FIRST, AND WE'LL WIN LIKE WE ALWAYS DO!
RIGHT!
IT FEELS WEIRD TO HOLD IT! IT'S LIKE YOUR SPIRIT IS LICKING A BATTERY.
THAT SOUNDS HORRIBLE!
CAN I TRY?
DO YOU REMEMBER WHAT THE RULES WERE? I WASN'T PAYING ATTENTION. DO WE WANT MORE ITEMS? OR LESS ITEMS?

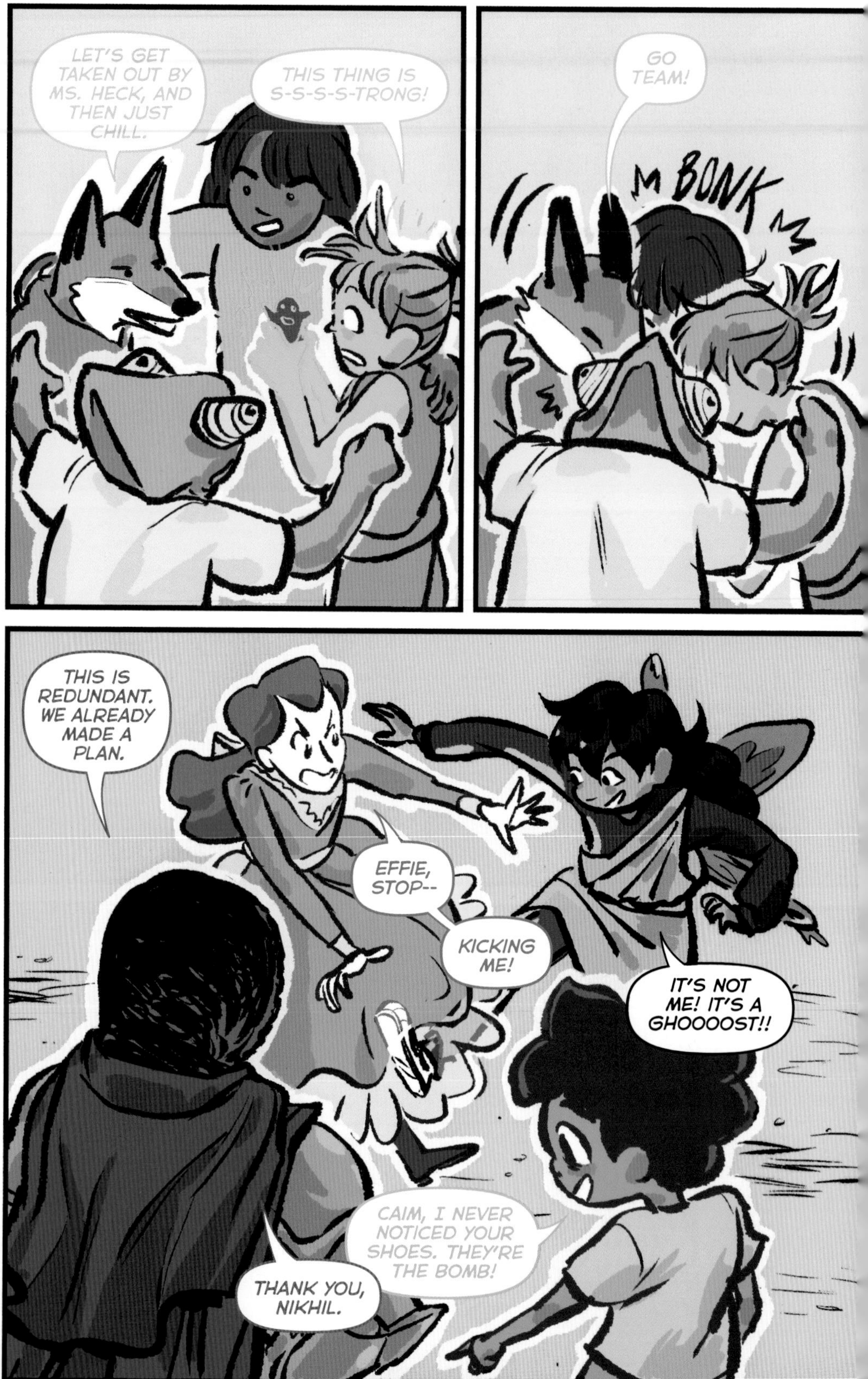
LET'S GET TAKEN OUT BY MS. HECK, AND THEN JUST CHILL.
THIS THING IS S-S-S-S-TRONG!
GO TEAM!
BONK
THIS IS REDUNDANT. WE ALREADY MADE A PLAN.
EFFIE, STOP--
KICKING ME!
IT'S NOT ME! IT'S A GHOOOOST!!
CAIM, I NEVER NOTICED YOUR SHOES. THEY'RE THE BOMB!
THANK YOU, NIKHIL.

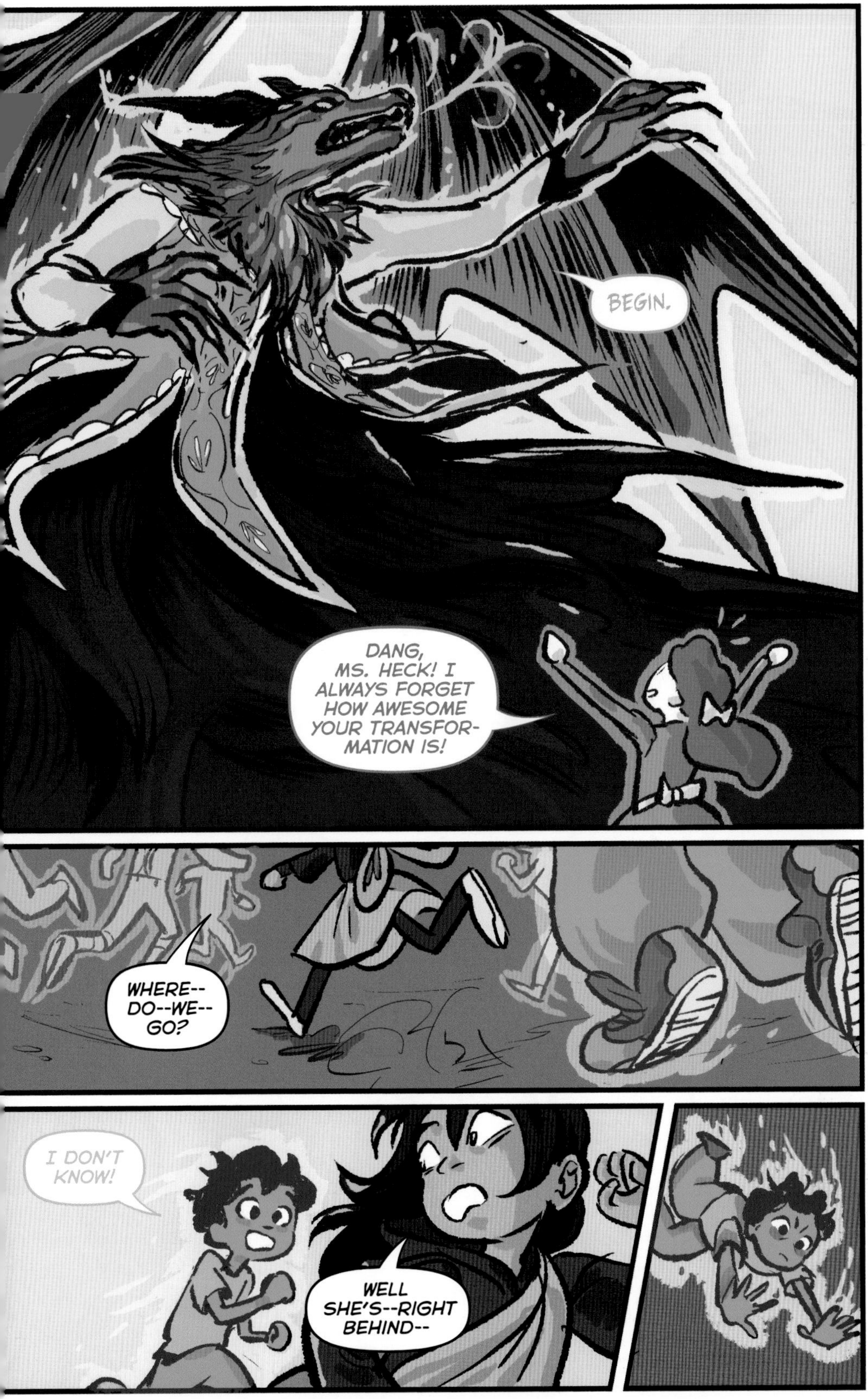
BEGIN.
DANG, MS. HECK! I ALWAYS FORGET HOW AWESOME YOUR TRANSFORMATION IS!
WHERE--DO--WE--GO?
I DON'T KNOW!
WELL SHE'S--RIGHT BEHIND--

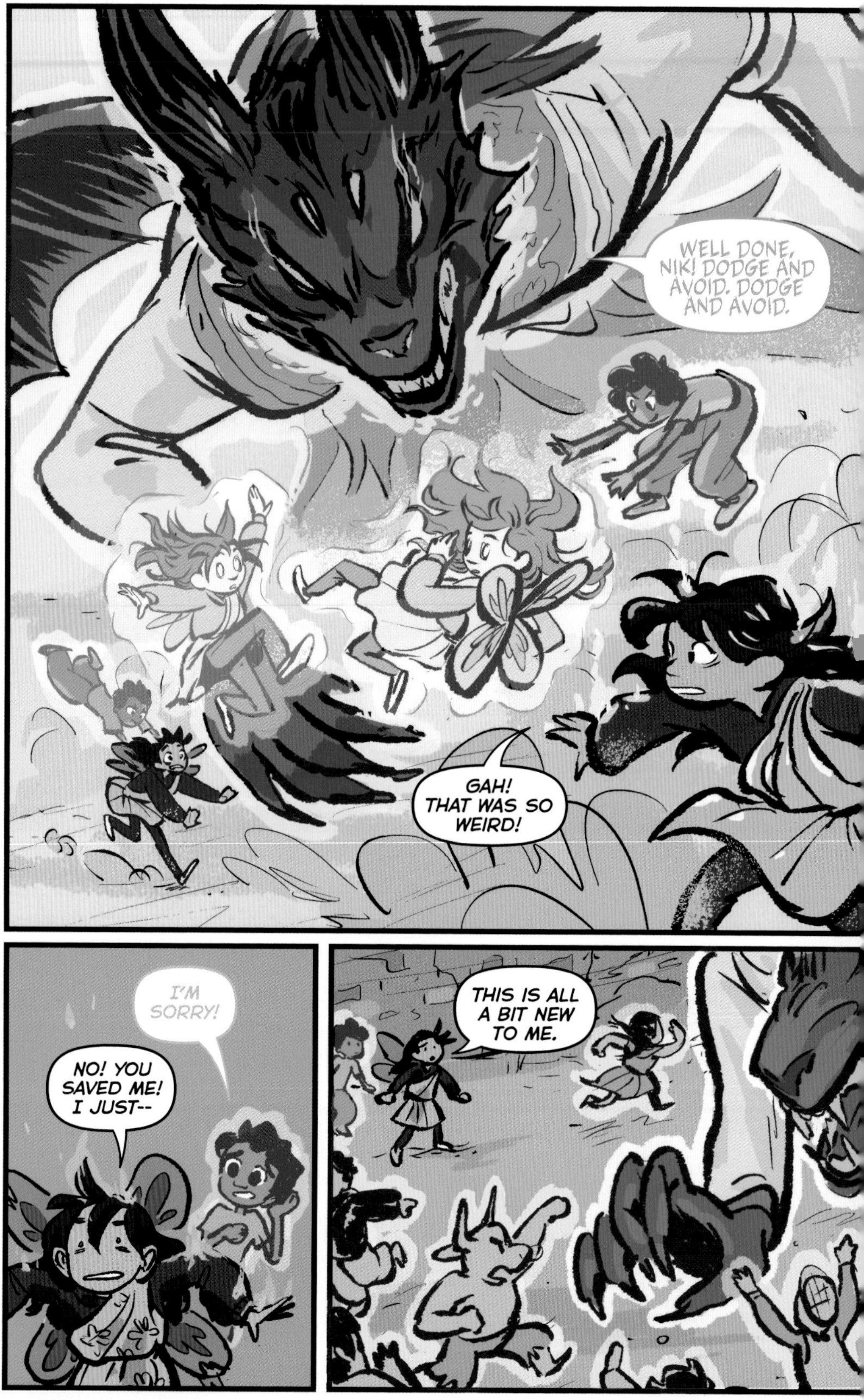
WELL DONE, NIK! DODGE AND AVOID. DODGE AND AVOID.
GAH! THAT WAS SO WEIRD!
I'M SORRY!
NO! YOU SAVED ME! I JUST--
THIS IS ALL A BIT NEW TO ME.

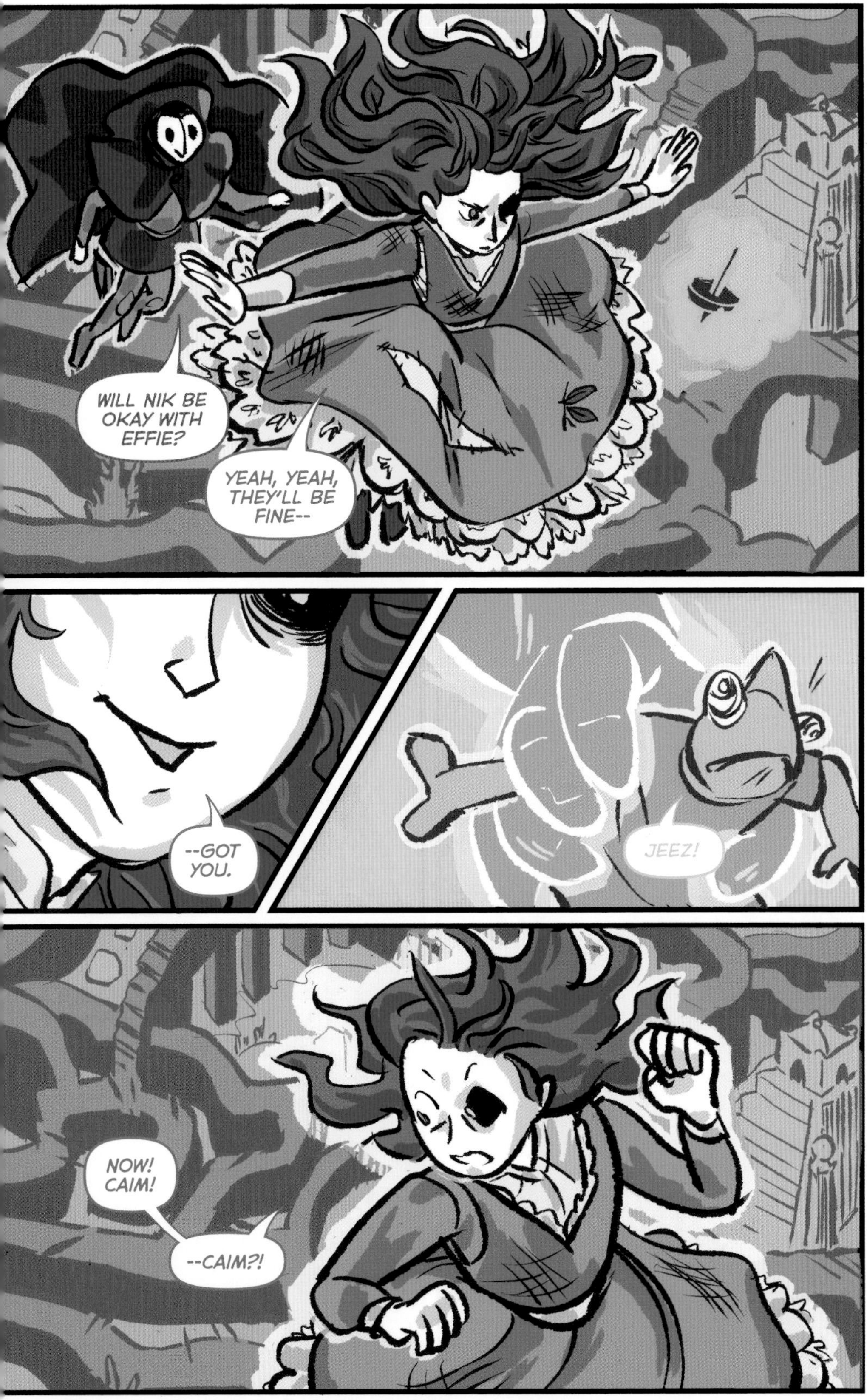
WILL NIK BE OKAY WITH EFFIE?
YEAH, YEAH, THEY'LL BE FINE--
--GOT YOU.
JEEZ!
NOW! CAIM!
--CAIM?!

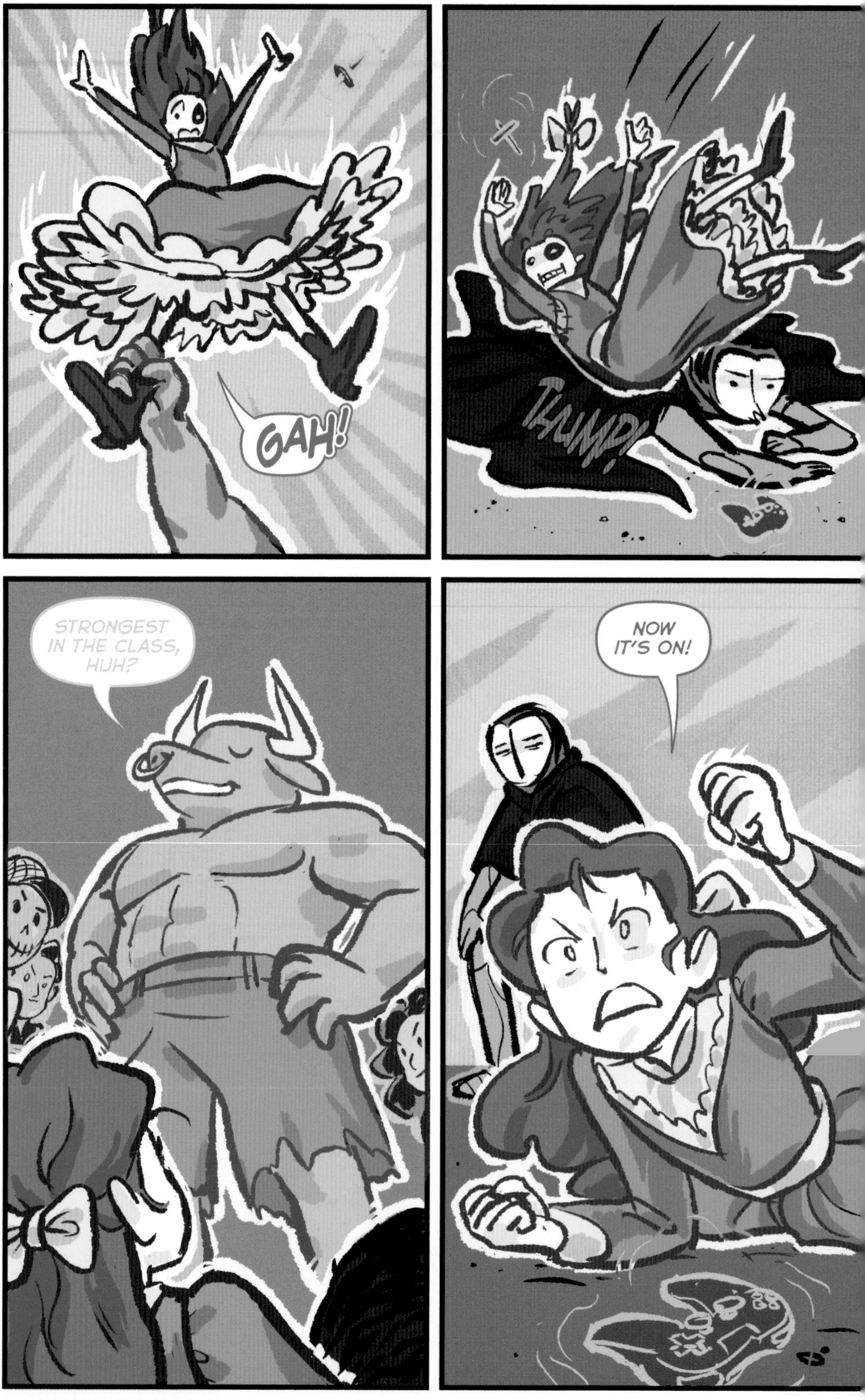
GAH!
THUMP!
STRONGEST IN THE CLASS, HUH?
NOW IT'S ON!

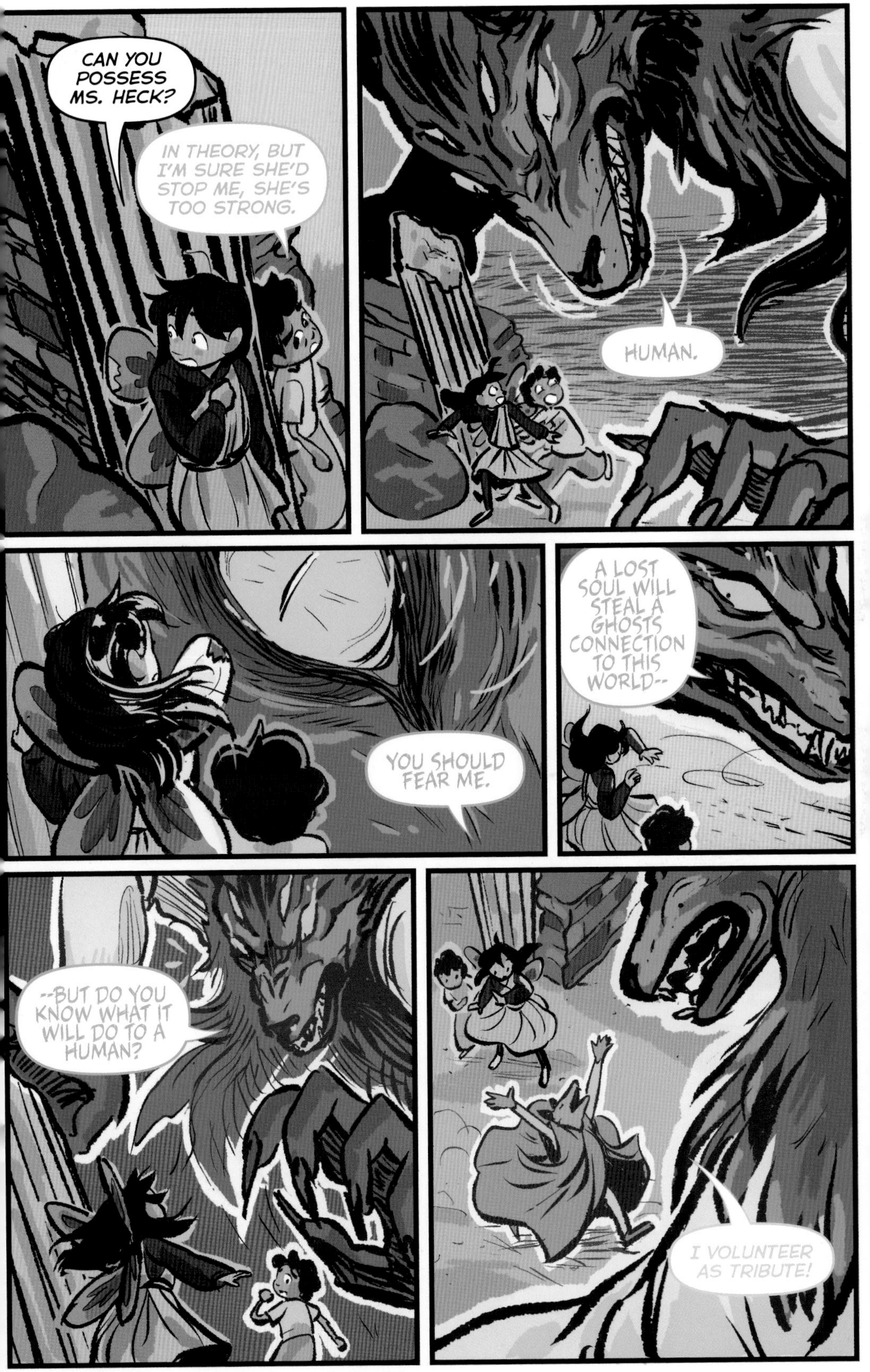
CAN YOU POSSESS MS. HECK?
IN THEORY, BUT I'M SURE SHE'D STOP ME, SHE'S TOO STRONG.
HUMAN.
YOU SHOULD FEAR ME.
A LOST SOUL WILL STEAL A GHOSTS CONNECTION TO THIS WORLD--
--BUT DO YOU KNOW WHAT IT WILL DO TO A HUMAN?
I VOLUNTEER AS TRIBUTE!

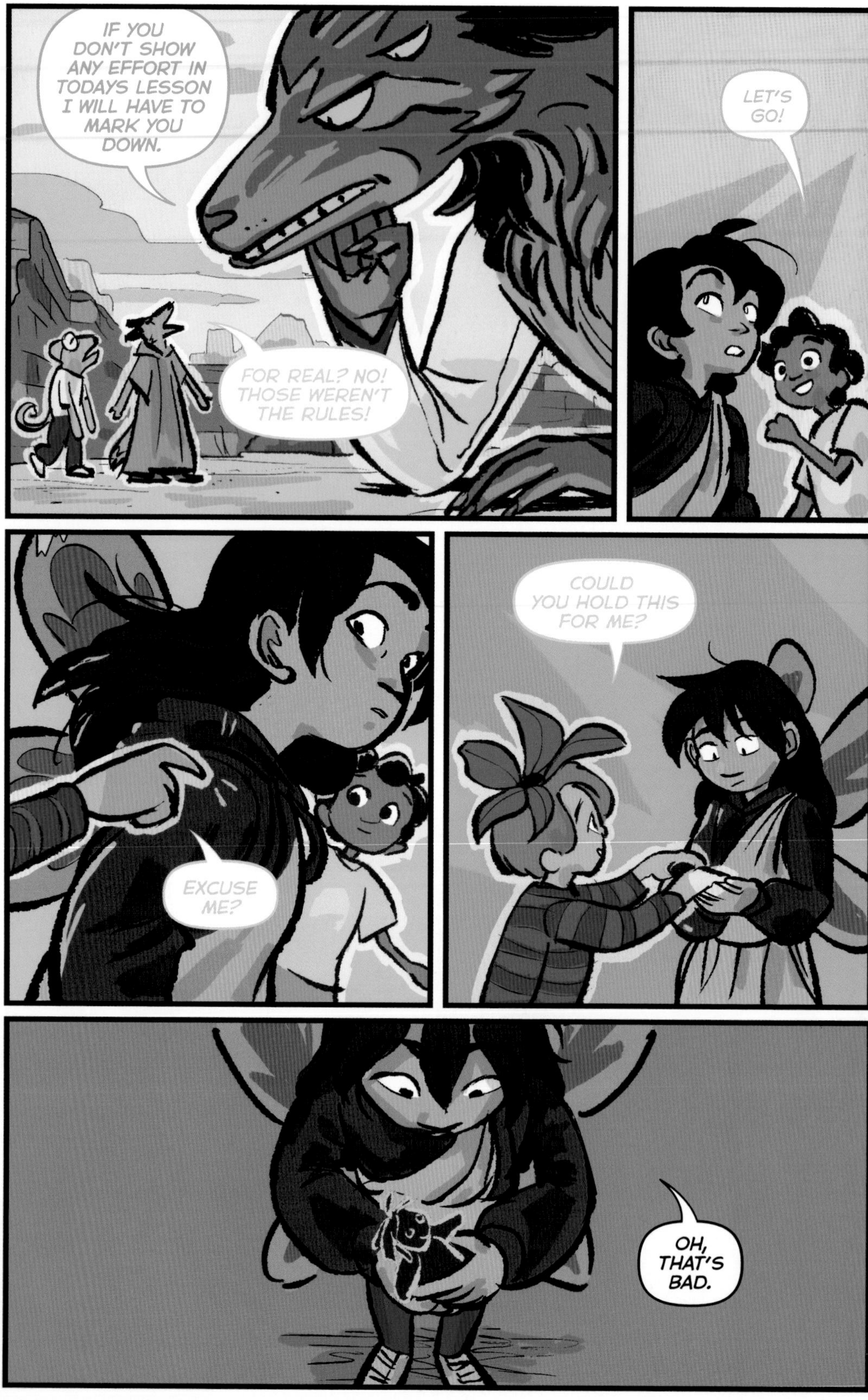
IF YOU DON'T SHOW ANY EFFORT IN TODAYS LESSON I WILL HAVE TO MARK YOU DOWN.
FOR REAL? NO! THOSE WEREN'T THE RULES!
LET'S GO!
EXCUSE ME?
COULD YOU HOLD THIS FOR ME?
OH, THAT'S BAD.

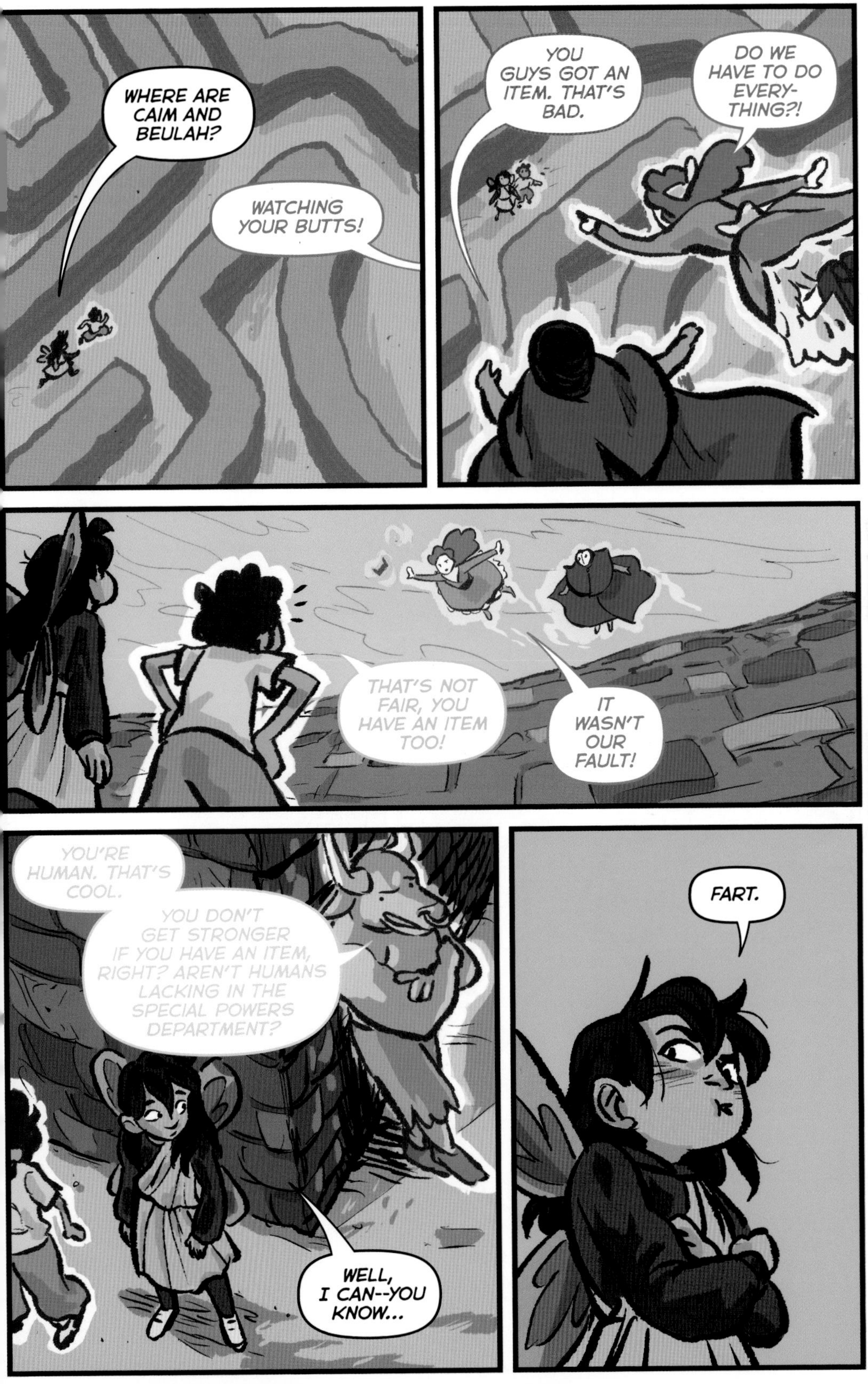
WHERE ARE CAIM AND BEULAH?
WATCHING YOUR BUTTS!
YOU GUYS GOT AN ITEM. THAT'S BAD.
DO WE HAVE TO DO EVERY-THING?!
THAT'S NOT FAIR, YOU HAVE AN ITEM TOO!
IT WASN'T OUR FAULT!
YOU'RE HUMAN. THAT'S COOL.
YOU DON'T GET STRONGER IF YOU HAVE AN ITEM, RIGHT? AREN'T HUMANS LACKING IN THE SPECIAL POWERS DEPARTMENT?
WELL, I CAN--YOU KNOW...
FART.

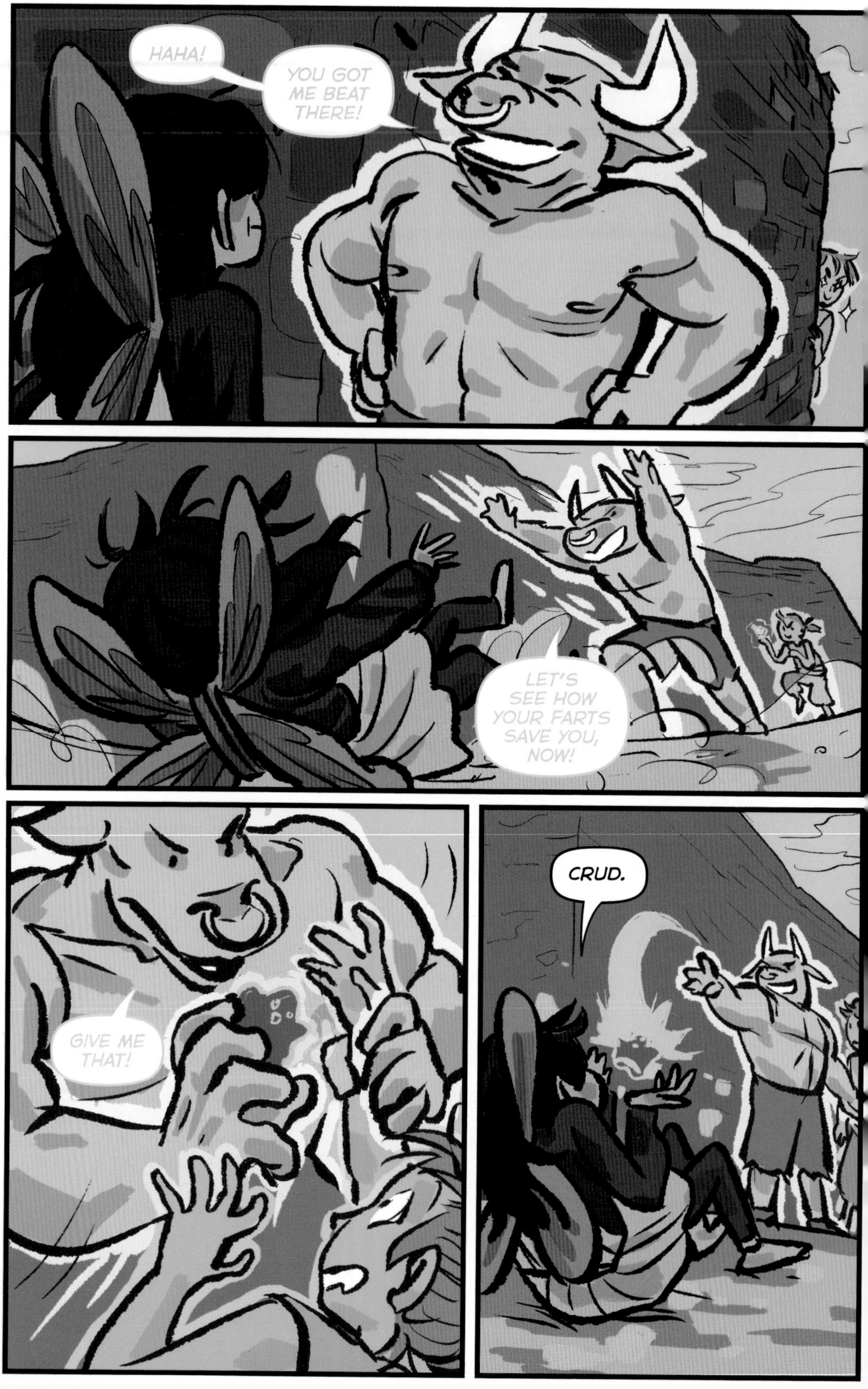
HAHA!
YOU GOT ME BEAT THERE!
LET'S SEE HOW YOUR FARTS SAVE YOU, NOW!
GIVE ME THAT!
CRUD.

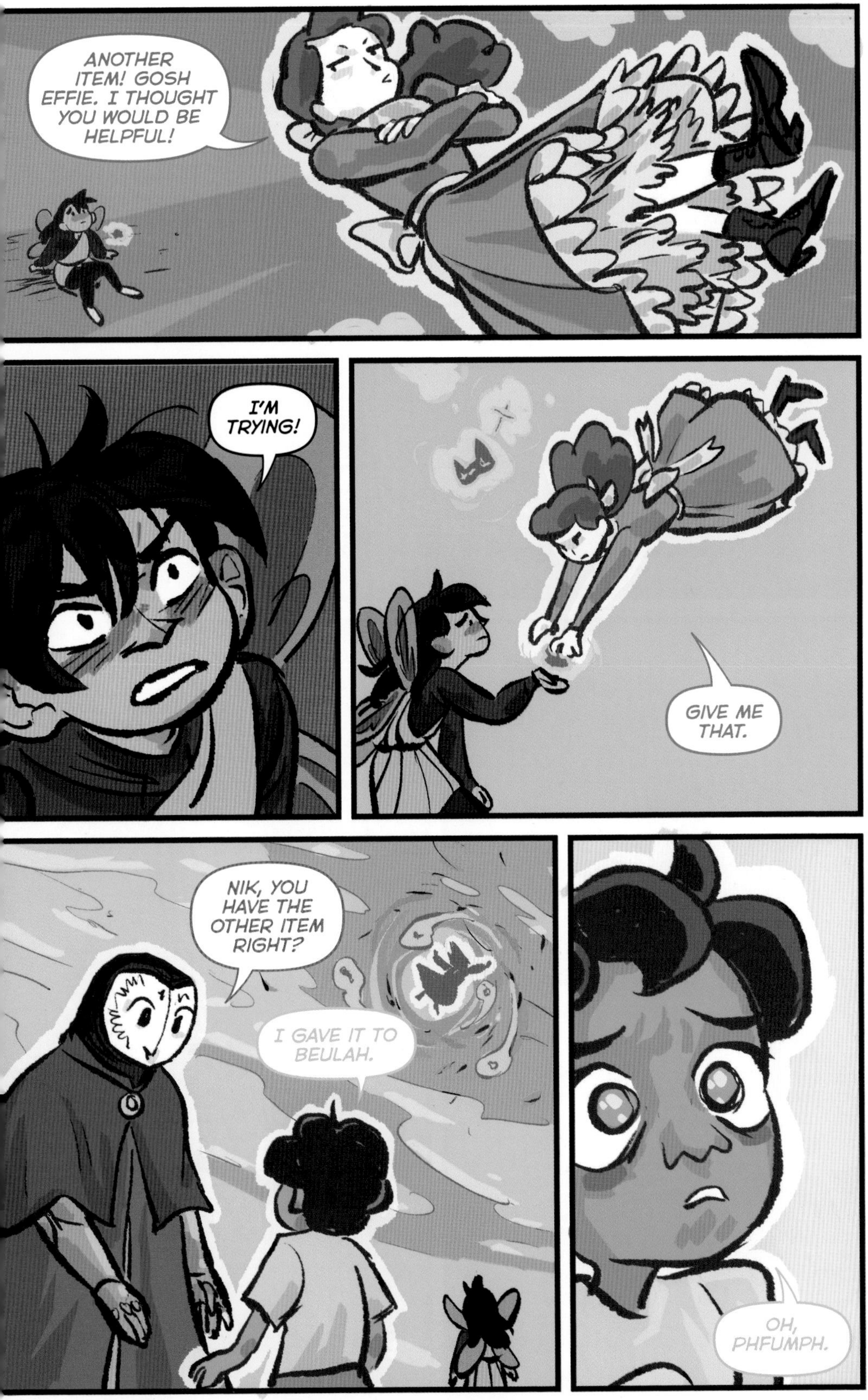
ANOTHER ITEM! GOSH EFFIE. I THOUGHT YOU WOULD BE HELPFUL!
I'M TRYING!
GIVE ME THAT.
NIK, YOU HAVE THE OTHER ITEM RIGHT?
I GAVE IT TO BEULAH.
OH, PHFUMPH.

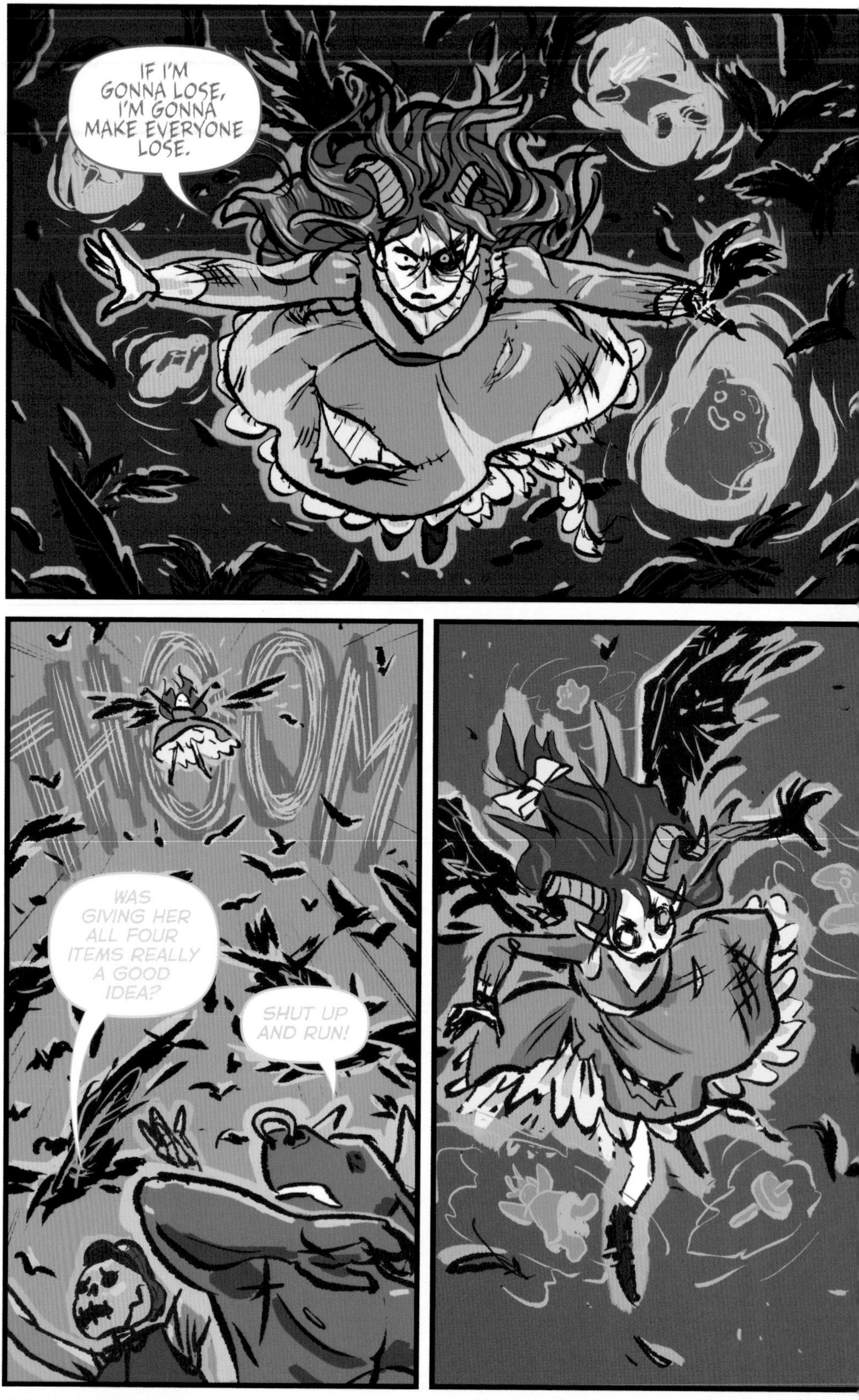

IF I'M GONNA LOSE, I'M GONNA MAKE EVERYONE LOSE.
THOOM
WAS GIVING HER ALL FOUR ITEMS REALLY A GOOD IDEA?
SHUT UP AND RUN!

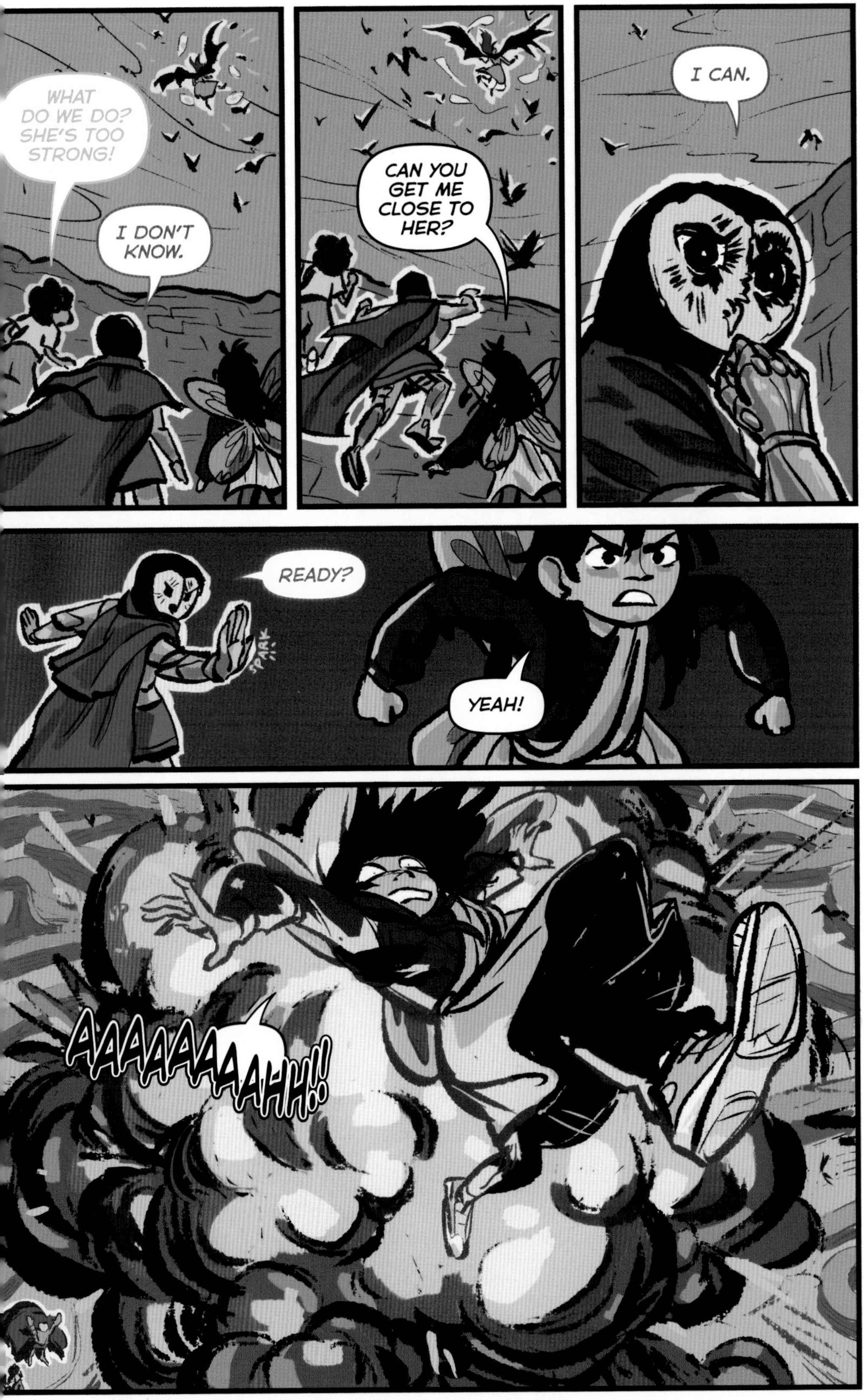
WHAT DO WE DO? SHE'S TOO STRONG!
I DON'T KNOW.
CAN YOU GET ME CLOSE TO HER?
I CAN.
READY?
SPARK
YEAH!
AAAAAAAAAHH!!

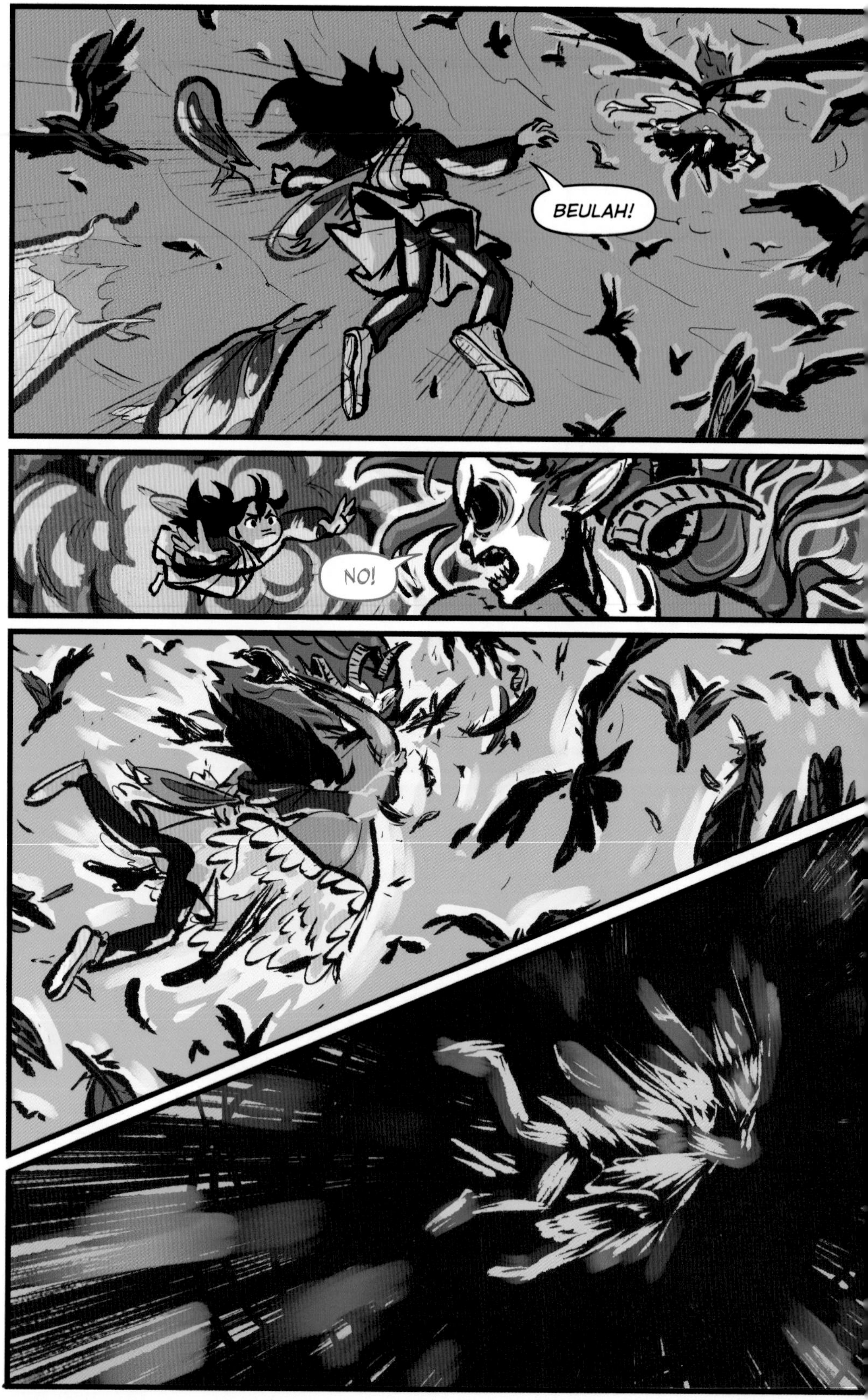
BEULAH!
NO!

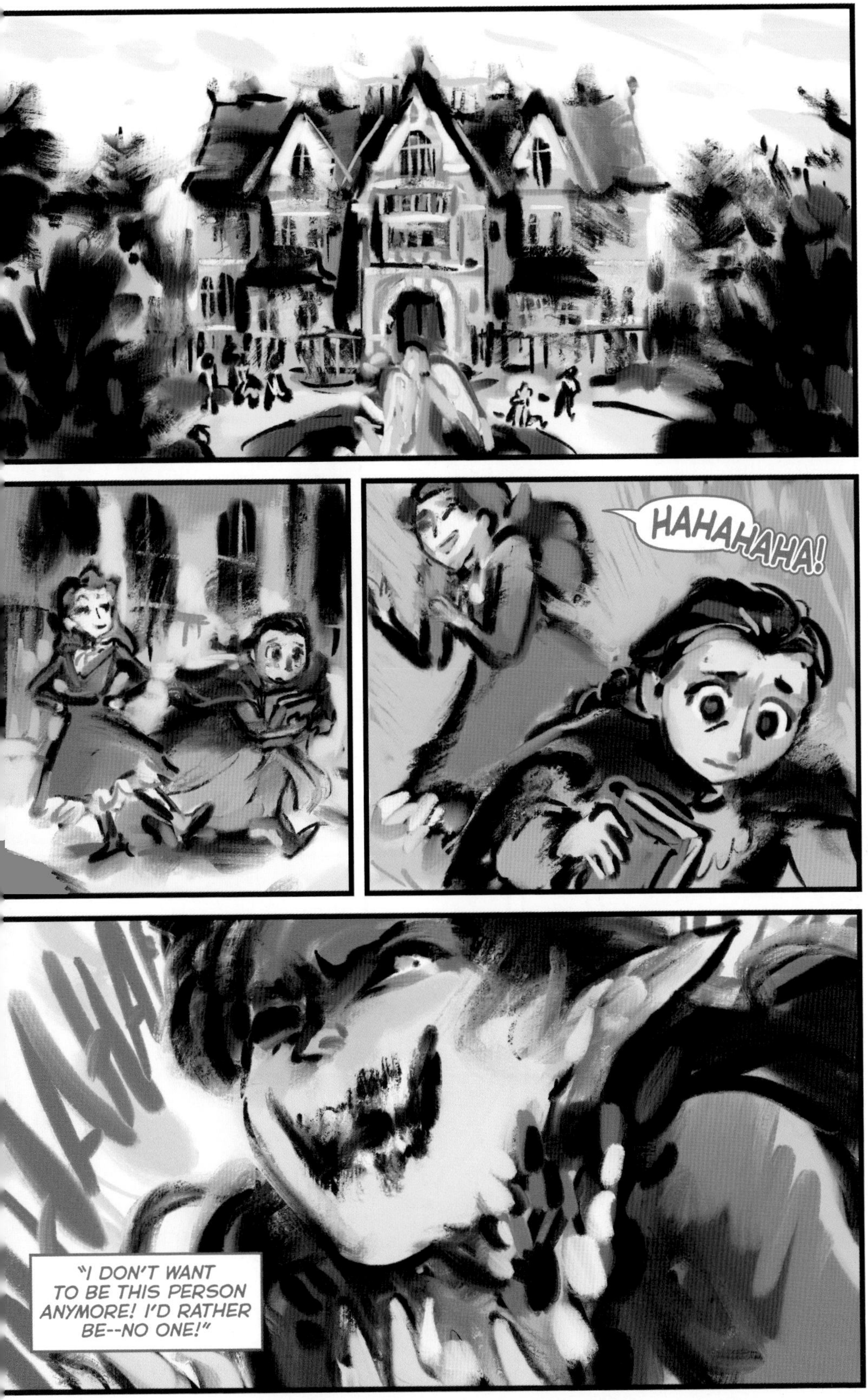
HAHAHAHA!
"I DON'T WANT TO BE THIS PERSON ANYMORE! I'D RATHER BE--NO ONE!"

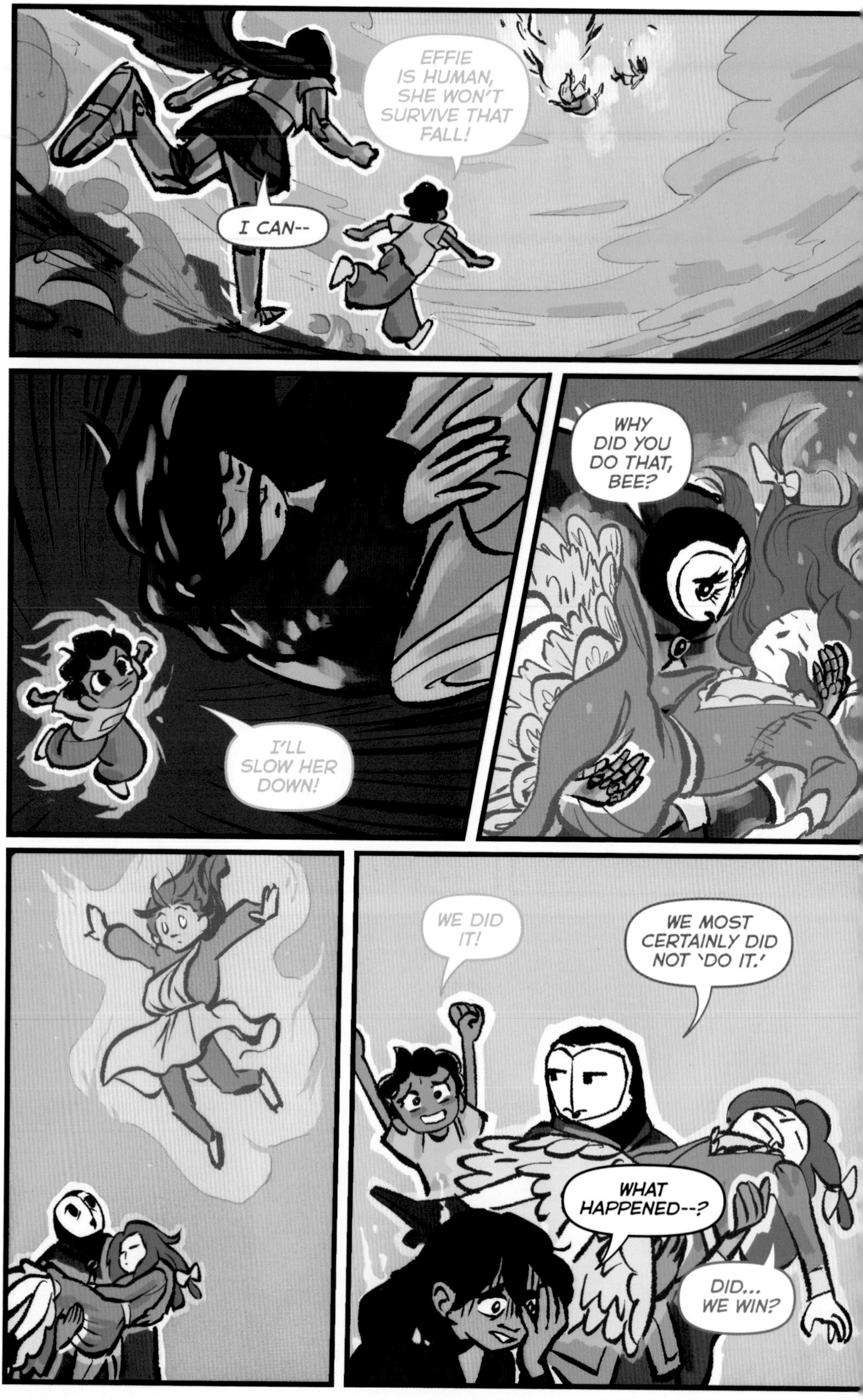
EFFIE IS HUMAN, SHE WON'T SURVIVE THAT FALL!
I CAN--
I'LL SLOW HER DOWN!
WHY DID YOU DO THAT, BEE?
WE DID IT!
WE MOST CERTAINLY DID NOT 'DO IT.'
WHAT HAPPENED--?
DID... WE WIN?

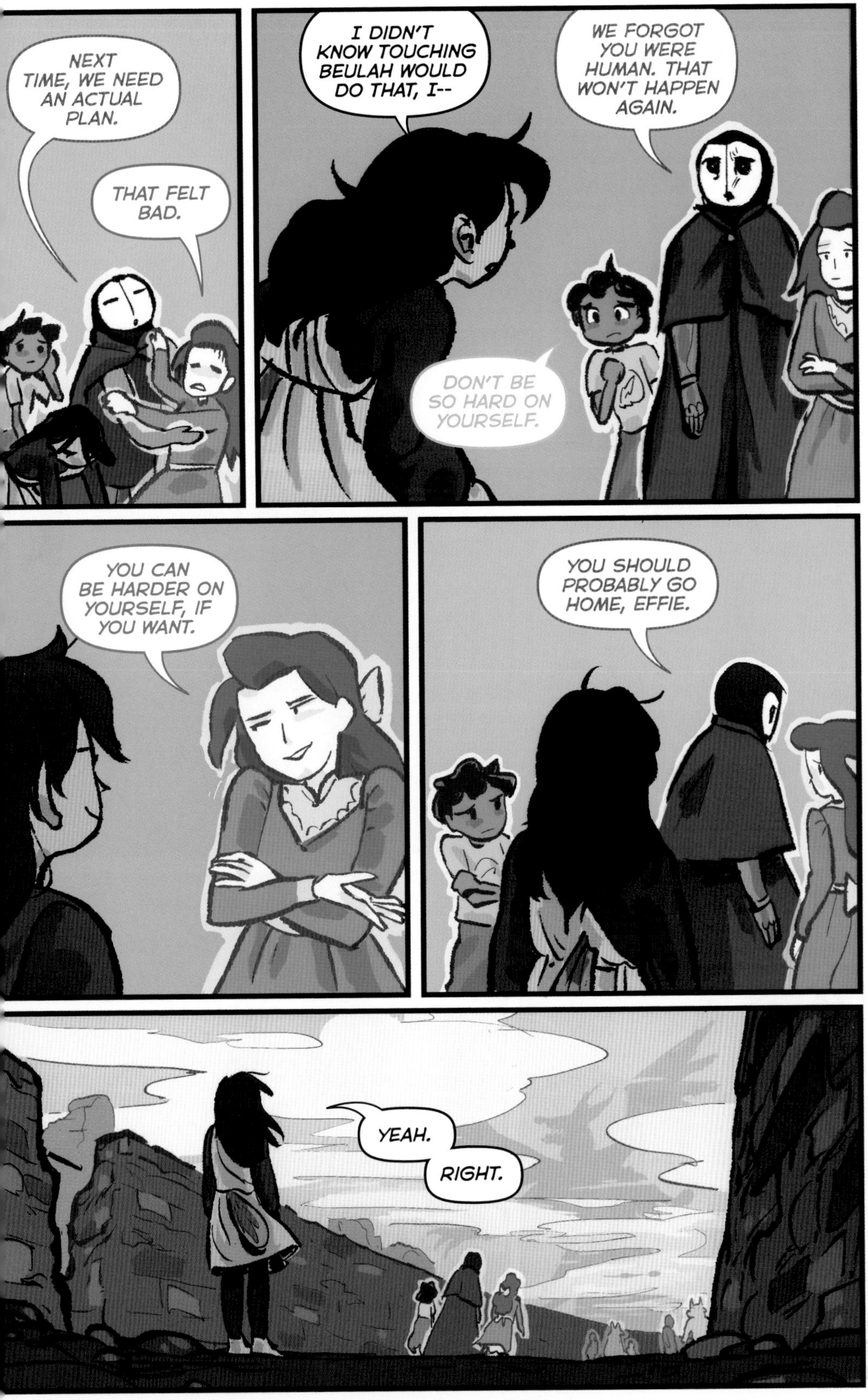
NEXT TIME, WE NEED AN ACTUAL PLAN.
THAT FELT BAD.
I DIDN'T KNOW TOUCHING BEULAH WOULD DO THAT, I--
WE FORGOT YOU WERE HUMAN. THAT WON'T HAPPEN AGAIN.
DON'T BE SO HARD ON YOURSELF.
YOU CAN BE HARDER ON YOURSELF, IF YOU WANT.
YOU SHOULD PROBABLY GO HOME, EFFIE.
YEAH.
RIGHT.

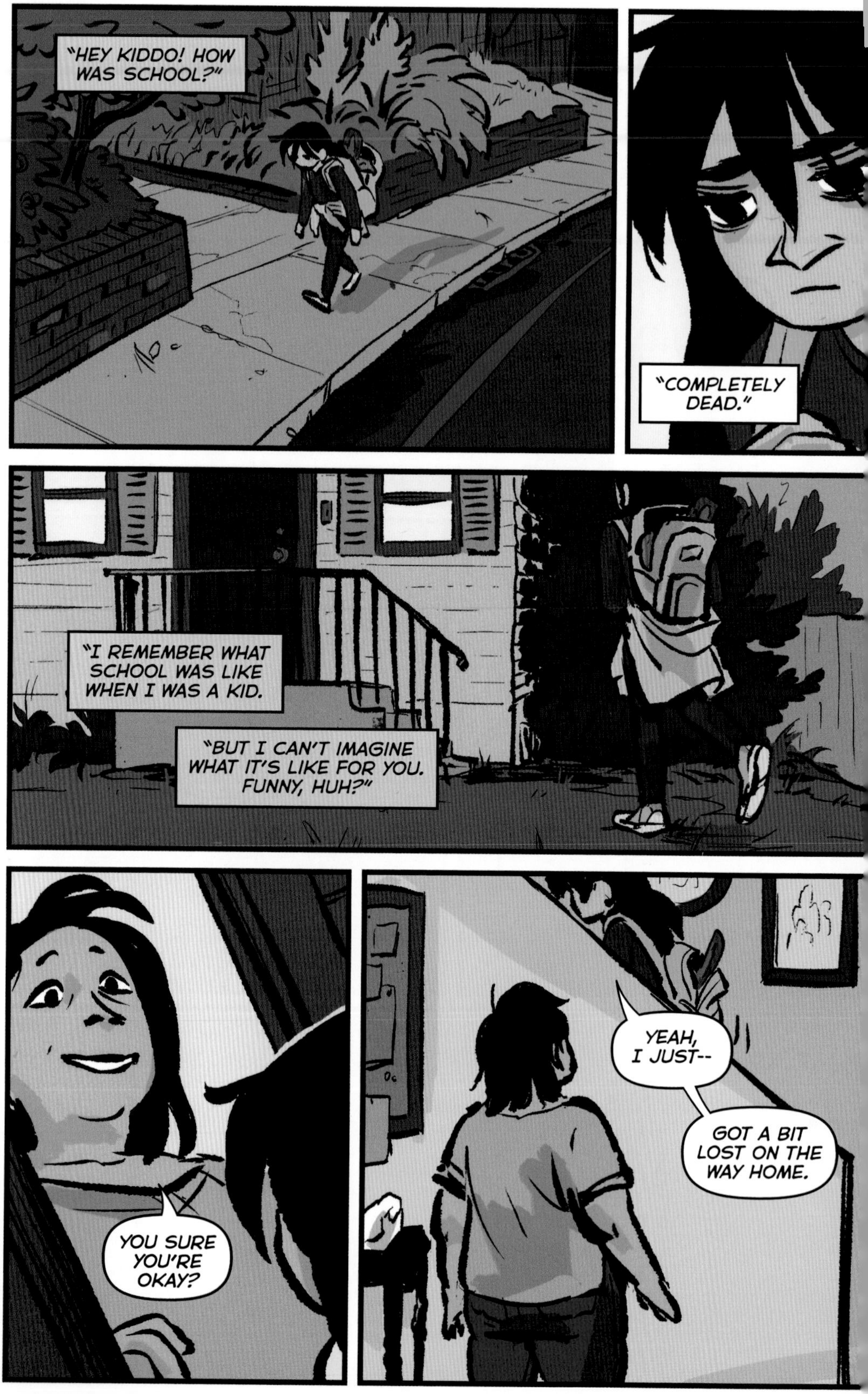

"HEY KIDDO! HOW WAS SCHOOL?"
"COMPLETELY DEAD."
"I REMEMBER WHAT SCHOOL WAS LIKE WHEN I WAS A KID.
"BUT I CAN'T IMAGINE WHAT IT'S LIKE FOR YOU. FUNNY, HUH?"
YOU SURE YOU'RE OKAY?
YEAH, I JUST--
GOT A BIT LOST ON THE WAY HOME.

"THERE'S ALWAYS TOMORROW, KIDDO. THE ONLY THING THAT MATTERS IS--"

"--YOU GOTTA TRY."

Things I'm good at	Things I not
	I

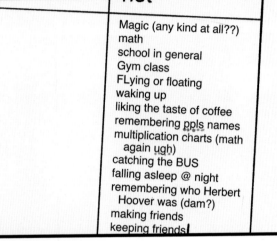

Magic (any kind at all??)
math
school in general
Gym class
FLying or floating
waking up
liking the taste of coffee
remembering ppls names
multiplication charts (math again ugh)
catching the BUS
falling asleep @ night
remembering who Herbert Hoover was (dam?)
making friends
keeping friends

good at

farting.

fa DELETE DELETE DEL

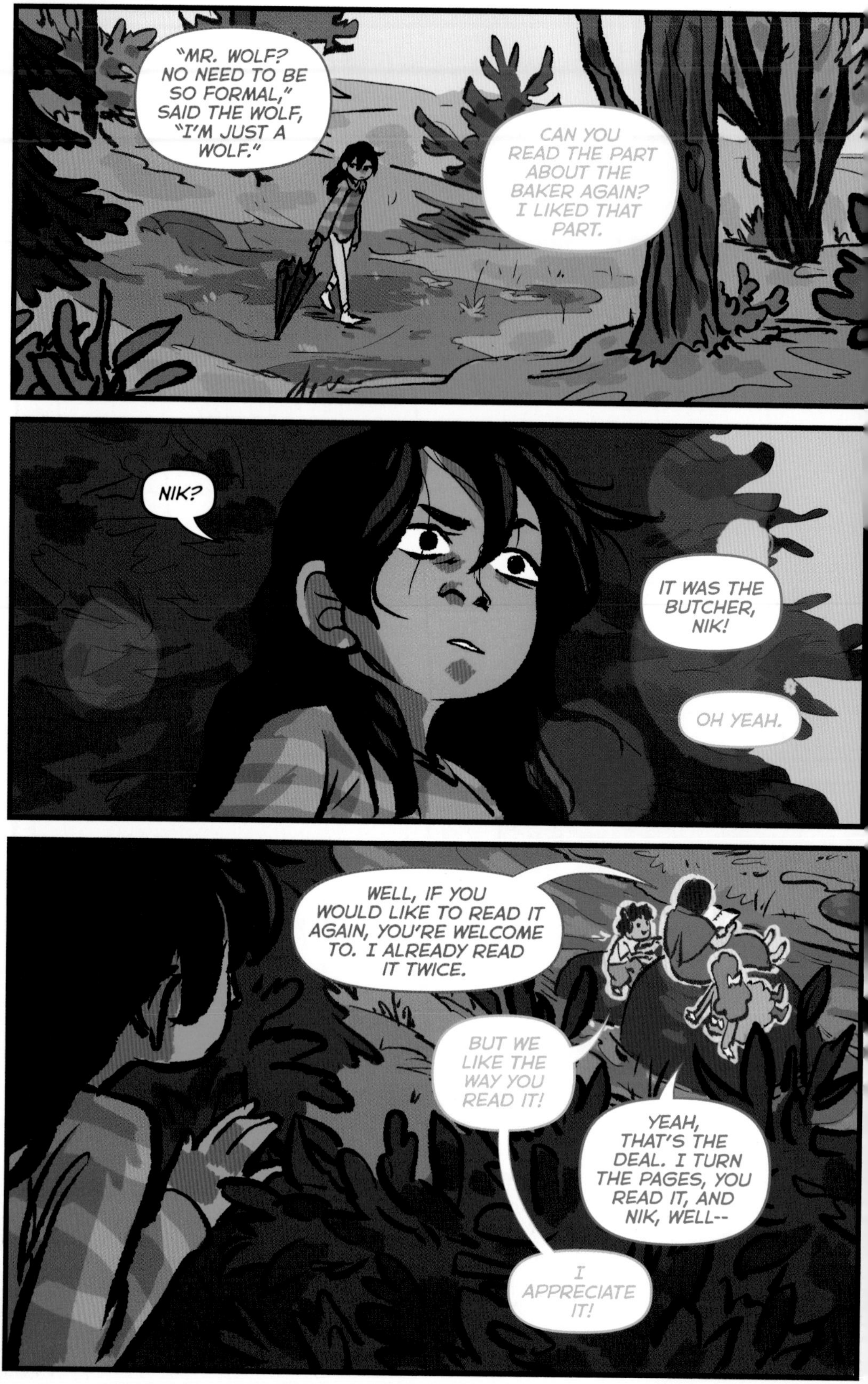
"MR. WOLF? NO NEED TO BE SO FORMAL," SAID THE WOLF, "I'M JUST A WOLF."
CAN YOU READ THE PART ABOUT THE BAKER AGAIN? I LIKED THAT PART.
NIK?
IT WAS THE BUTCHER, NIK!
OH YEAH.
WELL, IF YOU WOULD LIKE TO READ IT AGAIN, YOU'RE WELCOME TO. I ALREADY READ IT TWICE.
BUT WE LIKE THE WAY YOU READ IT!
YEAH, THAT'S THE DEAL. I TURN THE PAGES, YOU READ IT, AND NIK, WELL--
I APPRECIATE IT!

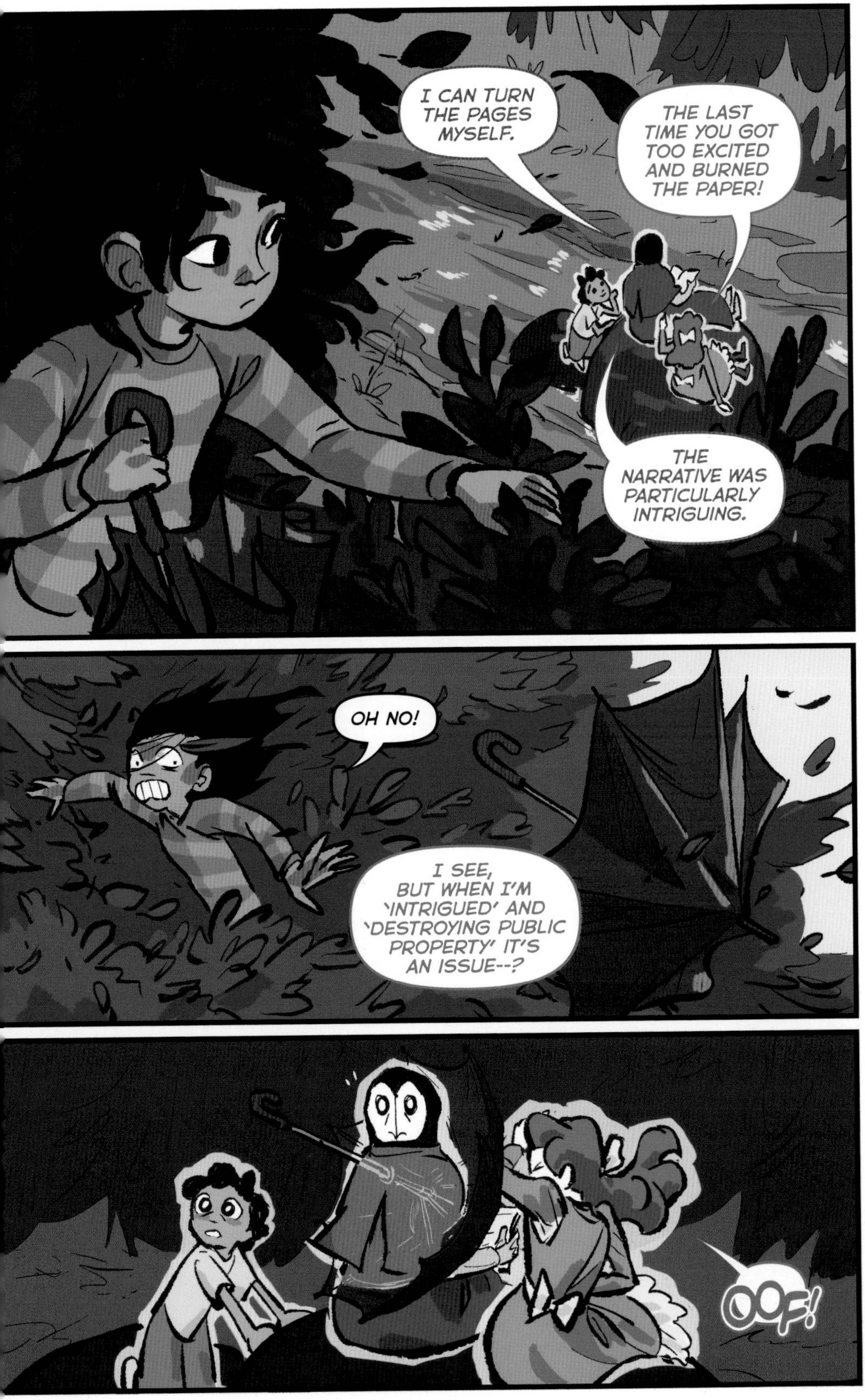
I CAN TURN THE PAGES MYSELF.
THE LAST TIME YOU GOT TOO EXCITED AND BURNED THE PAPER!
THE NARRATIVE WAS PARTICULARLY INTRIGUING.
OH NO!
I SEE, BUT WHEN I'M 'INTRIGUED' AND 'DESTROYING PUBLIC PROPERTY' IT'S AN ISSUE--?
OOF!

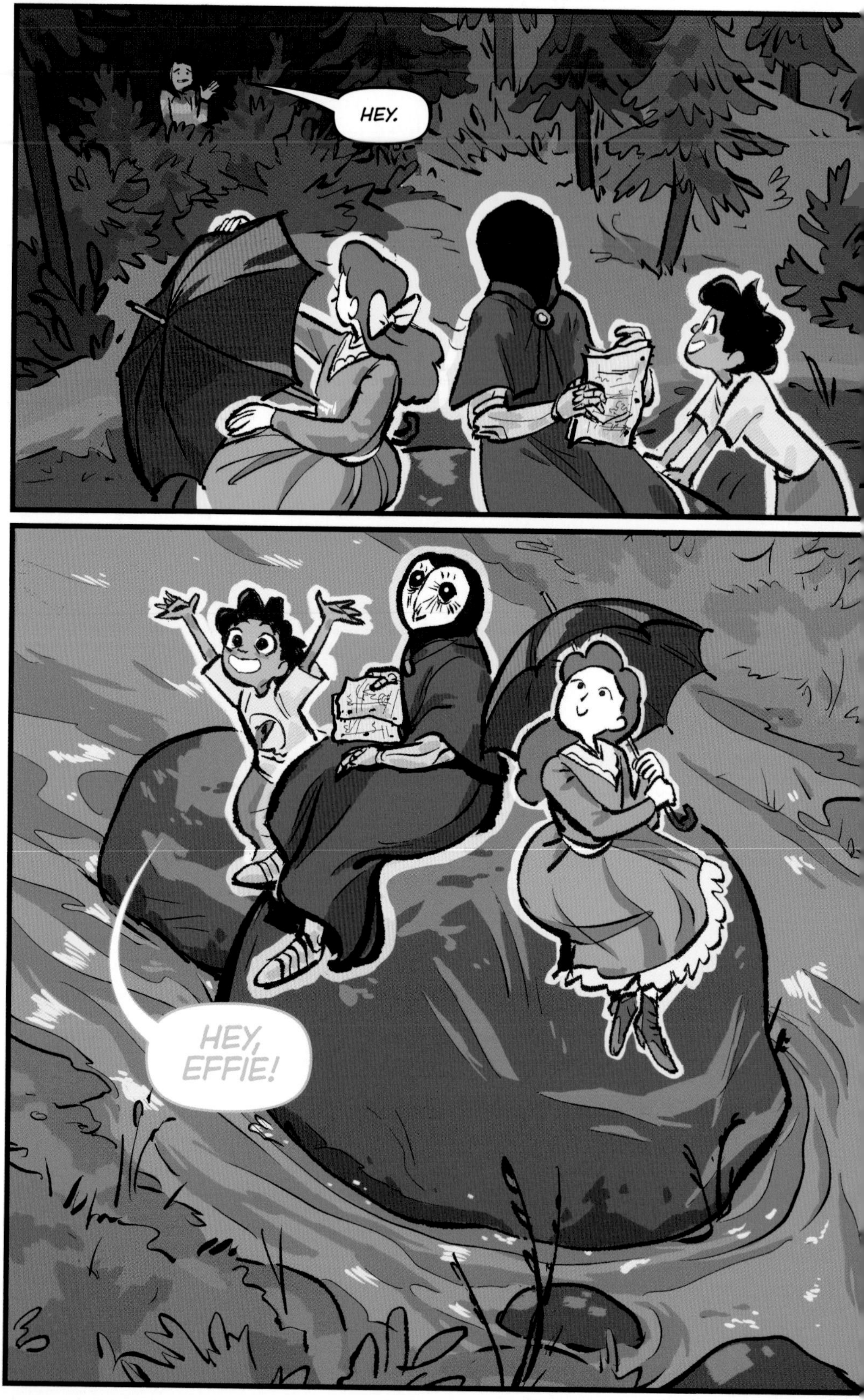
HEY.
HEY, EFFIE!

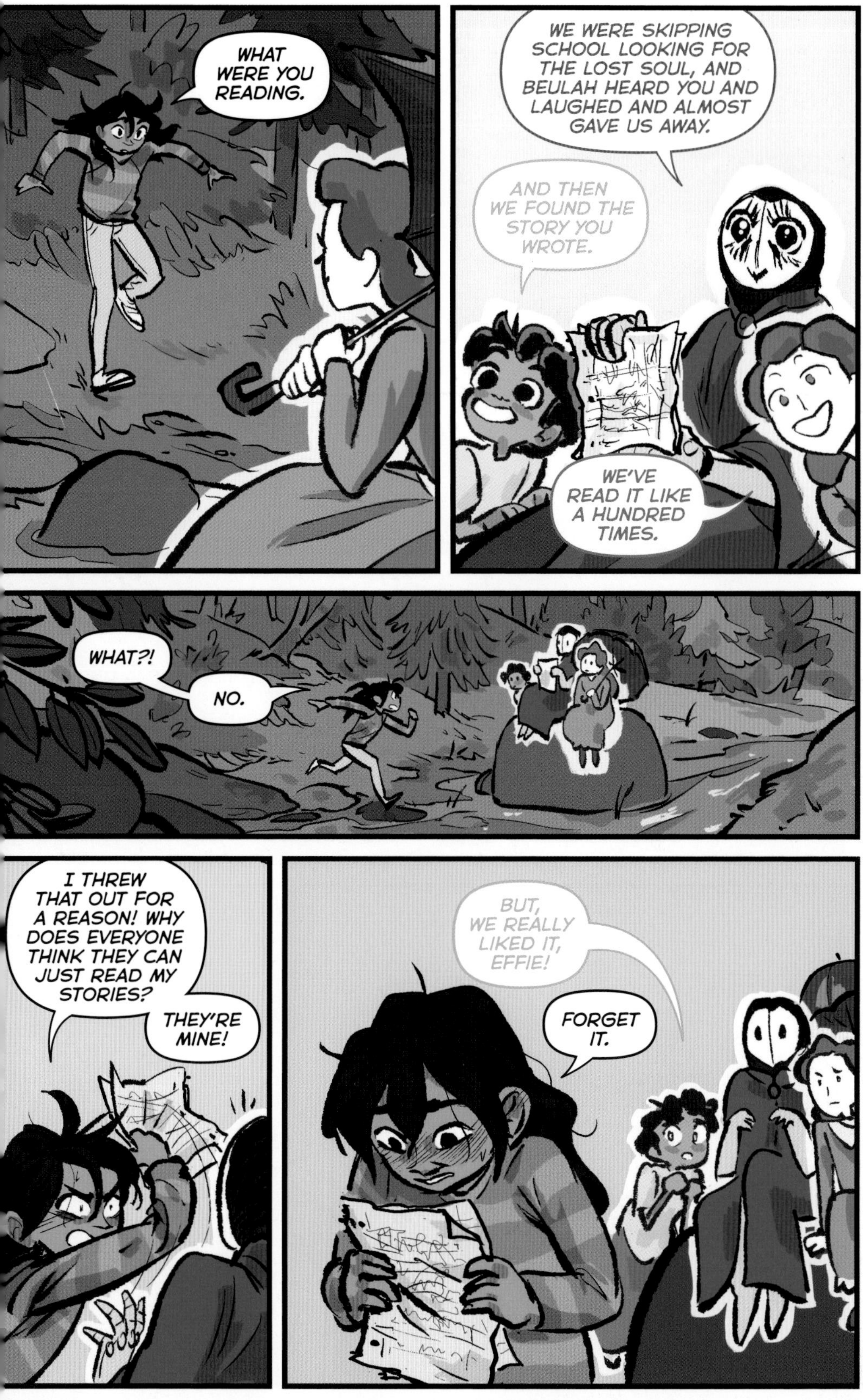
WHAT WERE YOU READING.
WE WERE SKIPPING SCHOOL LOOKING FOR THE LOST SOUL, AND BEULAH HEARD YOU AND LAUGHED AND ALMOST GAVE US AWAY.
AND THEN WE FOUND THE STORY YOU WROTE.
WE'VE READ IT LIKE A HUNDRED TIMES.
WHAT?!
NO.
I THREW THAT OUT FOR A REASON! WHY DOES EVERYONE THINK THEY CAN JUST READ MY STORIES?
THEY'RE MINE!
BUT, WE REALLY LIKED IT, EFFIE!
FORGET IT.

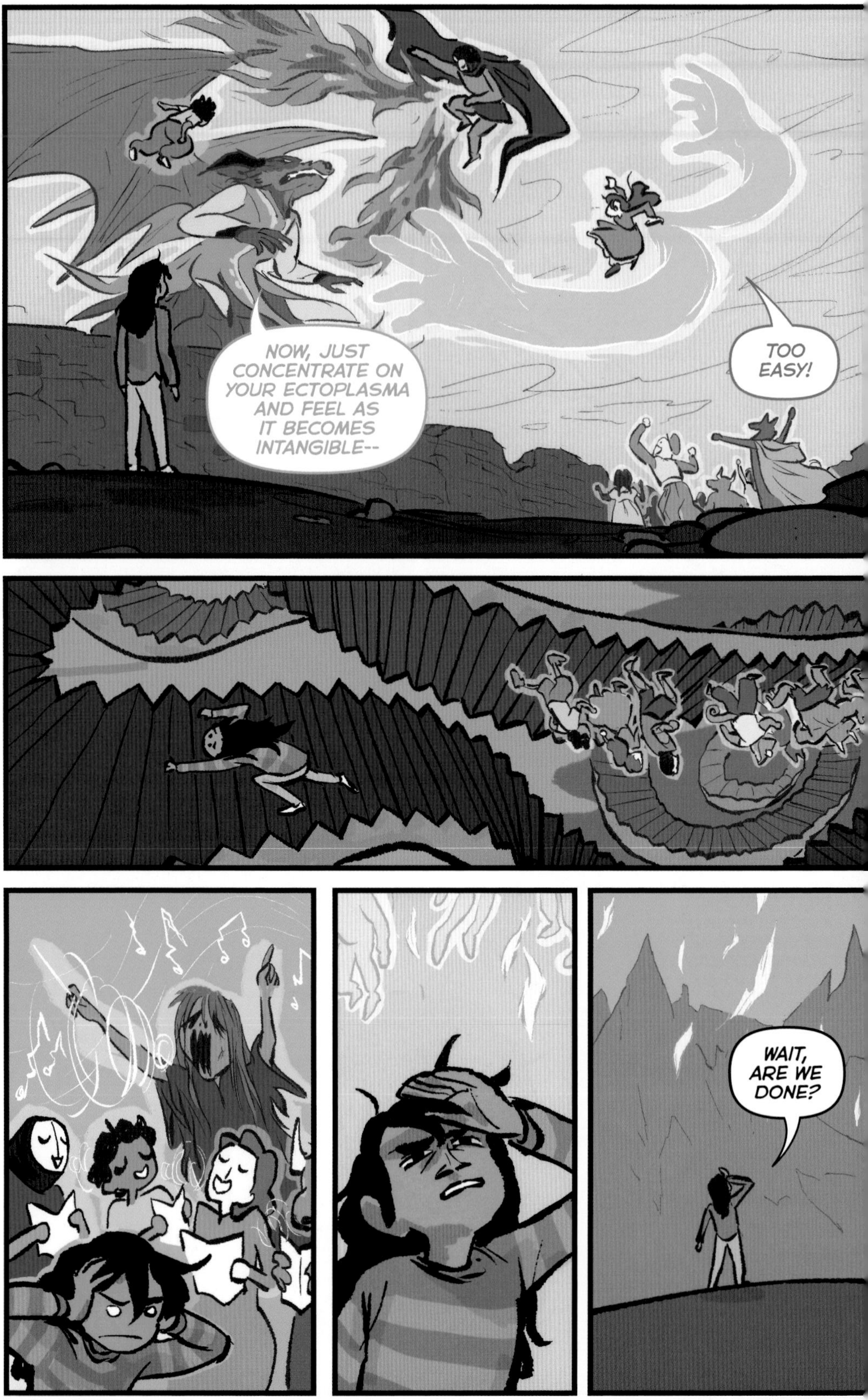
NOW, JUST CONCENTRATE ON YOUR ECTOPLASMA AND FEEL AS IT BECOMES INTANGIBLE--
TOO EASY!
WAIT, ARE WE DONE?

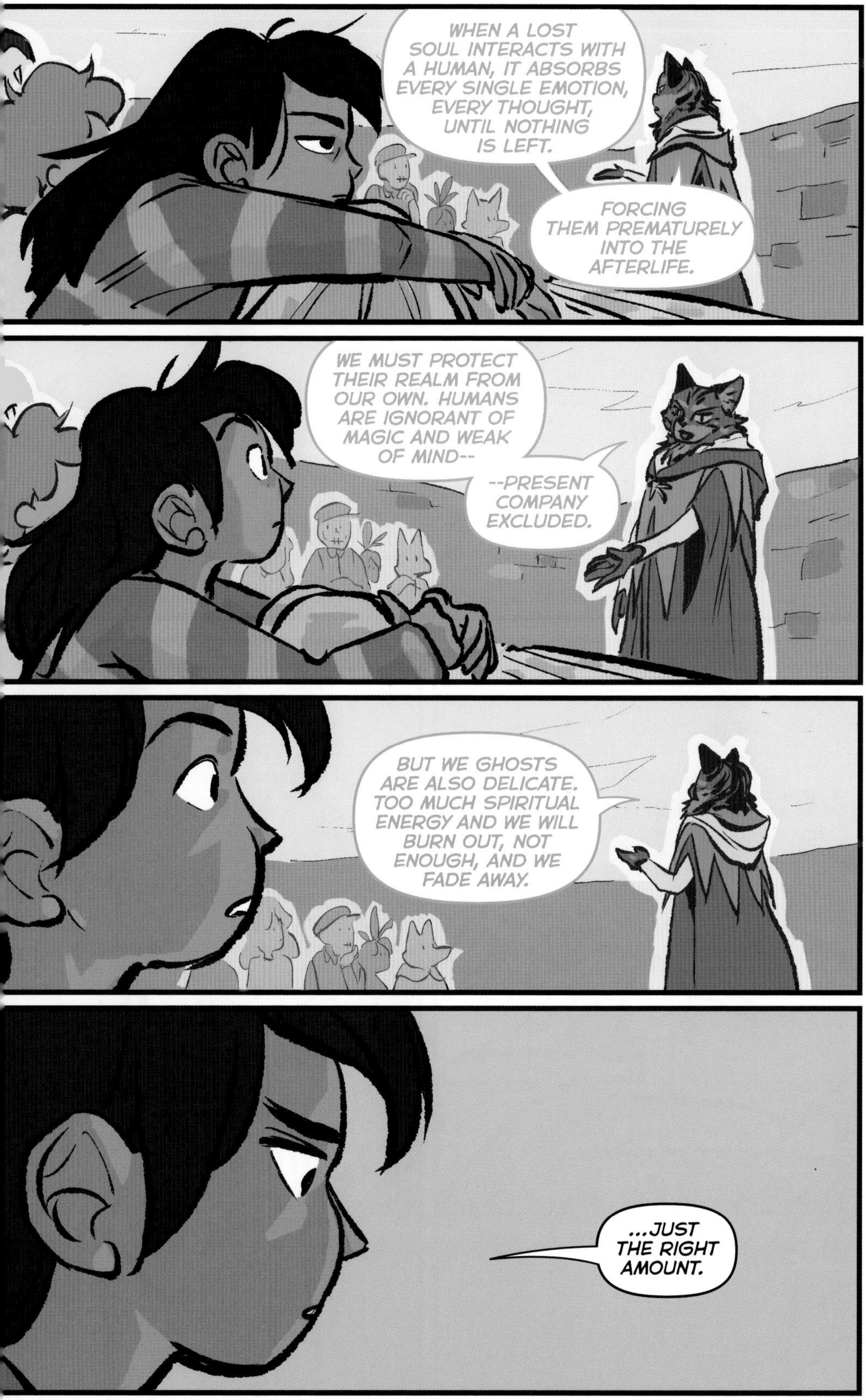

WHEN A LOST SOUL INTERACTS WITH A HUMAN, IT ABSORBS EVERY SINGLE EMOTION, EVERY THOUGHT, UNTIL NOTHING IS LEFT.
FORCING THEM PREMATURELY INTO THE AFTERLIFE.
WE MUST PROTECT THEIR REALM FROM OUR OWN. HUMANS ARE IGNORANT OF MAGIC AND WEAK OF MIND--
--PRESENT COMPANY EXCLUDED.
BUT WE GHOSTS ARE ALSO DELICATE. TOO MUCH SPIRITUAL ENERGY AND WE WILL BURN OUT, NOT ENOUGH, AND WE FADE AWAY.
...JUST THE RIGHT AMOUNT.

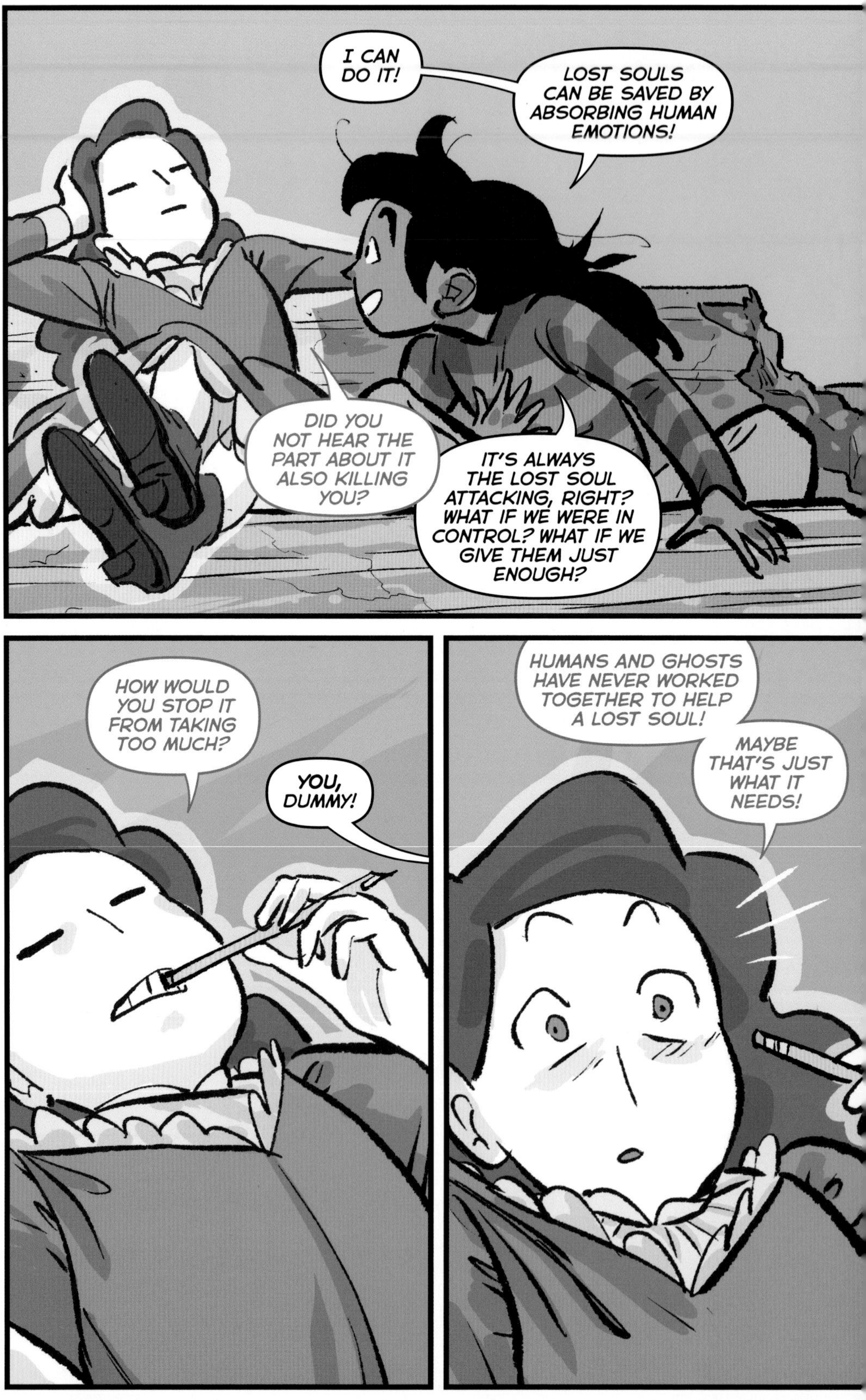

I CAN DO IT!
LOST SOULS CAN BE SAVED BY ABSORBING HUMAN EMOTIONS!
DID YOU NOT HEAR THE PART ABOUT IT ALSO KILLING YOU?
IT'S ALWAYS THE LOST SOUL ATTACKING, RIGHT? WHAT IF WE WERE IN CONTROL? WHAT IF WE GIVE THEM JUST ENOUGH?
HOW WOULD YOU STOP IT FROM TAKING TOO MUCH?
YOU, DUMMY!
HUMANS AND GHOSTS HAVE NEVER WORKED TOGETHER TO HELP A LOST SOUL!
MAYBE THAT'S JUST WHAT IT NEEDS!

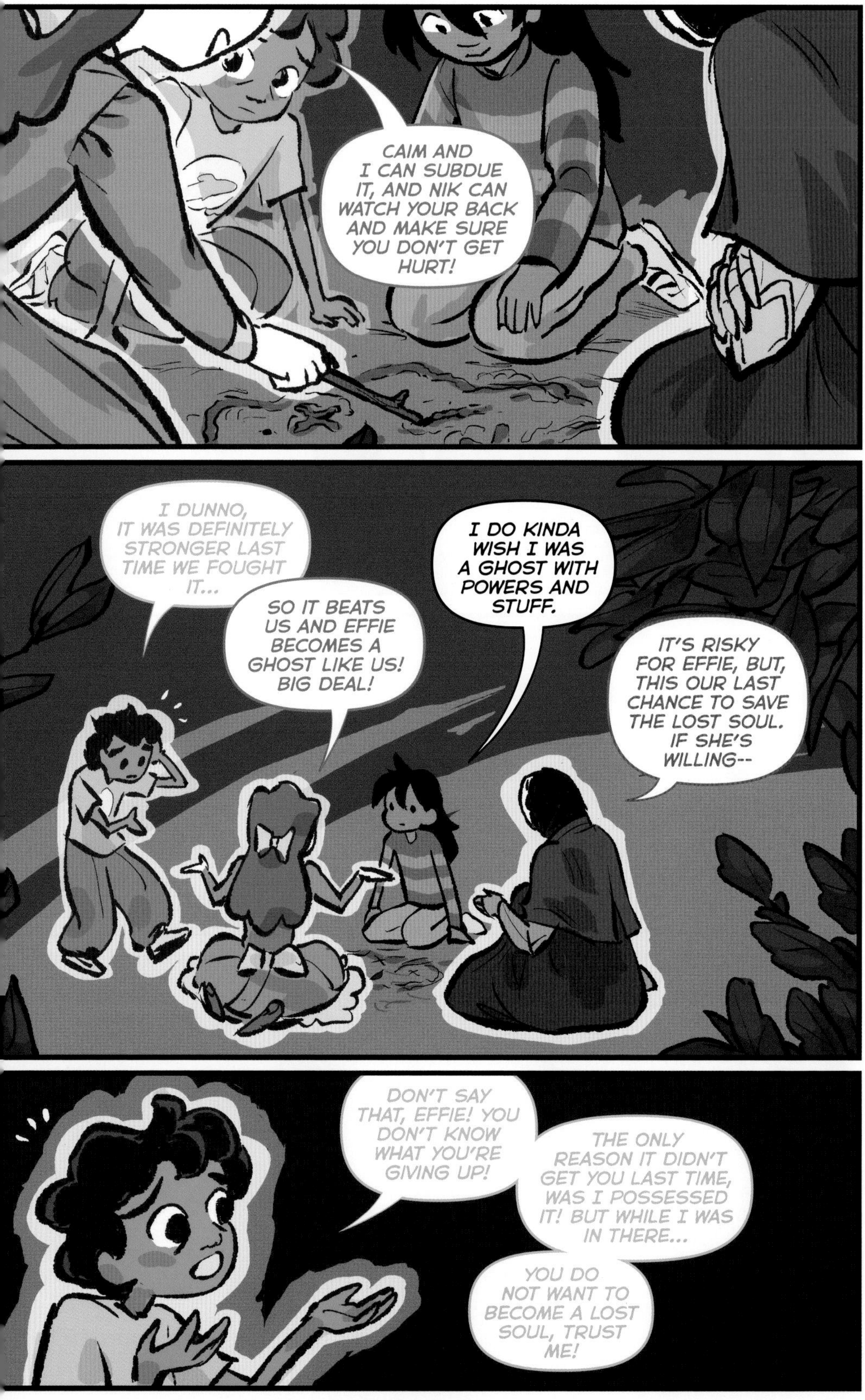
CAIM AND I CAN SUBDUE IT, AND NIK CAN WATCH YOUR BACK AND MAKE SURE YOU DON'T GET HURT!
I DUNNO, IT WAS DEFINITELY STRONGER LAST TIME WE FOUGHT IT...
SO IT BEATS US AND EFFIE BECOMES A GHOST LIKE US! BIG DEAL!
I DO KINDA WISH I WAS A GHOST WITH POWERS AND STUFF.
IT'S RISKY FOR EFFIE, BUT, THIS OUR LAST CHANCE TO SAVE THE LOST SOUL. IF SHE'S WILLING--
DON'T SAY THAT, EFFIE! YOU DON'T KNOW WHAT YOU'RE GIVING UP!
THE ONLY REASON IT DIDN'T GET YOU LAST TIME, WAS I POSSESSED IT! BUT WHILE I WAS IN THERE...
YOU DO NOT WANT TO BECOME A LOST SOUL, TRUST ME!

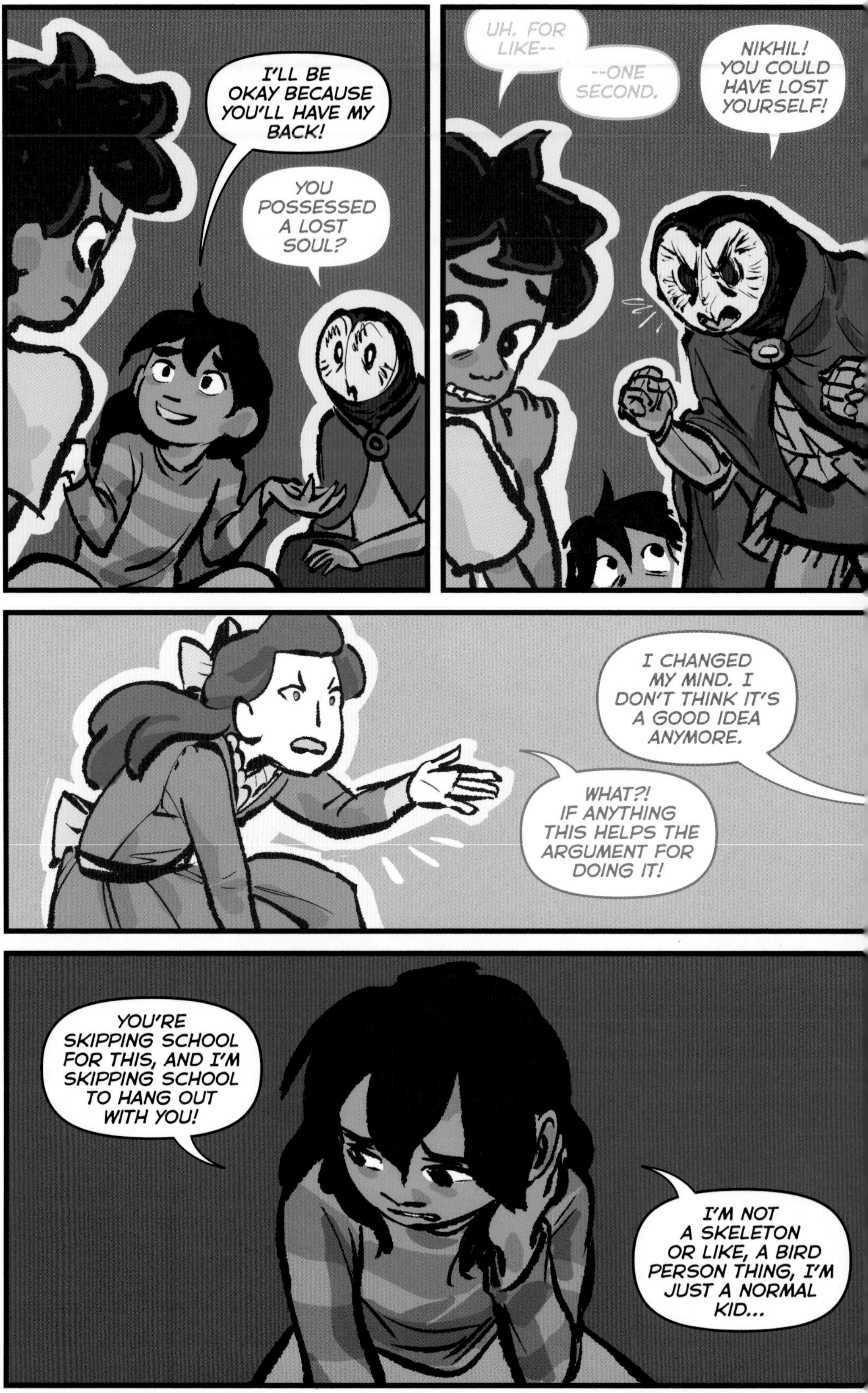
I'LL BE OKAY BECAUSE YOU'LL HAVE MY BACK!
YOU POSSESSED A LOST SOUL?
UH. FOR LIKE--
--ONE SECOND.
NIKHIL! YOU COULD HAVE LOST YOURSELF!
I CHANGED MY MIND. I DON'T THINK IT'S A GOOD IDEA ANYMORE.
WHAT?! IF ANYTHING THIS HELPS THE ARGUMENT FOR DOING IT!
YOU'RE SKIPPING SCHOOL FOR THIS, AND I'M SKIPPING SCHOOL TO HANG OUT WITH YOU!
I'M NOT A SKELETON OR LIKE, A BIRD PERSON THING, I'M JUST A NORMAL KID...

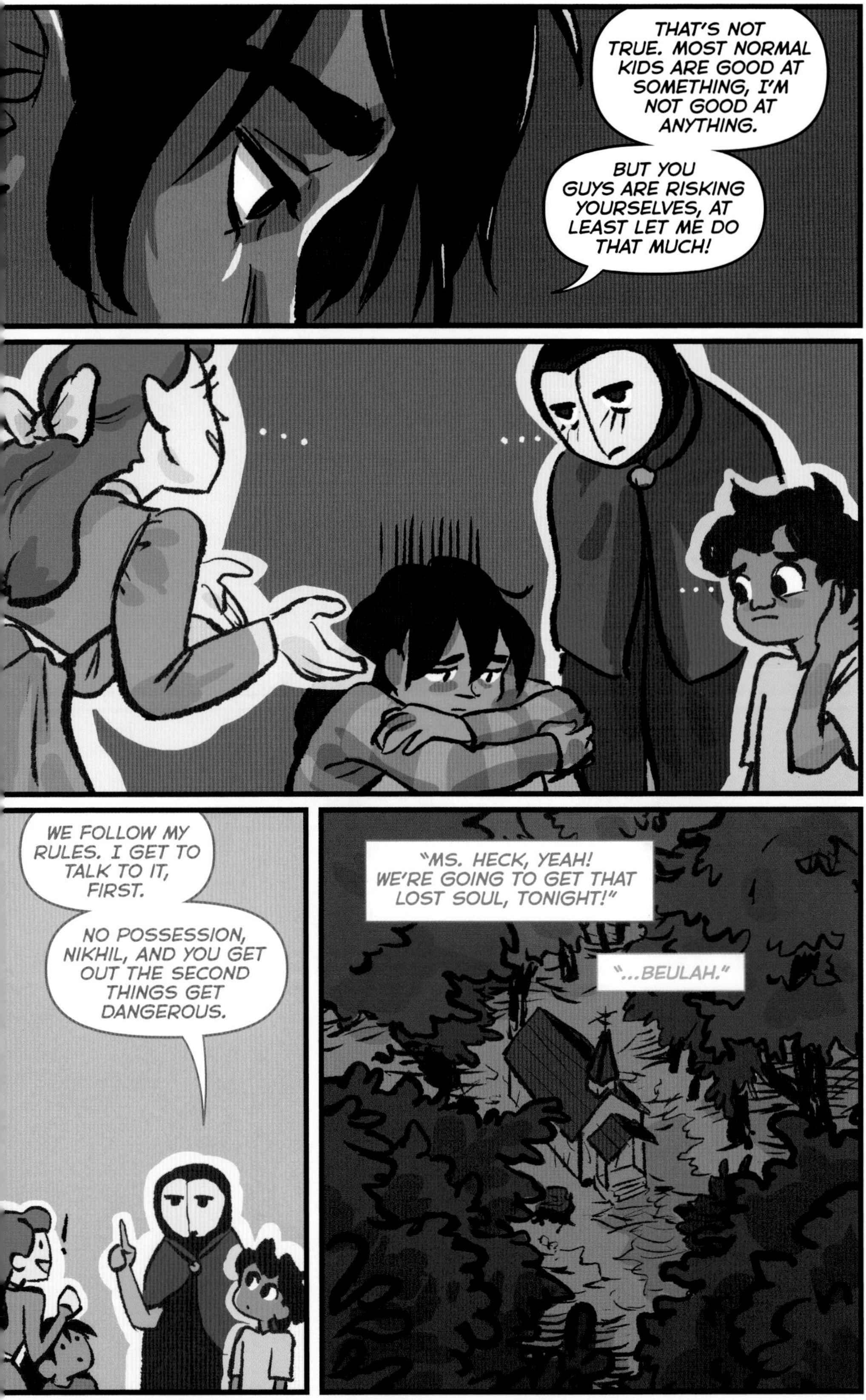
THAT'S NOT TRUE. MOST NORMAL KIDS ARE GOOD AT SOMETHING, I'M NOT GOOD AT ANYTHING.
BUT YOU GUYS ARE RISKING YOURSELVES, AT LEAST LET ME DO THAT MUCH!
...
...
...
WE FOLLOW MY RULES. I GET TO TALK TO IT, FIRST.
NO POSSESSION, NIKHIL, AND YOU GET OUT THE SECOND THINGS GET DANGEROUS.
!
"MS. HECK, YEAH! WE'RE GOING TO GET THAT LOST SOUL, TONIGHT!"
"...BEULAH."

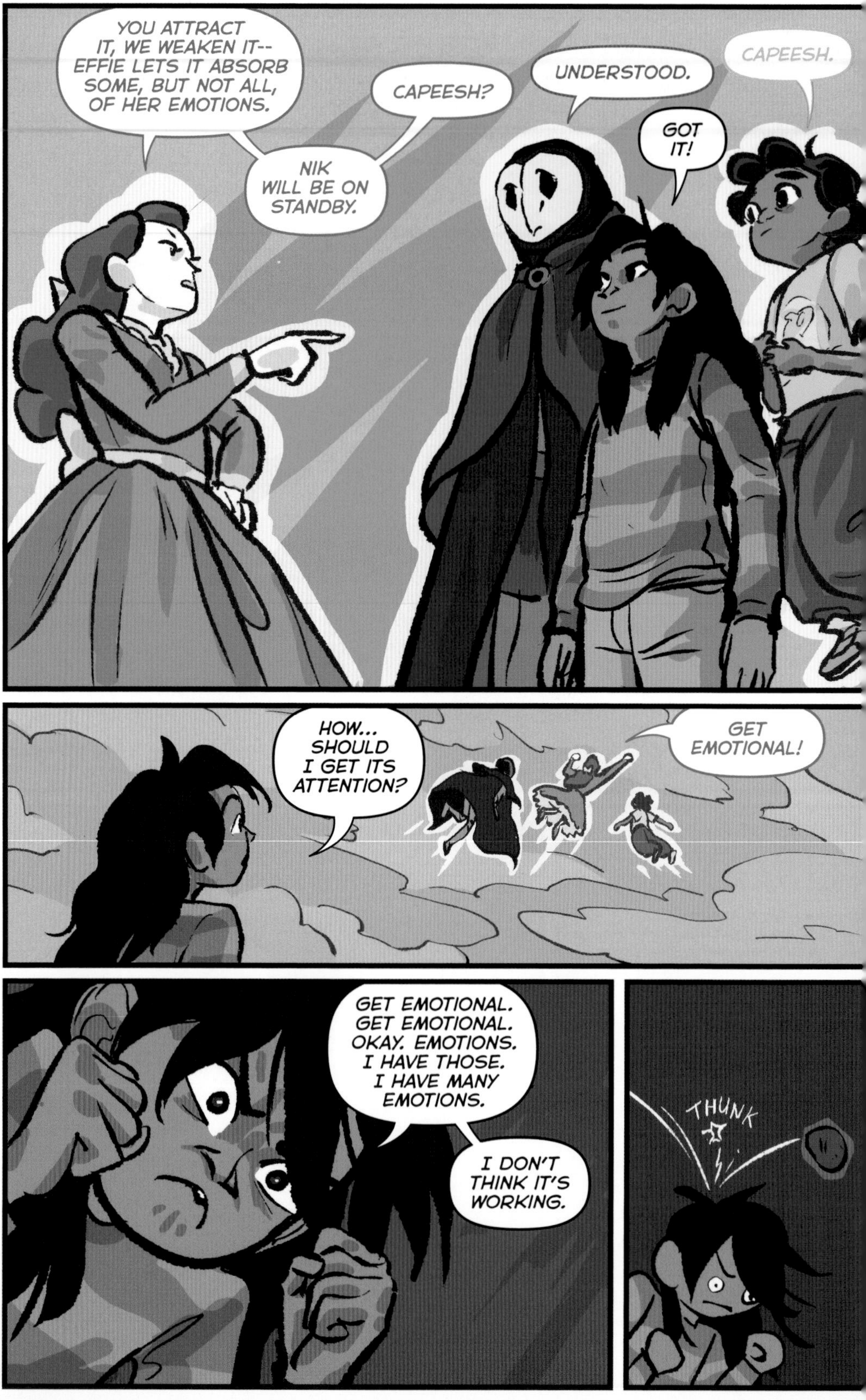
YOU ATTRACT IT, WE WEAKEN IT-- EFFIE LETS IT ABSORB SOME, BUT NOT ALL, OF HER EMOTIONS.
NIK WILL BE ON STANDBY.
CAPEESH?
UNDERSTOOD.
GOT IT!
CAPEESH.
HOW... SHOULD I GET ITS ATTENTION?
GET EMOTIONAL!
GET EMOTIONAL. GET EMOTIONAL. OKAY. EMOTIONS. I HAVE THOSE. I HAVE MANY EMOTIONS.
I DON'T THINK IT'S WORKING.
THUNK

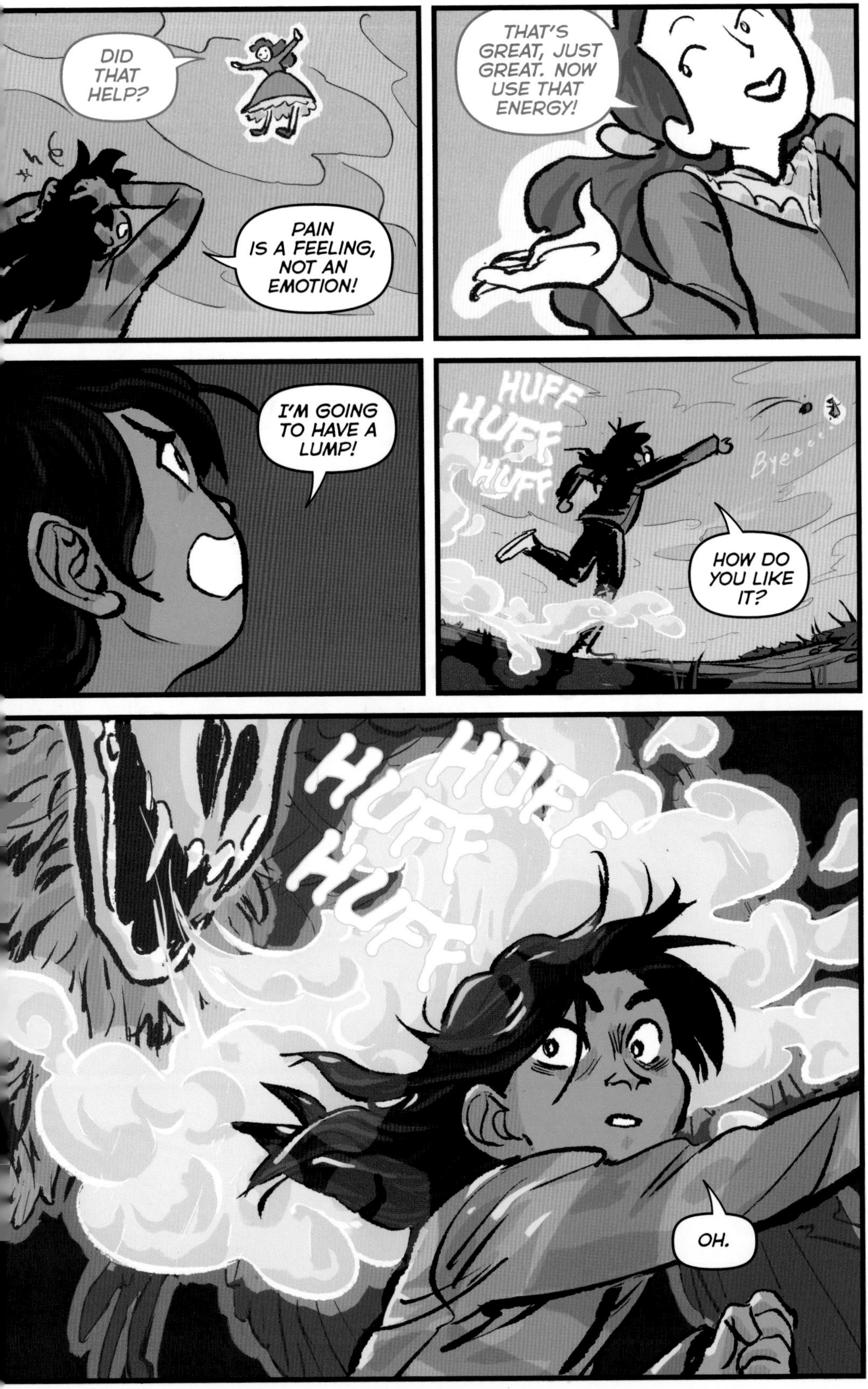
DID THAT HELP?
PAIN IS A FEELING, NOT AN EMOTION!
THAT'S GREAT, JUST GREAT. NOW USE THAT ENERGY!
I'M GOING TO HAVE A LUMP!
HUFF HUFF HUFF
Byeeee...
HOW DO YOU LIKE IT?
HUFF HUFF HUFF
OH.

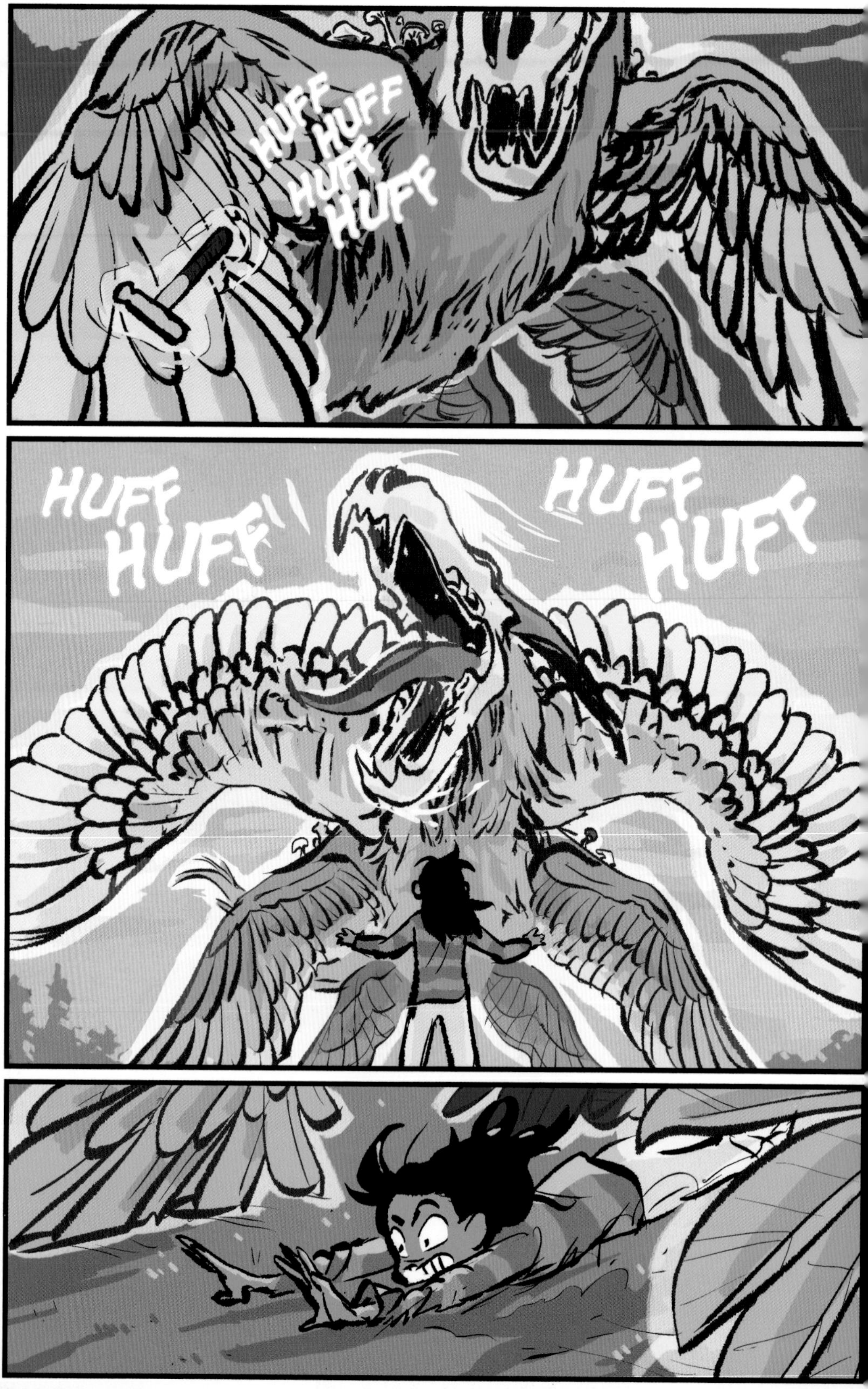
HUFF
HUFF
HUFF
HUFF
HUFF
HUFF
HUFF
HUFF

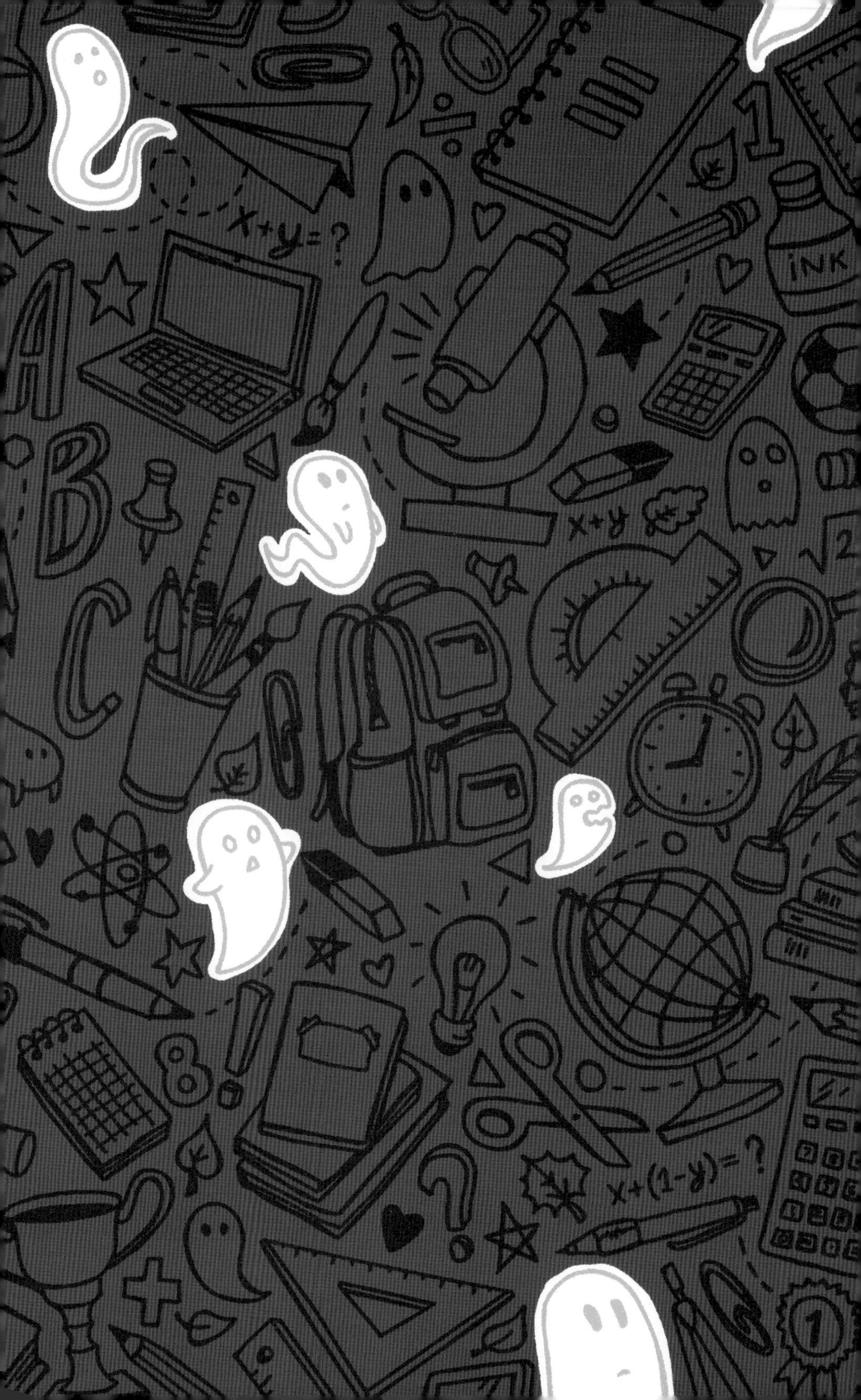
x+y=?
iNK
x+y
x+(1-y)=?

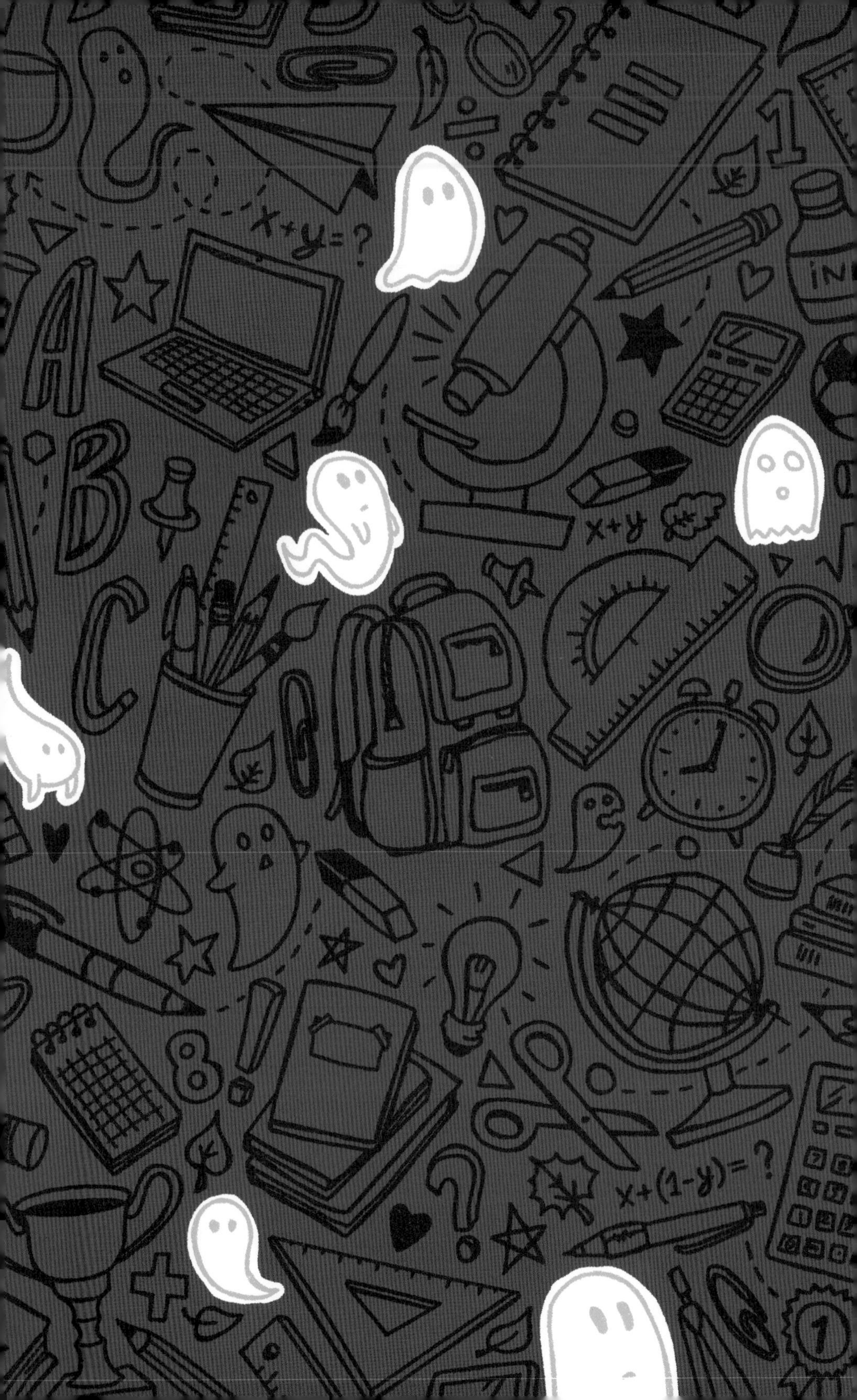
x+y=?
x+y
x+(1-y)=?

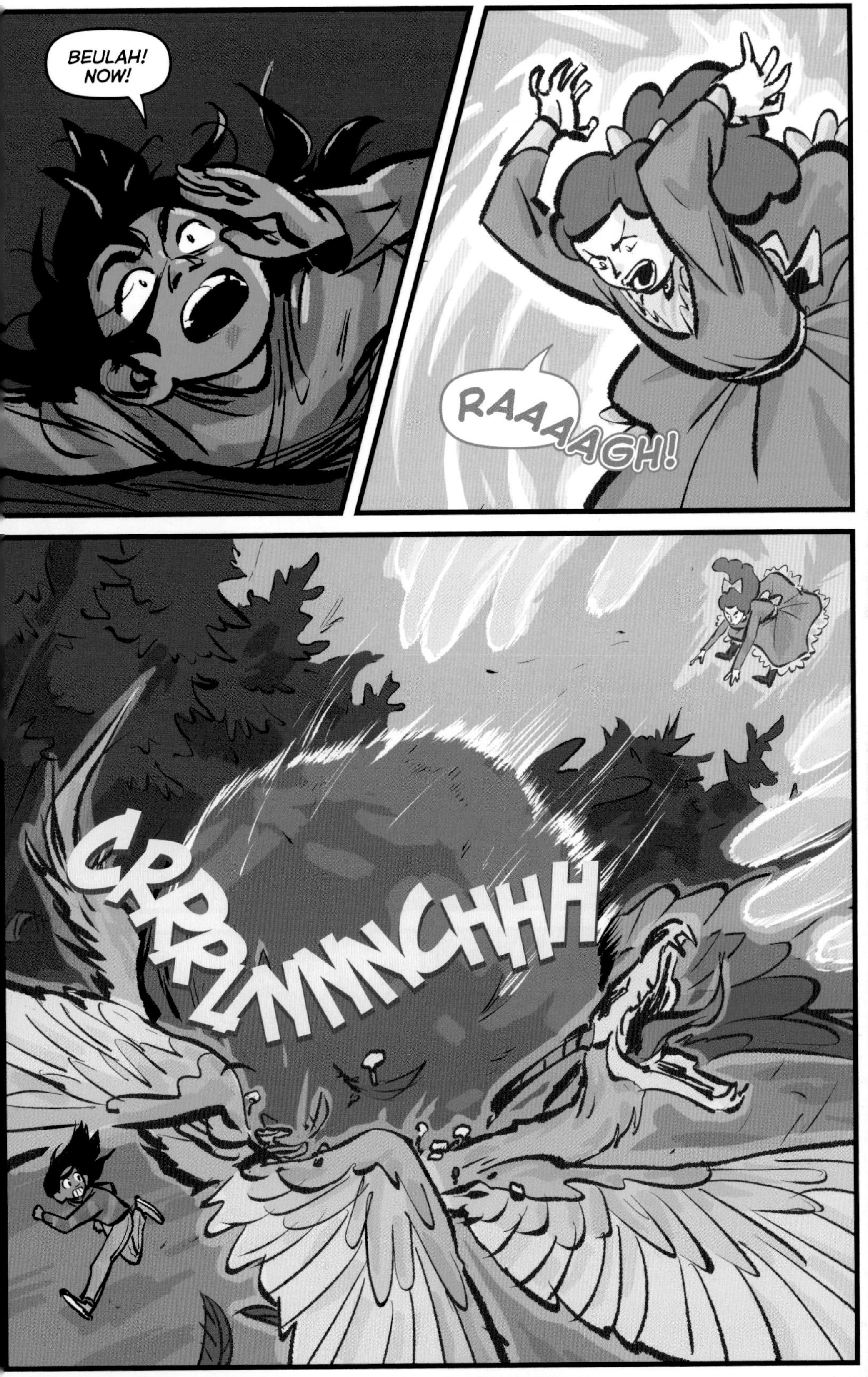
BEULAH! NOW!
RAAAAAGH!
CRRUNNNCHHH

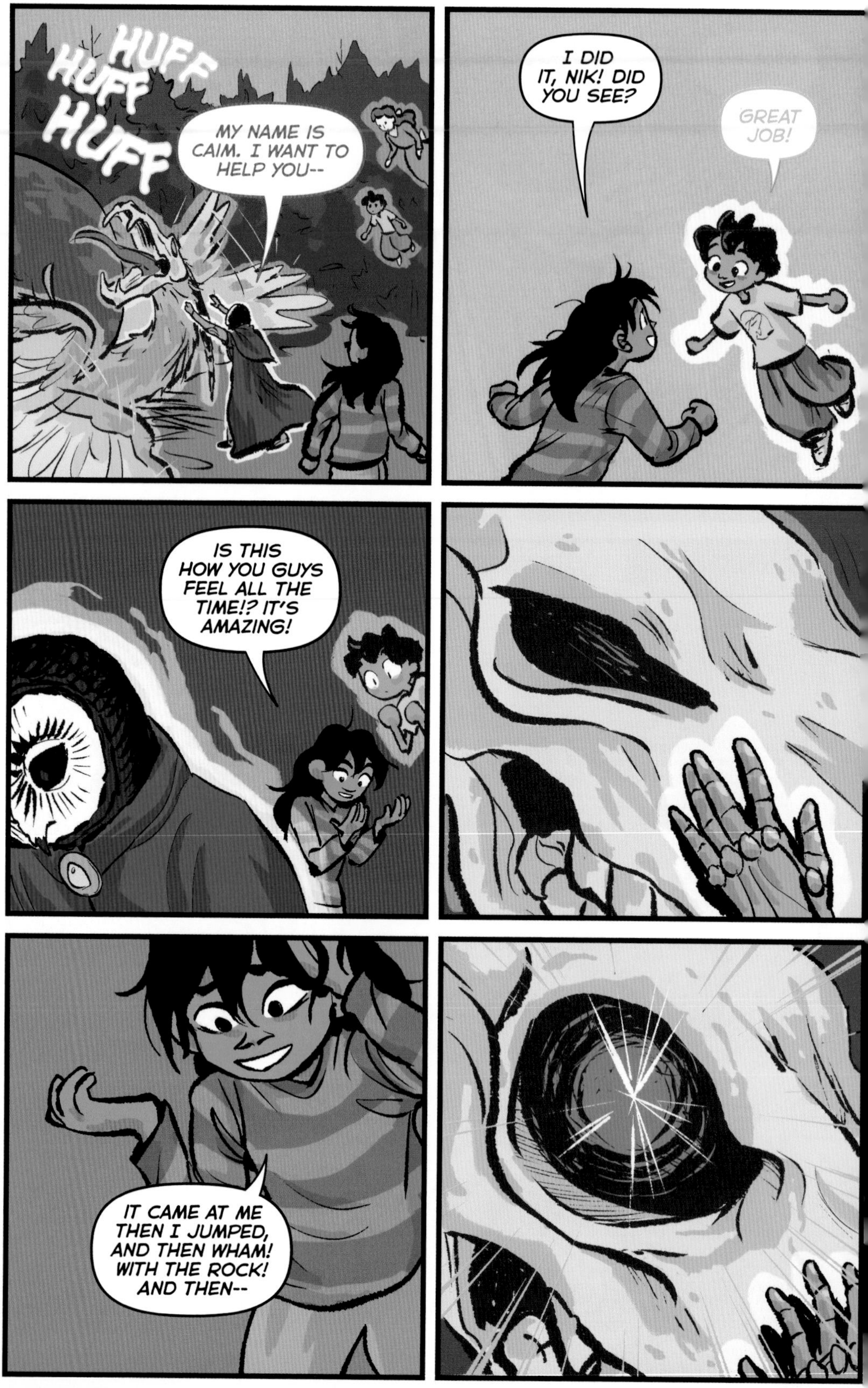
HUFF HUFF HUFF
MY NAME IS CAIM. I WANT TO HELP YOU--
I DID IT, NIK! DID YOU SEE?
GREAT JOB!
IS THIS HOW YOU GUYS FEEL ALL THE TIME!? IT'S AMAZING!
IT CAME AT ME THEN I JUMPED, AND THEN WHAM! WITH THE ROCK! AND THEN--

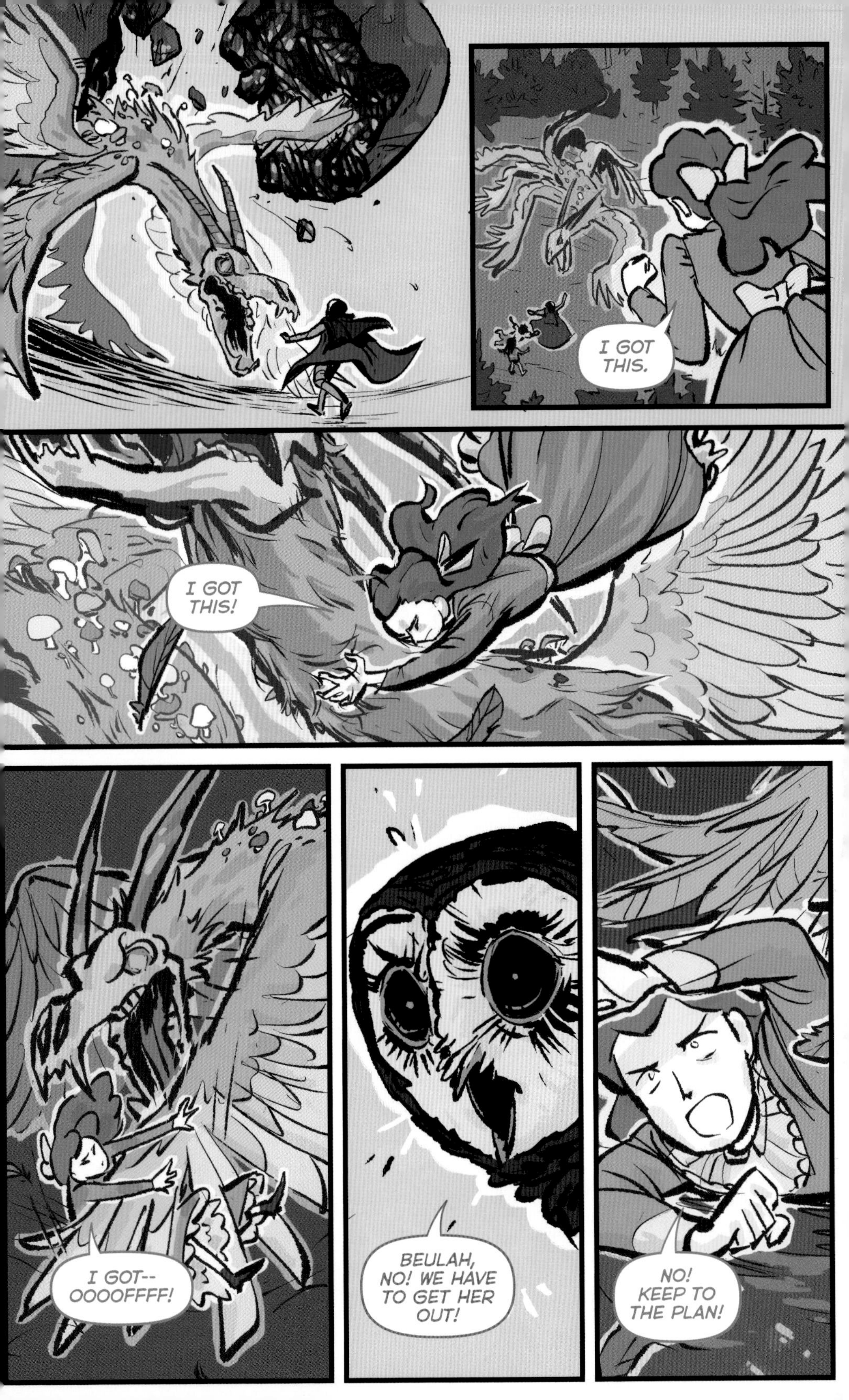
I GOT THIS.
I GOT THIS!
I GOT-- OOOOFFFF!
BEULAH, NO! WE HAVE TO GET HER OUT!
NO! KEEP TO THE PLAN!

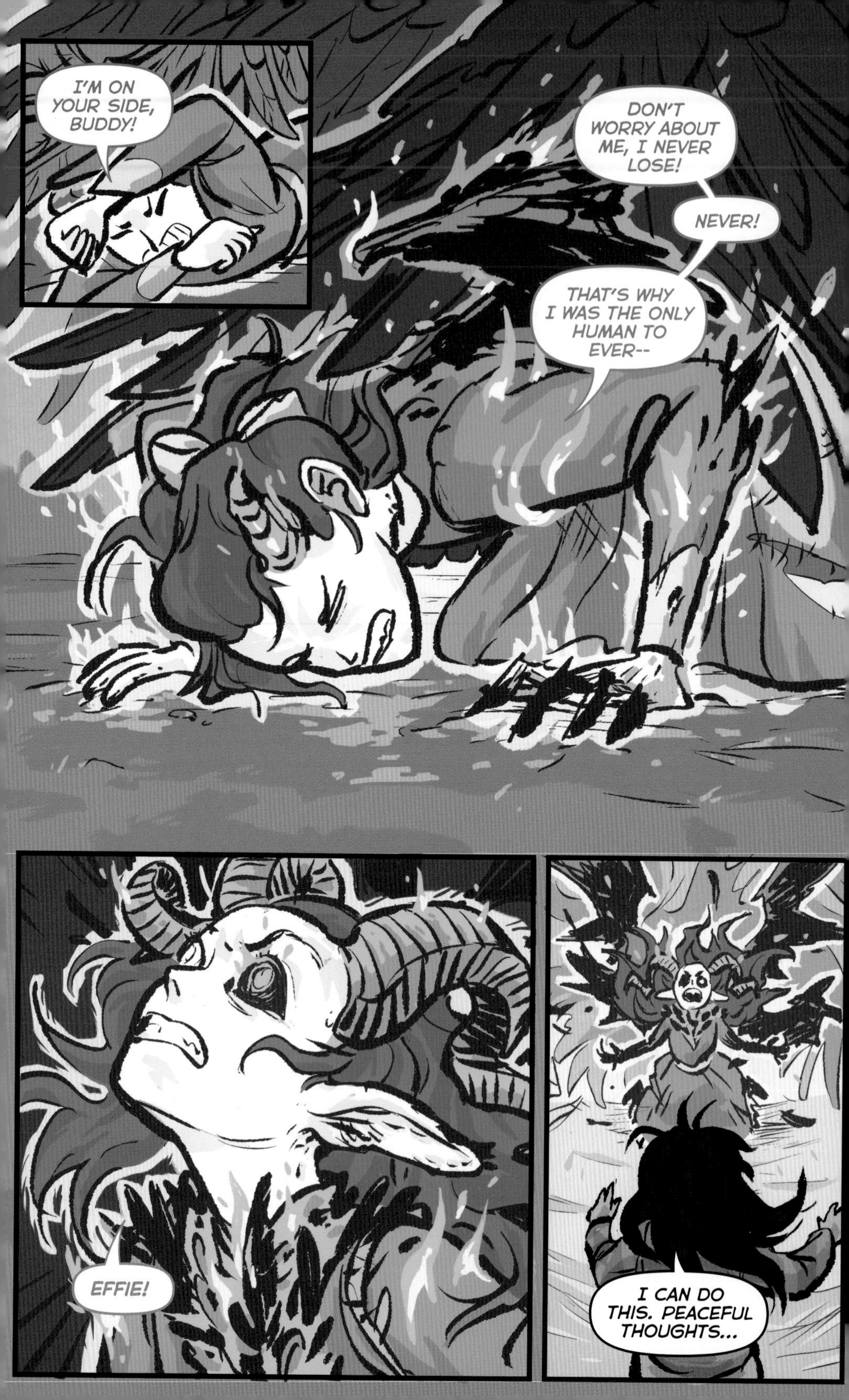
I'M ON YOUR SIDE, BUDDY!
DON'T WORRY ABOUT ME, I NEVER LOSE!
NEVER!
THAT'S WHY I WAS THE ONLY HUMAN TO EVER--
EFFIE!
I CAN DO THIS. PEACEFUL THOUGHTS...

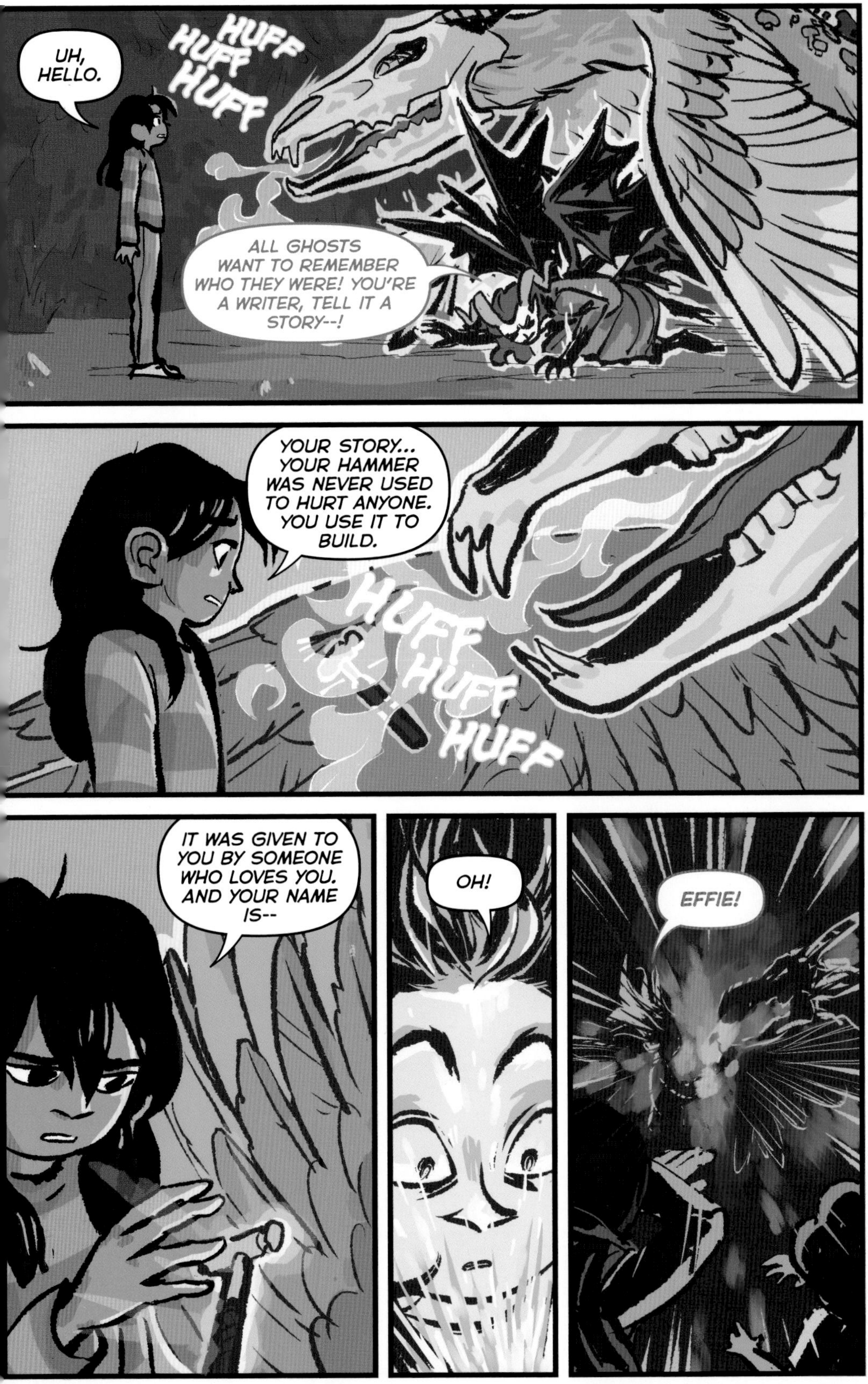
UH, HELLO.
HUFF HUFF HUFF
ALL GHOSTS WANT TO REMEMBER WHO THEY WERE! YOU'RE A WRITER, TELL IT A STORY--!
YOUR STORY... YOUR HAMMER WAS NEVER USED TO HURT ANYONE. YOU USE IT TO BUILD.
HUFF HUFF HUFF
IT WAS GIVEN TO YOU BY SOMEONE WHO LOVES YOU. AND YOUR NAME IS--
OH!
EFFIE!

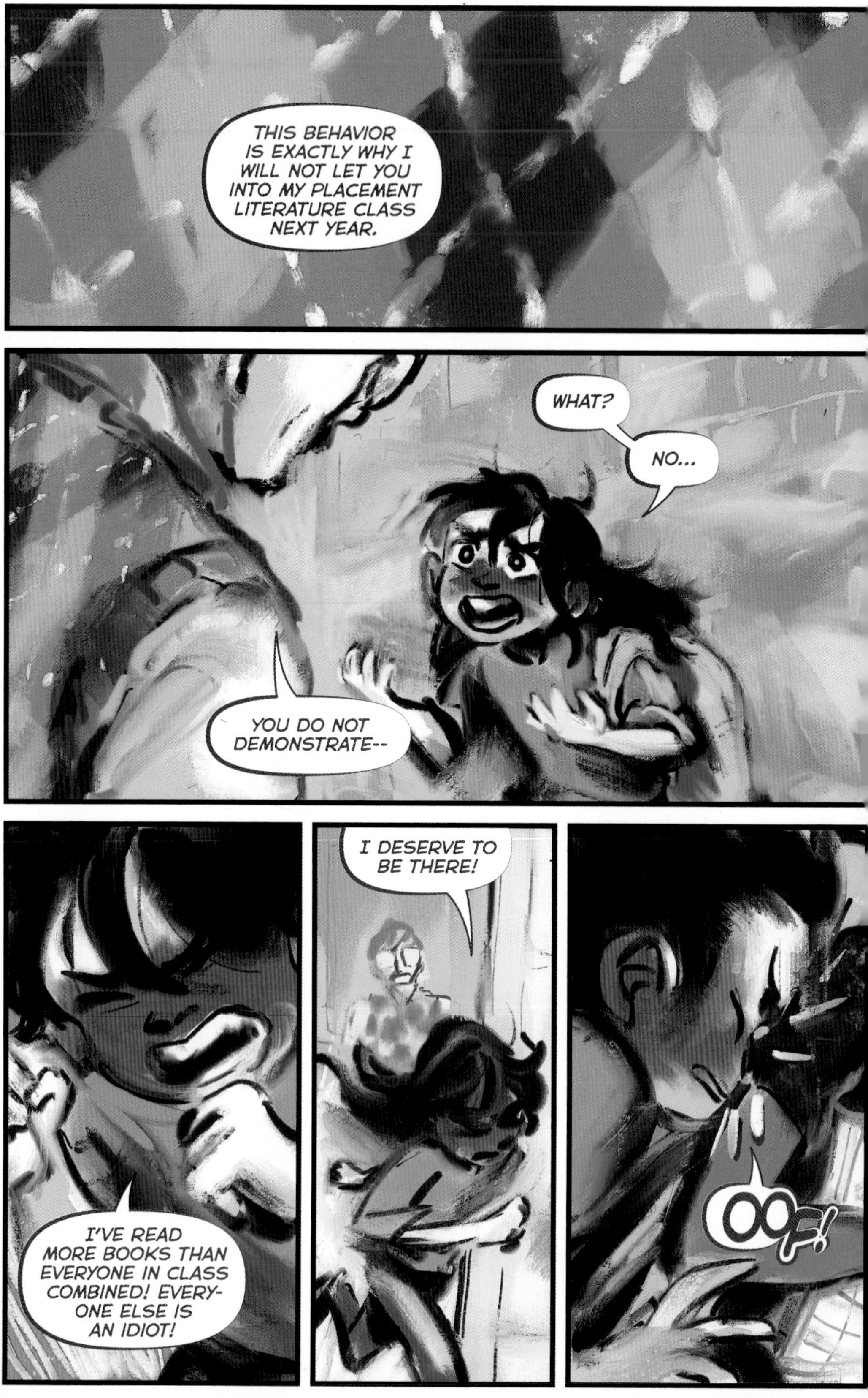
THIS BEHAVIOR IS EXACTLY WHY I WILL NOT LET YOU INTO MY PLACEMENT LITERATURE CLASS NEXT YEAR.
WHAT?
NO...
YOU DO NOT DEMONSTRATE--
I'VE READ MORE BOOKS THAN EVERYONE IN CLASS COMBINED! EVERY-ONE ELSE IS AN IDIOT!
I DESERVE TO BE THERE!
OOF!

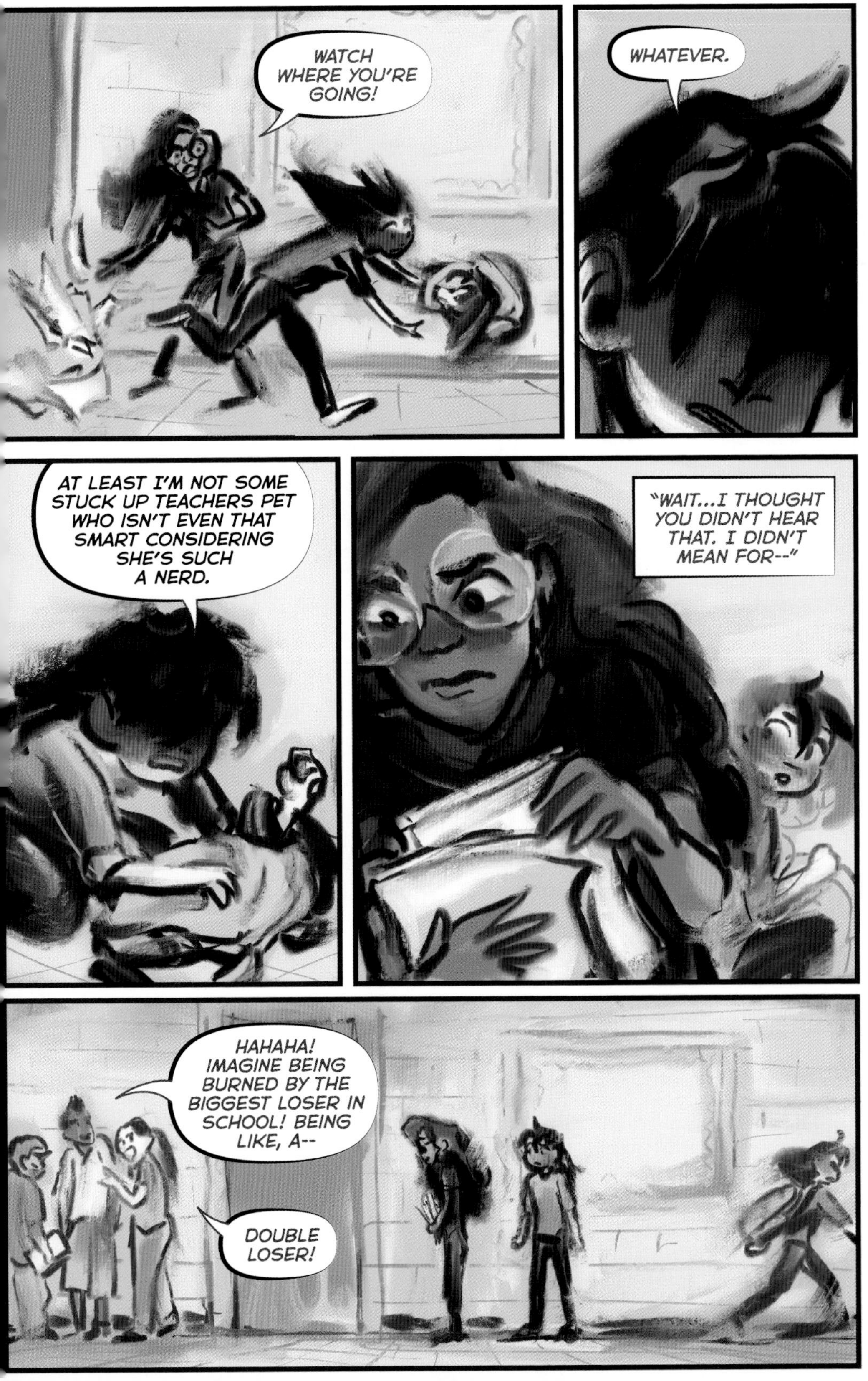
WATCH WHERE YOU'RE GOING!
WHATEVER.
AT LEAST I'M NOT SOME STUCK UP TEACHERS PET WHO ISN'T EVEN THAT SMART CONSIDERING SHE'S SUCH A NERD.
"WAIT...I THOUGHT YOU DIDN'T HEAR THAT. I DIDN'T MEAN FOR--"
HAHAHA! IMAGINE BEING BURNED BY THE BIGGEST LOSER IN SCHOOL! BEING LIKE, A--
DOUBLE LOSER!

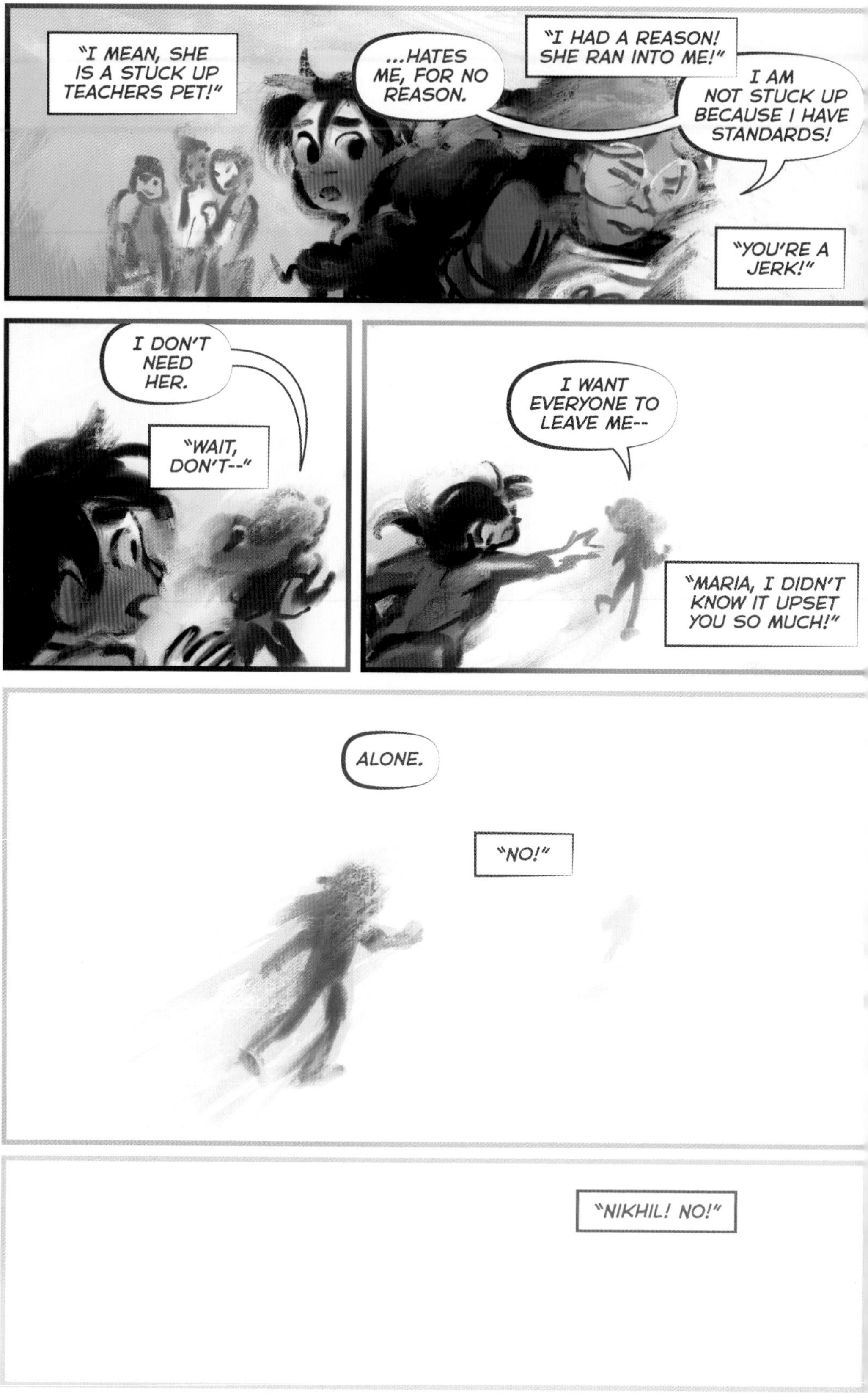
"I MEAN, SHE IS A STUCK UP TEACHERS PET!"
...HATES ME, FOR NO REASON.
"I HAD A REASON! SHE RAN INTO ME!"
I AM NOT STUCK UP BECAUSE I HAVE STANDARDS!
"YOU'RE A JERK!"
I DON'T NEED HER.
"WAIT, DON'T--"
I WANT EVERYONE TO LEAVE ME--
"MARIA, I DIDN'T KNOW IT UPSET YOU SO MUCH!"
ALONE.
"NO!"
"NIKHIL! NO!"

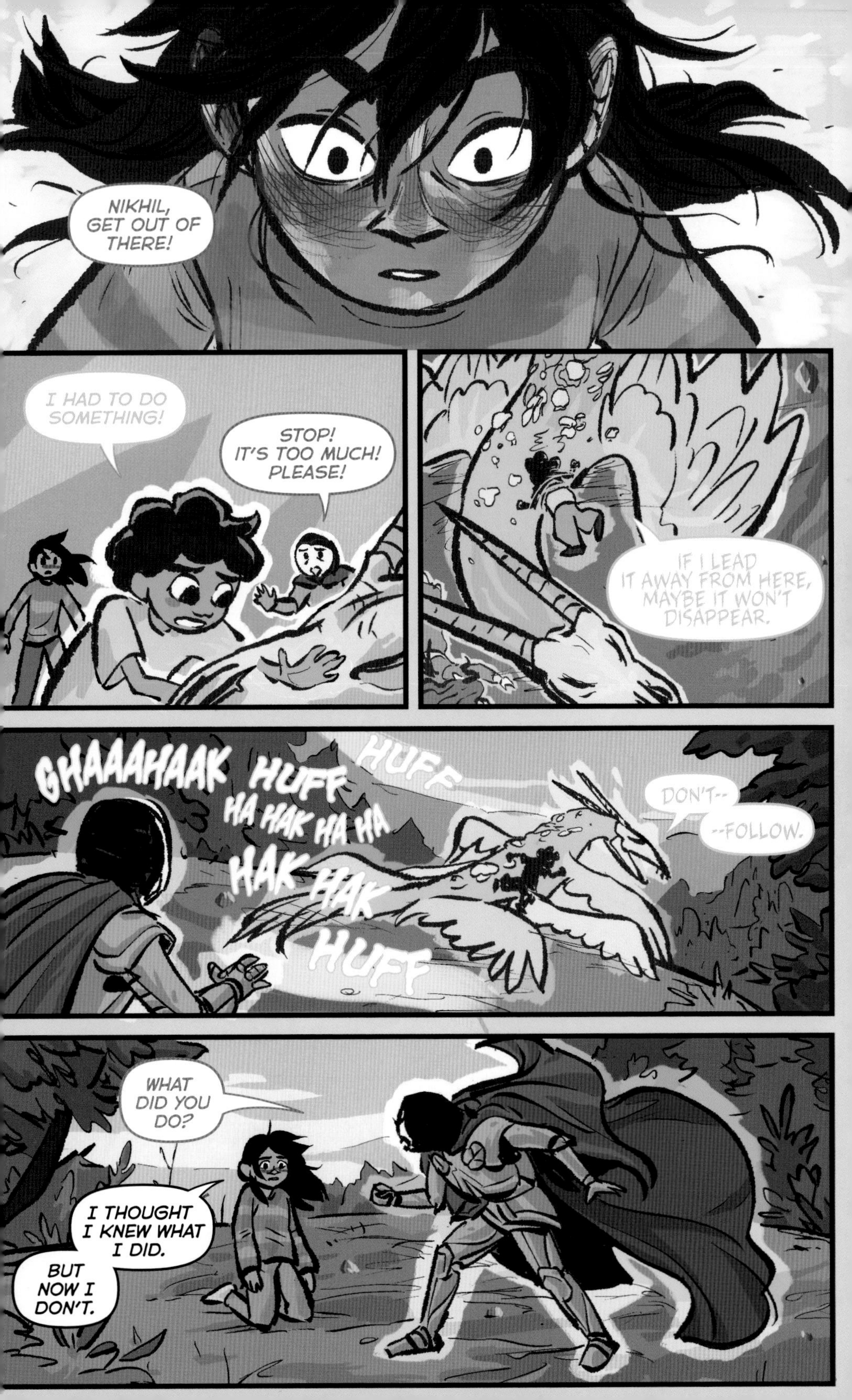
NIKHIL, GET OUT OF THERE!
I HAD TO DO SOMETHING!
STOP! IT'S TOO MUCH! PLEASE!
IF I LEAD IT AWAY FROM HERE, MAYBE IT WON'T DISAPPEAR.
GHAAAHAAK
HUFF
HUFF
HA HAK HA HA
HAK HAK
HUFF
DON'T--
--FOLLOW.
WHAT DID YOU DO?
I THOUGHT I KNEW WHAT I DID.
BUT NOW I DON'T.

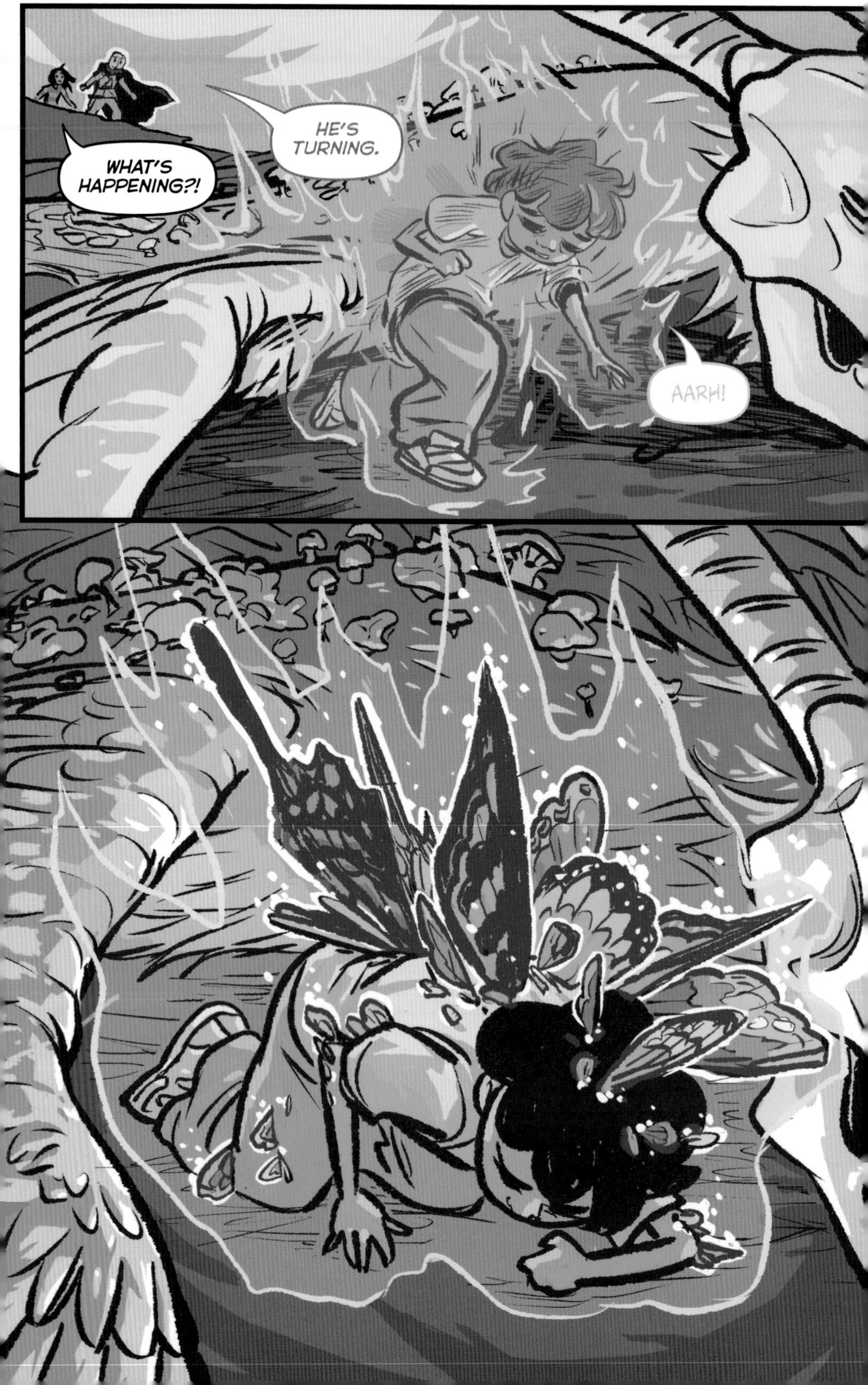
WHAT'S HAPPENING?!
HE'S TURNING.
AARH!

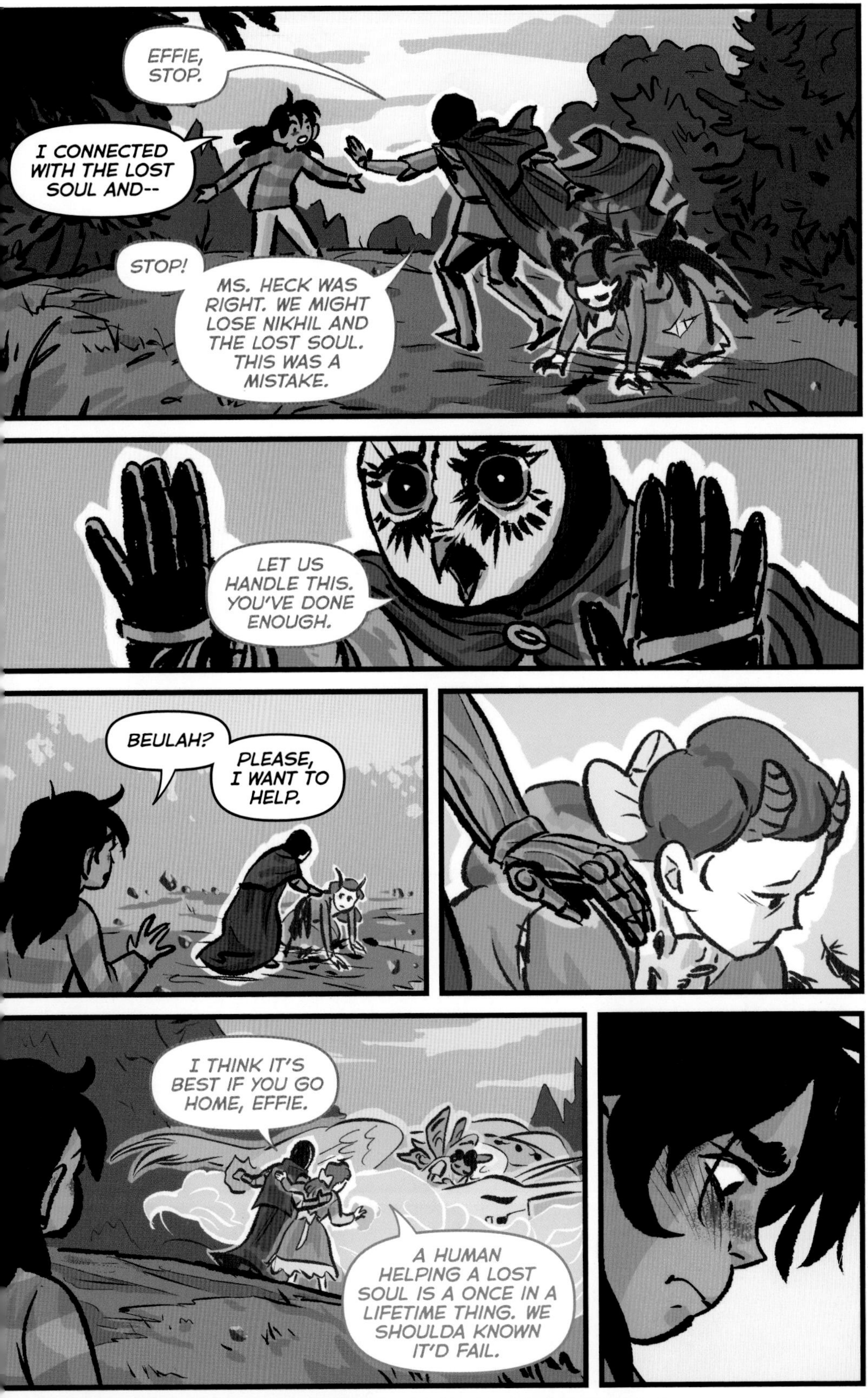
EFFIE, STOP.
I CONNECTED WITH THE LOST SOUL AND--
STOP!
MS. HECK WAS RIGHT. WE MIGHT LOSE NIKHIL AND THE LOST SOUL. THIS WAS A MISTAKE.
LET US HANDLE THIS. YOU'VE DONE ENOUGH.
BEULAH?
PLEASE, I WANT TO HELP.
I THINK IT'S BEST IF YOU GO HOME, EFFIE.
A HUMAN HELPING A LOST SOUL IS A ONCE IN A LIFETIME THING. WE SHOULDA KNOWN IT'D FAIL.

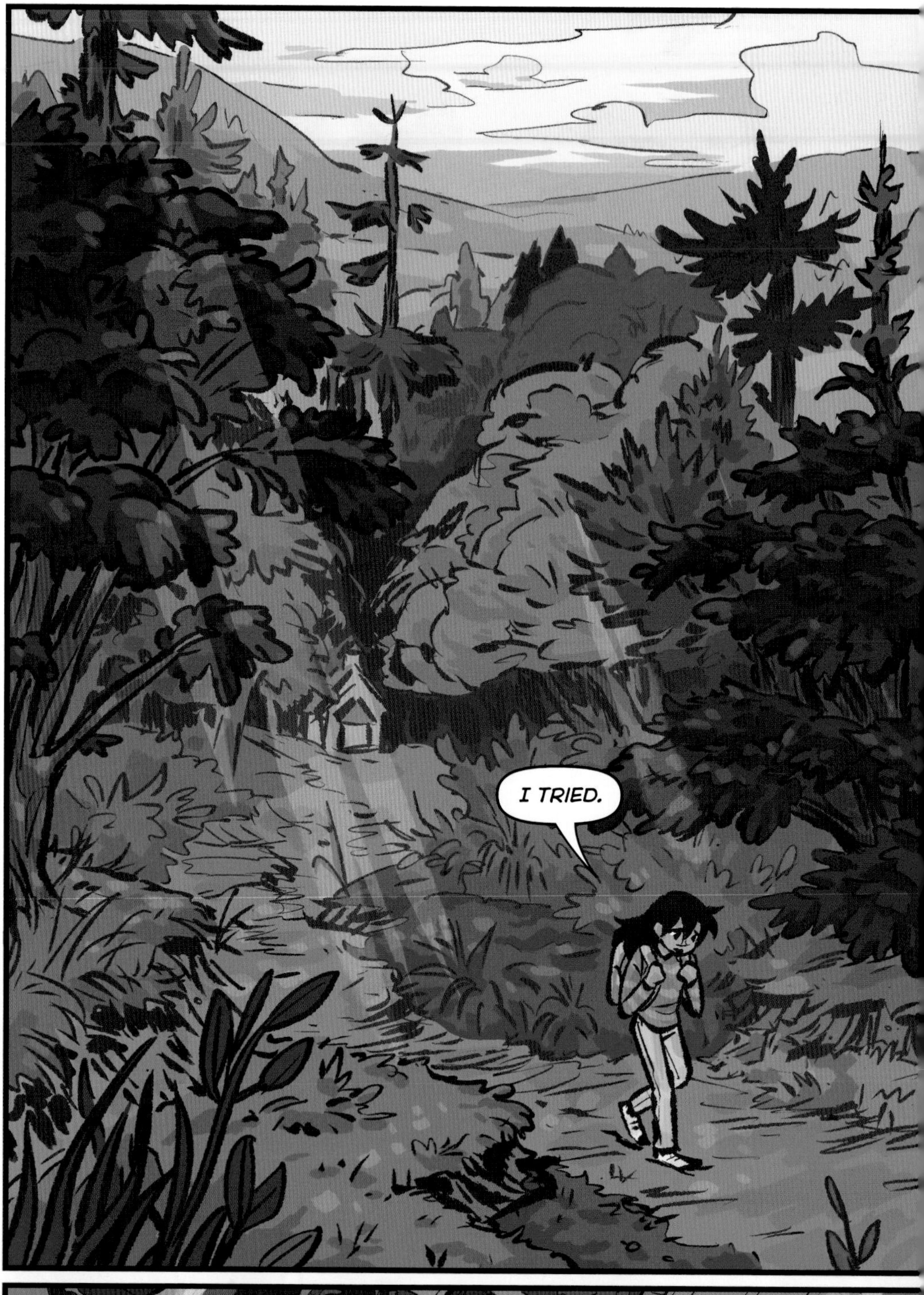
I TRIED.

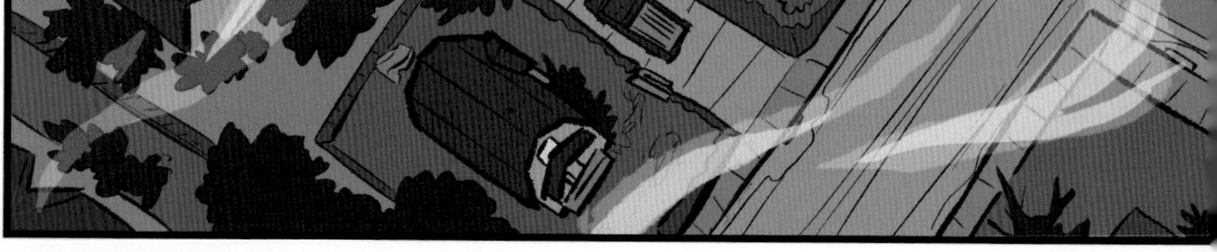

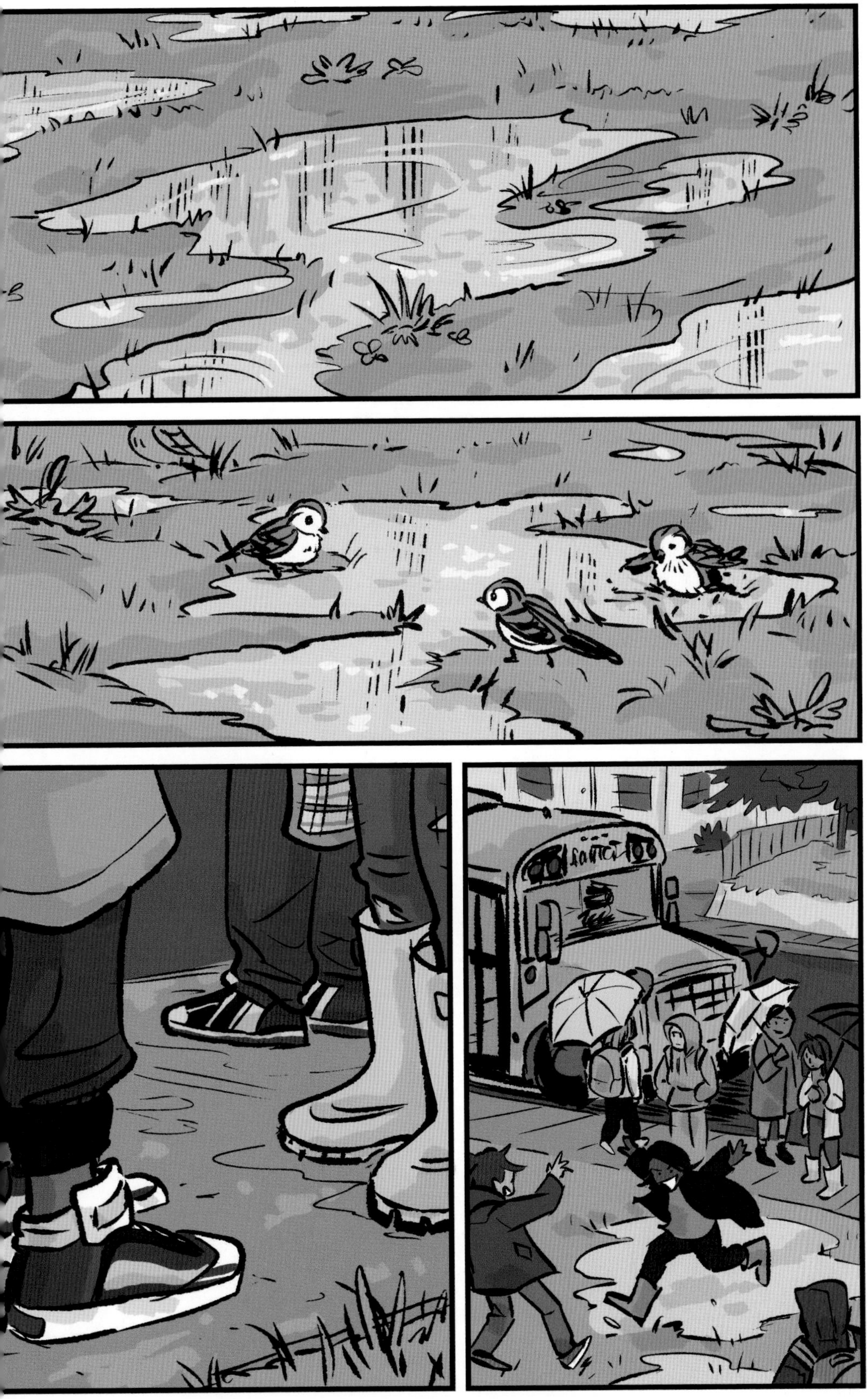

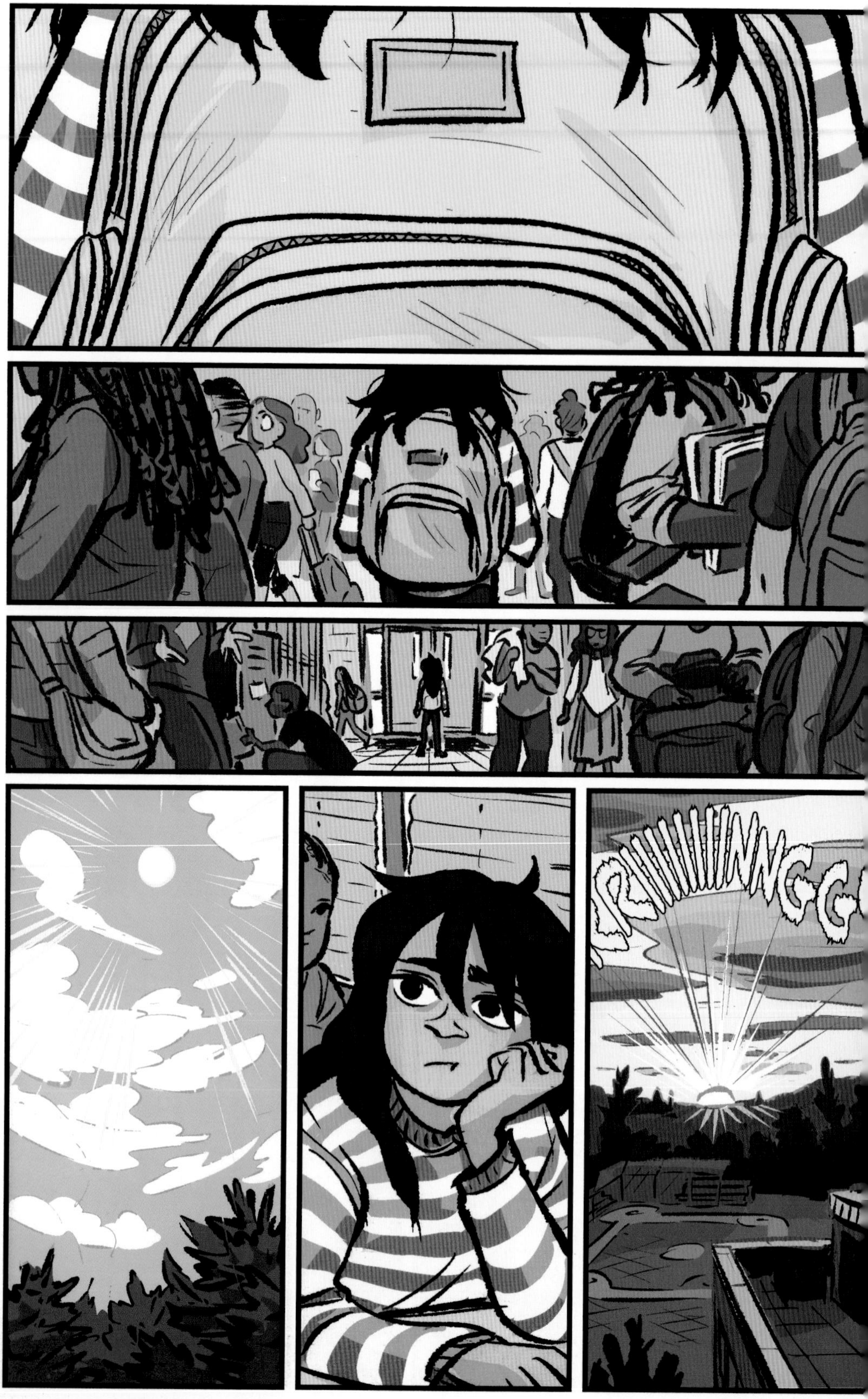
RIIIIIIIINNGG

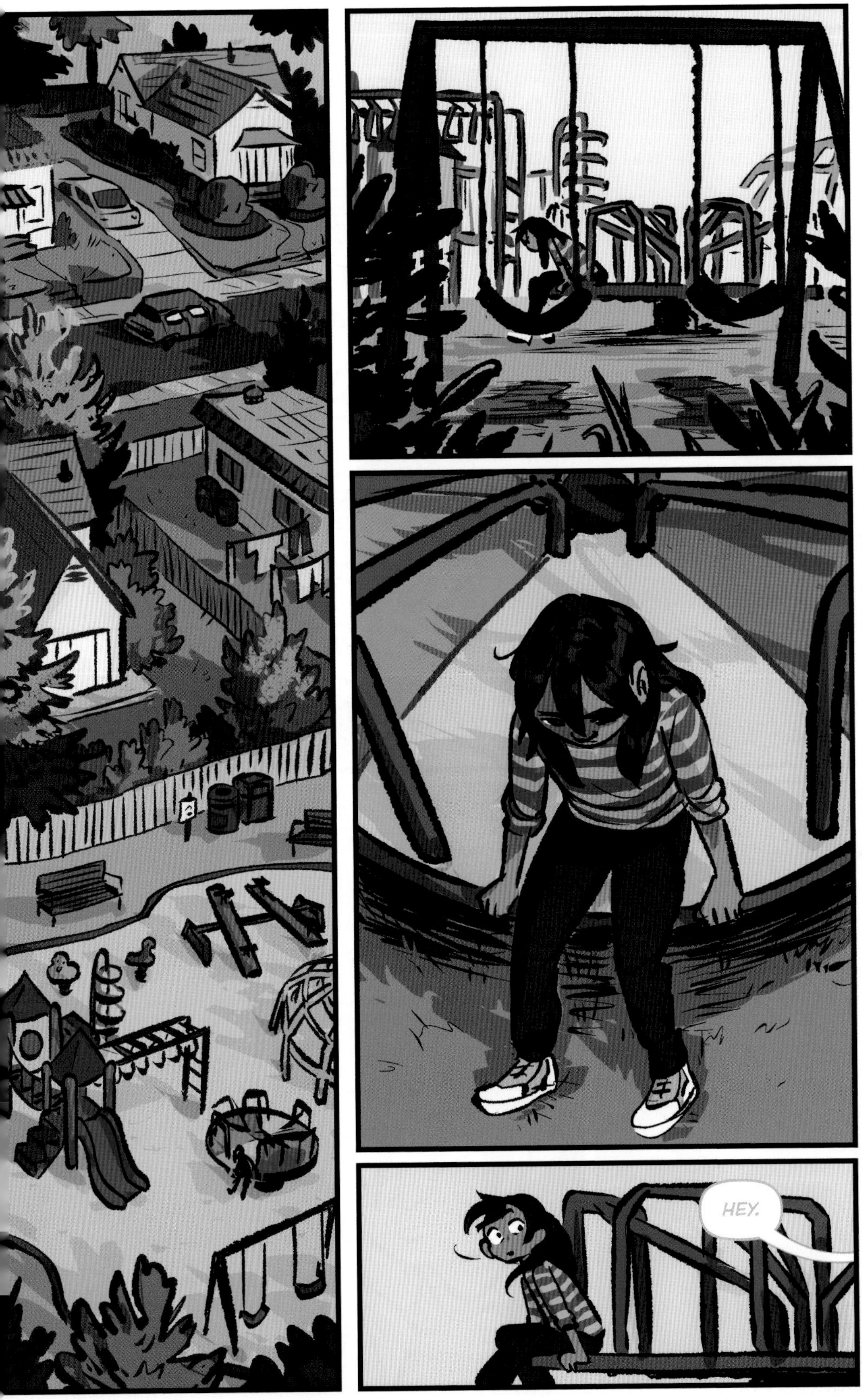
HEY.

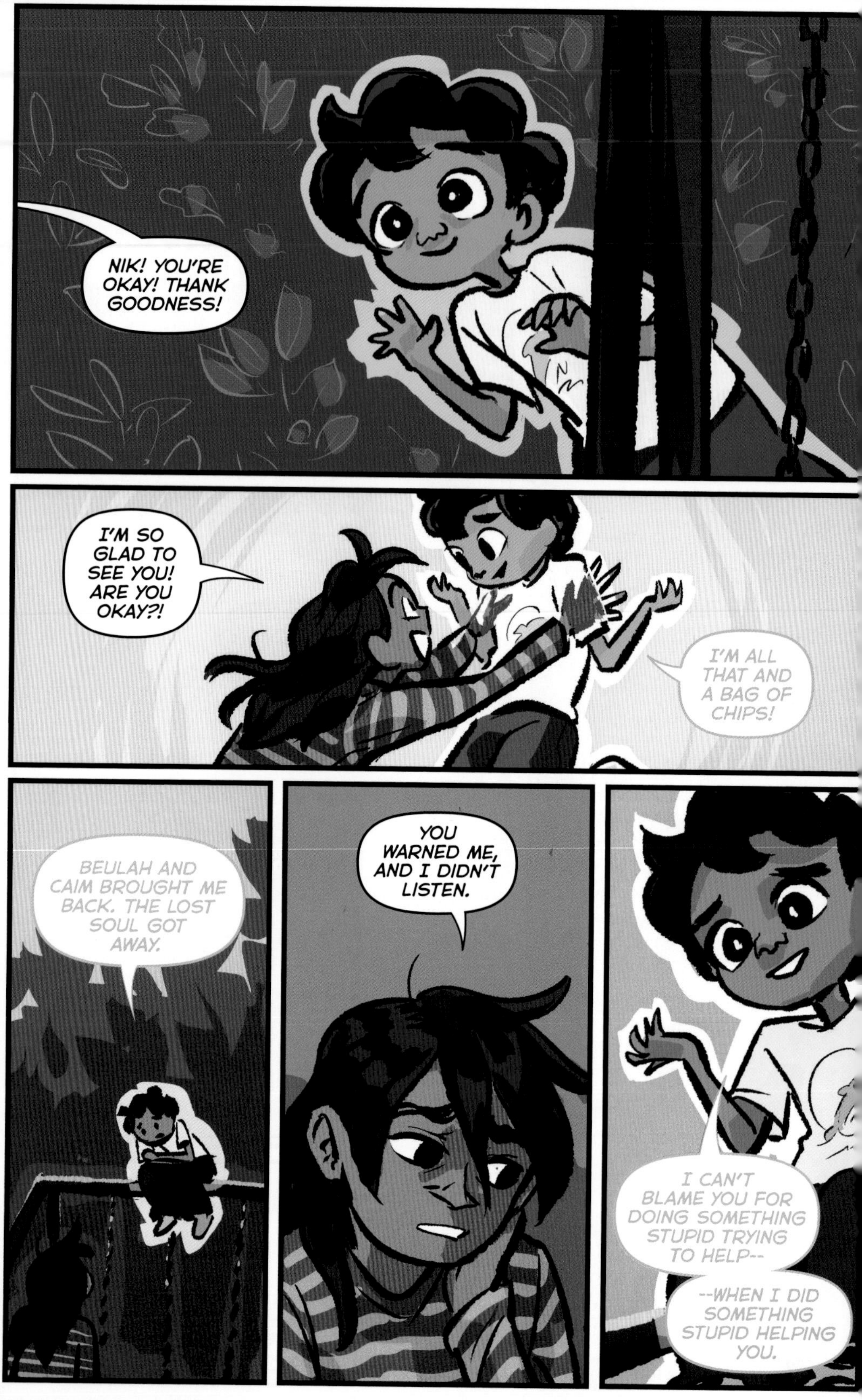
NIK! YOU'RE OKAY! THANK GOODNESS!
I'M SO GLAD TO SEE YOU! ARE YOU OKAY?!
I'M ALL THAT AND A BAG OF CHIPS!
BEULAH AND CAIM BROUGHT ME BACK. THE LOST SOUL GOT AWAY.
YOU WARNED ME, AND I DIDN'T LISTEN.
I CAN'T BLAME YOU FOR DOING SOMETHING STUPID TRYING TO HELP--
--WHEN I DID SOMETHING STUPID HELPING YOU.

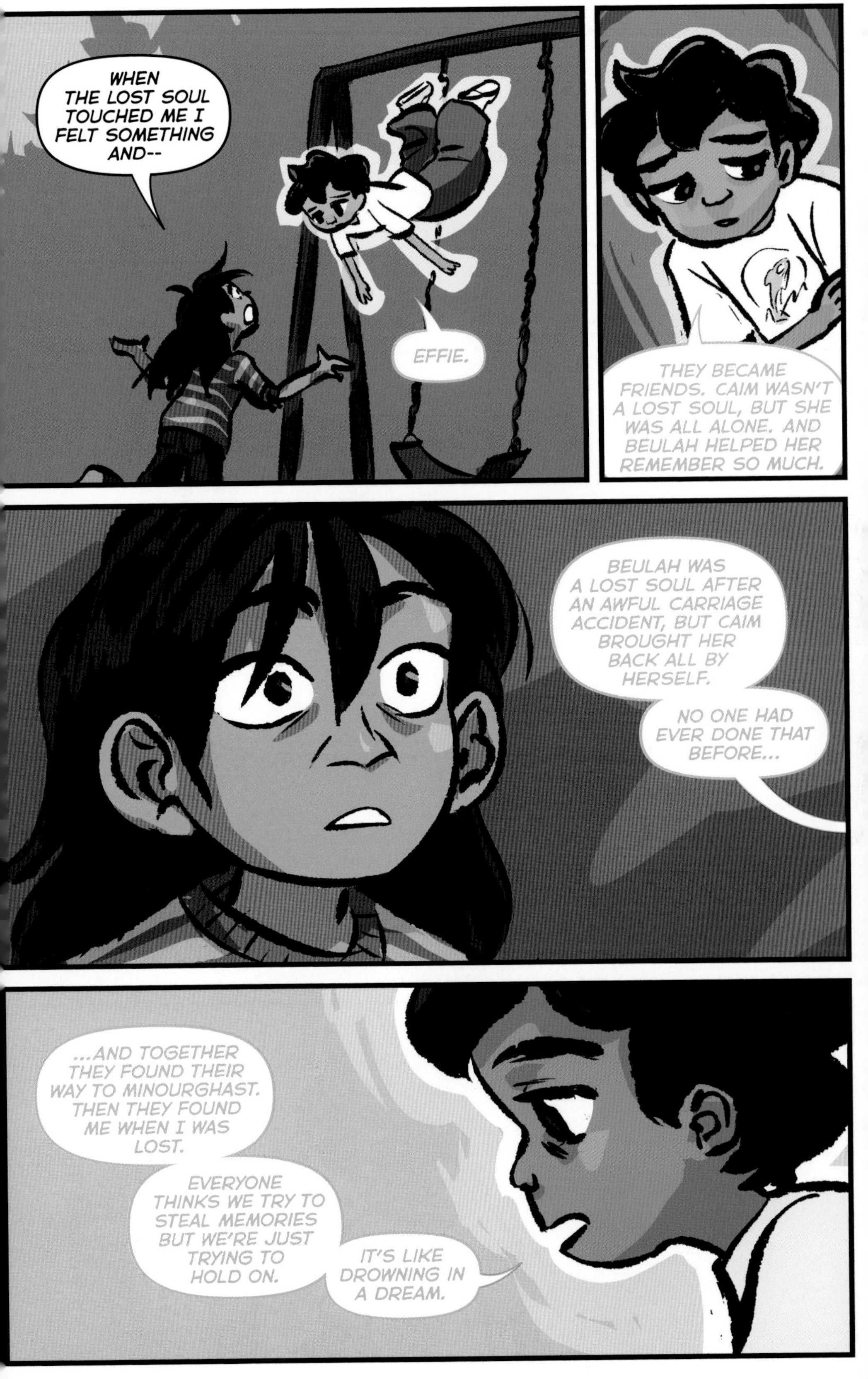
WHEN THE LOST SOUL TOUCHED ME I FELT SOMETHING AND--
EFFIE.
THEY BECAME FRIENDS. CAIM WASN'T A LOST SOUL, BUT SHE WAS ALL ALONE. AND BEULAH HELPED HER REMEMBER SO MUCH.
BEULAH WAS A LOST SOUL AFTER AN AWFUL CARRIAGE ACCIDENT, BUT CAIM BROUGHT HER BACK ALL BY HERSELF.
NO ONE HAD EVER DONE THAT BEFORE...
...AND TOGETHER THEY FOUND THEIR WAY TO MINOURGHAST. THEN THEY FOUND ME WHEN I WAS LOST.
EVERYONE THINKS WE TRY TO STEAL MEMORIES BUT WE'RE JUST TRYING TO HOLD ON.
IT'S LIKE DROWNING IN A DREAM.

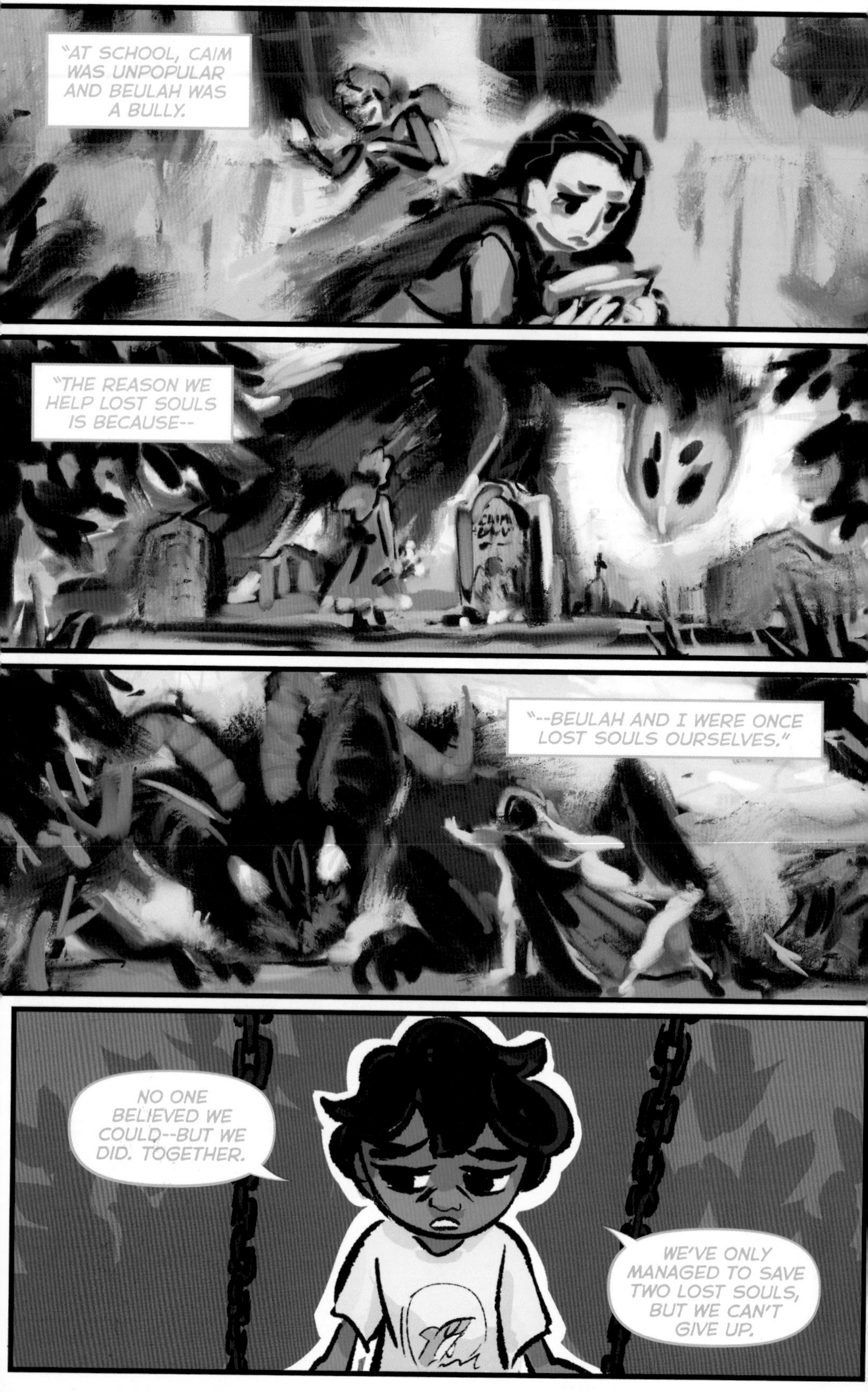
"AT SCHOOL, CAIM WAS UNPOPULAR AND BEULAH WAS A BULLY.
"THE REASON WE HELP LOST SOULS IS BECAUSE--
"--BEULAH AND I WERE ONCE LOST SOULS OURSELVES."
NO ONE BELIEVED WE COULD--BUT WE DID. TOGETHER.
WE'VE ONLY MANAGED TO SAVE TWO LOST SOULS, BUT WE CAN'T GIVE UP.

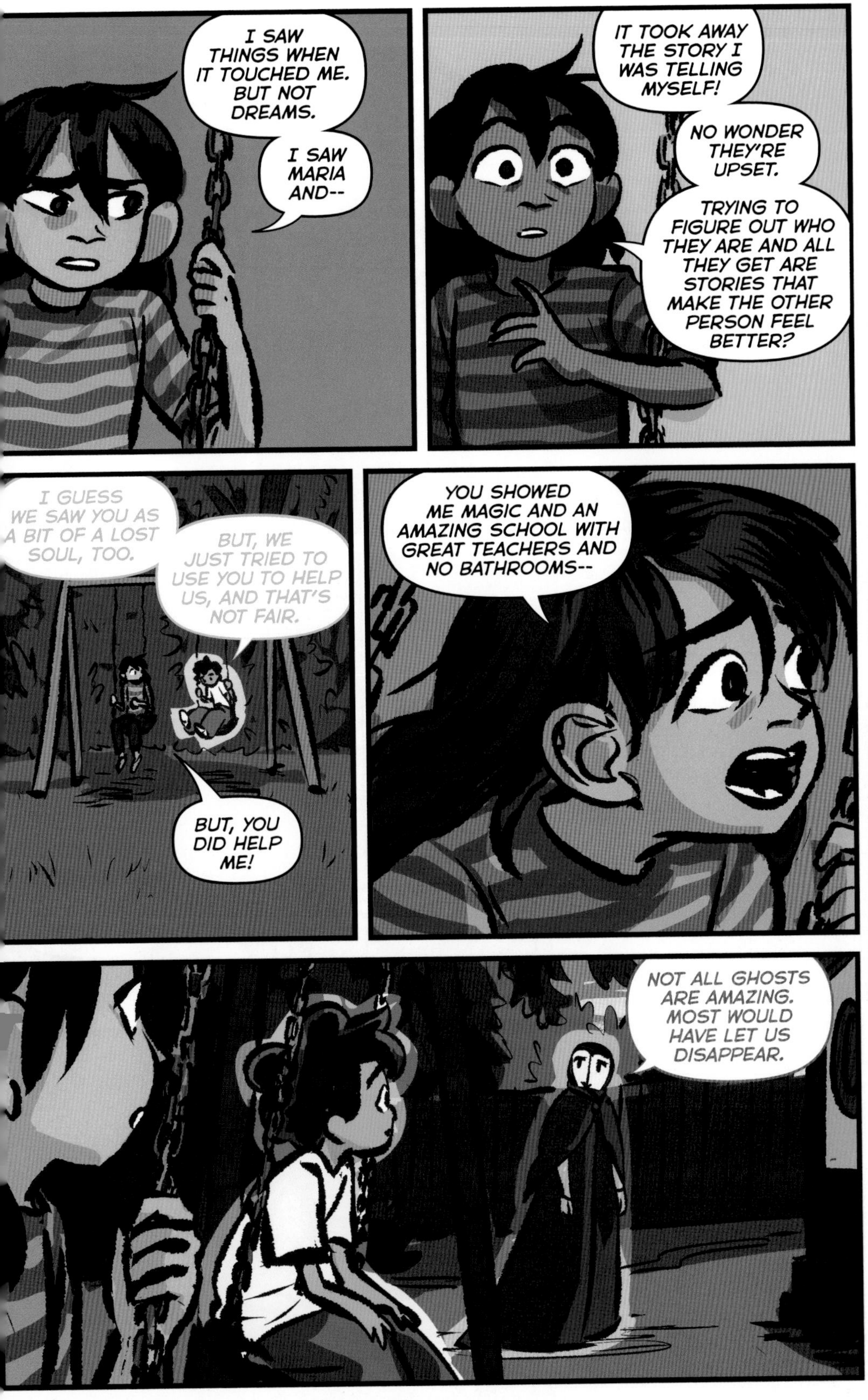
I SAW THINGS WHEN IT TOUCHED ME. BUT NOT DREAMS.
I SAW MARIA AND--
IT TOOK AWAY THE STORY I WAS TELLING MYSELF!
NO WONDER THEY'RE UPSET.
TRYING TO FIGURE OUT WHO THEY ARE AND ALL THEY GET ARE STORIES THAT MAKE THE OTHER PERSON FEEL BETTER?
I GUESS WE SAW YOU AS A BIT OF A LOST SOUL, TOO.
BUT, WE JUST TRIED TO USE YOU TO HELP US, AND THAT'S NOT FAIR.
BUT, YOU DID HELP ME!
YOU SHOWED ME MAGIC AND AN AMAZING SCHOOL WITH GREAT TEACHERS AND NO BATHROOMS--
NOT ALL GHOSTS ARE AMAZING. MOST WOULD HAVE LET US DISAPPEAR.

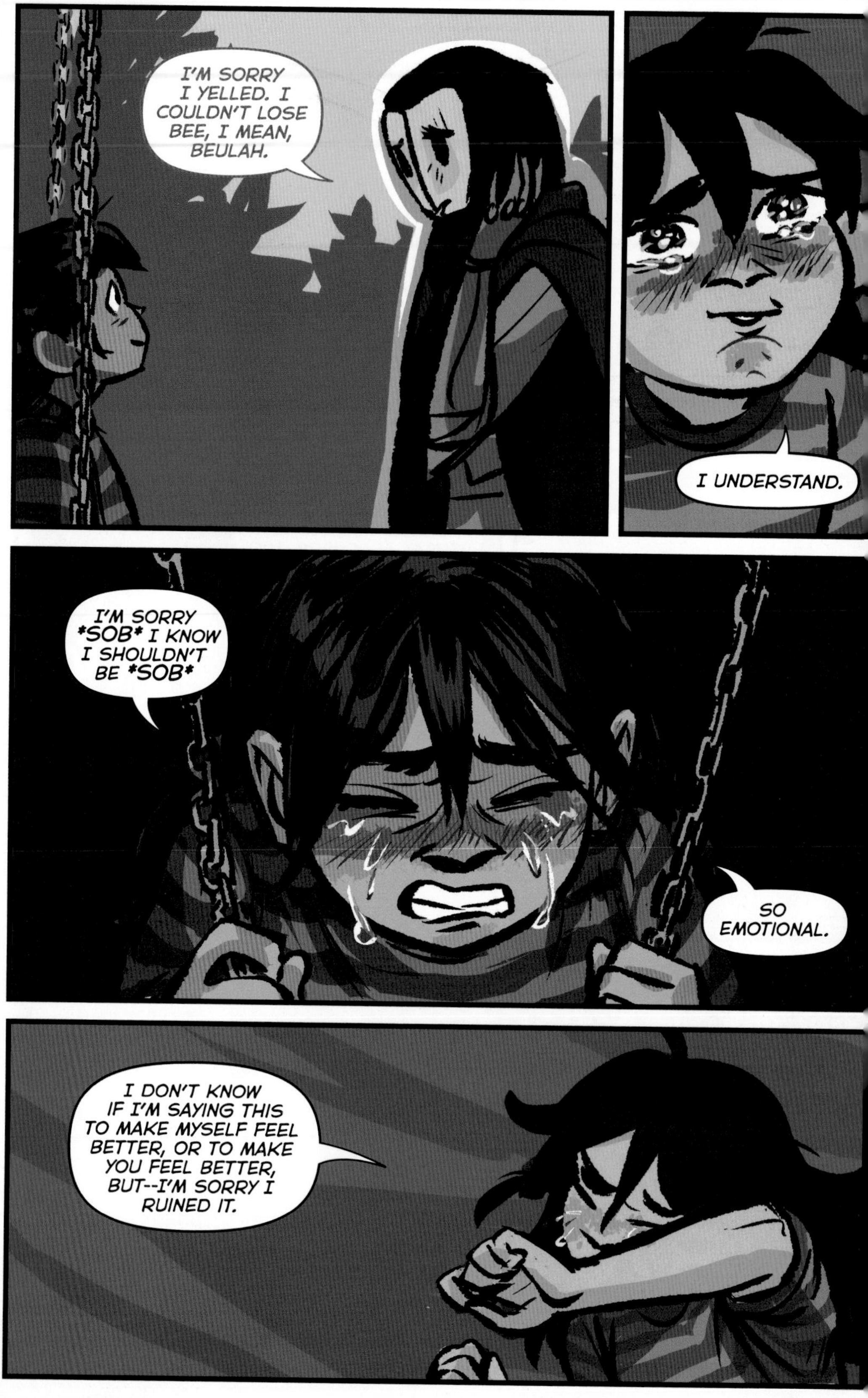
I'M SORRY I YELLED. I COULDN'T LOSE BEE, I MEAN, BEULAH.
I UNDERSTAND.
I'M SORRY *SOB* I KNOW I SHOULDN'T BE *SOB*
SO EMOTIONAL.
I DON'T KNOW IF I'M SAYING THIS TO MAKE MYSELF FEEL BETTER, OR TO MAKE YOU FEEL BETTER, BUT--I'M SORRY I RUINED IT.

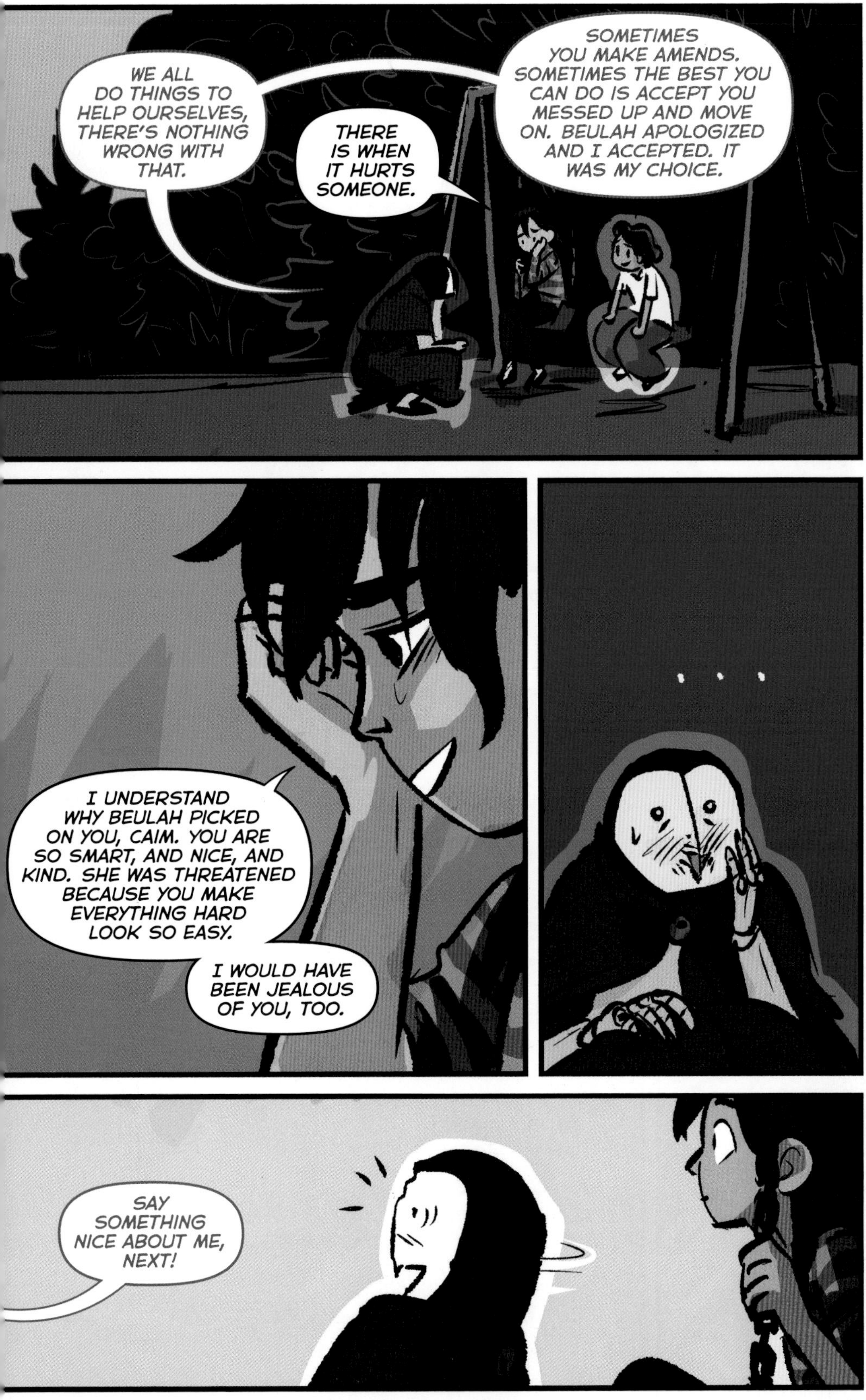
WE ALL DO THINGS TO HELP OURSELVES, THERE'S NOTHING WRONG WITH THAT.
THERE IS WHEN IT HURTS SOMEONE.
SOMETIMES YOU MAKE AMENDS. SOMETIMES THE BEST YOU CAN DO IS ACCEPT YOU MESSED UP AND MOVE ON. BEULAH APOLOGIZED AND I ACCEPTED. IT WAS MY CHOICE.
I UNDERSTAND WHY BEULAH PICKED ON YOU, CAIM. YOU ARE SO SMART, AND NICE, AND KIND. SHE WAS THREATENED BECAUSE YOU MAKE EVERYTHING HARD LOOK SO EASY.
I WOULD HAVE BEEN JEALOUS OF YOU, TOO.
...
SAY SOMETHING NICE ABOUT ME, NEXT!

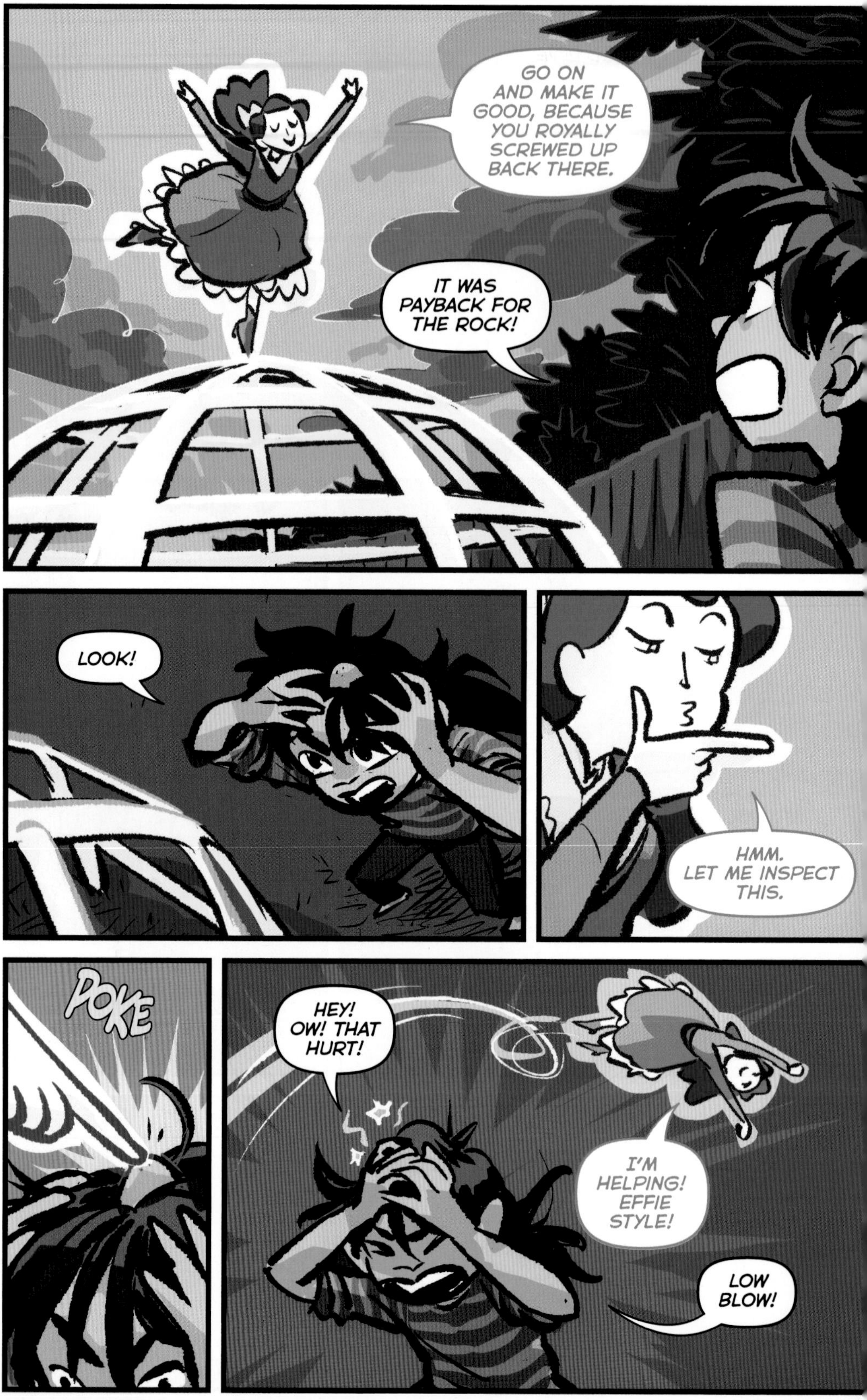
GO ON AND MAKE IT GOOD, BECAUSE YOU ROYALLY SCREWED UP BACK THERE.
IT WAS PAYBACK FOR THE ROCK!
LOOK!
HMM. LET ME INSPECT THIS.
POKE
HEY! OW! THAT HURT!
I'M HELPING! EFFIE STYLE!
LOW BLOW!

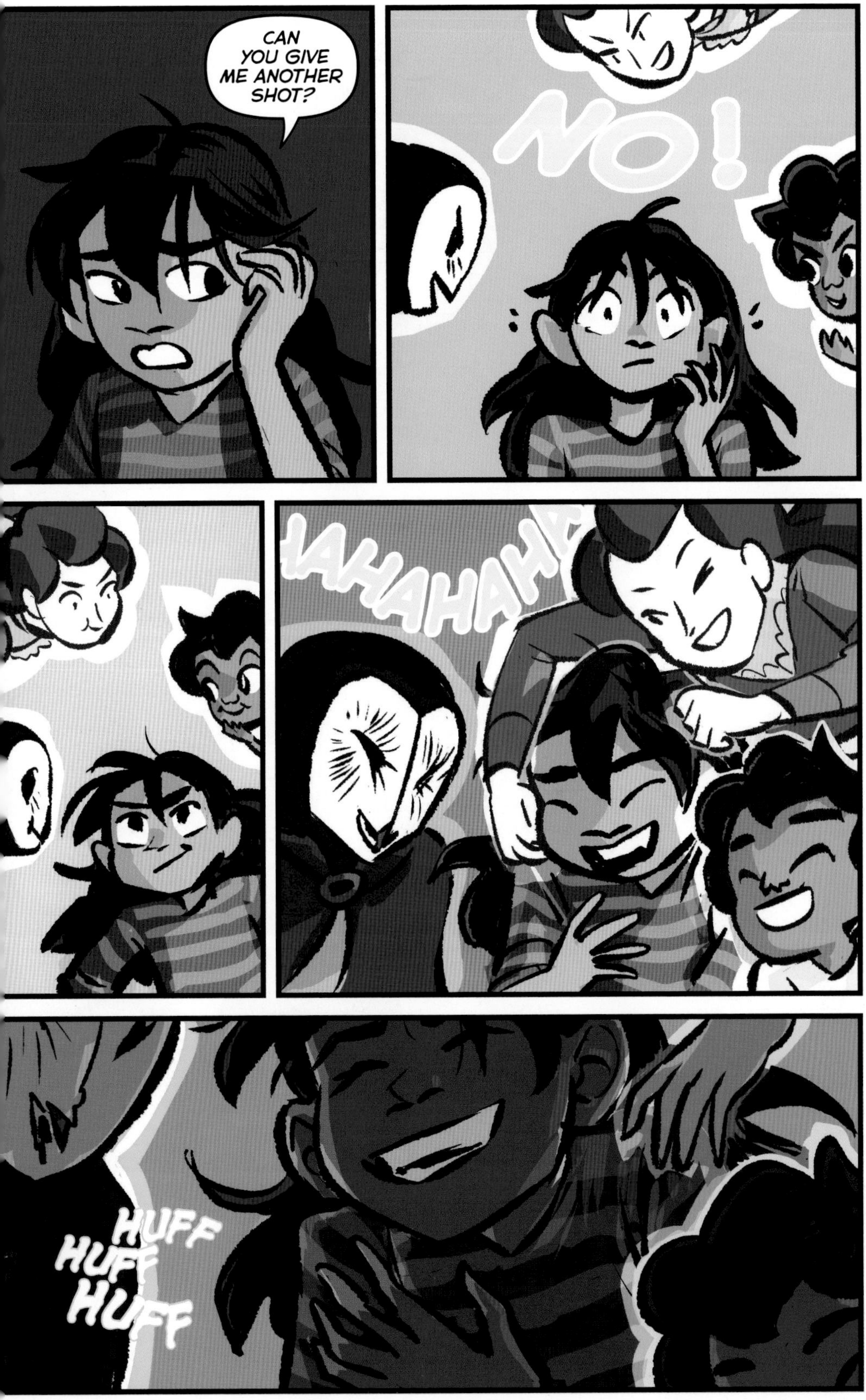
CAN YOU GIVE ME ANOTHER SHOT?
NO!
HAHAHAHAHA
HUFF
HUFF
HUFF

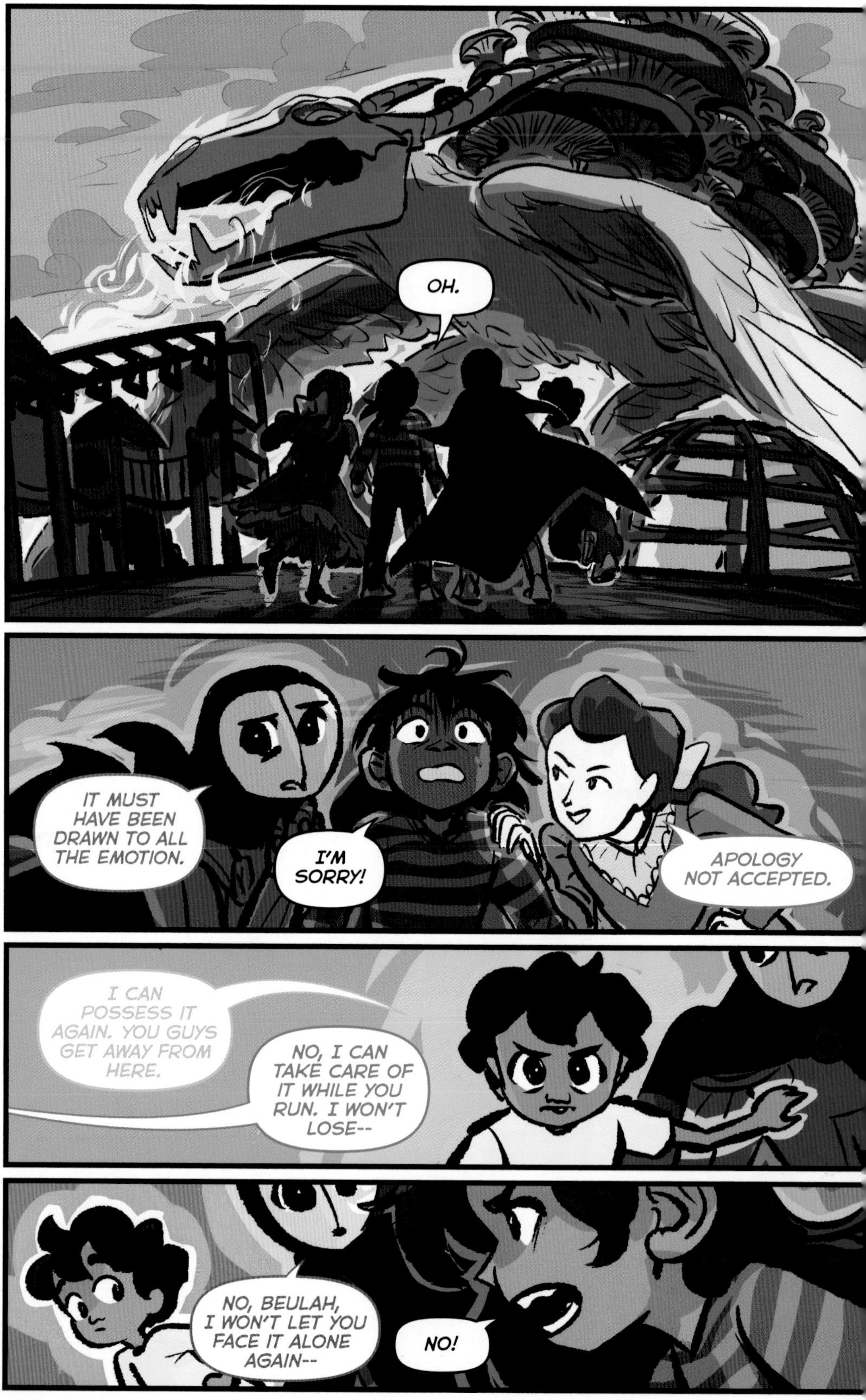
OH.
IT MUST HAVE BEEN DRAWN TO ALL THE EMOTION.
I'M SORRY!
APOLOGY NOT ACCEPTED.
I CAN POSSESS IT AGAIN. YOU GUYS GET AWAY FROM HERE.
NO, I CAN TAKE CARE OF IT WHILE YOU RUN. I WON'T LOSE--
NO, BEULAH, I WON'T LET YOU FACE IT ALONE AGAIN--
NO!

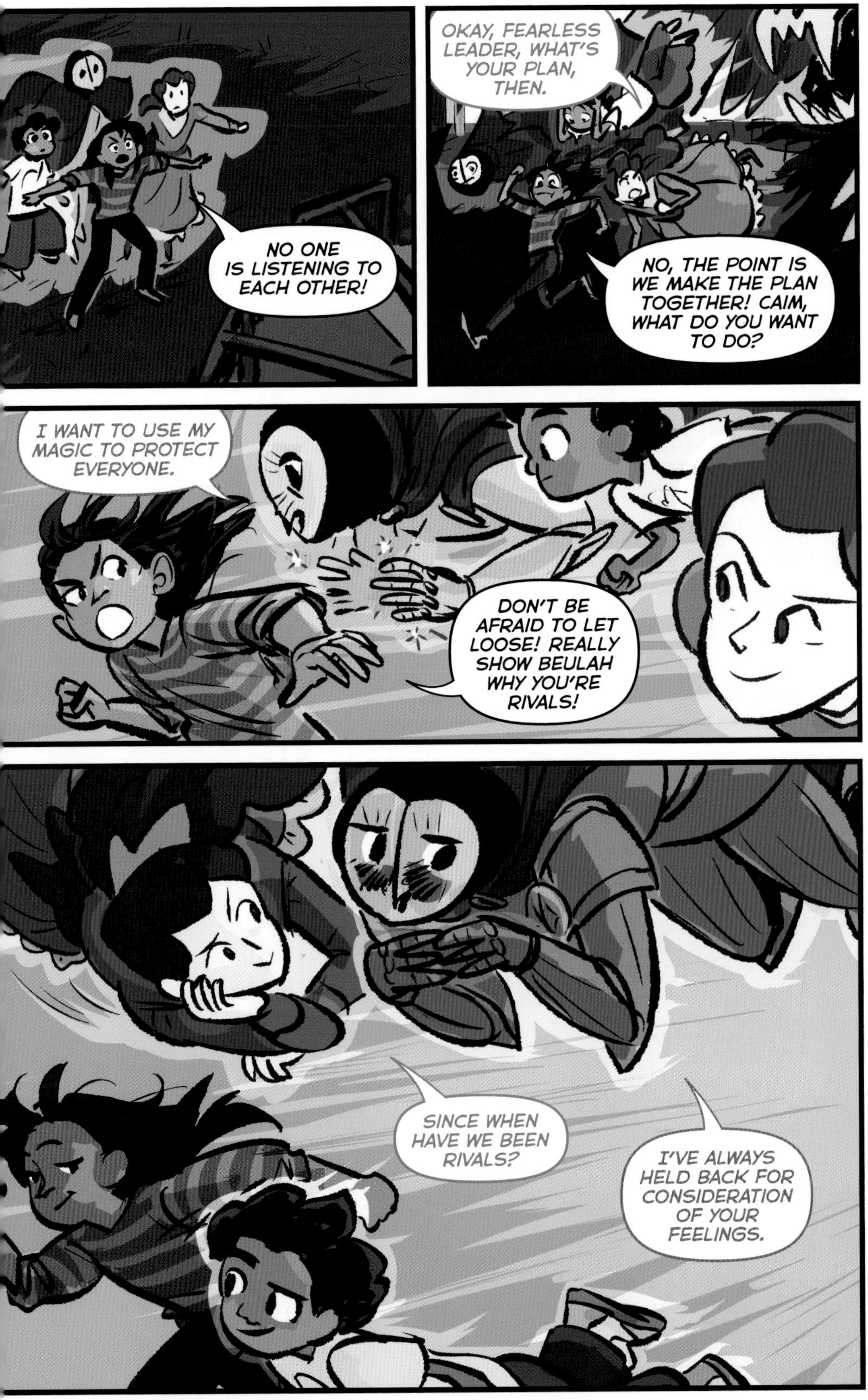
NO ONE IS LISTENING TO EACH OTHER!
OKAY, FEARLESS LEADER, WHAT'S YOUR PLAN, THEN.
NO, THE POINT IS WE MAKE THE PLAN TOGETHER! CAIM, WHAT DO YOU WANT TO DO?
I WANT TO USE MY MAGIC TO PROTECT EVERYONE.
DON'T BE AFRAID TO LET LOOSE! REALLY SHOW BEULAH WHY YOU'RE RIVALS!
SINCE WHEN HAVE WE BEEN RIVALS?
I'VE ALWAYS HELD BACK FOR CONSIDERATION OF YOUR FEELINGS.

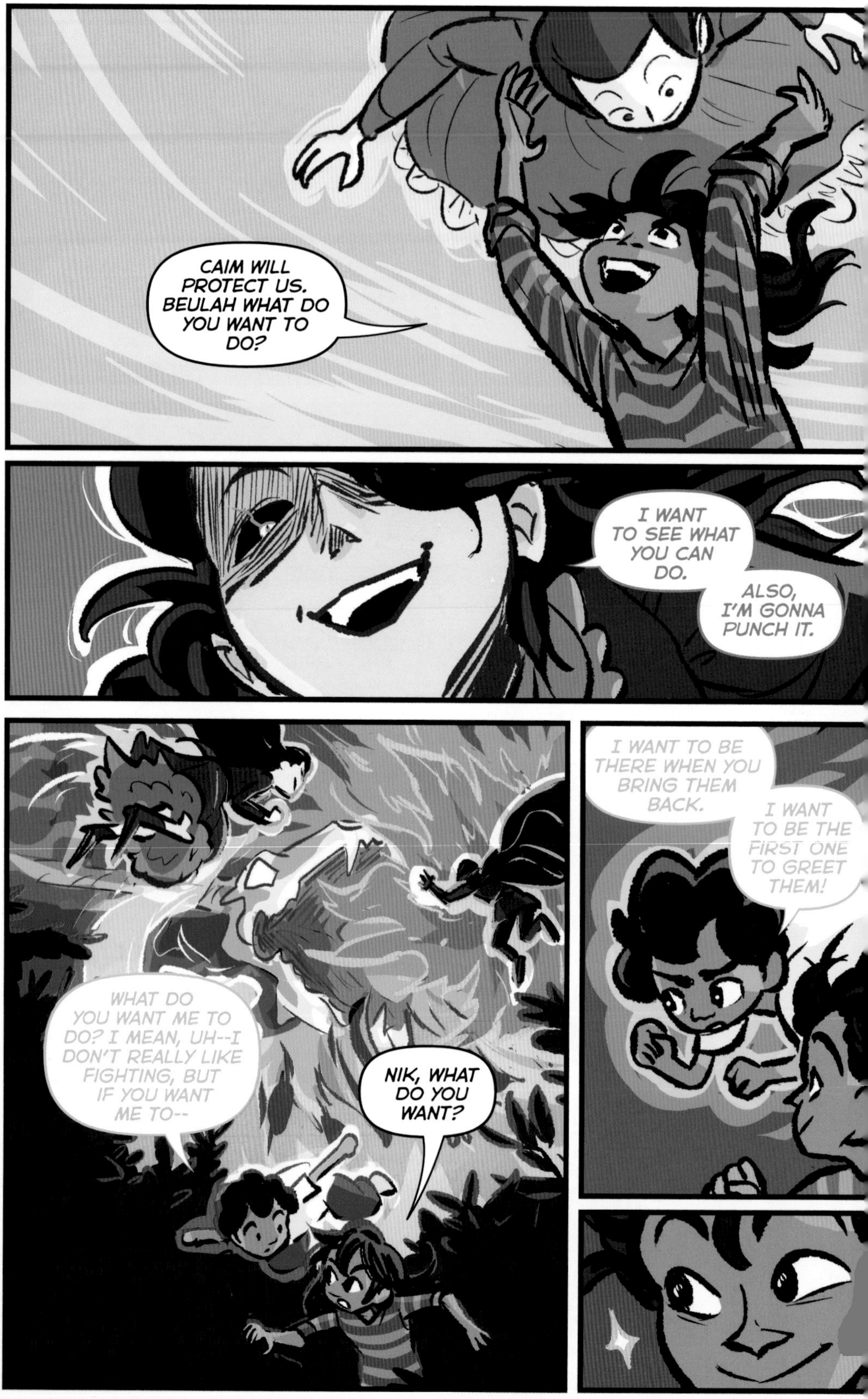
CAIM WILL PROTECT US. BEULAH WHAT DO YOU WANT TO DO?
I WANT TO SEE WHAT YOU CAN DO.
ALSO, I'M GONNA PUNCH IT.
NIK, WHAT DO YOU WANT?
WHAT DO YOU WANT ME TO DO? I MEAN, UH--I DON'T REALLY LIKE FIGHTING, BUT IF YOU WANT ME TO--
I WANT TO BE THERE WHEN YOU BRING THEM BACK.
I WANT TO BE THE FIRST ONE TO GREET THEM!

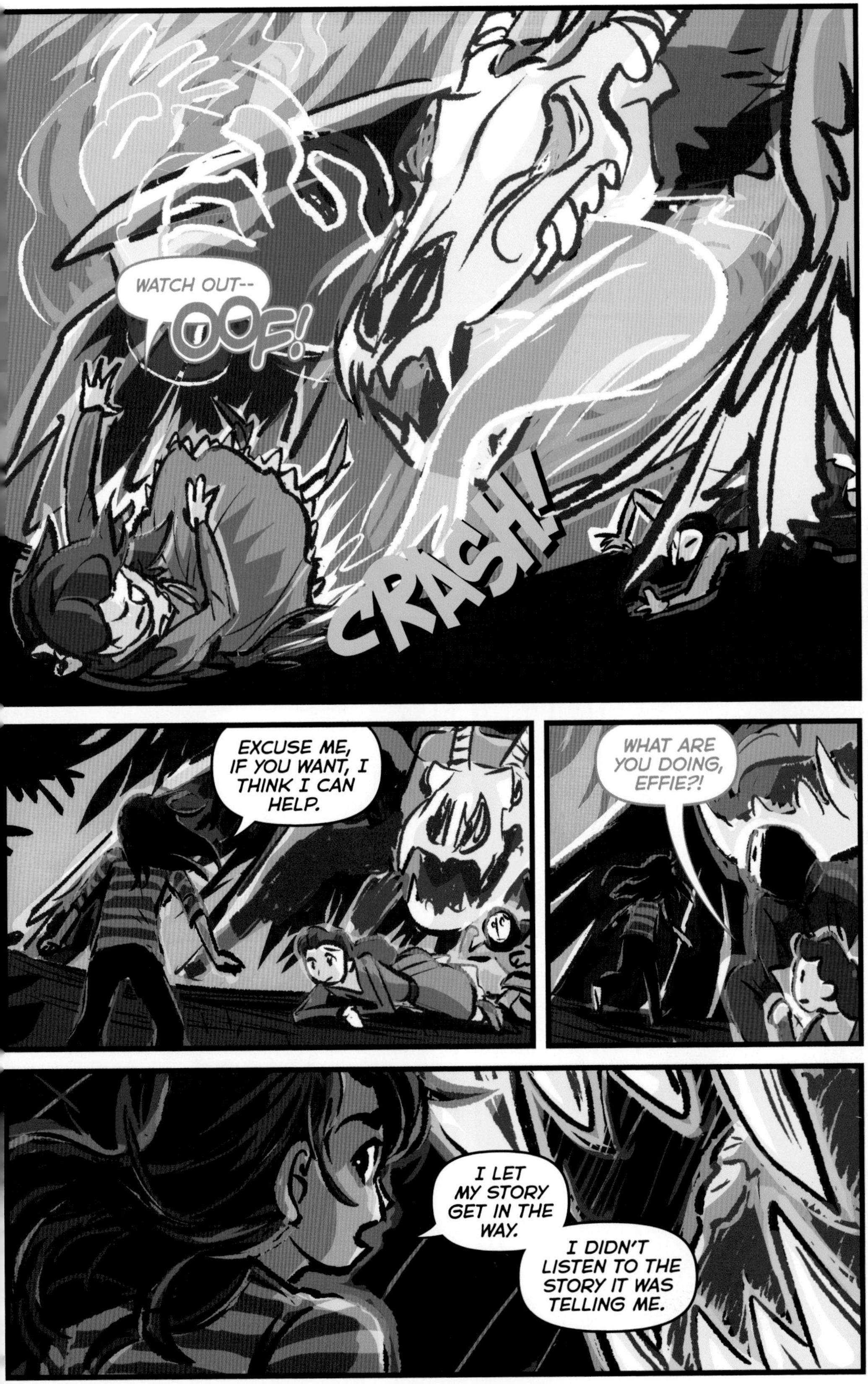
WATCH OUT--
OOF!
CRASH!
EXCUSE ME, IF YOU WANT, I THINK I CAN HELP.
WHAT ARE YOU DOING, EFFIE?!
I LET MY STORY GET IN THE WAY.
I DIDN'T LISTEN TO THE STORY IT WAS TELLING ME.

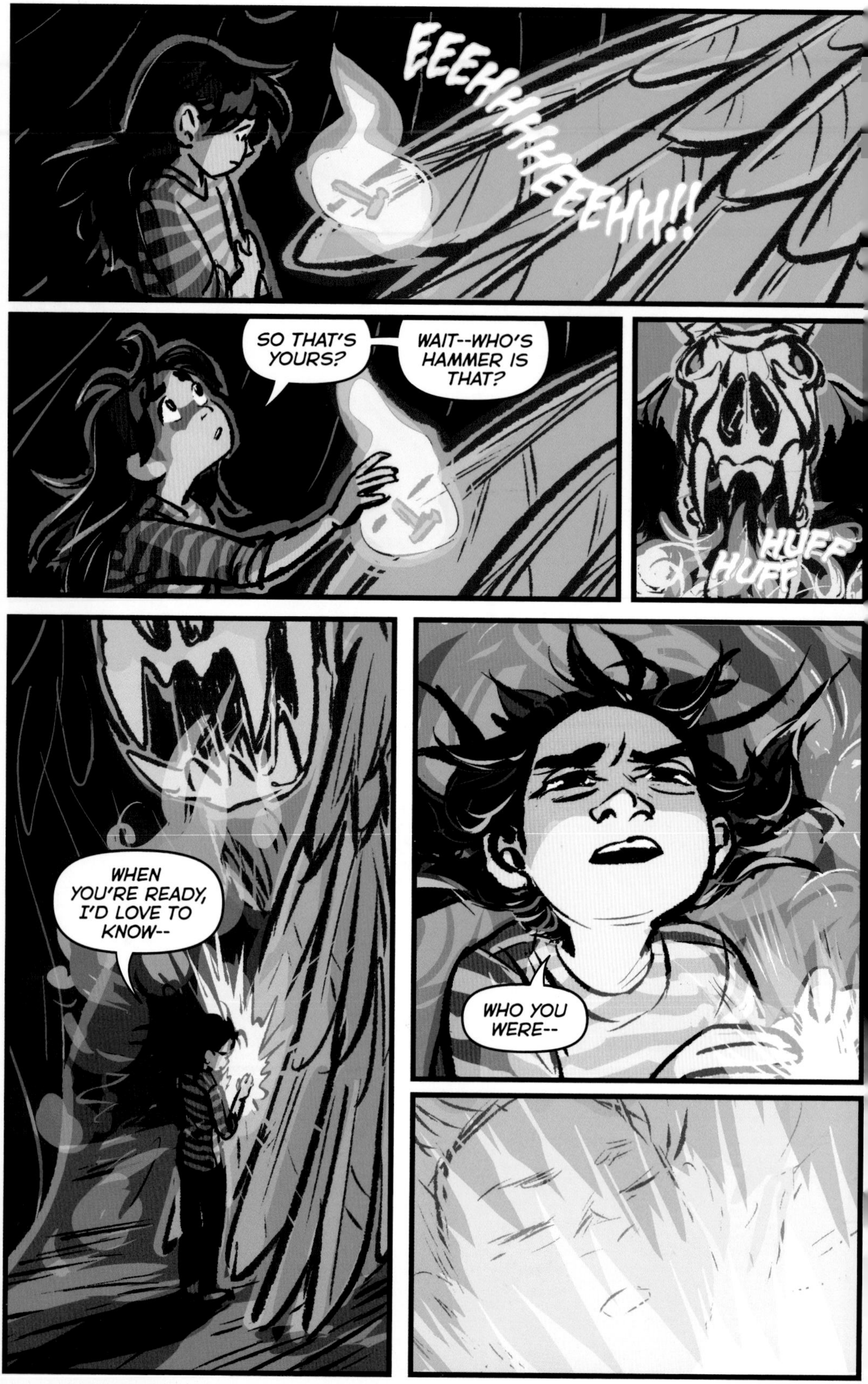
EEEHHHHEEEEHH!!
SO THAT'S YOURS?
WAIT--WHO'S HAMMER IS THAT?
HUFF
HUFF
WHEN YOU'RE READY, I'D LOVE TO KNOW--
WHO YOU WERE--

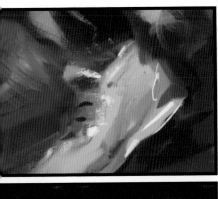

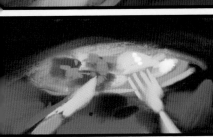
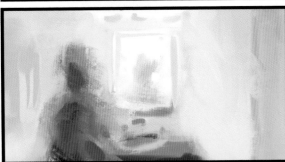

GAAARRRGHHHHUFF HUFF HUFF

WHY DIDN'T IT WORK?!

...THEY CAN'T REMEMBER.

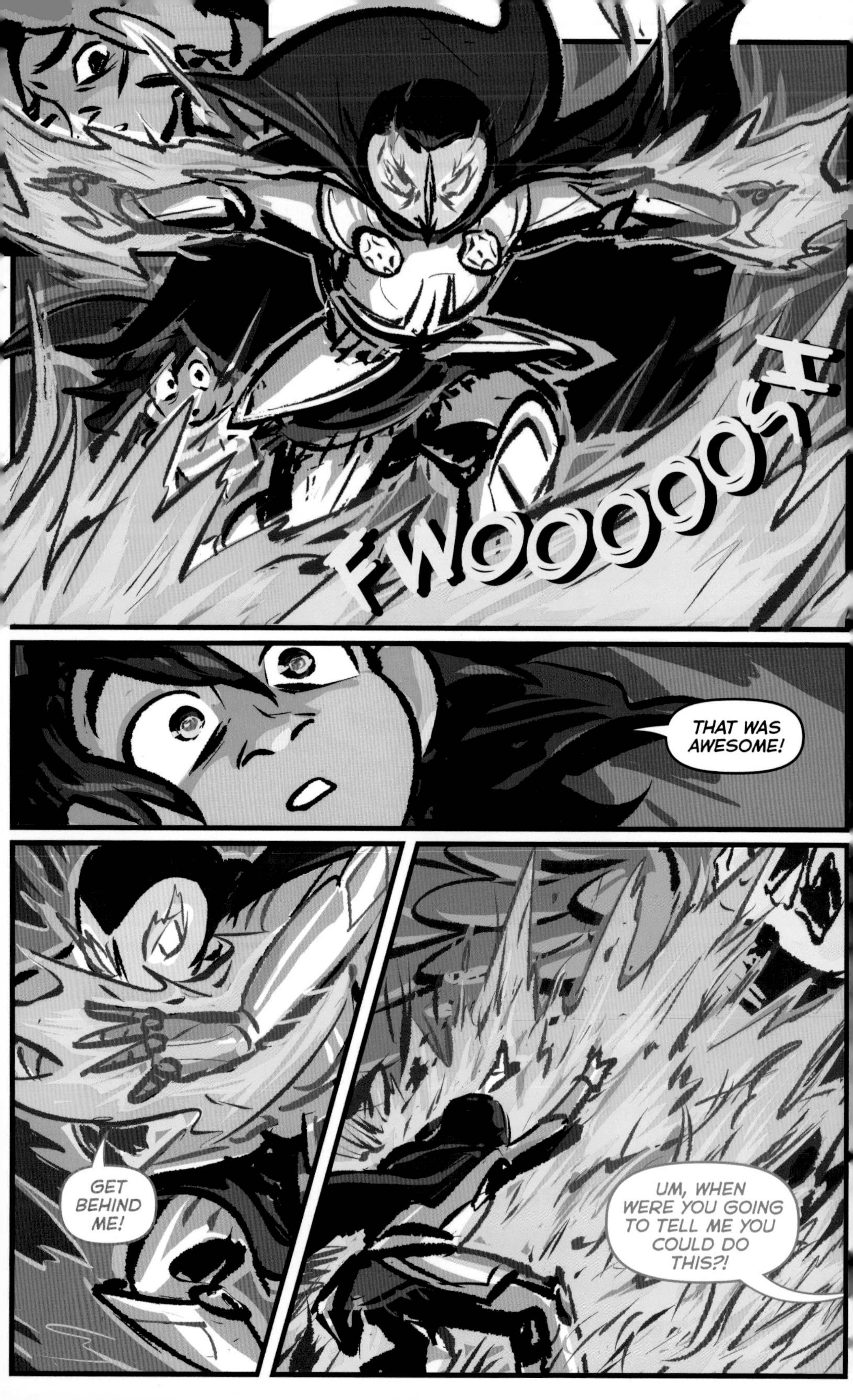
FWOOOOOOSH!
THAT WAS AWESOME!
GET BEHIND ME!
UM, WHEN WERE YOU GOING TO TELL ME YOU COULD DO THIS?!

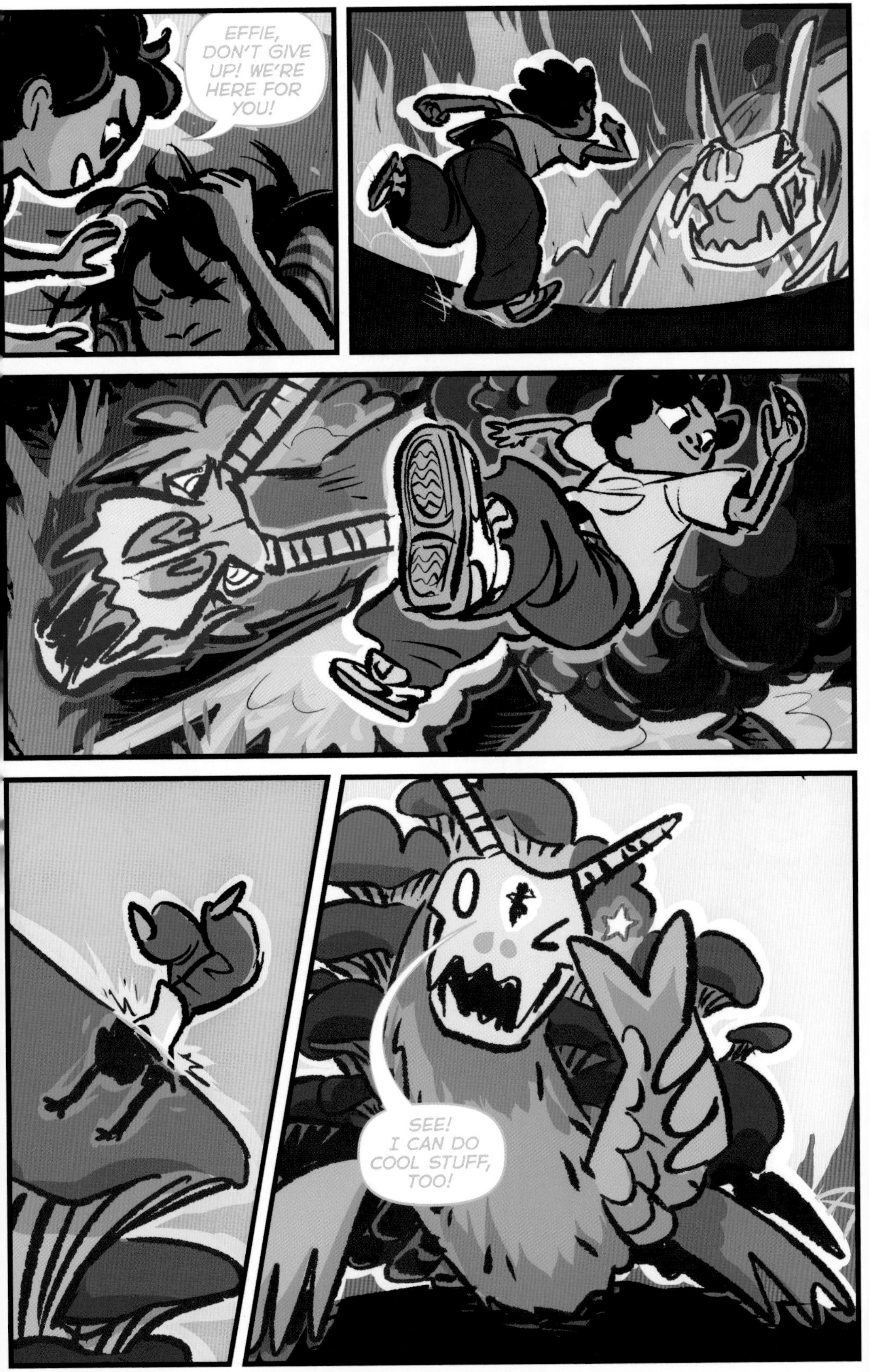
EFFIE, DON'T GIVE UP! WE'RE HERE FOR YOU!
SEE! I CAN DO COOL STUFF, TOO!

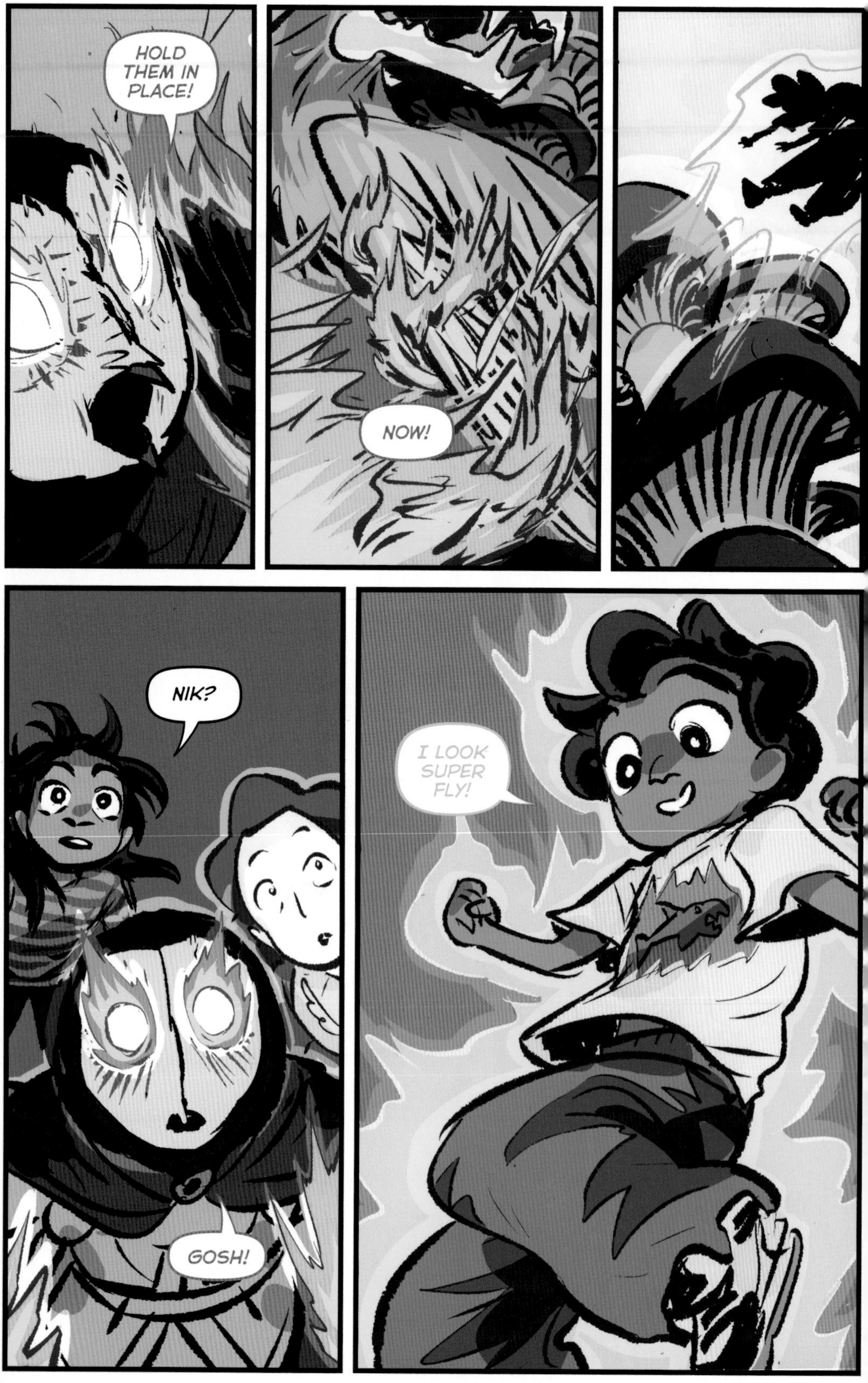
HOLD THEM IN PLACE!
NOW!
NIK?
GOSH!
I LOOK SUPER FLY!

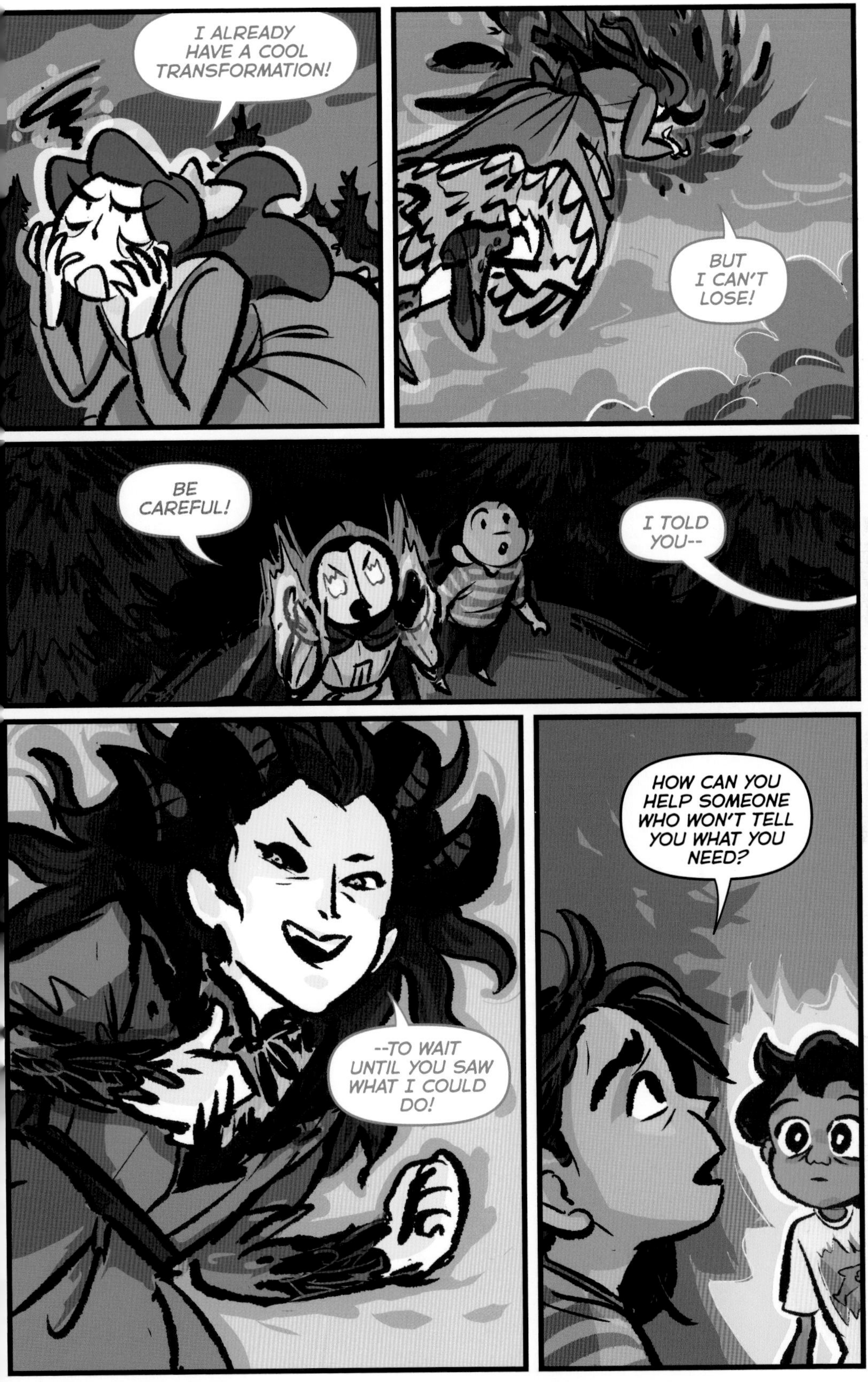
I ALREADY HAVE A COOL TRANSFORMATION!
BUT I CAN'T LOSE!
BE CAREFUL!
I TOLD YOU--
--TO WAIT UNTIL YOU SAW WHAT I COULD DO!
HOW CAN YOU HELP SOMEONE WHO WON'T TELL YOU WHAT YOU NEED?

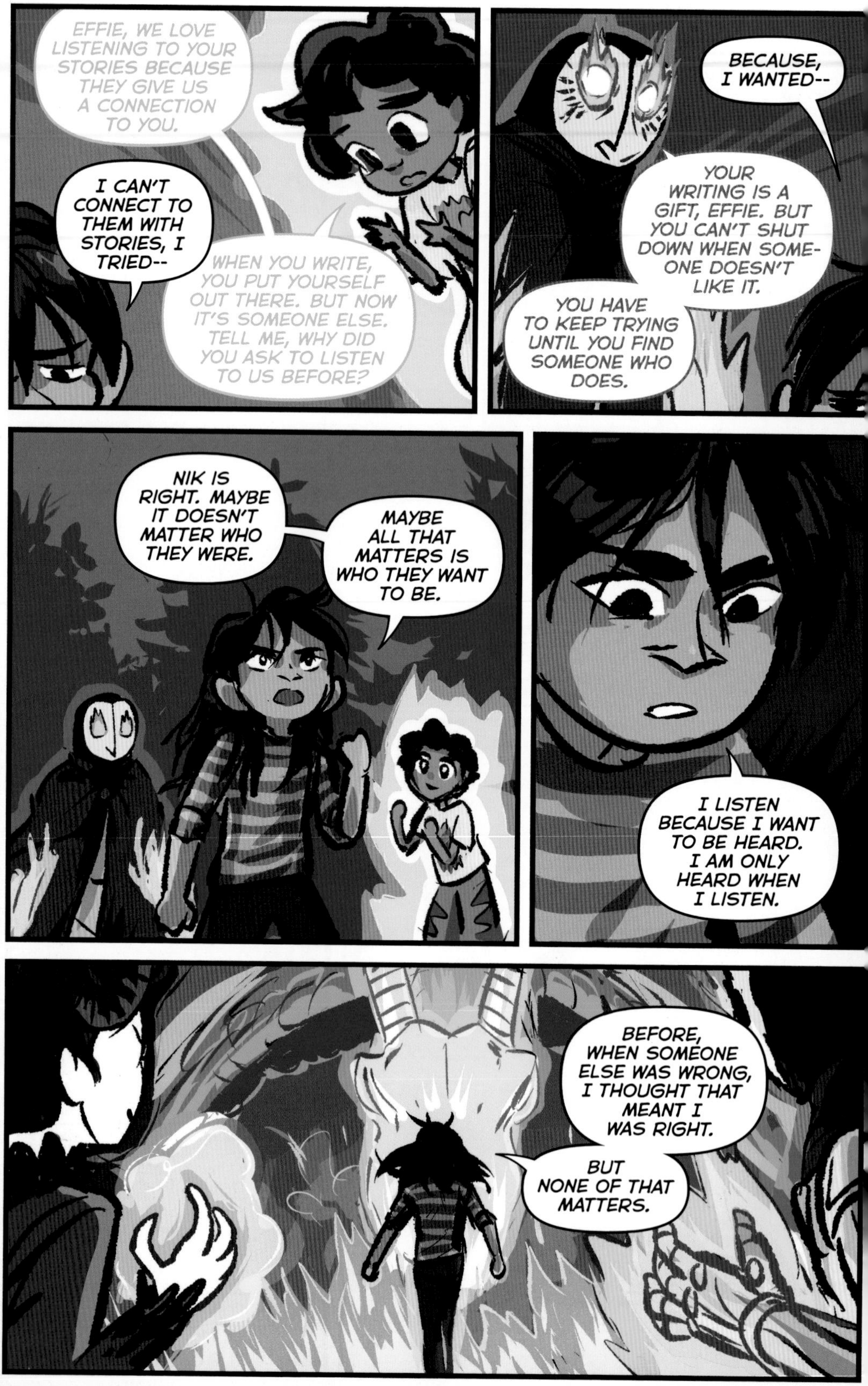
EFFIE, WE LOVE LISTENING TO YOUR STORIES BECAUSE THEY GIVE US A CONNECTION TO YOU.
I CAN'T CONNECT TO THEM WITH STORIES, I TRIED--
WHEN YOU WRITE, YOU PUT YOURSELF OUT THERE. BUT NOW IT'S SOMEONE ELSE. TELL ME, WHY DID YOU ASK TO LISTEN TO US BEFORE?
BECAUSE, I WANTED--
YOUR WRITING IS A GIFT, EFFIE. BUT YOU CAN'T SHUT DOWN WHEN SOME-ONE DOESN'T LIKE IT.
YOU HAVE TO KEEP TRYING UNTIL YOU FIND SOMEONE WHO DOES.
NIK IS RIGHT. MAYBE IT DOESN'T MATTER WHO THEY WERE.
MAYBE ALL THAT MATTERS IS WHO THEY WANT TO BE.
I LISTEN BECAUSE I WANT TO BE HEARD. I AM ONLY HEARD WHEN I LISTEN.
BEFORE, WHEN SOMEONE ELSE WAS WRONG, I THOUGHT THAT MEANT I WAS RIGHT.
BUT NONE OF THAT MATTERS.

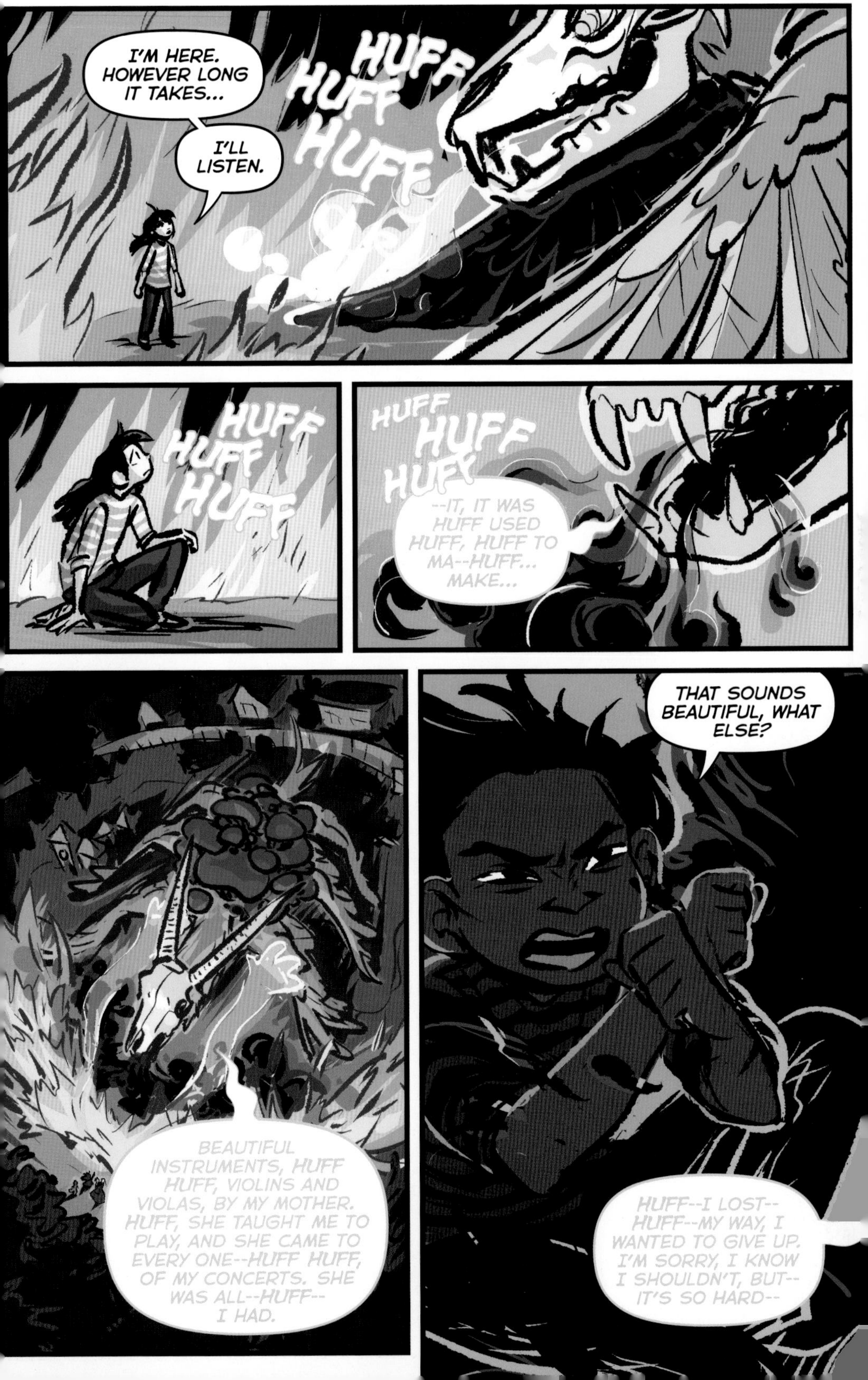
I'M HERE. HOWEVER LONG IT TAKES...
I'LL LISTEN.
HUFF HUFF HUFF
HUFF HUFF HUFF
HUFF HUFF HUFF
--IT, IT WAS HUFF USED HUFF, HUFF TO MA--HUFF... MAKE...
BEAUTIFUL INSTRUMENTS, HUFF HUFF, VIOLINS AND VIOLAS, BY MY MOTHER. HUFF, SHE TAUGHT ME TO PLAY, AND SHE CAME TO EVERY ONE--HUFF HUFF, OF MY CONCERTS. SHE WAS ALL--HUFF-- I HAD.
THAT SOUNDS BEAUTIFUL, WHAT ELSE?
HUFF--I LOST-- HUFF--MY WAY, I WANTED TO GIVE UP. I'M SORRY, I KNOW I SHOULDN'T, BUT-- IT'S SO HARD--

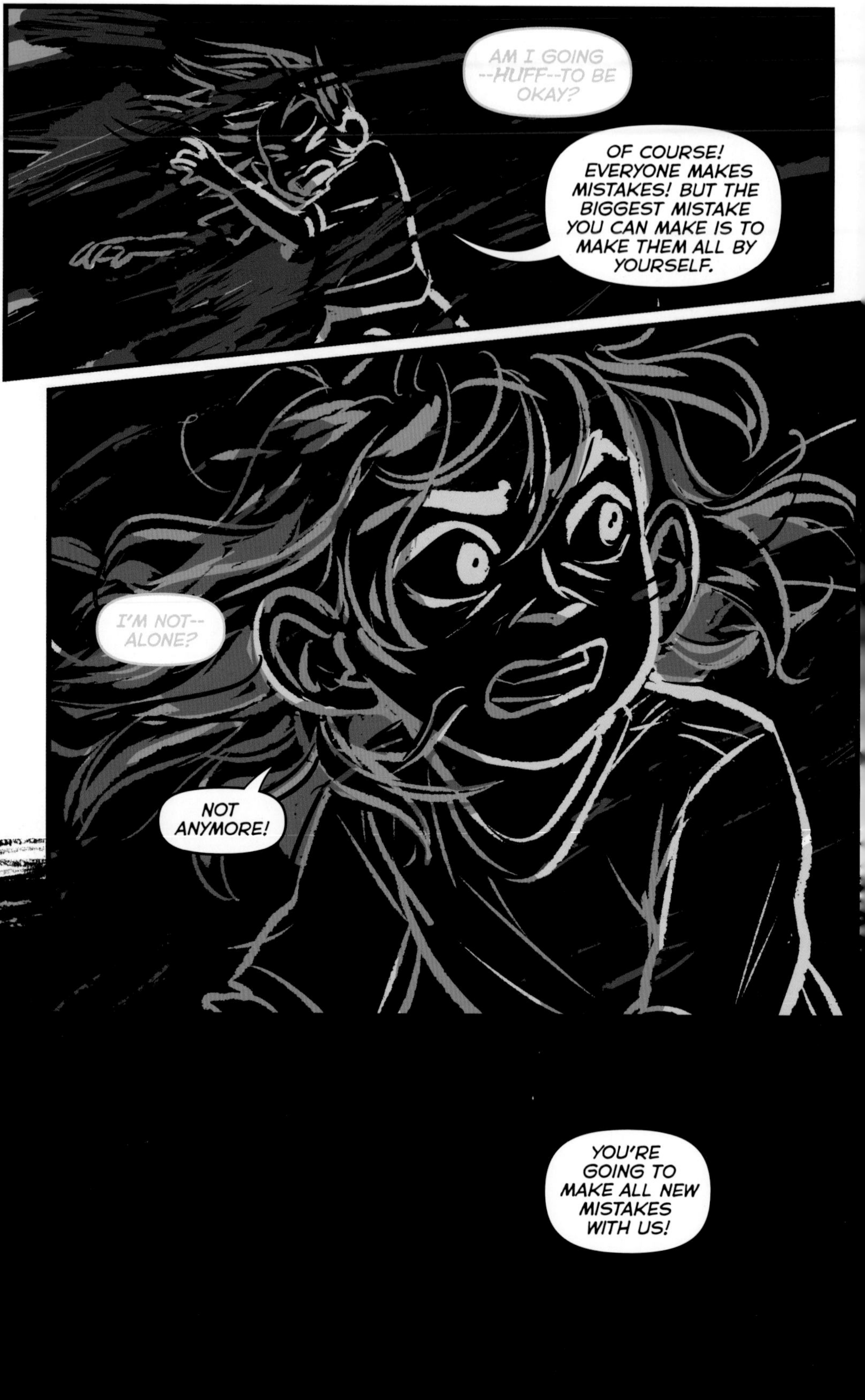
AM I GOING --HUFF--TO BE OKAY?
OF COURSE! EVERYONE MAKES MISTAKES! BUT THE BIGGEST MISTAKE YOU CAN MAKE IS TO MAKE THEM ALL BY YOURSELF.
I'M NOT-- ALONE?
NOT ANYMORE!
YOU'RE GOING TO MAKE ALL NEW MISTAKES WITH US!

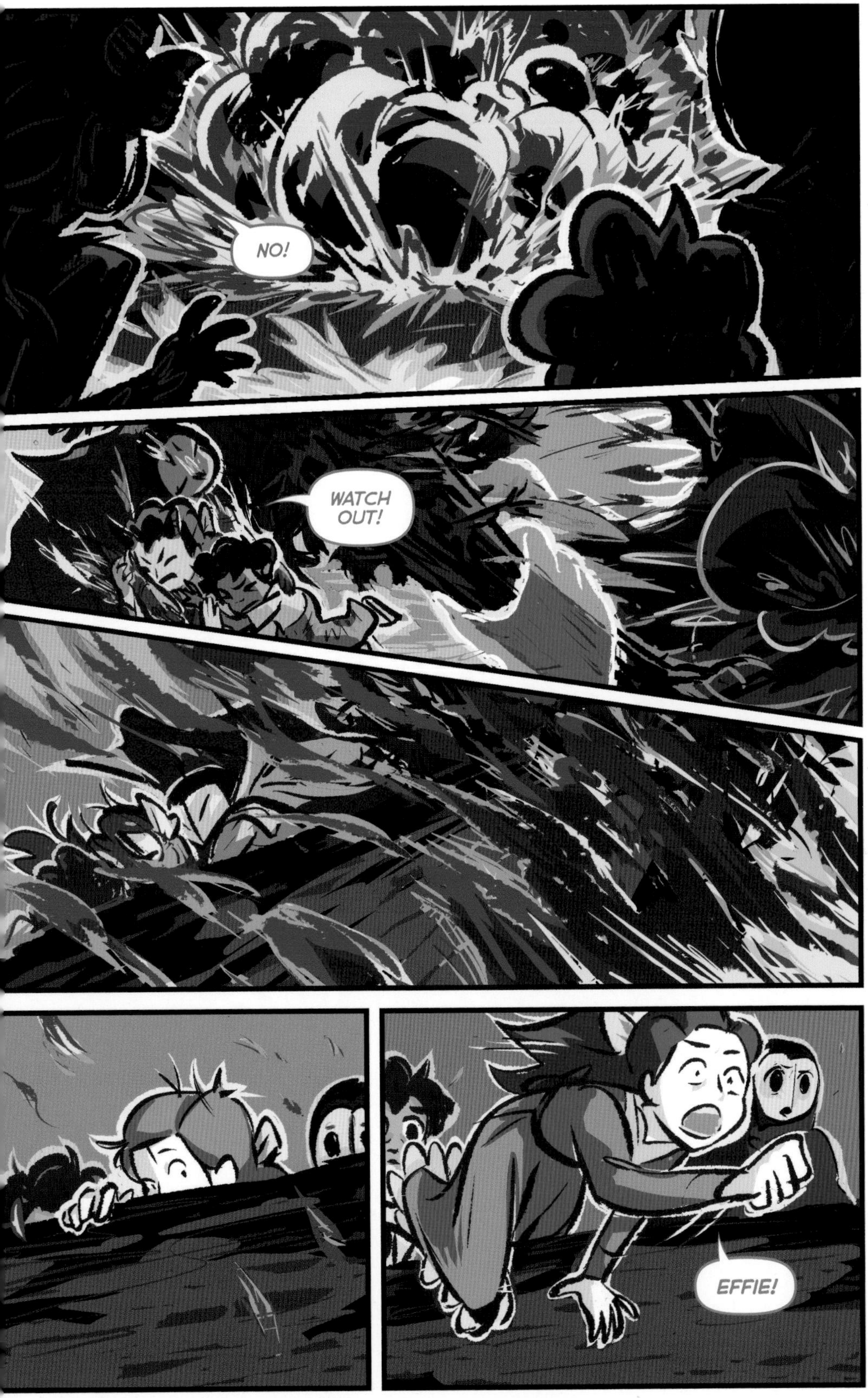
NO!
WATCH OUT!
EFFIE!

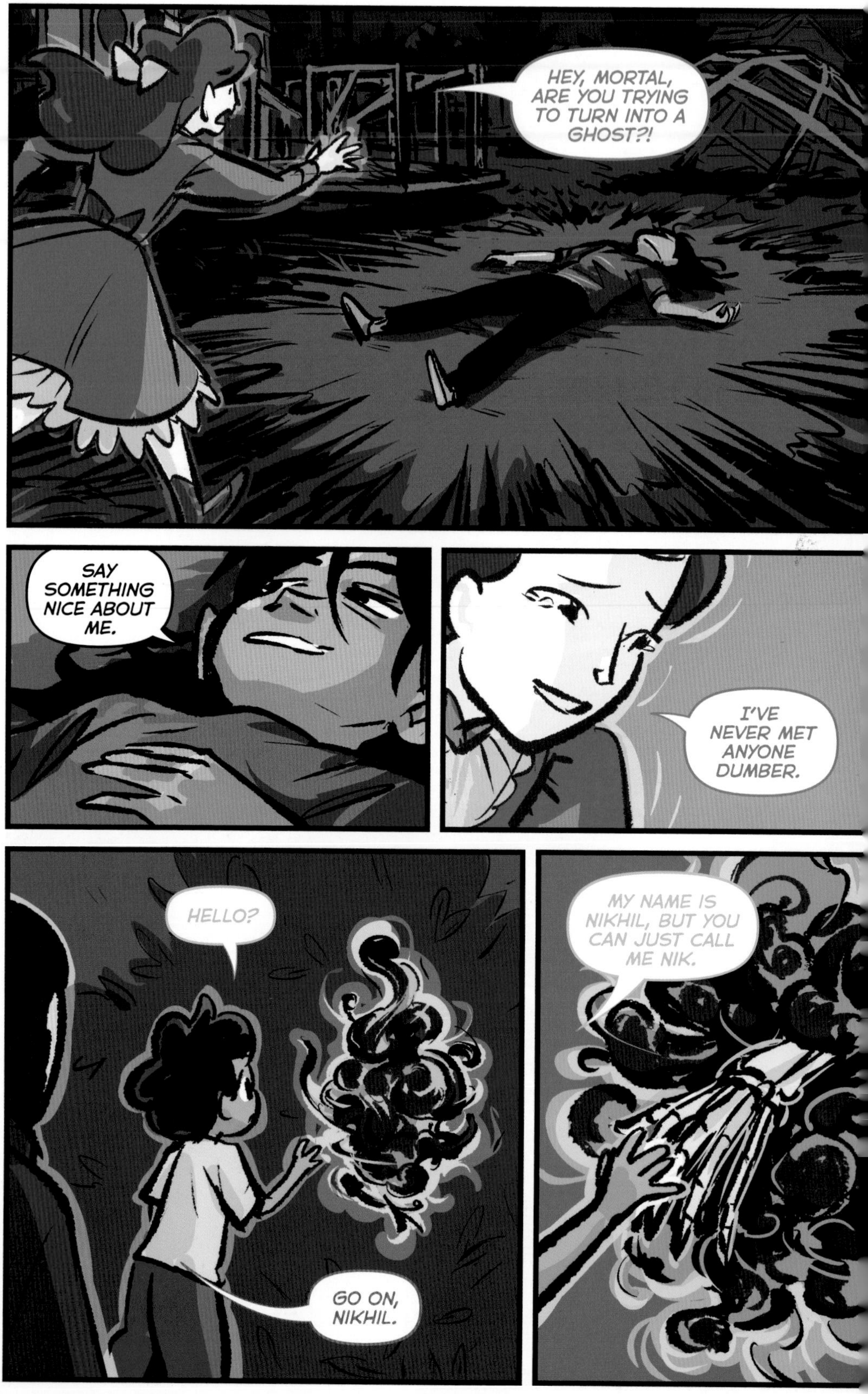
HEY, MORTAL, ARE YOU TRYING TO TURN INTO A GHOST?!
SAY SOMETHING NICE ABOUT ME.
I'VE NEVER MET ANYONE DUMBER.
HELLO?
GO ON, NIKHIL.
MY NAME IS NIKHIL, BUT YOU CAN JUST CALL ME NIK.

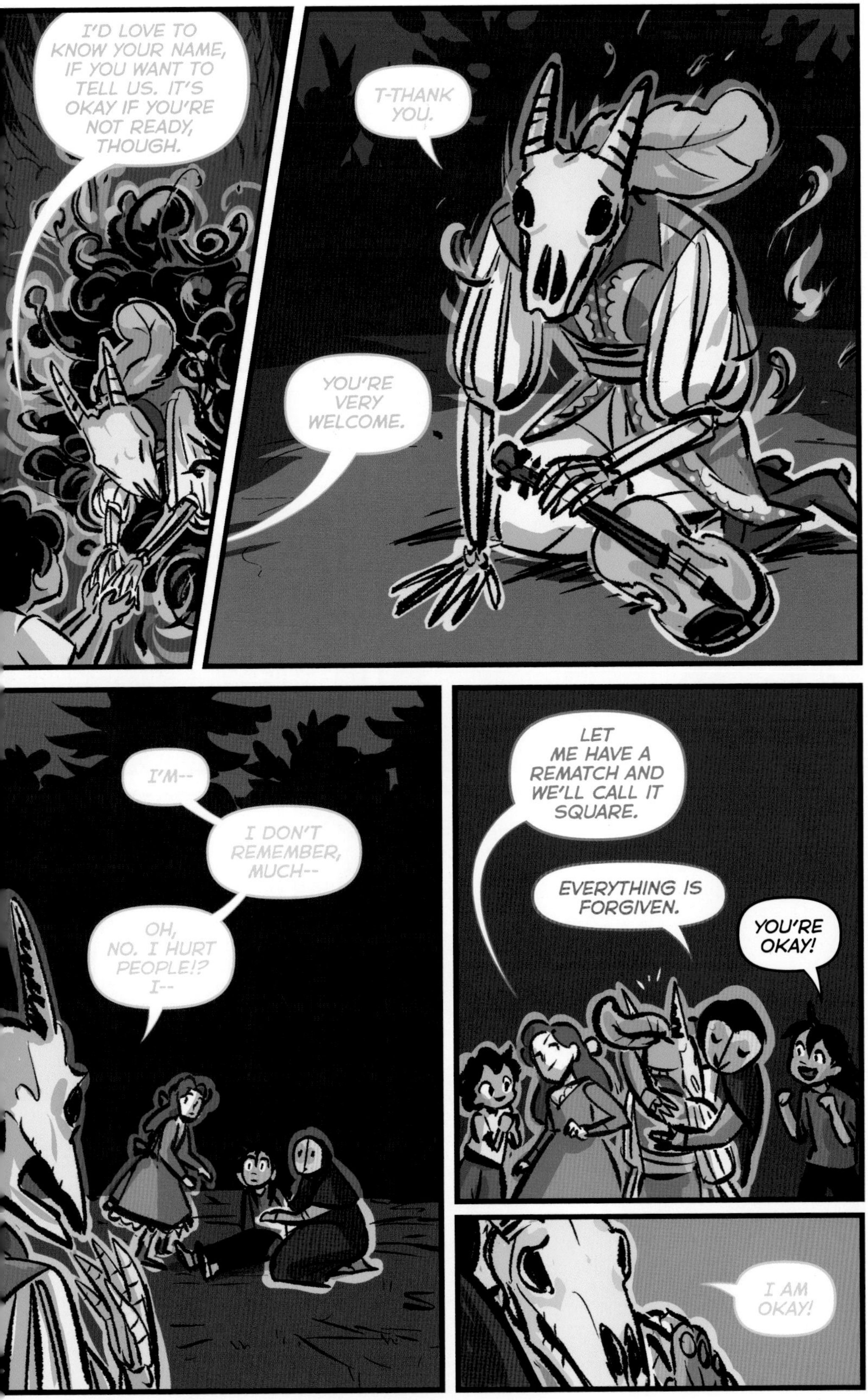
I'D LOVE TO KNOW YOUR NAME, IF YOU WANT TO TELL US. IT'S OKAY IF YOU'RE NOT READY, THOUGH.
T-THANK YOU.
YOU'RE VERY WELCOME.
I'M--
I DON'T REMEMBER, MUCH--
OH, NO. I HURT PEOPLE!? I--
LET ME HAVE A REMATCH AND WE'LL CALL IT SQUARE.
EVERYTHING IS FORGIVEN.
YOU'RE OKAY!
I AM OKAY!

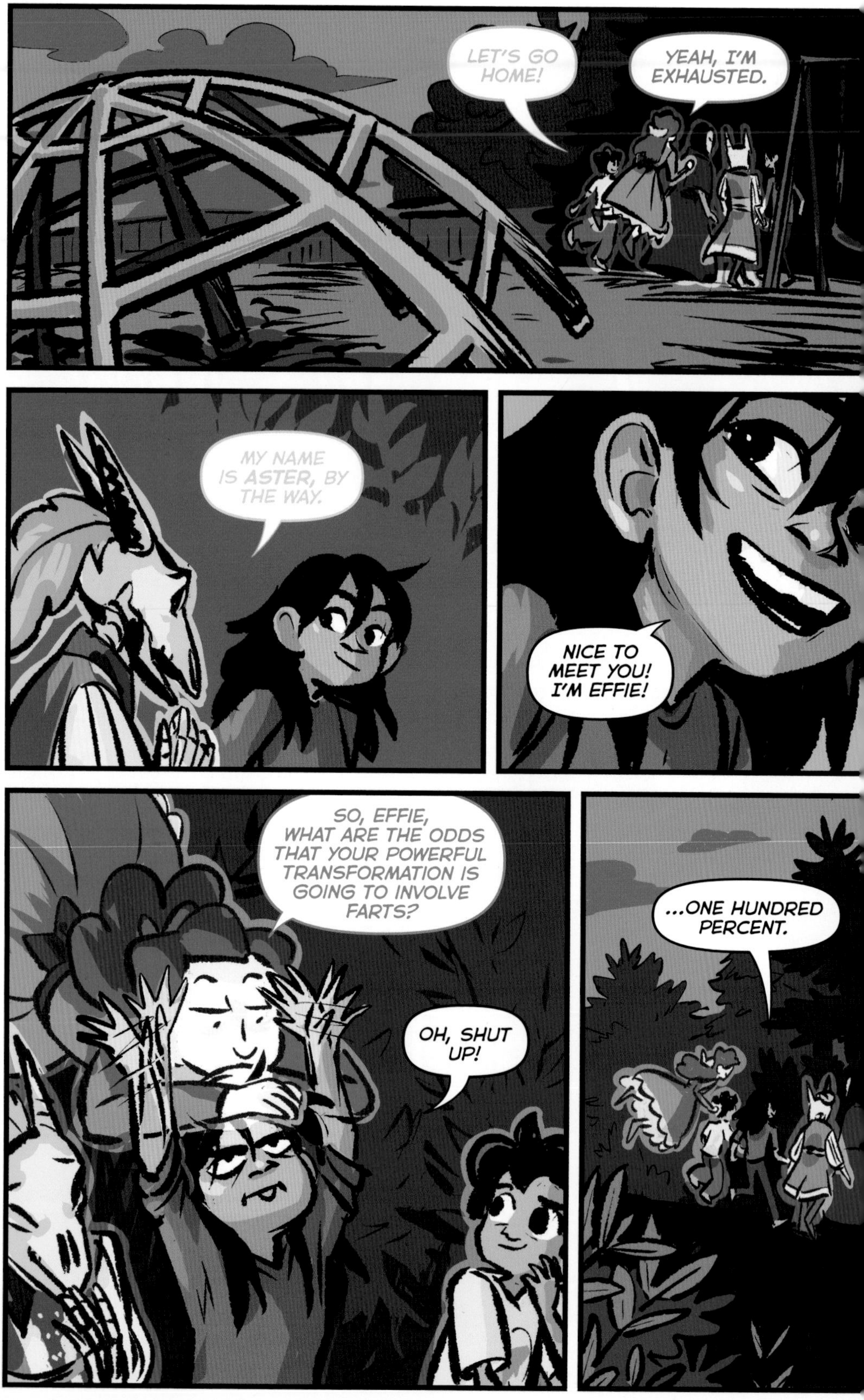
LET'S GO HOME!
YEAH, I'M EXHAUSTED.
MY NAME IS ASTER, BY THE WAY.
NICE TO MEET YOU! I'M EFFIE!
SO, EFFIE, WHAT ARE THE ODDS THAT YOUR POWERFUL TRANSFORMATION IS GOING TO INVOLVE FARTS?
OH, SHUT UP!
...ONE HUNDRED PERCENT.

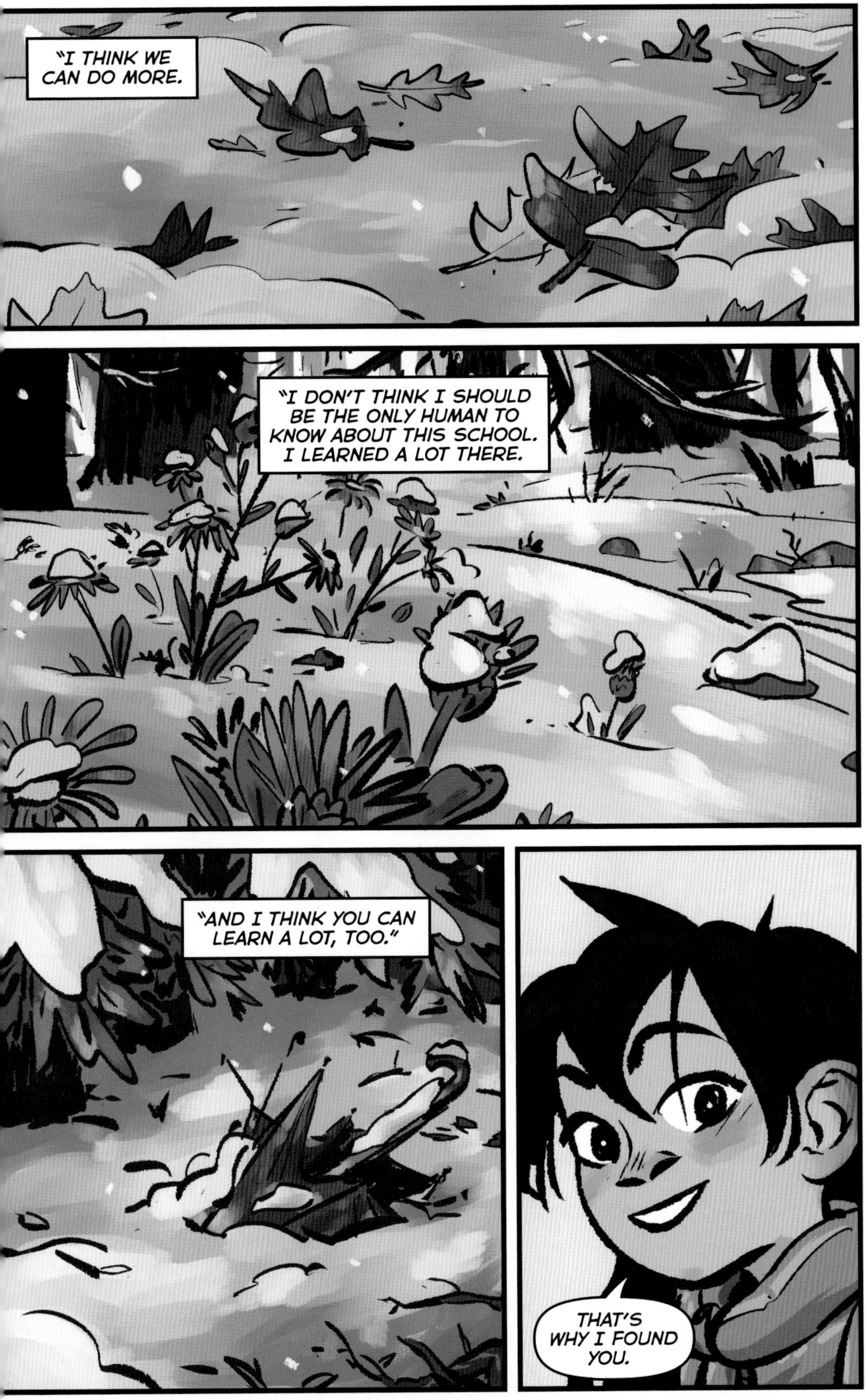
"I THINK WE CAN DO MORE.
"I DON'T THINK I SHOULD BE THE ONLY HUMAN TO KNOW ABOUT THIS SCHOOL. I LEARNED A LOT THERE.
"AND I THINK YOU CAN LEARN A LOT, TOO."
THAT'S WHY I FOUND YOU.

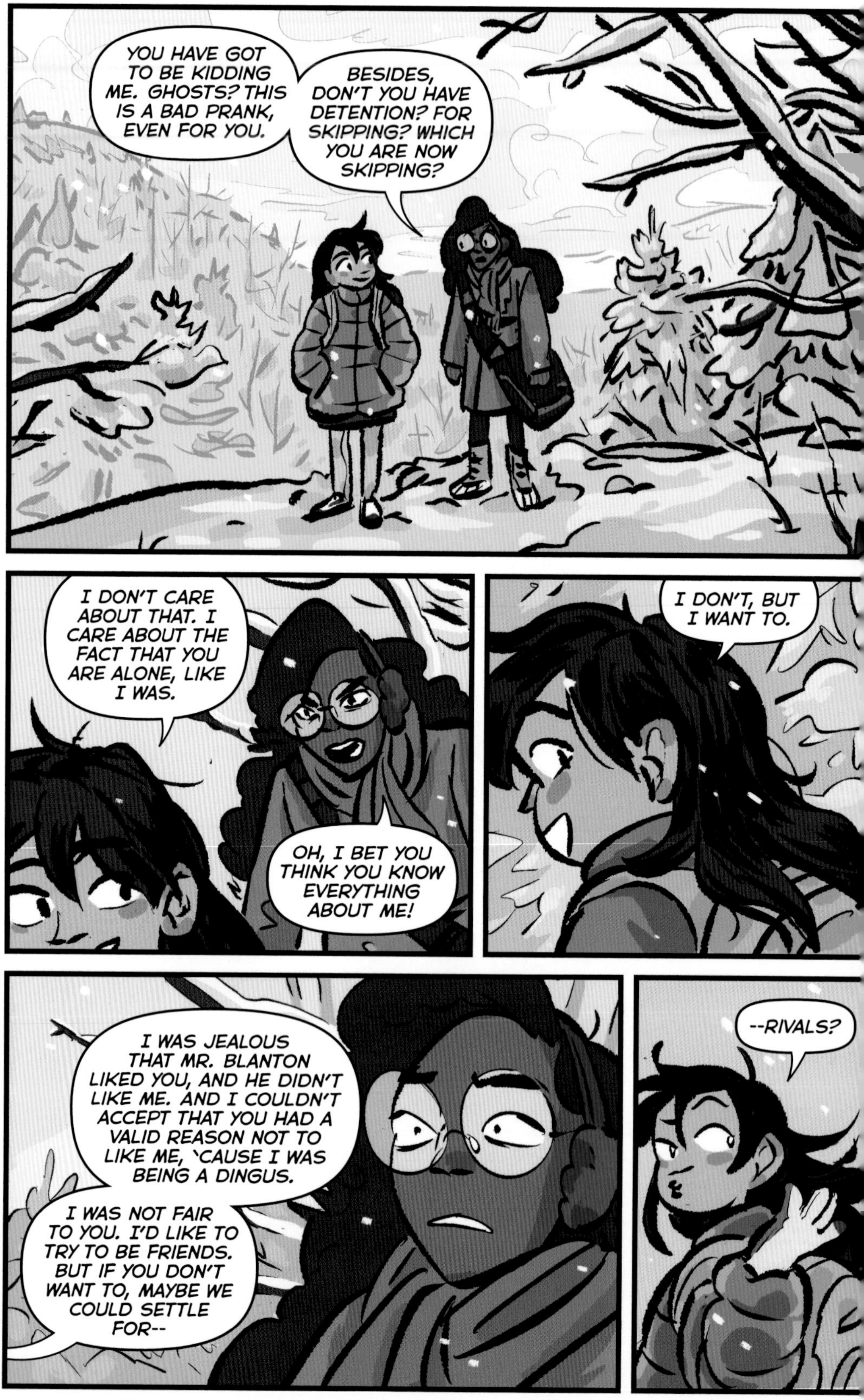
YOU HAVE GOT TO BE KIDDING ME. GHOSTS? THIS IS A BAD PRANK, EVEN FOR YOU.
BESIDES, DON'T YOU HAVE DETENTION? FOR SKIPPING? WHICH YOU ARE NOW SKIPPING?
I DON'T CARE ABOUT THAT. I CARE ABOUT THE FACT THAT YOU ARE ALONE, LIKE I WAS.
OH, I BET YOU THINK YOU KNOW EVERYTHING ABOUT ME!
I DON'T, BUT I WANT TO.
I WAS JEALOUS THAT MR. BLANTON LIKED YOU, AND HE DIDN'T LIKE ME. AND I COULDN'T ACCEPT THAT YOU HAD A VALID REASON NOT TO LIKE ME, 'CAUSE I WAS BEING A DINGUS.
I WAS NOT FAIR TO YOU. I'D LIKE TO TRY TO BE FRIENDS. BUT IF YOU DON'T WANT TO, MAYBE WE COULD SETTLE FOR--
--RIVALS?

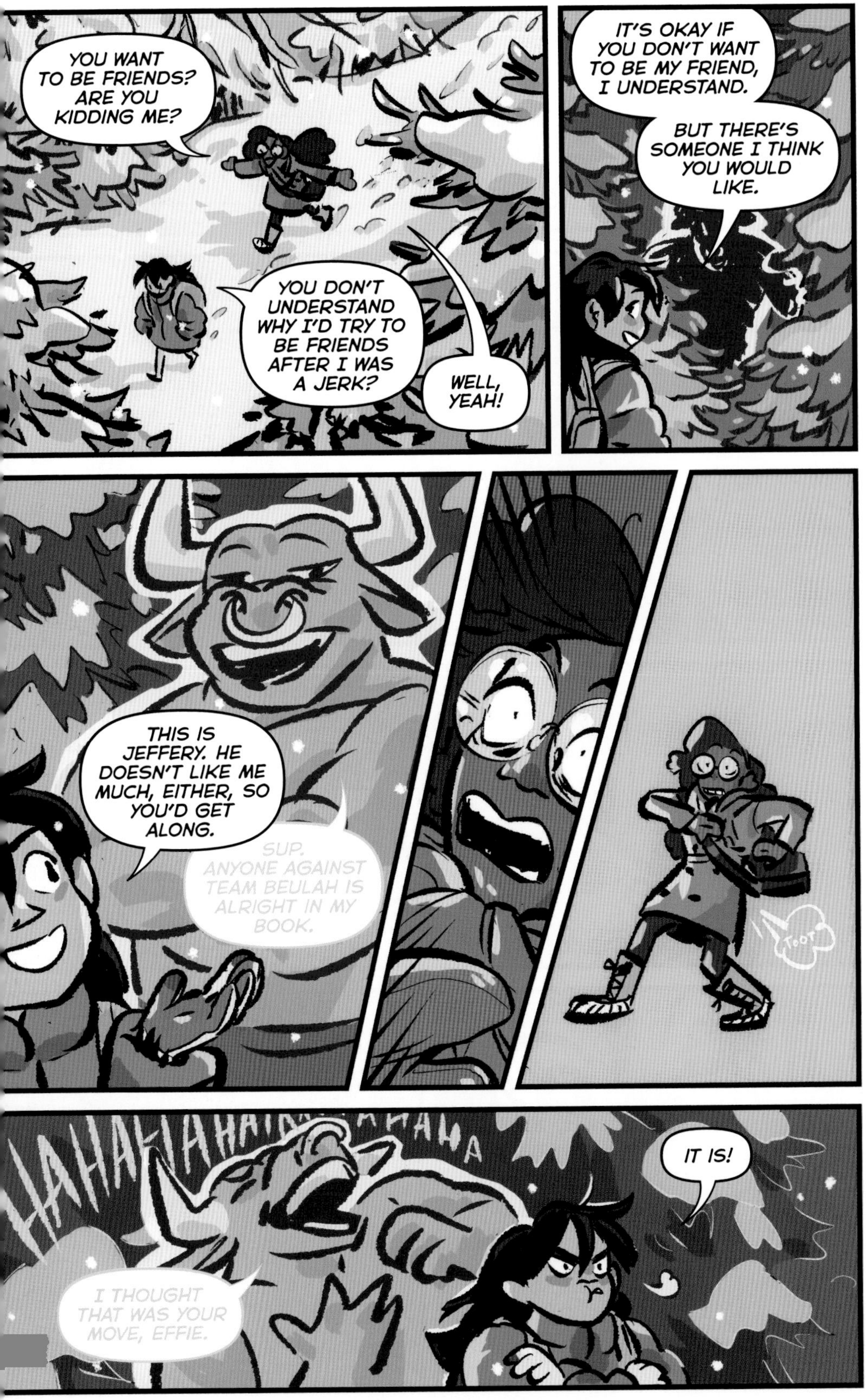
YOU WANT TO BE FRIENDS? ARE YOU KIDDING ME?
YOU DON'T UNDERSTAND WHY I'D TRY TO BE FRIENDS AFTER I WAS A JERK?
WELL, YEAH!
IT'S OKAY IF YOU DON'T WANT TO BE MY FRIEND, I UNDERSTAND.
BUT THERE'S SOMEONE I THINK YOU WOULD LIKE.
THIS IS JEFFERY. HE DOESN'T LIKE ME MUCH, EITHER, SO YOU'D GET ALONG.
SUP. ANYONE AGAINST TEAM BEULAH IS ALRIGHT IN MY BOOK.
TOOT
IT IS!
I THOUGHT THAT WAS YOUR MOVE, EFFIE.

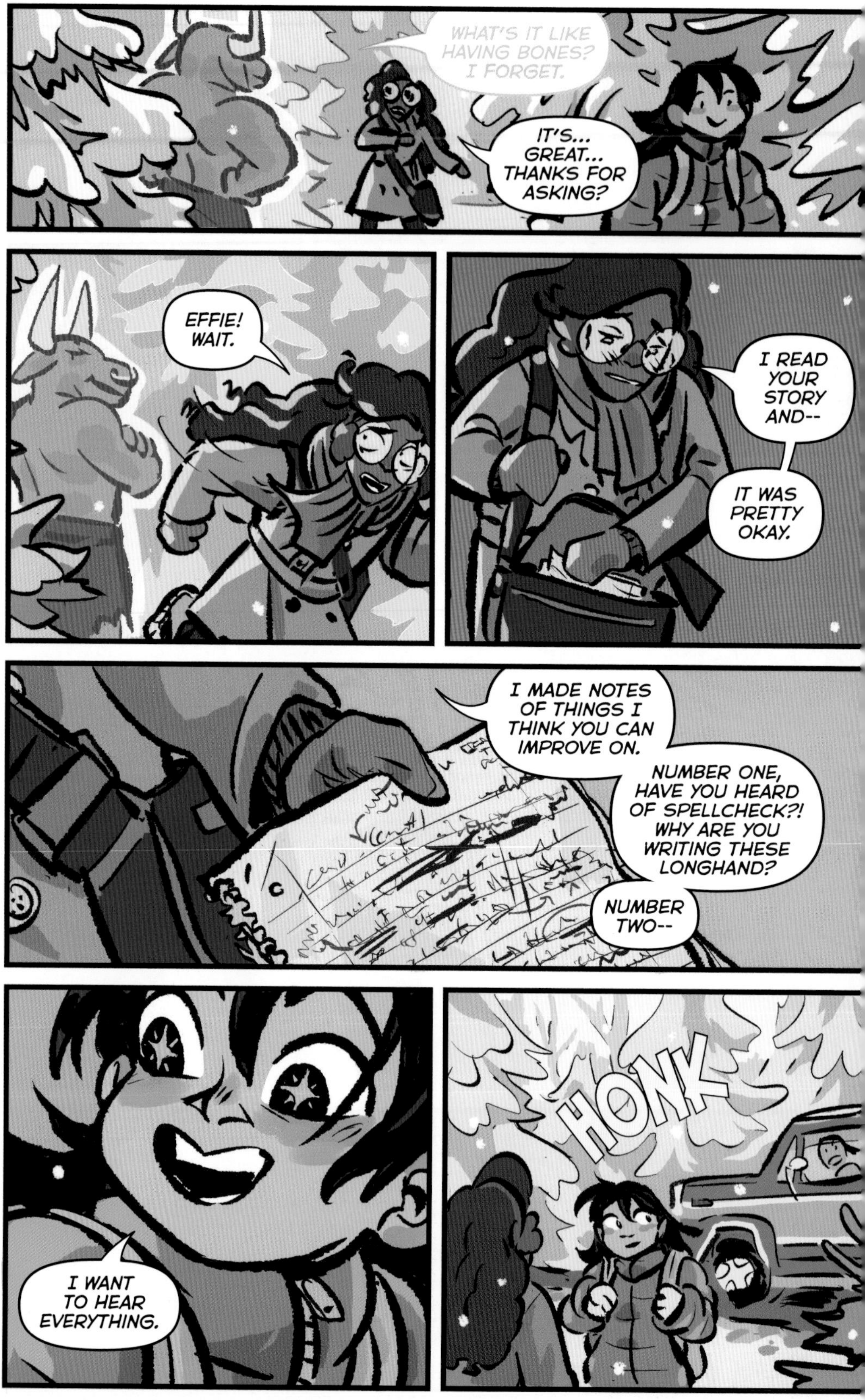

WHAT'S IT LIKE HAVING BONES? I FORGET.
IT'S... GREAT... THANKS FOR ASKING?
EFFIE! WAIT.
I READ YOUR STORY AND--
IT WAS PRETTY OKAY.
I MADE NOTES OF THINGS I THINK YOU CAN IMPROVE ON.
NUMBER ONE, HAVE YOU HEARD OF SPELLCHECK?! WHY ARE YOU WRITING THESE LONGHAND?
NUMBER TWO--
I WANT TO HEAR EVERYTHING.
HONK

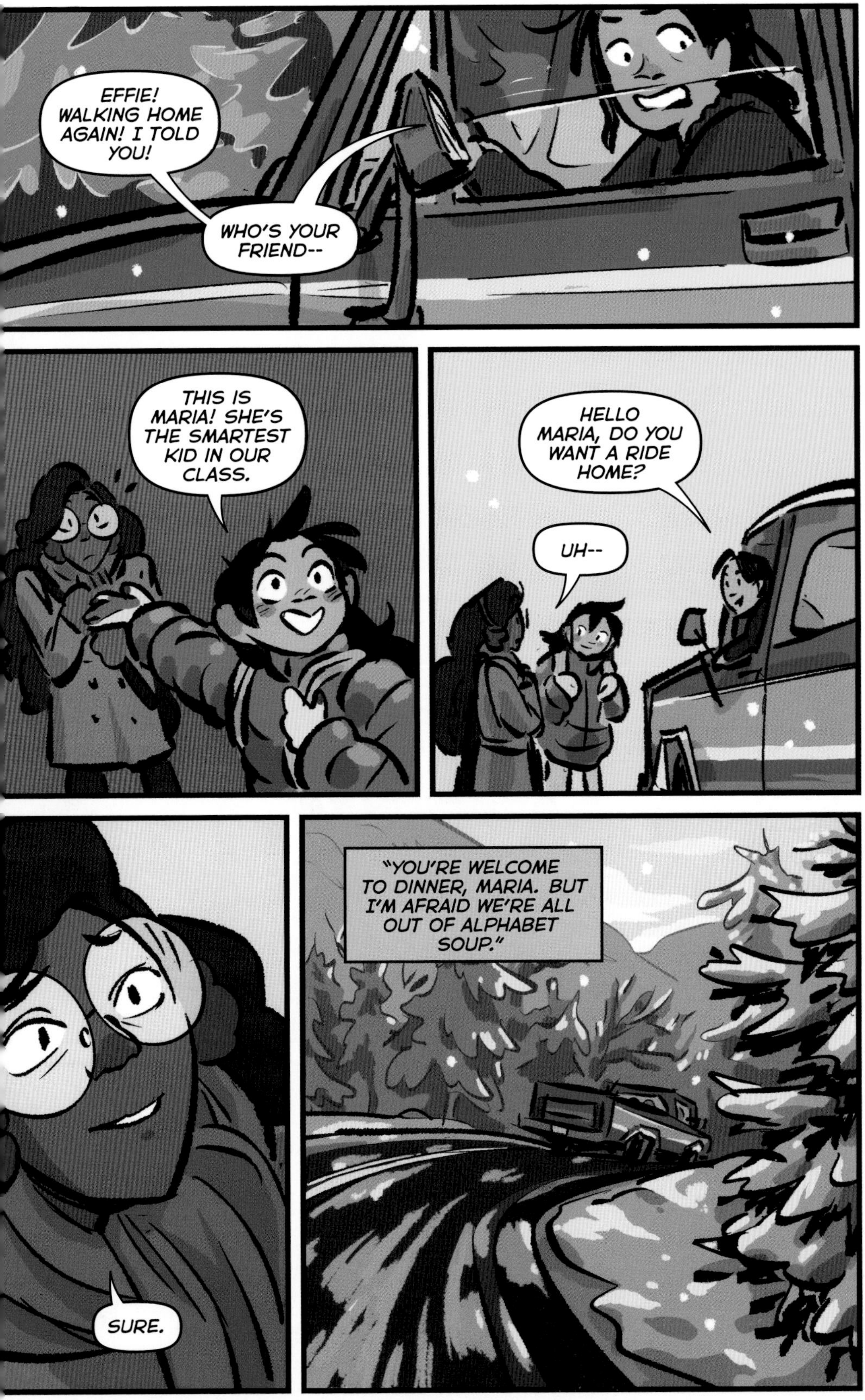
EFFIE! WALKING HOME AGAIN! I TOLD YOU!
WHO'S YOUR FRIEND--
THIS IS MARIA! SHE'S THE SMARTEST KID IN OUR CLASS.
HELLO MARIA, DO YOU WANT A RIDE HOME?
UH--
SURE.
"YOU'RE WELCOME TO DINNER, MARIA. BUT I'M AFRAID WE'RE ALL OUT OF ALPHABET SOUP."

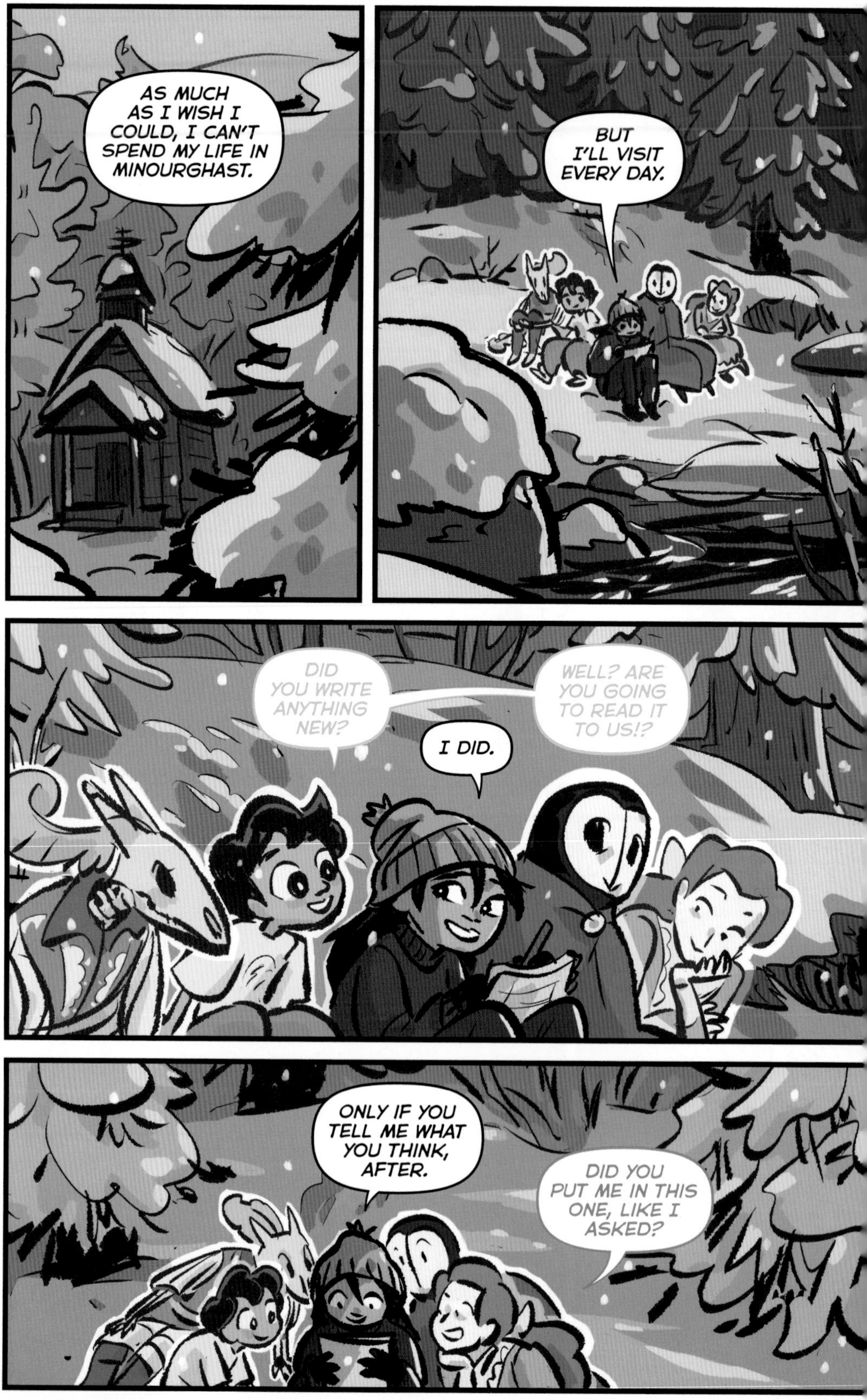
AS MUCH AS I WISH I COULD, I CAN'T SPEND MY LIFE IN MINOURGHAST.
BUT I'LL VISIT EVERY DAY.
DID YOU WRITE ANYTHING NEW?
WELL? ARE YOU GOING TO READ IT TO US!?
I DID.
ONLY IF YOU TELL ME WHAT YOU THINK, AFTER.
DID YOU PUT ME IN THIS ONE, LIKE I ASKED?

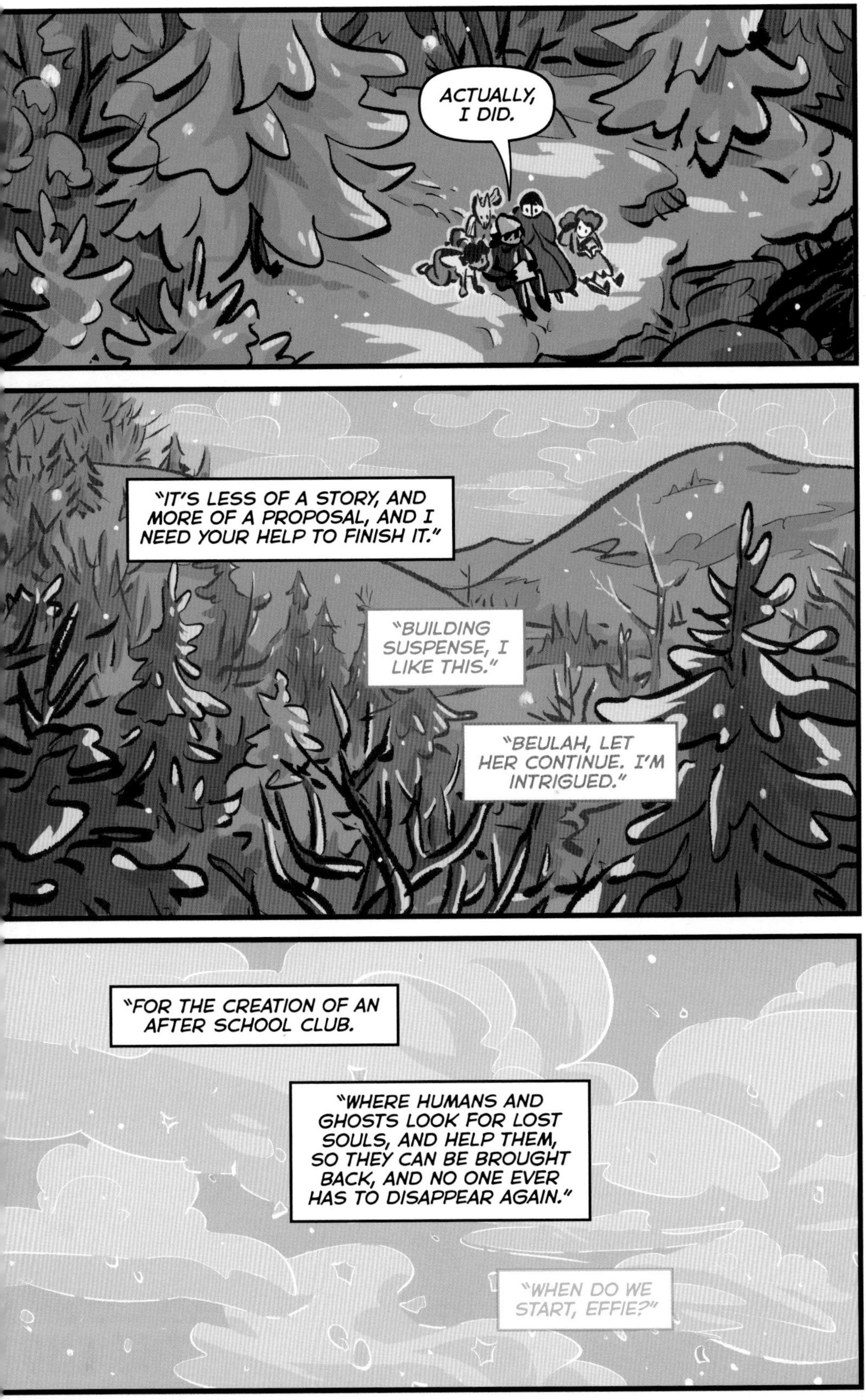

ACTUALLY, I DID.
"IT'S LESS OF A STORY, AND MORE OF A PROPOSAL, AND I NEED YOUR HELP TO FINISH IT."
"BUILDING SUSPENSE, I LIKE THIS."
"BEULAH, LET HER CONTINUE. I'M INTRIGUED."
"FOR THE CREATION OF AN AFTER SCHOOL CLUB.
"WHERE HUMANS AND GHOSTS LOOK FOR LOST SOULS, AND HELP THEM, SO THEY CAN BE BROUGHT BACK, AND NO ONE EVER HAS TO DISAPPEAR AGAIN."
"WHEN DO WE START, EFFIE?"

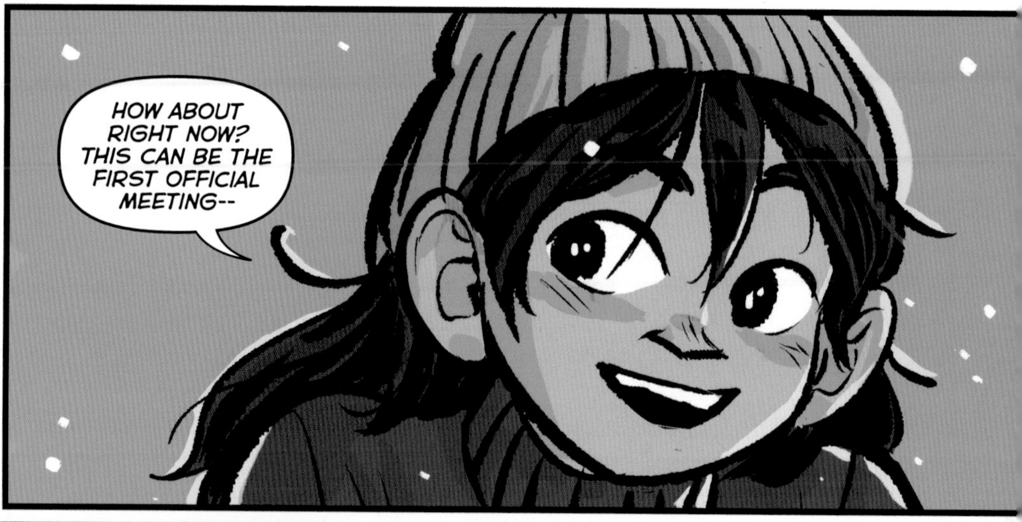
HOW ABOUT RIGHT NOW? THIS CAN BE THE FIRST OFFICIAL MEETING--

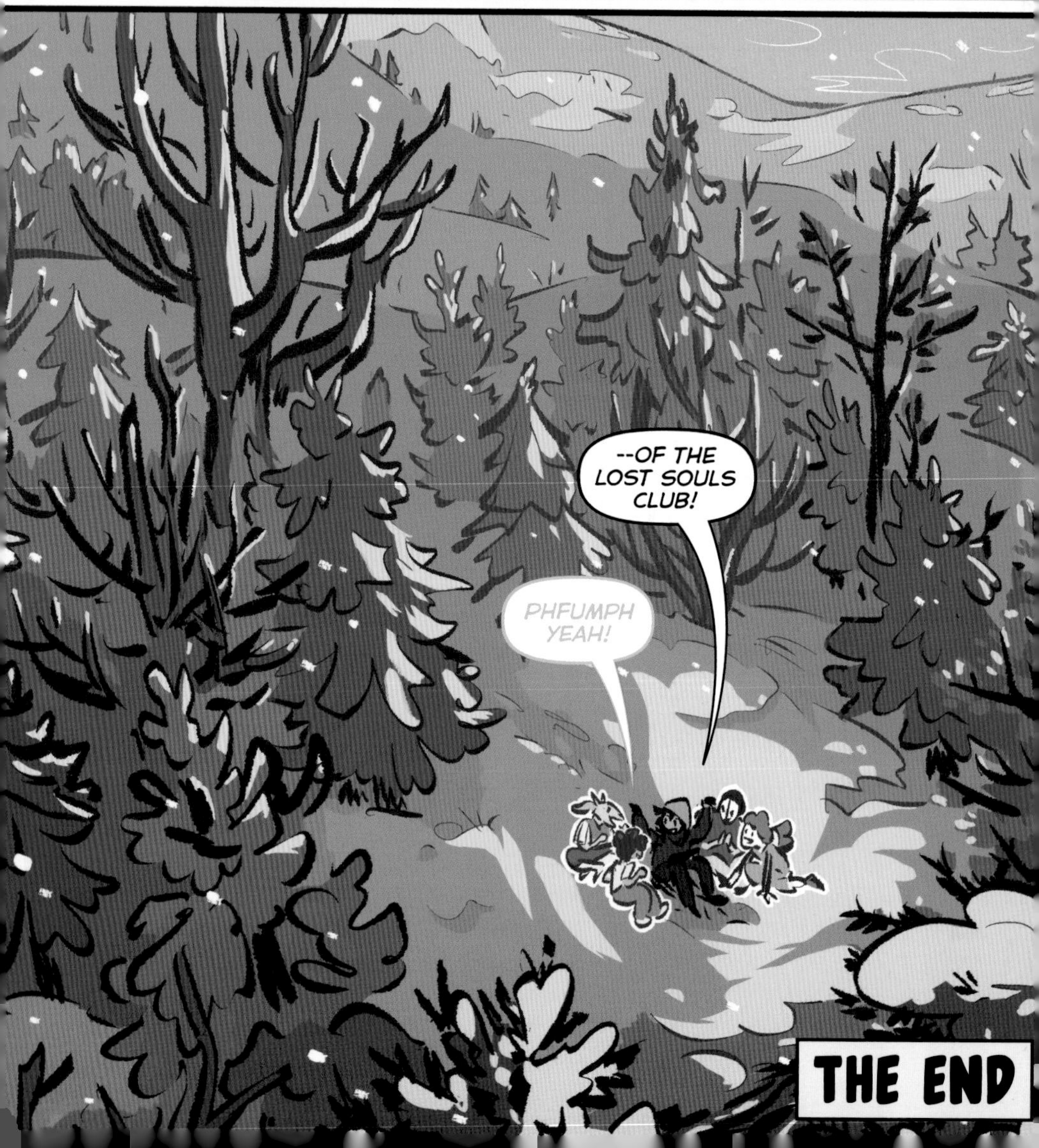
--OF THE LOST SOULS CLUB!
PHFUMPH YEAH!
THE END

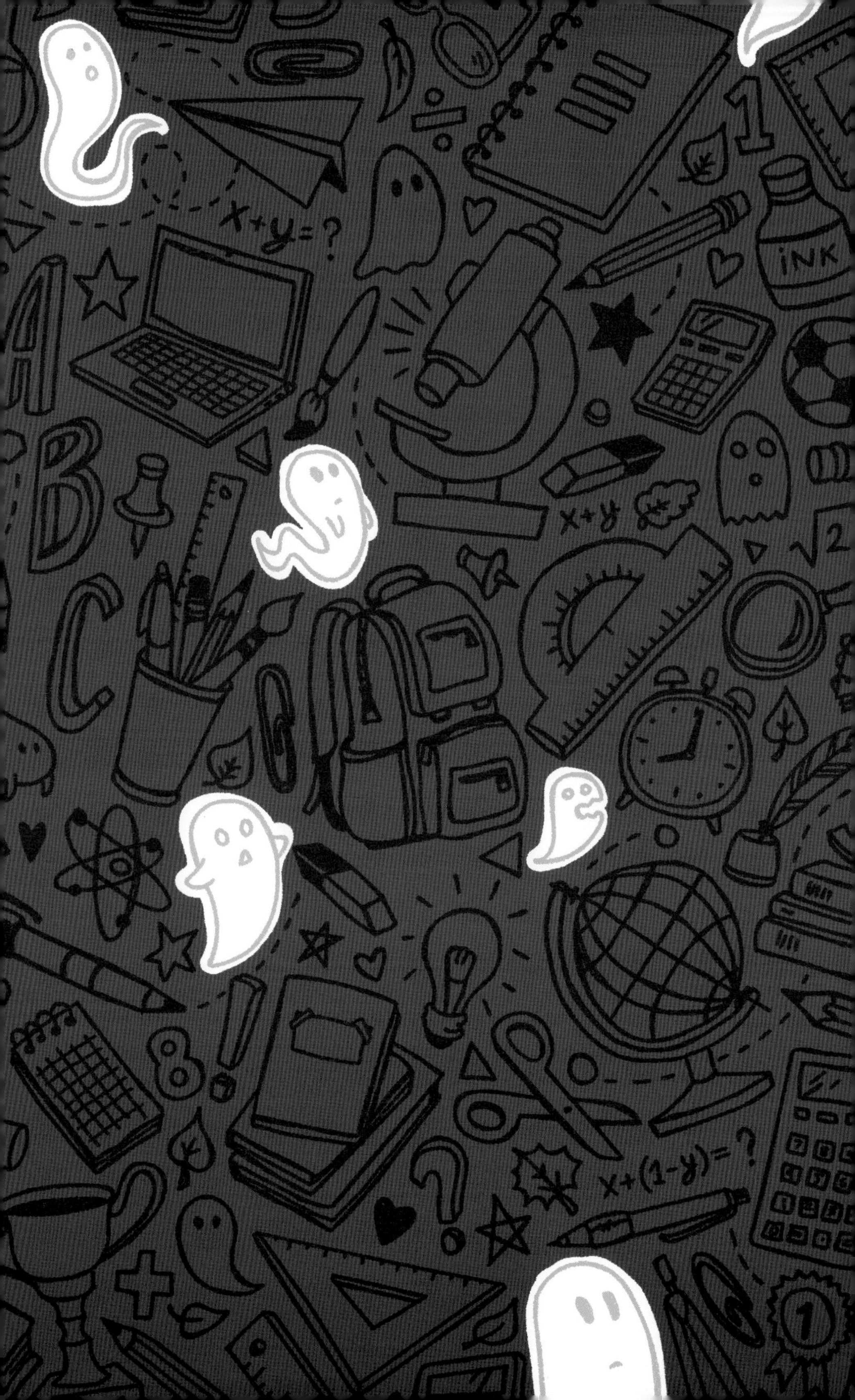
x+y=?
iNK
x+y
x+(1-y)=?

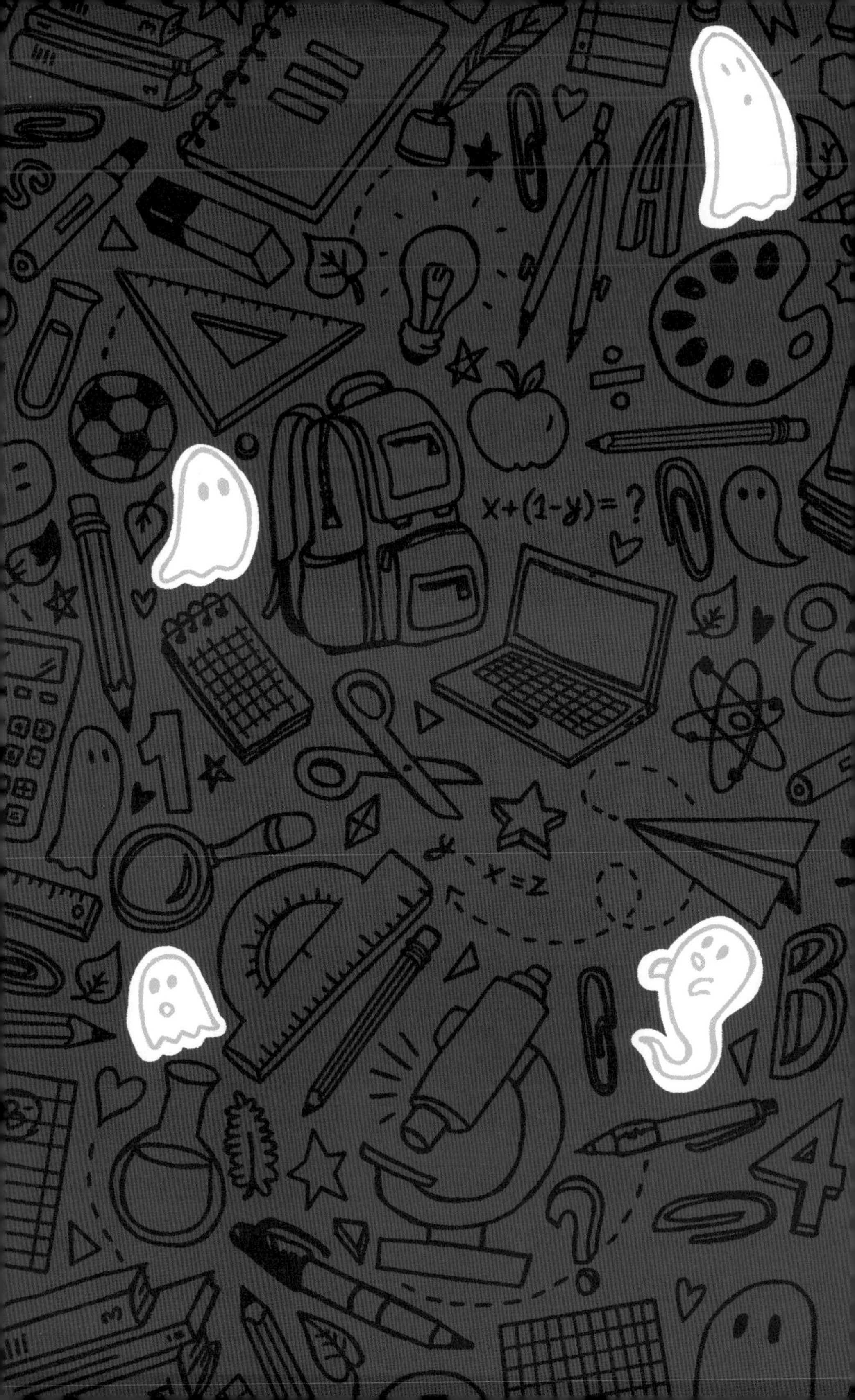
X+(1-y)=?

About the Authors

S.M. Vidaurri was born and raised in northern New Jersey. He lives and works in New York. He received a BFA in Illustration from the University of the Arts in Philadelphia. His apartment is filled with cats, romance novels and peach iced tea.

Hannah Krieger is making her publishing debut with *All My Friends Are Ghosts*, but has been drawing comics from her quiet home in North Carolina for several years. From the illustration assets she created for award-winning 2016 video game documentary *Man Vs Snake*, to her personal webcomics *Camodad* and *Psychic Mansion*, Hannah's affinities for everything ridiculous and/or spooky can be consistently found in her work.

DISCOVER
EXPLOSIVE NEW WORLDS

Adventure Time
Pendleton Ward and Others
Volume 1
ISBN: 978-1-60886-280-1 | $14.99 US
Volume 2
ISBN: 978-1-60886-323-5 | $14.99 US
Adventure Time: Islands
ISBN: 978-1-60886-972-5 | $9.99 US

The Amazing World of Gumball
Ben Bocquelet and Others
Volume 1
ISBN: 978-1-60886-488-1 | $14.99 US
Volume 2
ISBN: 978-1-60886-793-6 | $14.99 US

Brave Chef Brianna
Sam Sykes, Selina Espiritu
ISBN: 978-1-68415-050-2 | $14.99 US

Mega Princess
Kelly Thompson, Brianne Drouhard
ISBN: 978-1-68415-007-6 | $14.99 US

The Not-So Secret Society
Matthew Daley, Arlene Daley,
Wook Jin Clark
ISBN: 978-1-60886-997-8 | $9.99 US

Over the Garden Wall
Patrick McHale, Jim Campbell
and Others
Volume 1
ISBN: 978-1-60886-940-4 | $14.99 US
Volume 2
ISBN: 978-1-68415-006-9 | $14.99 US

Steven Universe
Rebecca Sugar and Others
Volume 1
ISBN: 978-1-60886-706-6 | $14.99 US
Volume 2
ISBN: 978-1-60886-796-7 | $14.99 US

Steven Universe & The Crystal Gems
ISBN: 978-1-60886-921-3 | $14.99 US

Steven Universe: Too Cool for School
ISBN: 978-1-60886-771-4 | $14.99 US

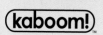

AVAILABLE AT YOUR LOCAL COMICS SHOP AND BOOKSTORE
To find a comics shop in your area, visit www.comicshoplocator.com
WWW.**BOOM-STUDIOS**.COM